Housekeepers
Say I Do!

SUSAN MEIER

Published in Great Britain 2013
by Mills & Boon, an imprint of Harlequin (UK) Limited,
Eton House, 18-24 Paradise Road, Richmond, Surrey TW9 1SR

HOUSEKEEPERS SAY I DO!
© Harlequin Enterprises II B.V./S.à.r.l 2013

Maid for the Millionaire, Maid for the Single Dad and *Maid in Montana* were first published in Great Britain by Harlequin (UK) Limited

Maid for the Millionaire © Linda Susan Meier 2010
Maid for the Single Dad © Linda Susan Meier 2010
Maid in Montana © Linda Susan Meier 2009

ISBN: 978 0 263 90559 5
ebook ISBN: 978 1 472 00132 0

05-0713

ROM
Pbk

Harlequin (UK) policy is to use papers that are natural, renewable and recyclable products and made from wood grown in sustainable forests. The logging and manufacturing processes conform to the legal environmental regulations of the country of origin.

Printed and bound in Spain by Blackprint CPI, Barcelona

MAID FOR
THE MILLIONAIRE

BY
SUSAN MEIER

Susan Meier spent most of her twenties thinking she was a job-hopper—until she began to write and realized everything that had come before was only research! One of eleven children, with twenty-four nieces and nephews and three kids of her own, Susan has had plenty of real-life experience watching romance blossom in unexpected ways. She lives in western Pennsylvania with her wonderful husband, Mike, three children and two overfed, well-cuddled cats, Sophie and Fluffy. You can visit Susan's website at www.susanmeier.com.

**Special thanks to Denise Meyers,
who lets me talk out my ideas…**

CHAPTER ONE

PINK UNDERWEAR?

Grimacing, Cain Nestor tossed his formerly white cotton briefs into the washing machine and slammed the door closed. Damn it! He should have stopped at the mall the night before and bought new ones, but it had been late when his private plane finally landed in Miami. Besides, back in Kansas he had done his own laundry plenty of times. He couldn't believe he'd forgotten so much in twelve years that he'd end up with pink underwear, but apparently he had.

Tightening the knot of the towel at his waist, he stormed out of the laundry room and into the kitchen just as the back door opened. From the pretty yellow ruffled apron that was the trademark of Happy Maids, he knew that his personal assistant Ava was one step ahead of him again. He'd been without a housekeeper since the beginning of February, three long weeks ago. Though Ava had interviewed, he'd found something wrong with every person she'd chosen—his maid lived in and a man couldn't be too careful about whom he let stay in his home—but the lack of clean underwear had clearly proven he'd hit a wall.

Leave it to his assistant to think of the stopgap measure. She'd hired a cleaning service.

Ready to make an apology for his appearance, Cain caught his once-a-week housekeeper's gaze and his heart froze in his chest. His breathing stopped. His thigh muscles turned to rubber.

"Liz?"

Though her long black hair had been pulled into a severe bun at her nape and she'd lost a few pounds in the three years since he'd seen her, he'd know those catlike green eyes anywhere.

"Cain?"

A million questions danced through his head, but they were quickly replaced by recriminations. She'd quit a very good job in Philadelphia and moved with him to Miami when she'd married him. Now, she was a maid? Not even a permanently employed housekeeper. She was a fill-in. A stopgap measure.

And it was his fault.

He swallowed. "I don't know what to say."

Liz Harper blinked a few times, making sure her eyes were not deceiving her and she really was seeing her ex-husband standing wrapped in only a towel in the kitchen of the house that was her first assignment for the day. He hadn't changed a bit in three years. His onyx eyes still had the uncanny ability to make her feel he could see the whole way to her soul. He still wore his black hair short. And he still had incredible muscles that rippled when he moved. Broad shoulders. Defined pecs. And six-pack abs. All of which were on display at the moment.

She licked her suddenly dry lips. "You could start by

saying, 'Excuse my nakedness. I'll just run upstairs and get a robe.'"

Remarkably, that made him laugh, and myriad memories assaulted her….

The day they'd met on the flight from Dallas to Philadelphia…

How they'd exchanged business cards and he'd called her cell phone even before she was out of the airport…

How they'd had dinner that night, entered into a long-distance relationship, made love for the first time on the beach just beyond his beautiful Miami home, and married on the spur of the moment in Las Vegas.

And now she was his housekeeper.

Could a woman fall any farther?

Worse, she wasn't in a position where she could turn down this job.

"Okay. I'll just—"

"Do you think—"

They stopped. The scent of his soap drifted to her and she realized he hadn't changed brands. More memories danced through her head. The warmth of his touch. The seriousness of his kiss.

She cleared her throat. "You first."

He shook his head. "No. Ladies first."

"Okay." She pulled in a breath. She didn't have to tell him her secrets. Wouldn't be so foolish again as to trust him with her dreams. If everything went well, she wouldn't even have to see him while she did her job. "Are you going to have a problem with this?"

He gripped his towel a little tighter. "You working for me or chatting about you working for me while I stand here just about naked?"

Her cheeks heated. The reminder that he was naked under one thin towel caused her blood to simmer with anticipation. For another two people that might be ridiculous three years after their divorce, but she and Cain had always had chemistry. Realistically, she knew it wouldn't simply disappear. After all, it had been strong enough to coax a normally sensible Pennsylvania girl to quit her dream job and follow him to Miami, and strong enough that a typically reclusive entrepreneur had opened up and let her into his life.

"Me working here for you until you hire a new maid." She motioned around the kitchen. The bronze and tan cut-glass backsplash accented tall cherrywood cabinets and bright stainless-steel appliances. "Is *that* going to be a problem?"

He glanced at the ceramic tile floor then back up at her. "I've gotta be honest, Liz. It does make me feel uncomfortable."

"Why? You're not supposed to be here when I am. In fact, I was told you're usually at the office by eight. It's a fluke that we've even run into each other. And I need this job!"

"Which is exactly why I feel bad."

That changed her blood from simmering with chemistry to boiling with fury. *"You feel sorry for me?"*

He winced. "Not sorry, per se—"

"Then sorry, per what?" But as the words tumbled out of her mouth she realized what was going on. Three steps got her to the big center island of his kitchen. "You think I fell apart when our marriage did and now I can only get a job as a maid?"

"Well—"

Three more steps had her standing in front of him.

"Honey, I *own* this company. I am the original Happy Maid."

She was tall enough that she only had to tilt her head slightly to catch his gaze, but when she did she regretted it. His dark eyes told her their closeness had resurrected their chemistry for him, too. Heat and need tightened her insides. Her breathing stuttered out of her chest. The faint scent of soap she'd sniffed while at the door hit her full force bringing back wonderful, painful memories.

He stepped away and broke eye contact. "Nice try."

"Call your personal assistant." When her voice came out as a breathy whisper, Liz paused and gulped some air to strengthen it. "I'm the one she dealt with. I signed the contract."

"If you're the owner, why are *you* cleaning my house?" He stopped. His sharp black eyes narrowed. "You're spying."

"On you? Really? After three years?" She huffed out a sound of disgust and turned away, then whirled to face him again. "You have got to be the most vain man in the world! I was hired through your assistant. She didn't give me your name. She hired me to clean the house of the CEO of Cain Corporation. I never associated you with Cain Corporation. Last I heard your company name was Nestor Construction."

"Nestor Construction is a wholly owned subsidiary of Cain Corporation."

"Fantastic." She pivoted and walked back to the center island. "Here's the deal. I have six employees and enough work for seven. But I can't hire the people I need and work exclusively in the office until I get enough work for eight." She also wouldn't tell him that she was scrambling to employ every woman from A Friend Indeed, a charity that provided temporary housing for women who needed a second chance. He didn't understand charities. He most certainly didn't understand second chances.

"Then my profit margins will allow me to take a salary while I spend my days marketing the business and the expansions I have planned."

"Expansions?"

"I'm getting into gardening and pool cleaning." She combed her fingers through the loose hair that had escaped the knot at her nape. "Down the road. Right now, I'm on the cusp with the maid service. I seriously need thirty more clients."

He whistled.

"It's not such a stretch in a city like Miami!"

"I'm not whistling at the difficulty. I'm impressed. When did you get into this?"

She hesitated then wondered why. It shouldn't matter. "Three years ago."

"You decided to start a company after we divorced?"

She raised her chin. She would not allow him to make her feel bad for her choices. "No. I took a few cleaning jobs to support myself when I moved out and it sort of blossomed."

"I offered you alimony."

"I didn't want it." Squaring her shoulders, she caught his gaze. Mistake. She'd always imagined that if she ever saw him again, their conversation would focus on why she'd left him without a word of explanation. Instead the floodgates of their chemistry had been opened, and she'd bet her last cent neither one of them was thinking about their disagreements. The look in his dark eyes brought to mind memories of satin sheets and days spent in bed.

"In a year I had enough work for myself and another maid full-time. In six more months I had four employees. I stayed level like that until I hit a boom again and added two employees. That's when I realized I could turn this business into something great."

"Okay, then."

"Okay?"

"I get it. I know what it's like to have a big idea and want to succeed." He turned away. "And as you said, our paths won't cross."

"So this is really okay?"

"Yeah. It's okay." He faced her again with a wince. "You wouldn't happen to be doing laundry first, would you?"

"Why?"

"I sort of made fifty percent of my underwear pink."

She laughed, and visions of other times, other laughter, assailed her and she felt as if she were caught in a time warp. Their marriage had ended so badly she'd forgotten the good times and now suddenly here they were all at the forefront of her mind. But that was wrong. Six years and buckets of tears had passed since the "good times" that nudged them to get married the week they'd accompanied friends to Vegas for their elopement. Only a few weeks after their hasty wedding, those good times became few and far between. By the time she left him they were nonexistent.

And now she was his maid.

"Is the other fifty percent in a basket somewhere?"

"Yes." He hooked a thumb behind him. "Laundry room."

"Do you have about an hour's worth of work you can do while you wait?"

"Yes."

"And you'll go to your office or study or to your bedroom to do that."

"I have an office in the back."

"Great. I'll get on the laundry."

A little over an hour later, Cain pulled his Porsche into the parking space in front of the office building he owned. He jumped out, marched into the lobby and headed for the private elevator in the back. He rode it to the top floor, where it opened onto his huge office.

"Ava!"

He strode to his desk, dropping his briefcase on the small round conference table as he passed it. He'd managed not to think about Liz as she moved around his home, vacuuming while the washing machine ran, then the dryer. To her credit, she hadn't saunteered into his office and dumped a clean pair of tidy-whities on the document he was reviewing. She'd simply stepped into the room, announced that the laundry had been folded and now sat on his bed. But it was seeing the tidy stack on his black satin bed-spread that caused unwanted emotions to tumble through him.

When they were married she'd insisted on doing laundry. She hadn't wanted a maid. She had stayed home and taken care of him.

As he'd stared at the neat pile, the years had slid away. Feelings he'd managed to bury had risen up like lava. She'd adored him and he'd worshipped her. He hadn't slept with a woman before her or one since who had made him feel what Liz could. And now she was in his house again.

Which was wrong. Absolutely, totally and completely wrong. For a woman who'd adored him and a man who'd worshipped her, they'd hurt each other beyond belief in the last year of their marriage. She hadn't even left a note when she'd gone. Her attorney had contacted him. She hadn't wanted his money, hadn't wanted to say goodbye. She simply wanted to be away from him, and he had been relieved when she left. It was wrong—wrong, wrong, wrong—for them to even be in the same room! He couldn't believe he'd agreed to this, but being nearly naked had definitely thrown him off his game.

Underwear in his possession, he had dressed quickly, thinking he'd have to sneak out, wondering if it would be prudent to have Ava call her and ask her to assign another of her employees to his house. But as she promised, she was nowhere to be seen when he left.

"Just a bit curious, Ava," he said when his short, slightly chubby, fifty-something-assistant stepped into his office. "Why'd you choose Happy Maids?"

She didn't bat an eye. "They come highly recommended and they're taking new clients." She peered at him over the rim of her black frame glasses. "Do you know how hard it is to get a good maid in Miami?"

"Apparently very hard or I'd have one right now."

"I've been handling my end. It's you who—" Her face froze. "Oh." Her eyes squeezed shut. "You were there when the maid arrived, weren't you?"

"Naked, in a towel, coming out of my laundry room."

She pressed her hand to her chest. "I'm so sorry."

He studied her face for signs that she knew Liz was his ex-wife, but her blue eyes were as innocent as a kitten's.

"I should have realized that you'd sleep late after four days of traveling." She sank to the sofa just inside the door. "I'm sorry."

"It's okay."

"No. Seriously. I am sorry. I know how you hate dealing with people." She bounced off the sofa and scampered to the desk. "But let's not dwell on it. It's over and it will never happen again." Changing the subject, she pointed at the mail on his desk. "This stack is the mail from the week. This stack is the messages I pulled off voice mail for you. This stack is messages I took for you. People I talked to." She looked up and smiled. "And I'll call the maid and tell her not to come until after nine next week."

"She's fine." She was. Now that his emotions were under control again, logic had kicked in. The fact that she wasn't around when he left the house that morning proved she didn't want to see him any more than he wanted to see her. If there was one thing he knew about Liz, it was that she was honest. If she said he'd never see her, she'd do everything in her power to make it so. That, at least, hadn't changed. Though she was the one to leave, the disintegration of their marriage had been his fault. He didn't want to upset her over a non-problem. He'd upset her enough in one lifetime.

"No. No. Let me call," Ava chirped happily. "I know that you don't like to run into people. You don't like to deal with people at all. That's my job, remember?"

"I can handle one maid."

Her expression skewed into one of total confusion. "Really?"

The skepticism in her voice almost made him want to ask her why she'd question that. But she was right. Her job was to keep little things away from him. Not necessarily people, but nitpicky tasks. It was probably a mistake that she'd said people. But whatever the reason she'd said it, it was irrelevant.

"I won't have to deal with her. I'll be out of my house by seven-thirty next week. It won't be a problem."

"Okay." She nodded eagerly, then all but ran from the room.

As Cain sank into his office chair, he frowned, Ava's words ringing in his head. Had it been a mistake when she said she knew he didn't like dealing with people or was he really that hard to get along with?

Once again, irrelevant. He got along just fine with the people he needed to get along with.

He reached for the stack of mail. All of it had been opened by Ava and sorted according to which of his three companies it pertained to. He read documents, correspondence and bids for upcoming projects, until he came to an envelope that hadn't been opened.

He twisted it until he could read the return address and he understood why. It was from his parents. His birthday had come and gone that week. Of course, his parents hadn't forgotten. Probably his sister hadn't, either. But he had.

He grabbed his letter opener, slit the seal and pulled out four inches of bubble wrap that protected a framed picture. Unwinding the bubble wrap—his dad always went a bit overboard—he exposed the picture and went still.

The family photo.

He leaned back in his chair, rubbed his hand across his chin.

The sticky note attached to the frame said, *Thought you might like this for your desk. Happy birthday.*

He tried to simply put it back in the envelope, but couldn't. His eyes were drawn to the people posing so happily.

His parents were dressed in their Sunday best. His sister wore an outfit that looked like she'd gotten it from somebody's trash—and considering that she'd been sixteen at the time, he suspected she might have. Cain wore a suit as did his brother, Tom, his hand on Cain's shoulder.

"If you get into trouble," Tom had said a million times, "you call me first. Not Mom and Dad. I'll get you out of it, then we'll break the news to the wardens."

Cain sniffed a laugh. Tom had always called their parents the wardens. Or the guards. Their parents were incredibly kind, open-minded people, but Tom loved to make jokes. Play with words. He'd had the type of sense of humor that made him popular no matter where he went.

Cain returned the picture to its envelope. He knew what his dad was really saying when he suggested Cain put the picture on his desk. Six years had gone by. It was time to move on. To remember in a good way, not sadly, that his older brother, the kindest, funniest, smartest of the Nestors, had been killed three days before his own wedding, only three weeks after Cain and Liz had eloped.

But he wasn't ready.

He might never be.

CHAPTER TWO

"ARE YOU KIDDING ME?" Carrying boxes of groceries up the walk to the entrance of one of the homes owned by A Friend Indeed, Ellie "Magic" Swanson turned to face Liz. Her amber-colored eyes were as round as two full moons.

"Nope. My first client of the day was my ex-husband."

She hadn't meant to tell Ellie about Cain, but it had slipped out, the way things always seemed to slip out with Ellie. She was a sweet, smart, eager twenty-two-year-old who had gotten involved with the wrong man and desperately needed a break in life. Liz had given her a job only to discover that it was Liz who benefited from the relationship more than Ellie did. Desperate for a second chance, Ellie had become an invaluable employee. Which is why Liz didn't merely provide cleaning services and grocery delivery services for A Friend Indeed, she also tried to give a job to every woman staying at the shelter homes who wanted one. She firmly believed in second chances.

Ellie shouldered open the back door, revealing the outdated but neat and clean kitchen. "How can that happen?"

"His assistant, Ava, hired us to clean the house of the CEO of Cain Corporation."

"And you didn't know your ex-husband was CEO of Cain Corporation?"

Liz set her box of groceries on the counter. "When we were married he only owned Nestor Construction. Apparently in three years he's branched out. Moved to a bigger house, too." In some ways it hurt that he'd sold the beach house they'd shared, but in others it didn't surprise her. He'd been so lost, so despondent after the death of his brother, that he'd thrown even more of into his work than before. The much larger house on the beach had probably been a reward for reaching a goal.

Ellie walked out of the pantry where she had begun storing canned goods, her beautiful face set in firm lines and her long blond curls bouncing. "I'll take his house next week."

"Are you kidding? He'll think I didn't come back because I was intimidated." She pointed her thumb at her chest. "I'm going. Besides, I have something else for you." She opened her shoulder-strap purse and rifled through its contents. After finding the employment application of a young woman, Rita, whom she'd interviewed the night before, she handed it to Ellie.

"What do you think?"

"Looks okay to me." She glanced up. "You checked her references?"

"Yes. But she's staying at one of our Friend Indeed houses. I thought you might know her."

Ellie shook her head. "No."

"Well, you'll be getting to know her next week. As soon as we're through here, we'll drop by the house she and her kids are using and tell her she's got the job and that she'll be working with you."

"You want me to train her?"

"My goal is to get myself out of the field and into the office permanently." Such as it was. The desk and chairs were secondhand. The air-conditioning rarely worked. The tile on the floor needed replacing. The only nice features of the crowded room were the bright yellow paint on the walls and the yellow-and-black area rug she'd found to cover most of the floor. But she was much better off than the women who came to A Friend Indeed, and working with them kept her grounded, appreciative of what she had, how far she'd come. It wasn't so long ago that her mom had run from her abusive father with her and her sisters. The second chance they'd found because of a shelter had changed the course of not just her mom's life, but also her life and her sisters'.

"To do that, I have to start teaching you to be my new second in command."

Pulling canned goods from the box on the counter, Ellie glanced up again.

Liz smiled. "The promotion comes with a raise."

Ellie's mouth fell open and she dropped the cans before racing to Liz to hug her. "I will do the best job of anybody you've ever seen!"

"I know you will."

"And seriously, I'll take your ex-husband's house."

"I'm fine. My husband wasn't abusive, remember? Simply distant and upset about his brother's death." She shrugged. "Besides, our paths won't cross. We'll be fine."

Liz reassured Ellie, but she wasn't a hundred percent

certain it was true. Though she and Cain wouldn't run into each other, she'd be touching his things, seeing bits and pieces of his life, opening old wounds. But she needed the job. A recommendation from Cain or his assistant could go a long way to getting the additional clients she needed. She wanted to expand. She wanted to be able to employ every woman who needed a second chance. To do that, she had to get more business.

Liz and Ellie finished storing the groceries and made a quick sweep through the house to be sure it was clean. A new family would be arriving later that afternoon to spend a few weeks regrouping before they moved on to a new life.

Satisfied that the house was ready for its new occupants, Liz led Ellie through the garage to the Happy Maids vehicle. The walk through the downstairs to the garage reminded her that she was content, happy with her life. She was smarter now and more confident than she had been when she was married. Surely she could handle being on the periphery of Cain's life.

The following Friday morning when it was time to clean Cain's house again, she sat in the bright yellow Happy Maids car a few houses down from Cain's, telling herself it wouldn't matter what she found. If the cupboards were bare, she wouldn't worry about whether or not he was eating. She would assume he was dining out. If his mail sat unopened, she'd dust around it. Even if there were lace panties between the sheets, she would not care.

Fortified, she waited until he pulled his gorgeous black Porsche out of his driveway and headed in the other direction. But just as their encounter the week before had brought back memories of happier times, seeing him in the Porsche reminded her of their rides along the ocean. With the convertible top down. The wind whipping her hair in all directions.

She squeezed her eyes shut. Their marriage had been abysmal. He was a withdrawn workaholic. Though his brother's death had caused him to stop talking almost completely, she'd seen signs that Cain might not be as involved in their relationship as she was during their six-month courtship. Canceled plans. Meetings that were more important than weekends with her. It had been an impulsive, reckless decision to marry. When she was his girlfriend, he at least tried to make time for her when she visited from Philadelphia. When she became his wife, he didn't feel the need to do that and she'd been miserably alone. When they actually did have time together, he'd been antsy, obviously thinking about his company and the work he could be doing. He'd never even tried to squeeze her into his life. So why wasn't she remembering that?

Fortified again, she slid the Happy Maids car into his drive and entered his house. As she'd noticed the week before, there were no personal touches. No pictures. No awards. No memorabilia.

Glancing around, she realized how easy it would be to pretend it was the home of a stranger. Releasing any thought of Cain from her mind and focusing on doing the best possible job for her "client," she cleaned quickly and efficiently. When she was done, she locked up and left as if this job were any other.

The following week, she decided that her mistake the Friday before had been watching him leave for work, seeing him in "their" beautiful Porsche. So she shifted his house from the first on her list to the second, and knew he was already gone by the time she got there. As she punched that week's code into the alarm to disable it and unlocked the kitchen door, she once again blanked her mind of any thought of Cain, pretending this was the house of a stranger.

Tossing the first load of laundry into the washer, she thought she heard a noise. She stopped, listened, but didn't hear it again. She returned to the kitchen and didn't hear any more noise, but something felt off. She told herself she was imagining things, stacked dishes in the dishwasher and turned it on.

She spent the next hour cleaning the downstairs in between trips to the laundry room. When the laundry was folded, she walked up the cherrywood staircase to the second floor. Humming a bit, happy with how well she was managing to keep her focus off the house's owner, she shouldered open the master bedroom door and gasped.

Damn.

"Who is it?"

The scratchy voice that came from the bed didn't sound like Cain's at all. But even in the dim light of his room, she could see it was him.

"It's me. Liz. Cleaning your house."

"Liz?"

His weak voice panicked her and she set the stack of clean laundry on the mirrored vanity and raced to the bed. His dark hair was soaked with sweat and spiked out in all directions. Black stubble covered his chin and cheeks.

"My *wife*, Liz?" he asked groggily.

"Ex-wife." She pressed her hand to his forehead. "You're burning up!"

Not waiting for a reply, she rushed into the master bathroom and searched through the drawers of the cherrywood vanity of the double sinks looking for something that might help him. Among the various toiletries, she eventually found some aspirin. She ran tap water into the glass and raced back to the bed.

Handing two aspirin and the water to him, she said, "Here."

He took the pills, but didn't say anything. As he passed the water glass back to her, he caught her gaze. His dark eyes were shiny from the effects of the fever, so she wasn't surprised when he lay down and immediately drifted off to sleep again.

She took the glass downstairs and put it in the sink. Telling herself to forget he was in the bedroom, she finished cleaning but couldn't leave in good conscience without checking up on him.

When she returned to the bedroom, Cain still slept soundly. She pressed her hand to his forehead again and frowned. Even after the aspirin, he was still burning up and he was so alone that it felt wrong to leave him. She could call his assistant but somehow that didn't seem right, either. An assistant shouldn't have to nurse him through the flu.

Technically an ex-wife shouldn't, either, but with his family at least a thousand miles away in Kansas, she was the lesser of two evils.

Sort of.

Tiptoeing out of the room, she pulled her cell phone from her apron pocket and dialed Ellie.

"Hey, sweetie." Ellie greeted her, obviously having noted the caller ID.

"Hey, Ellie. Is Rita with you?"

"Sure is. Doing wonderfully I might add."

"That's good because I think I need to have her take over my jobs this afternoon."

"On her own?"

"Is that a problem?"

Ellie's voice turned unexpectedly professional. "No. She'll be great."

"Good."

"Um, boss, I know where you are, remember? Is there anything going on I should know about?"

"No. I'm fine. I just decided to take the afternoon off." Liz winced. She hadn't actually lied. She was taking time off; she simply wasn't going to do something fun as Ellie suspected.

"No kidding! That's great."

"Yeah, so I'll be out of reach for the rest of the day. Give the other girls a call and instruct them to call you, not me, if they have a problem."

"On it, boss!" Ellie said, then she laughed. "This is so exciting!"

Liz smiled, glad Ellie was enjoying her new responsibilities. "I'll see you tomorrow."

She closed her cell phone then ambled to the kitchen. She'd promised herself she wouldn't care if he had food or not, but with him as sick as he was, he had to at least have chicken broth and orange juice. Finding neither, she grabbed her purse and keys and headed to the grocery store where she purchased flu medicine, orange juice, chicken broth and a paperback book.

She put everything but the flu meds and book away, then she grabbed a clean glass from the cupboard and tiptoed upstairs again. He roused when she entered.

"Liz?"

"Yes. I have flu meds. You interested?"

"God, yes."

"Great. Sit up."

She poured one dose of the flu meds into the little plastic cup and held it out to him. He swallowed the thick syrup and handed the cup back before lying down again.

As she took the medicine to the bathroom, a bubble of fear rose up in her. Caring for him had the potential to go so wrong. Not because she worried that they'd get involved again. Tomorrow, she would forget all about this, if only because even pondering being involved with him would bring back painful memories.

But she knew Cain. He hated owing people, and if she stayed too long or did too much, he'd think he owed her. When he believed he owed somebody he could be like a dog with a bone. Being beholden made him feel weak. He was never weak. Which made her caring for him when he was sick a double threat. Not only had he been weak, but she'd seen him weak. He'd *have* to make this up to her.

Of course, with him as sick as he was, she could hope he wouldn't remember most of this in the morning.

Everything would be fine.

With a peek at the bed to be sure he was asleep, she left the room and went to the Happy Maids car. In the trunk, she found a pair of sweatpants and a tank top. She changed out of her yellow maid uniform in one of the downstairs bathrooms then she took her book and a glass of orange juice into the study. Reclining on the sofa, she made herself comfortable to read.

She checked on him every hour or so. Finding him sleeping soundly every time, she slid out of the room and returned to the study. But just as she was pulling the door closed behind her on the fourth trip, he called out to her.

"Where are you going?"

She eased the door open again and walked over to the bed. "Cain? Are you okay?"

"I'm fine." He sat up. "Come back to bed."

Realizing the fever had him hallucinating or mixing up the past and present, she smiled and went into the bathroom to get him some water. She pressed the glass to his lips. "Sip."

As she held the glass to his mouth, he lifted his hand to the back of her thigh and possessively slid it up to her bottom.

Shock nearly caused her to spill water all over him. She hadn't even dated since she left him, and the feeling of a man's hand on her behind was equal parts startling and wonderful.

He smiled up at her. "I'm better."

Ignoring the enticing warmth spiraling through her, she tried to sound like an impartial nurse when she said, "You're hallucinating."

His hand lovingly roamed her bottom as his fever-glazed eyes gazed up at her longingly. "Please. I seriously feel better. Come back to bed."

His last words were a hoarse whisper that tiptoed into the silent room, the yearning in them like a living thing. She reminded herself that this wasn't Cain. The Cain she'd married was a cold, distant man. But a little part of her couldn't help admitting that this was the man she'd always wished he would be. Loving. Eager for her. Happy to be with her.

Which scared her more than the hand on her bottom. Wishing and hoping were what had gotten her into trouble in the first place—why she'd married him that impulsive day in Vegas. On that trip, he'd been so loving, so sweet, so happy that she'd stupidly believed that if they were married, if she didn't live a thousand miles away, they wouldn't have to spend the first day of each of their trips getting reacquainted. He'd be comfortable with her. Happy.

And for three weeks they had been. Then his brother had died, forcing him to help his dad run the family business in Kansas through e-mails and teleconference calls, as he also ran Nestor Construction. Their marriage had become one more thing in his life that he had to do. A burden to him.

That's what she had to remember. She'd become a burden to him.

She pulled away, straightening her shoulders. She wasn't anybody's burden. Not ever.

"Go back to sleep."

She returned to the study and her book, but realized that in her eagerness to get out of the room she'd forgotten to give him another dose of medicine. So she returned to his room and found him sleeping peacefully. Not wanting to disturb him, she took a seat on the chair by the window. The next time he stirred, she'd be there to give him the meds. She opened her book and began to read in the pale light of the lamp behind her.

Cain awakened from what had been the worst night of his life. Spasms of shivers had overtaken him in between bouts of heat so intense his pillow was wet with sweat. He'd thrown up. All his muscles ached. But that wasn't the half of it. He'd dreamed Liz had taken his temperature, given him medicine and walked him to and from the bathroom.

With a groan, he tossed off the covers and sat up in bed. He didn't want to remember the feeling of her palm on his forehead, the scent of her that lingered when she had hovered over him or the wave of longing that swept through him just imagining that she was back in his life. He pulled in a breath. How could he dream about a woman who'd left him without a word of explanation? A woman who was in his bed one day and gone without a word the next?

Because he'd been a fool. That's how. He'd lost her because he was always working, never had time for her, and grieving his brother. No matter how she'd left, he couldn't blame her. She was innocent of any wrongdoing…and that was why he still wanted her.

As his eyes adjusted, he noticed soft light spilling toward him from across the room. He must have left the bathroom light on. He looked to the left and saw Liz watching him from his reading chair.

He licked his dry lips. She was so beautiful. Silhouetted in the pale light from the bathroom, she looked ethereal. Her long black hair floated around her, accenting her smooth, perfect alabaster skin. She wore sweatpants and a tank top, and he realized she'd turned off the air-conditioning. Probably because of his shivering.

Still, her being in his bedroom didn't make sense. They'd divorced three years ago.

"Why are you here?" he demanded. "*How* are you here?"

"I'm your maid, remember?"

"My maid?"

"Your assistant hired Happy Maids to clean your house once a week—"

He closed his eyes and lay down again, as it all came back to him. "Yeah. I remember."

"You were pretty sick when I got here Friday morning."

"Friday morning?" He sat up again and then groaned when his stiff muscles protested. "What day is it?"

"Relax. It's early Saturday morning."

He peered over. "You've been here all night?"

She inclined her head. "You were very sick. I didn't feel comfortable leaving you."

He fell back to the pillow. "Honest Liz."

"That's why hundreds of people let me and my company into their homes every week to clean. My reputation precedes me."

He could hear the smile in her voice and fought a wave of nostalgia. "I guess thanks are in order."

"You're welcome."

"And I probably owe you an apology for fondling your butt."

"Oh, so you remember that?"

This time she laughed. The soft sound drifted to him, smoothed over him, made him long for everything he'd had and lost.

Which made him feel foolish, stupid, *weak*. She was gone. He had lost her. He could take total blame. But he refused to let any mistake make him weak.

"You know what? I appreciate all the help you've given me, but I think I can handle things from here on out."

"You're kicking me out?"

"I'm not kicking you out. I'm granting you a pardon. Consider this a get-out-of-jail-free card."

"Okay." She rose from the chair. Book under her arm, she headed for the door. But she stopped and glanced back at him. "You're sure?"

He'd expect nothing less from her than absolute selflessness. Which made him feel like an absolute creep. He tried to cover that with a smile so she wouldn't even have a hint of how hard just seeing her was for him. "I'm positive. I feel terrific."

"Okay."

With that she opened the door and slipped out. When the door closed behind her, he hung his head. It had been an accident of fate that he'd gotten the flu the very day she was here to clean his house. But he wasn't an idiot. His reaction to her proved that having her back in his life—even as a temporary employee—wasn't going to work. The weeks it took Ava to find a permanent maid would be filled with a barrage of memories that would overwhelm him with intense sadness one minute and yearning for what might have been the next.

He should get rid of her. That's what his common sense was telling him to do. But in his heart he knew he owed her. For more than just staying with him while he was sick. He should have never talked her into marrying him.

CHAPTER THREE

IT WAS FIVE O'CLOCK when Liz finally fell into bed. Ellie called her around eleven, reminding her that they were taking Amanda Gray and her children, the family who had moved into the Friend Indeed house the weekend before, to the beach.

She slogged out from under the covers and woke herself up in the shower. She pulled a pair of shorts and a navy-blue-and-white striped T-shirt over her white bikini, and drove to Amanda's temporary house. Ellie's little blue car was already in the driveway. She pushed out into the hot Miami day and walked around back to the kitchen door.

"Mrs. Harper!" Amanda's three-year-old daughter Joy bounced with happiness as Liz entered and she froze.

Liz had been part of the welcoming committee when Amanda and her children had arrived at the house, but until this very second she hadn't made the connection that Joy was about the age her child would have been.

Her child.

Her heart splintered. She should have a child right now. But she didn't. She'd lost her baby. Lost her marriage. Lost everything in what seemed like the blink of an eye.

Swallowing hard, she got rid of the lump in her throat. The barrage of self-pity that assailed her wasn't just unexpected; it was unwanted. She knew spending so much time with Cain had caused her to make the connection between her baby and Joy. But that didn't mean she had to wallow in it. Her miscarriage had been three years ago. She'd had therapy. She might long for that child with every fiber of her being, but, out of necessity, she'd moved on.

Amanda, a tall redhead with big blue eyes, corrected her daughter. "It's Ms. Harper, not Mrs."

"That's okay," Liz said walking into the kitchen, knowing she had to push through this. If she was going to work in the same city as her ex, she might not be able to avoid him. She most definitely couldn't avoid all children the same age her child would have been. Being in contact with both might be a new phase of her recovery.

She could handle this. She *would* handle this.

"Smells great in here."

"I made French toast," Ellie said, standing at the stove. "Want some?"

"No. We're late." She peeked into the picnic basket she'd instructed Ellie to bring. "When we get to the beach, I'll just eat some of the fruit you packed."

"Okay." Ellie removed her apron and hung it in the pantry. "Then we're ready to go."

Amanda turned to the hall. "I'll get Billy."

Billy was a sixteen-year-old who deserted them the second the two cars they drove to the beach stopped in the public parking lot. Obviously expecting his desertion, Amanda waved at his back as he ran to a crowd of kids his own age playing volleyball.

Amanda, Ellie and Liz spent the next hours building a sand castle with Joy who was thrilled with all the attention. Around four o'clock, Ellie and Amanda left the sand to set up a picnic under their umbrella.

Joy smiled up at Liz. "Do you like sand?"

She gazed down at the adorable cherub. The wind tossed her thin blond locks. Her blue eyes sparkled. Now that Liz was over the shock of realizing Joy and her baby would have been close to the same age, she felt normal again. Strong. Accepting of that particular sadness in her life. That was the difference between her and Cain. She'd dealt with her loss. She hadn't let it turn her into someone who couldn't connect with people.

"I love the beach. I'm happy to have someone to share it with."

Joy nodded enthusiastically. "Me, too!"

They ate the sandwiches and fruit Ellie had packed for dinner, then Joy fell asleep under the umbrella. Obviously relaxed and happy, Amanda lay beside her daughter and closed her eyes, too.

"So what did you do yesterday?" Ellie singsonged in the voice that told Liz she knew something out of the ordinary had happened the day before.

Liz peered over at Ellie. Did the woman have a sixth sense about everything? "Not much."

"Oh, come on. You never take a day off. I know something happened."

Liz grabbed the bottle of sunscreen and put her attention to applying it. Knowing Ellie wouldn't let her alone unless she told her something, she said, "I was taking care of a sick friend."

Ellie nudged her playfully. "So? Who was this friend?"

"Just a friend."

"A man!"

"I said nothing about a man."

Ellie laughed. "You didn't need to. The fact that you won't give me a name or elaborate proves I'm right."

How could she argue with that?

Ellie squeezed her shoulder. "I'm proud of you."

"Don't make a big deal out of it."

Ellie laughed gaily. "Let's see. You not only took a day off, but you were with a man and I'm not supposed to make a big deal out of it?"

"No, you're not. Because I'm never going to see him again."

"How do you know?"

"Because I know."

"Okay, then." Ellie closed her eyes and her face scrunched comically.

"What are you doing?"

"Wishing that you'd see him again."

"You might not want to do that."

"Oh, I think I do."

"The man was my ex."

Ellie's eyes popped open. "Oh, Liz! Damn it. You should have told me that before I wished. You know how powerful my wishes can be."

"That's why I told you now. You need to take it back."

"I can't."

"Yeah, well, you'd better or you're going to break your record of wishes granted. Because I'm not going to see him again."

Stupidly, that made her sad. She'd loved Cain with her whole heart and soul, but his brother had died and he'd gone into his shell. She'd tried to hang in there with him, to be there when he reached the point that he could work through his pain and withdrawal, but he never had. And then one day she realized she was pregnant. She knew in her heart that Cain wasn't ready for a child, so she'd waited a few weeks, hoping that if she were further along the pregnancy would seem more real to him. Maybe even be a cause for joy.

But she'd miscarried before she'd had a chance to tell him and suddenly she was the one unable to function. She knew she needed help. At the very least she needed someone to talk to. She couldn't talk to Cain. She wouldn't have been able to handle it if he had dismissed the loss of the little life so precious to her. So she'd gone. Their marriage had been in shambles anyway. The miscarriage simply pointed out what she already knew. Cain wasn't emotionally available.

Ending their marriage had been the right thing to do. She'd gotten therapy, moved on and made a wonderful life for herself.

And he'd moved on. Achieved the success he'd always wanted.

There was nothing to be sad about.

She spent most of the rest of the day in the ocean with Joy, until all thoughts of her miscarriage and her ex-husband had receded. Through the week, occasionally something would remind her of her short pregnancy or her doomed marriage, but she ruthlessly squelched the urge to feel sorry for herself until by Friday, she didn't have a second thought about going to Cain's house to clean. The past was the past. She'd moved on, into the future.

Assuming he'd already gone to work, Liz simply pulled the Happy Maids car into his driveway, bounced out and let herself into his kitchen.

But when she turned from pulling her key from the door, she saw Cain standing over a tall stack of waffles.

"Good morning."

She froze.

They weren't supposed to run into each other. That was why she thought she could keep this job. But three of her four cleaning trips to his house, he'd been home. Without even knowing it, he'd dredged up memories that she'd had to deal with. Emotions she'd thought long dead. Now here he was again.

Still, she wouldn't make an argument of it. She could say a few words of casual conversation, as she walked to the door on the other side of the kitchen and slipped out of the room to clean another section of the house.

"You must be really hungry."

He laughed. "I am. But these are for you." He shrugged. "A thank-you for helping me last weekend."

She froze. She should have expected this. She *had* expected this. She knew he hated owing anyone.

She sucked in a quiet breath. Not only did she not want to spend time with him, but she hadn't eaten waffles since their fateful trip to Vegas. Mostly because she didn't want to remember that wonderful time. *That* Cain wasn't the real Cain. Neither was this guy who'd made her waffles. He didn't want to thank her as much as he felt guilty that she'd helped him the week before and wouldn't let that "debt" go unpaid.

"That's not necessary."

"I know it's not necessary, but I *want* to thank you."

"You did thank me. The words are enough."

He sighed. "Just sit down and have a waffle."

"No!" Because the single word came out so angrily, she smiled to soften it. "Thanks, but no."

Their gazes held for a few seconds. She read the confusion in his dark eyes. He didn't understand why she wouldn't eat breakfast with him. They'd been so happy the one and only time they'd had waffles together. And maybe that's why he'd chosen them?

Regret rose up in her, but regret was a foolish emotion. She couldn't change who he was. She couldn't change the fact that she'd lost their child. And she refused to be pulled into believing the nice side of him was in control. That would only lead to more heartache. Neither one of them wanted that.

She turned and walked away. "I'll get started upstairs while you eat."

Cain pretended her refusal to eat his thank-you waffles hadn't bothered him. Being incredibly busy at work, it was easy to block out the memory. But Saturday morning he took his boat out, and alone on the water with nothing to keep him company but his thoughts, he was miserable.

Liz was without a doubt the kindest woman in the world and he had hurt her. He'd hurt her enough that she couldn't even force herself to be polite and eat breakfast with him.

When she'd left him three years before, he'd experienced a bit of remorse, but mostly he was relieved. He'd quickly buried both emotions under work—as he always did. But sitting on the ocean, with the sun on his face and the truth stirring his soul, he knew he had to make it up to her. All of it. The quick marriage, the horrible three years together, the bitter divorce and probably the pain she'd suffered afterward.

He owed her. And he hated owing anyone. But her refusal had shown him that she didn't want a grand gesture. Hell, she didn't want any gesture at all. Still, he needed to ease his own conscience by doing something for her. And he would. He simply wouldn't let her know he was doing it.

On Sunday morning, he got her phone number from Ava and tried calling her. He needed no more than a ten-minute conversation with her. He was very, very good at figuring out what people wanted or needed. That was part of what had made him so successful at negotiating. In ten minutes, he could figure out what anyone wanted or needed and then he could use that knowledge to negotiate for what *he* wanted. The situation with Liz was no different. He wanted to ease his conscience and could do that by simply finding a need and filling it for her. Anonymously, of course. Then his conscience would be clear. He could fall out of her life again, and they both could go back to the new lives they'd created without each other.

His call went directly to voice mail, so he tried calling her on Monday morning. That call also went to voice mail. Not wanting to make a fool of himself by leaving a hundred unanswered messages, he waited for Friday to roll around. She might not take his calls, she might not have eaten the breakfast he'd prepared the week before, but she couldn't avoid him in his own house if he really wanted to talk to her.

And he did. In only a few minutes, he could ascertain what was important to her, get it and ease his conscience. If he had to follow her around while she dusted, he would.

Realizing she might not enter if she saw he was still home, Cain stayed out of sight until he heard the bip, bip, bip of his alarm being disabled. He waited to hear the back door open and close, then he stepped into the kitchen.

"Liz."

The woman in the yellow maid's apron turned. "Mr. Nestor?"

"Oh, I'm sorry."

Well, if that didn't take the cake! Not only had she refused his thank-you waffles and ignored his calls, but now she'd sent someone else to clean his house?

He sucked in a breath to control his temper so he could apologize again to Liz's employee, then he drove to his office. He was done with pussyfooting around. Now, she'd deal with him on his terms.

He kept the five o'clock space on his calendar open assuming she and her employees met back at her office for some sort of debriefing at the end of the work week. At the very least, to get their weekly paychecks. Ava gave him the business address she'd gotten for Happy Maids and he jumped into his black Porsche.

With traffic, the drive took forty minutes, not the twenty he'd planned on. By the time he arrived at the office building housing Happy Maids, he saw a line of women in yellow aprons exiting. He quickly found a parking place for his car, but even before he could shut off his engine, Liz whizzed by him in an ugly green car.

Damn it!

Yanking on the Porsche's gearshift, he roared out of the parking space. He wasn't entirely sure it was a good idea to follow Liz home. She might take that as an invasion of privacy, but right at this moment, with the memory of her refusal to eat his waffles ringing in his head, and his embarrassment when he realized she'd given the job of cleaning his house to one of her employees adding fuel to the fire, he didn't give a damn.

He wanted to get this off his conscience and all he needed were ten minutes. But she wouldn't even give him ten minutes. So he'd have to take them. He wasn't sure how he'd explain his presence at her door, but he suddenly realized he had the perfect topic of conversation. He could calmly, kindly, ask her why she'd left their marriage without a word. Three years had gone by. The subject wasn't touchy anymore. At least not for him. He knew why she'd left. He'd been a lousy husband. This should be something she'd want to discuss. To get off her chest.

He wouldn't be mean. He'd say the words women loved to hear. That he wanted to talk. To clean their slate. For closure. So they could both move on completely. Actually, what he was doing was giving her a chance to vent. She'd probably be thrilled for it.

He grinned. He was a genius. Mostly because Liz was the kind of woman she was. She didn't rant and rail. Or even get angry. She'd probably quietly tell him that she'd left him because he had been a nightmare to live with, and he would humbly agree, not argue, showing her he really did want closure. All the while he'd be processing her house, looking for clues of what mattered to her, what she needed. So he could get it for her and wipe this off his conscience.

He wove in and out of traffic two car lengths behind her, not surprised when she drove to one of Miami's lower-middle-class neighborhoods. She identified with blue-collar people. Which was one of the reasons their marriage had been so stressful. She'd been afraid to come out of her shell. Afraid of saying or doing the wrong thing with his wealthy friends. Afraid, even, to plan their own parties.

She pulled her car onto the driveway of a modest home and jumped out. As she ducked into the one-car garage and disappeared, he drove in behind her.

He took a second to catch his breath and organize his thoughts. First he would apologize for being presumptuous when he made the waffles for her. Then he'd give her the spiel about wanting a clean slate—which, now that he thought about it, was true. He was here to help them move on. Then he'd do what he did best. He'd observe her surroundings, really listen to what she said and figure out what he could do for her.

Taking a few measured breaths, he got out of his car and started up the cracked cement sidewalk. He was amazingly calm by the time a little girl of about three answered the door after he rang the bell.

"Mom!" she screamed, turning and running back into the dark foyer. "It's a stranger!"

Cain blinked. His mouth fell open. Then his entire body froze in fear. Liz had a child? A child old enough to be…well, *his*?

Oh, dear God. That would explain why she'd left without a word. Why she'd avoided him—

Liz and a red-haired woman Cain didn't recognize raced into the hall leading to the foyer. The red-haired woman pushed the little girl behind her in a move that very obviously said this was her child, not Liz's.

Chastising his overactive imagination, Cain forced his breathing back to normal but it wasn't so easy to get his heart rate off red alert.

And Liz still barreled up the hall, looking ready for a fight. She was only a few feet in front of him before she recognized him.

"Oh. It's you." Sighing heavily, she turned to the redhead. "This is my ex-husband, Cain."

Still coming down from the shock of thinking he was a dad, he quickly said, "I'm here to apologize about the waffles last week."

"Apology accepted. Now leave."

Wow. She was a lot quicker on her feet than he'd remembered. "No. I can't. I mean, you didn't have to send another employee to clean my house today." Embarrassment twisted his tongue. He wasn't saying any of this well. Where was the control that helped him schmooze bankers, sweet-talk union reps and haggle with suppliers?

Gone. That's where. Because Liz wasn't a banker, union rep or supplier. She was a normal person. His ex-wife. Now he understood Ava's comments the day he'd discovered Liz was his temporary maid. He wasn't good at ordinary conversation with ordinary people. Business was his element. That was why he didn't have a personal life.

Still, he needed to talk to her.

He rubbed his hand across the back of his neck. "Could you give me ten minutes?"

"For what?"

He smiled as charmingly as he could, deciding to pretend this was a business conversation so he'd get some of his control back. "Ten minutes, Liz. That's all I want."

Liz sighed and glanced at the woman beside her.

She shrugged. "You could go outside to the patio."

Cain blanched. "This isn't your house?"

"No."

He squeezed his eyes shut in embarrassment, then addressed the redhead. "I'm sorry. Ms.—"

"It's Amanda." She shrugged. "And don't worry about it. It's not really my house, either."

"Then whose house is it?"

Liz motioned for him to follow her down the hall and into the kitchen. "I'll explain on the patio."

The little girl with the big blue eyes also followed them to the sliding glass door. Liz stopped short of exiting, stooping to the toddler's level. "Joy, you stay with your mom, okay?"

Grinning shyly, Joy nodded.

Liz smiled and hugged her fiercely, before she rose. Something odd bubbled up inside Cain, something he'd never once considered while they were married. Liz would make a wonderful mom. He'd known she'd wanted children, but after his brother's death, they'd never again discussed it. Was that why she'd left him without a word? And if it was—if what meant the most to her was having a child—how could he possibly make *that* up to her?

Without looking at him she said, "This way."

She led him to a small stone patio with an inexpensive umbrella-covered table. There was no pool, no outdoor kitchen. Just a tiny gas grill.

She sat at the table and he did the same. "Whose house is this?"

"It's owned by a charity." Lowering her voice to a whisper, she leaned in closer so he could hear her. "Look, Cain, I really can't tell you much, except this house belongs to a charity for women who need a second chance. They stay at houses like this until they can get on their feet."

Cain didn't have to work hard to read between the lines of what she'd said. He frowned. "She's been abused?"

Liz shushed him with a wave of her hand and whispered, "Yes." Lowering her voice even more she added, "Look, we don't like talking about this when we're with the clients. We're trying to establish them as any other member of their community. Not someone being supported by a charity. We want them to think of us as friends, not benefactors."

Following her direction to keep the conversation more private, Cain leaned closer to Liz. The light scent of her shampoo drifted over to him. The smoothness of her skin called him to touch. Memories tripped over themselves in his brain until he remembered this was how she'd been the day he'd met her on the plane. Sweet. Kind. Shy. Reluctant to talk. He'd had to draw her out even to get her to tell him the simplest things about herself.

That day he hadn't been bad at normal conversation. He'd wanted to sleep with her enough that he'd pushed beyond his inability to chitchat.

He rubbed his hand across the back of his neck. That was a bad connection to make with her sitting so close, smelling like heaven, while his own blood vibrated through his veins with recognition that this woman had once been his.

He cleared his throat. "So, this is a charity?"

"Yes." She winced.

He glanced around, confused. "What are *you* doing here?"

"Happy Maids donates housecleaning services when one of the Friend Indeed houses becomes vacant. I also stock the cupboards with groceries and cleaning supplies. I'm part of the committee that welcomes a woman to her new house and stays in her life to help her acclimate."

"A Friend Indeed?"

She nodded.

Processing everything she'd told him, Cain stayed silent. He'd accomplished his purpose. A woman who not only donated the services of her business, but also bought groceries, was obviously committed to this charity. Anything he did for A Friend Indeed would be a kindness to her. Clearly, they'd won her heart. So all he had to do was make a big contribution, and his conscience would be clear.

But figuring that out also meant he had nothing more to say.

He could try to make up a reason to talk to her, but he'd already proven chitchat wasn't his forte. Plus, that would only mean staying longer with the woman whose mere presence made him ache for what they'd had and lost. There was no point wanting what he couldn't have. They'd been married once. It had failed.

Exhaling a big breath, Cain rose. "I'm sorry I bothered you."

Her brow puckering in confusion, she rose with him. "I thought you wanted to talk."

"We just did." Rather than return to the kitchen and leave through the front door, he glanced around, saw the strip of sidewalk surrounding the house that probably led to the driveway and headed off.

His conscience tweaked again at the fact that he'd

confused her but he ignored it. The money he would donate would more than make up for it.

On Monday morning, he had Ava investigate A Friend Indeed. At first she found very little beyond their name and their registration as a charitable organization, then Cain called in a few favors and doors began to open. Though shrouded in secrecy, the charity checked out and on Friday morning Cain had Ava write a check and deliver it to the home of the president of the group's board of directors. She returned a few hours later chuckling.

"Ayleen Francis wants to meet you."

Cain glanced up from the document he was reading. "Meet me?"

She leaned against the door frame. "I did the usual spiel that I do when you have me deliver a check like this. That you admire the work being done by the group and want to help, but prefer to remain anonymous, et cetera. And she said that was fine but she wouldn't accept your check unless she met you."

Cain frowned. "Seriously?"

"That's what she said."

"But—" Damn it. Why did everything about Liz have to turn complicated? "Why would she want to meet me?"

"To thank you?"

Annoyed, he growled. "I don't need thanks."

Ava shrugged. "I have no idea what's going on. I'm just the messenger." She set the check and a business card on Cain's desk. "Here's the address. She said it would be wonderful if you could be there tonight at eight."

Cain snatched up the card and damned near threw it in the trash. But he stopped. He was *this* close to making it up to Liz for their marriage being a disaster. No matter how much he'd worked with his dad before he sold the family business in Kansas and retired, Cain had never been able to do enough to make up for his brother's death. His parents had accepted Tom's death as an accident and eventually Cain had, too. Sort of. As the driver of the car, he would always feel responsible. He'd never let go of that guilt. But he did understand it had been an accident.

But his troubled marriage wasn't an accident. He'd coerced Liz. Seduced her. More sexually experienced than she had been, he'd taken advantage of their chemistry. Used it. She hadn't stood a chance.

And he knew he had to make that up to her. Was he really going to let one oddball request stand in his way of finally feeling freed of the debt?

CHAPTER FOUR

ARRANGING HER NOTES for the executive board meeting for A Friend Indeed held the first Friday of the month, Liz sat at the long table in the conference room of the accounting firm that handled the finances for the charity. The firm also lent them space to hold their meetings because A Friend Indeed didn't want to waste money on an office that wouldn't often be used. Their work was in the field.

Ayleen Francis, a fiftysomething socialite with blond hair and a ready smile who was the president of the board, sat at the head of the table chatting with Ronald Johnson, a local man whose daughter had been murdered by an ex-boyfriend. A Friend Indeed had actually been Ron's brainchild, but it took Ayleen's money and clout to bring his dream to fruition.

Beside Ron was Rose Swartz, owner of a chain of floral shops. Liberty Myers sat next to Rose and beside Liz was Bill Brown. The actual board for the group consisted of sixteen members, but the six-person executive board handled most of the day-to-day decisions.

Waiting for Ayleen to begin the meeting, Liz handed the receipts for the groceries she'd purchased for

Amanda and her kids to Rose, the group's treasurer, as well as a statement for cleaning services. Liz donated both the food and the services, but for accounting purposes A Friend Indeed kept track of what each cost.

"Thank you, Liz," Rose said, her smile warm and appreciative. But before Liz could say you're welcome, someone entered behind her and a hush fell over the small group.

Ayleen rose just as Liz turned to see Cain standing in the door way. "I'm assuming you're Cain Nestor."

He nodded.

Ayleen smiled and turned to the group. "Everyone, this is Cain Nestor, CEO of Cain Corporation. He's visiting us this evening."

Shock and confusion rippled through Liz. She hadn't seen Cain in three years, now suddenly he was everywhere! Worse, she'd brought him here. She'd given him the name of the group when he followed her to Amanda's. She couldn't believe he was still pursuing the opportunity to thank her for staying with him while he was sick, but apparently he was and she didn't like it. She was over him. She wanted to stay over him!

"Just take a seat anywhere." Ayleen motioned to the empty seats at the end of the table.

Cain didn't move from the doorway. "Ms. Francis—"

Ayleen smiled sweetly. "Call me Ayleen."

"Ayleen, could we talk privately?"

"Actually, I don't say or do much for A Friend Indeed without my executive board present. That's why I asked your assistant to pass on the message for you to meet me here. If you'll let me start the meeting, I'll tell the group about your donation—"

Liz frowned. He'd made a donation? To *her* charity?

"My assistant was also supposed to tell you that the donation was to be kept confidential."

"Everything about A Friend Indeed is confidential." She motioned around the room. "Nothing about the group goes beyond the board of directors. Some things don't go beyond the six people at this table. However, none of us keeps secrets from the others. But if you don't care to stay for the meeting, then I'll simply tell the group I'm refusing your donation."

Cain gaped at her. "What?"

"Mr. Nestor, though we appreciate your money, what we really need is your help." She ambled to the conference-room door. "As I've already mentioned, everything about A Friend Indeed is confidential. That's out of necessity. We give women a place to stay after they leave abusive husbands or boyfriends." She smiled engagingly as she slid her arm beneath Cain's and guided him into the room.

"For their safety, we promise complete anonymity. But because we do promise complete anonymity to our clients, we can't simply hire construction firms to come and do repair work on our houses. As a result, several of them are in serious disrepair."

Liz sat up, suddenly understanding the point Ayleen was about to make. The group didn't need money as much as they needed skilled, trustworthy volunteers.

"The amount of your check is wonderful. But what we really need is help. If you seriously want to do something for this group, what we'd like is your time."

Cain glanced at Liz, then returned his gaze to Ayleen. "What are you saying?"

"I'm asking you to do some work for us."

He looked at Liz again. Her skin heated. Her heartbeat jumped to double-time. He was actually considering it.

For her.

Something warm and syrupy flooded her system. He'd never done anything like this. It was overkill as a thank-you for her helping him through the flu. Donating money was more within his comfort zone. Especially donating anonymously. A secret donation of money, no matter how big, was easy for him.

But A Friend Indeed didn't need his money as much as his help. And he was considering it.

Holding his gaze, Liz saw the debate in his eyes. He'd have to give up time, work with people. Ordinary people. Because someone from A Friend Indeed would have to accompany him. A stranger couldn't go to the home of one of their abused women alone.

But, his money hadn't been accepted. If he still wanted to do something nice for Liz, it would require his time. Something he rarely gave.

Continuing to hold Liz's gaze he said, "What would I have to do?"

Liz smiled. Slowly. Gratefully. She didn't care as much about a thank-you as she cared about A Friend Indeed. About the families in the homes that needed repairs. She'd been up close and personal with most of them, since her group was in charge of cleaning them for the families, and she knew just how bad some of the homes were.

Alyeen said, "Liz? What would he have to do?"

Liz faced Ayleen. "Cain paid his way through university working construction jobs in the summer. If he could spare the time, the house we moved Amanda into a few weeks ago has a lot of little things that need to be repaired."

"It's been years since I've done any hands-on construction. I can't make any promises without seeing the house."

Ayleen clapped her hands together with glee. "Understandable. I'll have Liz take you to Amanda's."

Liz's heart thumped. She wanted his help, the group *needed* his help, but she didn't want to have to be with him to get it.

"I'm not sure I can," Liz said at the same time that Cain said, "That's not necessary."

"You're a stranger to us," Ayleen firmly told Cain. "For the safety and assurance of our families, I want you with someone from the board at all times." She faced Liz. "Liz, you've been at Amanda's every weekend since she moved in anyway. And you obviously know Cain. You're the best person to accompany him to Amanda's tomorrow." She smiled at Liz. "Please."

Drat. She shouldn't have mentioned her knowledge about Cain's construction experience. But she had been amazed and grateful that he was willing to help. She'd be crazy or shrewish to refuse to do her part.

"Sure."

Ayleen maneuvered Cain into a seat, but not once did Liz even glance in his direction. It was one thing to appreciate the gift of his help, quite another to be stuck spending time with him. Worse, the whole idea that he'd be willing to actually work, *physically work*, to thank her for a few hours of caring for him gave her a soft fluttery feeling in her stomach.

She ignored it. They had to spend time together the next day. Maybe hours. She couldn't be all soft and happy—but she couldn't be angry with him, either. He was doing a huge favor for a charity that meant a great deal to her.

Of course he'd wanted to do it anonymously. Being with her probably wasn't a happy prospect for him any more than it was for her. With anybody else she'd be figuring out a way to make this deal palatable for them. So maybe that's what she needed to do with Cain. Find a way to make this easy for him, as if they were two friends working together for a charity.

The thought caused her brow to furrow. They'd never been friends. They'd been passionate lovers. A distant married couple. Hurt divorced people. But they'd never really been friends. They'd never even tried to be friends.

Maybe becoming friends was the real way for them to get beyond their troubled marriage? To pretend, even if only for a few hours, that the past was the past and from this point on they were two nice people trying to help each other.

Cain was already at Amanda's house the next morning when Liz arrived. Instead of his black Porsche, he waited for her in one of his Nestor Construction trucks. An old red one.

Keeping with her decision to treat him as she would a friend, she smiled and patted the side of the truck bed. "Wow. I haven't seen one of these in years."

He walked around the truck and Liz's smile disappeared as her mouth fell open slightly. She'd already noticed his T-shirt, but for some reason or another, the jeans he wore caught her off guard. He looked so young. So capable. So…sexy.

She cleared her throat, reminding herself that this was a new era for her and Cain. Friends. Two nice people working together for a charity.

"Mostly, we use Cain Corporation trucks now." He grinned. "But when I ran Nestor Construction, this one was mine." He patted the wheel well. "She was my first."

"Ah, a man and his truck." Eager to get out of the sun and to the reason they were here, Liz turned to the sidewalk. "Come on. This way."

They walked to the front door and Liz knocked. Joy answered, but Amanda was only a few feet behind her. She grabbed the giggling three-year-old and hoisted her into her arms. "Sorry about that."

Liz laughed. "Good morning, Joy," she said, tweaking the little girl's cheek as she passed.

Joy buried her face in Amanda's neck. "Morning."

Amanda looked pointedly at Cain. "And this is Cain?"

Cain held out his hand for shaking. "Sorry about our first meeting."

Amanda smiled. "That's okay. Neither one of us was in good form that day. Can I get you some coffee?"

Cain peered over at Liz.

Liz motioned for everyone to go into the kitchen. "Of course, we'd love some coffee."

When Amanda walked through the swinging door out of sight, Liz caught Cain's arm, holding him back. "If she offers something, take it. A lot of the women who come to us have little to no self-esteem. It makes them feel good about themselves to have coffee or doughnuts to offer. Take whatever she offers and eat it."

Looking sheepish and unsure, he nodded and everything inside Liz stilled. For the first time in their relationship she knew something he didn't. He needed her.

Their gazes caught.

Liz smiled, downplaying the reversal of their roles and seeking to reassure him.

The corners of his mouth edged up slowly in response, and his entire countenance changed. Crinkles formed around dark eyes that warmed.

The hallway suddenly felt small and quiet. The memory of how much she'd loved this man fluttered through her. With one step forward she could lay her palm on his cheek. Touch him. Feel his skin again. Feel connected to him in the only way they'd ever been connected. Touch.

But one touch always led to another and another and another. Which was probably why making love was the only way they'd bonded. They'd never had a chance to be friends. Never given themselves a chance to get to know each other.

Sad, really.

Instead of stepping forward, she stepped back, motioning to the door. "After you."

He shook his head. His voice was rich, husky when he said, "No. After you."

He'd been as affected by the moment as she had been. For a second she couldn't move, couldn't breathe, as another possibility for why he'd been so insistent on thanking her popped into her head. He hadn't forgotten their sexual chemistry any more than she had. They hadn't been good as a married couple, but they had been fantastic lovers. What if he was being kind, using this "thank you" as a first step to seducing her?

A sickening feeling rose up in her. He hadn't hesitated the first time. He'd done everything he'd had to do to get her to Miami, into his bed. Working for a charity was small potatoes compared to some of the things he'd done to woo her, including whisk her to Vegas and seduce her into marrying him.

Well, six years later she wasn't so foolish. So young. So inexperienced. If he dared as much as make a pass at her, he'd find himself with a new Friend Indeed employee as his liaison. He'd still have to fulfill his end of the bargain. He just wouldn't do it with her.

She headed for the swinging door. Cain followed. In the kitchen, Amanda already had three mugs of coffee on the table. The room was spotless and smelled of maple syrup. Amanda had the look of a woman who'd happily served her daughter breakfast.

Cain took a seat at the table. "We can use this time to talk about what you need me to do."

"You're doing the work?"

Liz caught Amanda's hand, forcing her gaze to hers for reassurance. "Yes. Cain worked in construction to put himself through university."

"And as a bartender and a grocery boy. I was also a waiter and amusement-park vendor." He smiled at Amanda as she sat. "School was four long years."

Amanda laughed.

Liz pulled her hand away. "So go ahead. Give Cain the list of things that need to be done."

"First, the plumbing."

He took a small notebook from his shirt pocket. "Okay."

"There are some places with missing baseboard."

"Uh-huh."

"The ceiling in the first bedroom has water marks."

Without looking up from his note taking, Cain said, "That's not good."

"And most of the walls need to be painted."

"You guys can help with that."

Liz hesitated. She didn't want to agree to time in the

same room with him, but from the sounds of the list Cain's work here wouldn't be a few hours. He'd be here for days and Liz would be, too. If she had to be here to oversee things, she might as well have something to do. Plus, the more she did, the sooner her time with Cain would be over.

"Sure."

Because Amanda had stopped listing repair items, Cain finally glanced up. "That's it?"

"Isn't that enough?"

"It's plenty. In fact," he said with a wince, "if those water marks are roof leaks, we've got a problem."

"Why?"

Cain caught Liz's gaze and her insides turned to gelatin again. But not because of chemistry. Because of fear. His eyes were soft, his expression grave. He wanted to do a good job. But he also had to be honest.

She'd only seen him look this way once. When she'd told him she couldn't plan a huge Christmas party he'd wanted to host for his business associates. She'd been afraid—terrified really—that she'd do something wrong, something simple, but so awful that she'd embarrass them both. He'd been angry first, but that emotion had flitted from his face quickly and was replaced by the expression he now wore. It had disappointed him that she couldn't do what he needed, but he had to be honest and admit he still wanted the party. So he'd hired someone to plan it for him.

He'd moved beyond it as if it wasn't a big deal. But the disappointment he'd felt in her lingered. Even now it reminded her that he knew they weren't good for each other as a couple. They didn't match. He wouldn't want to start something with her any more than she'd want to start something with him. No matter how sexually compatible they were, he wasn't here to seduce her. She actually felt a little foolish for even thinking it.

"A roof isn't a one-man job. Even with a crew a roof takes a few days. At the very least a weekend." He looked at Amanda. "But I'll choose the crew with care."

Amanda looked at Liz.

"We'll talk it over with Ayleen, but we can trust Cain. If he says he'll figure out a way to keep all this confidential, he'll do it." When it came to work Cain was as good as his word. "Plus, if Cain's okay with it, we'll only work weekends and you can take the kids to the beach or something. Not be around. Just to be sure no one sees you."

Amanda nodded. "Okay."

"Okay." Cain rose. "Let me take a quick look at all these things then I'll make a trip to the building supply store."

"Toilets are fixed. Showers all work," Cain said, wiping his hands on a paper towel as he walked into the kitchen.

Amanda had made grilled cheese sandwiches and tomato soup for lunch. Liz already sat at the table. Amanda was happily serving. He took a seat and Liz smiled at him. After walking through the house with him behaving like a contractor, not her ex-husband, not the man she shared unbelievable chemistry with, Liz was slightly annoyed with herself for even considering he was only here as part of a plan to seduce her. His work here might have begun as a way to thank her for caring for him, but now that he was here, he clearly wanted to do a good job. It almost seemed he'd forgotten their chemistry or that she had imagined his reaction as they stood in the hallway that morning.

Which was good. Excellent. And took her back to her plan of behaving like his friend.

"So this afternoon we paint?"

"I'd like to get the painting done before we put up new baseboards. With all the rooms that need to be painted, it's going to take a few days. So it would be best if we started immediately after we eat."

"Okay."

Liz took a sandwich from the platter Amanda passed to her and handed it to Cain. Things were good. Relaxed. The more she was in his company this way, the more confident and comfortable she felt around him.

"I'll do the ceilings," Cain said, taking three sandwiches. "You guys handle the walls."

Amanda grimaced. "I'm sorry. I scheduled a playdate for Joy. I didn't realize you'd need me this soon."

"It's all right," Liz said easily. "Cain and I will be fine."

She genuinely believed that, until Amanda and Joy left and suddenly she and Cain were alone with two gallons of paint, two paint trays and a few brushes and rollers. Why did fate always have to test her like this? Just because she'd become comfortable around him, that didn't mean she had to be tested an hour after the thought had formed in her brain.

"What's the protocol on this?" she asked, nervously flitting away from him.

"First, we put blue tape around the windows and doors and existing baseboards so we don't get any paint where we don't want it. Then I'll do the ceiling and you do the walls."

He went out to his truck and returned with a roll of blue tape. Swiftly, without a second thought and as if he weren't having any trouble being alone with her, he applied it on the wood trim around the windows.

"Wow. A person would never guess you hadn't done that in about ten years."

He laughed. "It's like riding a bike. It comes back to you."

He *was* at ease. He wasn't seeing her as anything but a work buddy. Surely, she could follow suit.

"I know but you really look like you were born to this. It's almost a shame you don't do it anymore."

"My end of things is equally important." He turned from the window. "Come here. Let me show you how simple it is."

She walked over to the window and he positioned her in front of it. Handing her the roll, he said, "Hook the end of the tape over the edge of the top molding and then just roll it down."

She did as he said but the tape angled inward and by the time she reached the bottom the edge was still bare.

"Here." Covering her hand with his, he showed her how to direct the roll as she moved it downward, so that the side of the woodwork was entirely covered by the tape.

Liz barely noticed. With his chest brushing her back and his arm sliding along her arm, old feelings burst inside her. The scent of him drifted to her and she squeezed her eyes shut. She had never met a man who caused such a riot inside her. She longed to turn around and snuggle into him, wrap her arms around him, simply enjoy the feeling of his big body against hers.

She stiffened. She had to get beyond this! If he could treat her like a coworker, she could treat him like a friend.

As if unfazed, he pulled away and walked to the paint. He poured some of the gray into one of the trays and white into the second one.

"Okay. I'm ceilings. You're walls. But first I'm going to do the edge where the wall meets the ceiling." He nodded at the tray of gray paint. "You take that and a roller and go nuts on the walls. Just stay away from the edges."

"With pleasure." She managed to make her voice sound light and friendly, but inside she was a mess. Especially since he seemed so cavalier. All this time she'd believed his attraction to her fueled her attraction to him. Now, she wasn't so sure. Oh, she still believed he was attracted to her. His attraction simply didn't control him.

And by God she wasn't going to let hers control her, either!

For the next ten minutes they were quiet. Cain took a brush and painted an incredibly straight, incredibly neat six-inch swatch at the top of the wall, ensuring that Liz wouldn't even accidentally get any gray paint on the ceiling.

Deciding she needed to bring them back to a neutral place or the silence would make her nuts by the end of the day she said, "How do you do that so fast, yet so well?"

"Lots and lots of practice," he said, preoccupied with pouring more white paint into his tray. "Don't forget I did this kind of work four summers in a row. That was how I knew I wanted to run a construction company. I learned to do just about everything and I actually knew the work involved when I read plans or specs."

"Makes sense." She rolled gray paint onto the far wall. She'd heard that story before, but now that she was a business owner she understood it and could respond to it.

"In a way, I got into cleaning for the same reason. Once I realized what would be required of my employees, it was easy to know who to choose for what jobs and also what to charge."

"And you did great."

His praise brought a lump to her throat. In the three years they were married he'd never praised her beyond her looks. He loved how she looked, how she smelled, how soft she was. But he'd never noticed her beyond that.

She cleared her throat. "Thanks."

Occupied with painting the ceiling, Cain quietly said, "You know this is going to be more than a one-day job."

"So you've said."

He winced. "More than a two-week job."

She stopped. "Really?"

"Because we can only work weekends, I'm thinking we're in this for a month. And we're kind of going to be stuck together."

"Are you bailing?"

"No!" His answer was sharp. He stopped painting and faced her. "No. But I have to warn you that I'm a little confused about how to treat you."

Relief stuttered through her. She didn't want him to seduce her, but she certainly didn't want to be the only one fighting an attraction. "I thought we were trying to behave like friends."

"I'm not sure how to do that."

"Most of the day you've been treating me like a coworker. Why don't you go back to that? Forget I'm your ex-wife."

He glanced over at her and all the air evaporated from Liz's lungs. The look he gave her was long and slow, as if asking how he could forget that they'd been married, been intimate.

Maybe that was the crux of their problem? Every time she looked at him something inside her stirred to life. She'd lived for three years without thinking about sex, but put him in the room with her and she needed to fan herself. Worse, through nearly three years of a bad marriage, they'd already proven they could be angry with each other, all wrong for each other and still pleasure each other beyond belief.

It was going to be difficult to pretend none of that mattered.

But they had to try.

She cleared her throat. "I could use a glass of water. Would you like one?"

"Please."

In the kitchen, she took two bottles of water from the refrigerator. She pressed the cool container against her cheek. Late March in southern Florida could be hot, but being in the same room with Cain was turning out to be even hotter.

Still, A Friend Indeed needed his help. Amanda deserved a pretty home for herself and her kids. Liz was also a strong, determined businesswoman who had handled some fairly tough trials through the three years of running her company. One little attraction wasn't going to ruin her.

Feeling better, she walked back to the living room, but stopped dead in the doorway. Reaching up to paint the ceiling, with his back to her, Cain stretched his T-shirt taut against his muscles. His jeans snugly outlined his behind. She swallowed. Memories of them in the shower and tangled in their sheets flashed through her brain.

She pressed the water bottle to her cheek again, pushing the pointless memories aside, and strode up behind him.

"Here."

He turned abruptly and a few drops of paint rained on her nose.

"Oops! Sorry. You kind of surprised me."

"It's okay."

He yanked a work hanky from his back pocket. "Let me get that."

Enclosing her chin in his big hand to hold her head still, he rubbed the cloth against her nose. Memories returned full force. Times he'd kissed her. Laughing on the beach before running into the house for mind-blowing sex. Falling asleep spooned together after.

He blinked. His hand stilled. Everything she was feeling was reflected in his dark eyes.

The world stopped for Liz. Holding his gaze, knowing exactly what he was remembering, feeling the thrum of her own heart as a result of the memories that poured through her brain, Liz couldn't move, couldn't breathe.

For ten seconds she was absolutely positive he was going to kiss her. The urge to stand on her tiptoes and accept a kiss was so strong she had to fight it with everything in her. But in the end, he backed away, his hand falling to his side.

Turning to the wall again, he said, "Another twenty minutes and I'll have the ceiling done. If you want to go put blue tape around the windows in the dining room we could probably get that room done today, too."

She stepped back. "Okay." She took another step backward toward the door. "Don't forget your water."

He didn't look up. "I won't."

Relief rattled through her. He'd just had a golden opportunity to kiss her, yet he'd stepped away.

She definitely wasn't the only one who wanted them to be friends, not lovers, or the only one who'd changed.

When Liz was gone, Cain lowered himself to the floor. Leaning against the old stone fireplace, he rubbed his hand down his face.

He could have kissed her. Not out of habit. Not out of instinct driven by happy memories. But because he wanted to. He *longed* to. She'd hardly left the house for their entire marriage. Now she was a business owner, a volunteer for a charity, a confident, self-sufficient woman. This new side of Liz he was seeing was very appealing. When he coupled her new personality with his blissful sexual memories, she was damned near irresistible.

But the clincher—the thing that almost took him over the top—was the way she looked at him as if she'd never stopped loving him. As if she wanted what he wanted. As if her entire body revved with anticipation, the way his did. As if her heart was open and begging.

He'd always known he was the problem in their marriage. And now that he was older and wiser, he desperately wanted to fix things. But he didn't want to hurt her again. He saw the trust in her eyes. Sweet, innocent trust. She was counting on him to do the right thing.

Part of him genuinely believed the right thing was to leave her alone. Let her get on with her life. Become the success she was destined to be.

The other part just kept thinking that she was his woman, and he wanted her back.

But he knew that was impossible.

CHAPTER FIVE

WHILE THEY WORKED, Amanda and Joy returned from Joy's playdate, and Amanda prepared a barbecue. Liz didn't realize she was cooking until the aroma of tangy barbeque sauce floated through the downstairs. Just the scent brought Liz to the patio. A minute later, Cain followed behind her.

"What is that smell?"

Amanda laughed. "It's my mother's special barbeque-sauce recipe. Have a seat. Everything's done."

A glance to the right showed the umbrella table had been set with paper plates and plastic utensils. A bowl of potato salad sat beside some baked beans and a basket of rolls.

Starving from all the work she'd done, Liz sat down without a second thought. Cain, however, debated. She couldn't imagine how a single man could turn down home cooking until she remembered their near miss with the kiss. Their gazes caught. He looked away.

She could guess what he was thinking. It was getting harder and harder to work together because the longer they were together the more tempted they were. But his stepping away from the kiss proved he was here to help, only to help, not to try to work his way back into her bed.

And that meant she was safe. But so was he. He simply didn't know that she was as determined as he was to get beyond their attraction. Perhaps even to be friends.

So maybe she had to show him?

"Come on, Cain. This smells too good to resist."

He caught her gaze and she smiled encouragingly. She tried to show him with her expression that everything was okay. They could be around each other, if he'd just relax.

He walked to the table. "You're right. Especially since I'd be going home to takeout."

He sat across the table from her, leaving the two seats on either side of her for Amanda and Joy.

She smiled. As long as they paid no attention to their attraction, they could work toward becoming friends. She would simply have to ignore the extreme sadness that welled in her heart, now that their glances would no longer be heated and they had both silently stated their intentions not to get involved again. Mourning something that hadn't worked was ridiculous. She didn't want to go back to what they had. Apparently neither did he. So at least trying to become friends would make the next few weeks easier.

"Where's Billy?"

"Beach with some friends," Amanda announced casually. Then she paused and grinned. "You can't believe how wonderful it feels to say that. We were always so worried about Rick's reaction to everything that most of the time we didn't talk. Telling him where Billy was was an invitation to get into an argument." She shook her head. "It was no way to live."

"No. It isn't."

That came from Cain and caused Liz's head to swivel in his direction. Not only was he not one to talk about such personal things, but his sympathetic tone was so unexpected she almost couldn't believe it was he who had spoken.

"Men who abuse anyone weaker than they are are scum." His voice gentled and he glanced at Amanda. "I'm glad you're safe."

Liz stared at him, suddenly understanding. He'd never been a bad person, simply an overly busy person who had never stopped long enough to pay attention to anything that didn't pop up in front of him. Amanda and her children were no longer an "issue" to him. They were people with names and faces and lives. It lightened Liz's heart that he didn't just recognize that; he genuinely seemed to care for them.

Still, the conversation could potentially dip into subjects too serious for Joy's ears. "Well, that's all over now," Liz said, turning to the little girl. "And how did you like your playdate?"

Joy leaned across the table. "It was fun. Maddie has a cat."

"A huge monster cat!" Amanda said, picking up the platter of chicken and spearing a barbecued breast. "I swear I thought it was a dog when I first saw it."

They laughed.

"Do you have a cat?" Joy asked Liz.

"No. No cat for me. I'm allergic."

"It means she can't be around them or she'll sneeze," Amanda explained to Joy as she passed the beans to Cain.

"I didn't know you were allergic to cats."

That was Cain. His words were soft, not sharp or ac-

cusatory, but trepidation rippled through her, reminding her of another reason she and Cain couldn't be
more than coworkers. She had bigger secrets than an
allergy to cats. From the day she'd met him she'd kept
her father's abuse a secret. Plus, she'd never told him
they'd created a child, and then she'd lost that child.

If they weren't with Amanda, this might have been
the time to tell him. They'd had a reasonably pleasant
afternoon. They'd both silently stated their intention not
to get involved, but to try to be friends. That had created
a kind of bond of honesty between them, which would
have made this the perfect time to at least tell him about
his child.

But they weren't alone.

Liz turned her attention to the platter of chicken that
had come her way. "You didn't have a cat. I didn't have
a cat. It never came up."

He accepted her answer easily, but shame buffeted
her, an unexpected result of spending so much time in
his company. With him behaving like a good guy, a normal guy, a guy who wanted to get beyond their sexual
chemistry and be friends, the secrets she'd kept in their
marriage suddenly seemed incredibly wrong.

She hadn't told him that her dad had abused her, her
mom and her sisters because at the time she was working to forget that. To build a life without her other life
hanging over her head. She hadn't told him about her
miscarriage because she'd needed help herself to accept
it. And she'd had to leave him to get that help.

But three years later, so far beyond both of those
problems that she could speak about each without
breaking down, she wondered about the wisdom of
having kept her secrets from him.

Would their marriage have been different if she'd admitted that as a child she'd been poor, hungry and constantly afraid?

Would *he* have been different if she'd turned to him for comfort in her time of need?

She'd never know the answer to, either, but the possibility that she could have changed her marriage, saved it, with a few whispered words, haunted her.

Sitting at the kitchen table of Amanda's house the next morning, finishing a cup of coffee after eating delicious blueberry pancakes, Liz smiled shakily at Cain as he stepped into the room. "Good morning."

"Good morning."

She might have kept secrets but she and Cain were now divorced, trying to get along while they worked together, not trying to reconcile. For that reason, she'd decided that the story of her abusive father could remain her secret. But as she had paced the floor the night before, working all this out in her brain, she realized how much she wanted to tell him about their baby.

When they divorced, she had been too raw and too hurt herself to tell him. By the time she'd gotten herself together, their paths never crossed. But now that their paths hadn't merely crossed, they were actually intersecting for the next several weeks; she couldn't keep the secret from him any more. He'd created a child. They'd lost that child. He deserved to know. And she wanted to tell him.

Which left her with two problems. When she'd tell him and how she'd tell him. She might be ready to share, but he might not be ready to hear it. She had to be alert for another opportunity like the one the day before…except when they were alone, not with other people.

Amanda turned from the stove. "Are you hungry, Cain? I'm making blueberry pancakes."

It was clear that Amanda reveled in the role of mom. Without the constant fear of her abusive husband she had blossomed. Joy was bright-eyed and happy, a little chatterbox who had entertained Liz all through breakfast. Amanda's only remaining problem was Billy, her sixteen-year-old son. They hadn't been away from their violent father long enough for any one of them to have adjusted, but once they had, Liz was certain Amanda would think of some way to connect with her son.

As far as Amanda's situation was concerned, Liz could relax…except for Cain, who hesitated just inside the kitchen door. Had he figured out she'd kept secrets bigger than an allergy to cats? Was he angry? Would he confront her? She couldn't handle that. Telling him about their baby had to be on her terms. That would be better for both of them. It would be horrible if he confronted her now.

Finally he said, "I've already eaten breakfast."

Relief wanted to rush out of her on a long gust of air, but she held it back. She'd instructed him to take everything Amanda offered. The day before he could have easily begged off her barbecue by saying it was time to go home. But he couldn't so easily walk away from breakfast when he would be staying all morning.

Amanda said, "That's okay. Just have some coffee." She reached for a mug from the cupboard by the stove, filled it and handed it to him. "Sit for a minute."

He took the coffee and he and Amanda ambled to chairs at the table, as Amanda's sixteen-year-old son Billy stepped into the room, music headphones in his ears. Totally oblivious to the people at the table, he walked to the refrigerator and pulled out the milk.

Amanda cast an embarrassed glance at her son. "Billy, at least say good-morning."

He ignored her.

She rose, walked over to him and took one of the headphones from his right ear. "Good morning," she singsonged.

Billy sighed. "Morning."

"Say good morning to our guests."

He scowled toward the table. "Good morning."

Liz had seen this a million times before. A teenager embarrassed that he had to count on a charity for a roof over his head frequently acted out. Especially the son of an abusive father. Even as Billy was probably glad to get away from his dad, he also missed him. Worse, he could be wondering about himself. If he was like his dad.

Liz's gaze slid to Cain. Billy was the kind of employee Cain hated. Troubled. He wanted only the best, both emotionally and physically, so he didn't have to deal with problems. His job was to get whatever construction project he had done and done right. He didn't have time for employee problems.

But after the way he'd reacted to Amanda's comment the day before, Liz knew he'd changed. At least somewhat. And he did have a soft spot for Amanda and her family. Billy was a part of that family. He desperately needed a positive male role model. If Cain simply behaved as he had the day before when he showed her how to use the blue tape and paint, Billy might actually learn something.

Plus, she and Cain wouldn't have to be in the same room.

She didn't want to spend the day worrying about

how and when she'd tell him about their child. She also couldn't simply blurt it out in an awkward silence, particularly since they might be alone in the room but they weren't alone in the house. She wanted the right opportunity again, but she also needed time to think it through so she could choose her words carefully. Not being around Cain would buy her time.

She took a breath then smiled at Billy. "We could sure use your help today. Especially Cain."

Amanda gasped and clasped her hands together. "What a wonderful idea! Do you know who Mr. Nestor is?"

Billy rolled his eyes. "No."

"He owns a construction company." Amanda all but glowed with enthusiasm. "I'll bet he could teach you a million things."

"I don't need to know a million things, Mom. Besides, I want to go to med school."

"And you're going to need money," Amanda pointed out. "Mr. Nestor put himself through university working construction."

Billy glared at Cain.

Cain shifted uncomfortably. "Construction isn't for everyone," he said, clearly unhappy to be caught in the middle. "I was also a bartender."

"But you're here now," Liz said, unable to stop herself. Her gaze roamed over to Cain's. "And you could teach him so much."

She let her eyes say the words she couldn't utter in front of the angry teen who desperately needed to at least see how a decent man behaved.

Cain pulled in a slow breath. Liz held hers. He'd changed. She knew he'd changed just from the sympathy he'd displayed to Amanda the day before. He could do this! All he had to do was say okay.

She held her breath as she held his gaze. His steely eyes bore into hers, but the longer their connection, the more his eyes softened.

Finally, he turned on his chair, facing Billy. "What I'm doing today isn't hard. So it might be a good place for you to start if you're interested in learning a few things."

"There! See!" Amanda clasped Billy on the shoulder. "It will be good for you."

Cain rose and motioned for Billy to follow him out of the kitchen. Liz stared after them, her heart pounding. No matter how much she wanted to believe he'd done that out of sympathy for Amanda's situation, she knew he'd done it for her.

She turned back to her coffee, smiled at Amanda, trying to appear as if nothing was wrong. But everything was wrong. First, spending time with him had caused her to realize he deserved to know he'd created and lost a child. Now he was softening, doing things she asked.

For the first time it occurred to her that maybe he wasn't changing because of their situation but to please her.

And if he was…Lord help them.

Ten minutes later Cain found himself in the living room with an angry, sullen teenager. He debated drawing him into conversation, but somehow he didn't think the charisma that typically worked on egotistical bankers and clever business owners would work with a kid. And the chitchat he was forcing himself to develop with Amanda and Liz hadn't served him all that well, either. He and Billy could either work in silence, or he could hit this kid with the truth.

"You know what? I don't like this any more than you do."

Surprised, Billy looked over.

"But your mom wants you here and every once in a while a man has to suck it up and do what his mom wants." Technically, he and Billy were in the same boat. He was in this room, with this angry boy, because he hadn't been able to resist the pleading in Liz's eyes. And that troubled him. He was falling for her again. Only this time it was different. This time he had nothing to prove professionally. No reason to back away. No way to erect walls that would allow him to be in a relationship and still protect his heart. She'd broken it once. She could do it again.

"If you'd kept your mouth shut I could have gotten out of this."

"How? By being a brat? That's a skill that'll really help you in the real world."

"I don't care about the real world."

Cain snorted. "No kidding." He slid his tape measure from his tool belt and walked to the wall. Holding the end of the tape against the wall, he waved the tape measure's silver container at Billy. "Take this to the other end of the wall."

Billy sighed, but took the tape box and did as Cain requested.

"What's the length?"

"Ten feet."

"Exactly ten feet?"

"I don't know."

Exasperated, but not about to let Billy know that and give him leverage to be a pain all day, Cain said, "Okay. Let's try this again. You hold this end against the wall. I'll get the number."

Without a word, Billy walked the tape back to Cain and they switched places.

He measured the length, told Billy to let go of his end and the tape snapped back into the silver container. He reached for one of the long pieces of trim he'd purchased the day before. It bowed when he lifted it and he motioned with his chin for Billy to grab the other end. "Get that, will you?"

Billy made a face, but picked up the wood.

Cain carried it to the miter box. The tools he had in his truck were from nearly ten years before. Though they weren't the latest technology they still worked. And maybe teaching this kid a little something today might be the best way to get his mind off Liz. About the fact that he didn't just want her, he was doing crazy things for her. About the fact that if he didn't watch himself, he'd be in so far that he'd be vulnerable again.

"You know, eventually you'll have to go to somebody for a job. You're not going to get through school on your good looks."

Adjusting the wood in the box, Cain made his end cuts. He gestured for Billy to help him take the piece of trim to the wall again. He snapped it into place and secured it with a few shots from a nail gun.

"I was thinking maybe I'd try the bartending thing like you did."

Surprised, Cain glanced over. He cautiously said, "Bartending is good when classes are in session and working nights fits into your schedule. But summers were when I made my tuition. To earn that much money, you have to have a job that pays. Construction pays."

Billy opened his mouth to say something, but snapped it shut. Cain unexpectedly itched to encourage him to talk, but he stopped himself. If the kid wanted to talk, he'd talk. Cain had no intention of overstepping his boundaries. He knew that Liz had set Billy up with him to be a good example, but he wasn't a therapist. Hell, he wasn't even much of a talker. He couldn't believe this kid had gotten as much out of him as he had.

"My dad was—is—in construction."

"Ah." No wonder Liz thought this would be such a wonderful arrangement.

"Look, kid, you don't have to be like your dad. You can be anybody, anything, you want." He glanced around the room. "Doing stuff like this," he said, bringing his words down to Billy's level, "gives you a way to test what you're good at while you figure out who you are." He paused then casually said, "You mentioned that you wanted to go to med school."

"It's a pipe dream. No way I'll swing that."

"Not with that attitude."

Billy snorted. "My mom *can't* help."

"Hey, I made my own way. You can, too." Motioning for Billy to pick up the next board, he casually eased them back into conversation. "Besides, it's a good life lesson. The construction jobs I took to pay for tuition pointed me in the direction of what I wanted to do with my life."

Seeing that Billy was really listening, Cain felt edgy. It would be so easy to steer this kid wrong. He wasn't a people person. He didn't know anything about being raised by an abusive father. There were a million different ways he could make a mistake.

"I think I want to be a doctor, but I'm not sure."

"You'll work that out." He motioned for Billy to grab the tape measure again. "Everything doesn't have to be figured out in one day. Take your time. Give yourself a break. Don't think you have to make all your decisions right now."

Oddly, his advice to Billy also relaxed him about Liz. Every decision didn't have to be made in a day. That's what had screwed them up in the first place. They jumped from seat mates in a plane to dating to sleeping together in a matter of days. Melting and doing her bidding just because she turned her pretty green eyes on him was as bad as working to seduce her the first day he'd met her.

Somehow he had to get back to behaving normally around his wife.

Ex-wife.

Maybe the first step to doing that would be to remember falling victim to their sexual attraction hadn't done anything except toss them into an unhappy marriage.

Just outside the door, Liz leaned against the wall and breathed an enormous sigh of relief. Two minutes after she suggested Billy help Cain she remembered they'd be using power tools—potential weapons—and she nearly panicked. But it appeared as if Billy and Cain had found a way to get along.

She and Amanda began painting the dining room but at eleven-thirty, they stopped to prepare lunch. At twelve they called Cain and Billy to the kitchen table and to her surprise they were chatting about a big project Cain's company had bid on when they walked to the sink to wash their hands.

They came to the table talking about how Cain's job is part math, part hand-holding and part diplomacy and didn't stop except to grab a bite of sandwich between sentences.

Liz smiled at Cain, working to keep their "friendship" going and determined not to worry about her secret until the time to tell him materialized, but Cain quickly glanced away, as if embarrassed.

When they'd finished eating, Billy and Cain went back to their work and Liz and Amanda cleaned the kitchen then resumed painting.

At five, Liz's muscles were pleasantly sore. She did manual labor for a living, but the muscles required for painting were different than those required for washing windows, vacuuming and dusting. Amanda planned to take her kids out to dinner so Cain and Liz had decided to leave to give them time to clean up before going out.

Still, as tired and sore as she was, she couldn't let Cain go without telling him she was proud of him. Billy needed him and he had cracked some barriers that Amanda had admitted she couldn't crack. After his wary expression when he glanced at her at lunch, she had to tell him how much he was needed, how good a job he was doing.

Leaning against the bed of his truck, waiting as he said goodbye to Amanda and Billy, she smiled as he approached.

"I'm not sure if you're embarrassed because you didn't want to help Billy or embarrassed that you did such a good job."

He tossed a saw into the toolbox in the bed of his truck. "He's a good kid."

"Of course he is. He just spent the first sixteen years of his life with a man who gave him a very bad impression of what a man's supposed to do. You were a good example today."

"Don't toss my hat in the ring for sainthood."

She laughed.

"I'm serious. If Billy had been a truly angry, truly rebellious teen, I would have been so far out of my league I could have done some real damage."

She sobered. He had a very good point. "I know."

He made a move to open his truck door and Liz stepped away. "I'm sorry."

Climbing into the truck, he shook his head. "No need to apologize. Let's just be glad it worked out."

She nodded. He started his truck and backed out of the driveway.

Liz stared after him. She'd expected him to either be angry that she'd set him up or to preen with pride. Instead, he'd sort of acted normally.

She folded her arms across her chest and watched his truck chug out of the neighborhood and an unexpected question tiptoed into her consciousness. Was acting normally his way of showing her they could be friends… Or his way of easing himself back into her life?

After all, he didn't have to be here, repairing Amanda's house. He could have refused when Ayleen asked him.

He also hadn't needed to befriend Billy. Yet, he'd responded to her silent plea and then did a bang-up job.

He also didn't have to interact with her. She was only here as a chaperone of sorts. Now that the work was going smoothly, he could ignore her.

So what was he doing?

CHAPTER SIX

"HAPPY MAIDS. Liz Harper speaking."

"Good morning, Ms. Harper. It's Ava from Cain Corporation. Mr. Nestor asked me to call."

Liz's heart did a somersault in her chest. Something was wrong. There was no reason for Cain to ask Ava to call except to reprimand her or fire her. Or maybe he'd finally found a full-time maid? It wasn't that she begrudged him help, but with Rita working now, bringing her staff up to seven, she needed every assignment she had and more.

"He's having some friends for a small dinner tonight—"

Liz's heart tumbled again and she squeezed her eyes shut. She wasn't fired. He was inviting her to a party! Oh God! He *was* trying to ease her back into his life.

"He's cooking."

Knowing Cain was very good at the grill, Liz wasn't surprised. But she still didn't want to go to a party at his house. Not when she was just about certain he was trying to get them back together.

"So he won't have a caterer to clean up. He's going

to need you to send someone tonight after the party to do that. He'll pay extra, of course."

Liz fell into her office chair, her cheeks flaming. So much for being invited to his party. He wanted her to *clean up*. She was his maid. Not a friend. Not a potential lover or date…or even an ex-wife. She was an employee.

He wasn't trying to ease her into his life. He wasn't even trying to show her they could be friends. He wasn't thinking that hard about it because in his mind there was no longer a question.

He didn't want her.

She swallowed again, easing the lump in her throat so she could speak. That was, after all, what she wanted.

"We'll be happy to clean up after the party."

"You'll only need one person."

No longer upset about the call itself, Liz noticed the pinched, tight tone of Ava's voice.

"It's a small party. Mr. Nestor and the partners of his new venture are gathering to have dinner before they sign a contract. He believes everyone will be gone by nine. Let me suggest you arrive around a quarter after nine."

The first time Liz had spoken with Ava, she'd been light, friendly, eager to get some housecleaning help for her boss. Today's stiff voice and formal tone puzzled Liz.

"A quarter after nine is fine."

She hung up the phone confused. Could Cain have told his assistant that Liz was his ex-wife? But why would he? What difference would it make? He never shared personal information with employees. Why start now?

Placing her fingers on her computer keyboard to begin inputting her workers' hours on a spreadsheet, she frowned. Even if he had told Ava Liz was his ex-wife, why would that upset his assistant?

And was that why she hadn't received any referrals from Ava?

She'd expected at least one person to call and say they'd been referred. That was how it worked in Liz's business. Maids had to be trusted. A word-of-mouth recommendation worked better than cold advertising. Yet, she'd gotten no recommendation from Cain.

She shook her head, dislodging those thoughts and getting her mind back on work. She didn't want to waste this precious time she had to do her paperwork fuming and speculating. With Rita working, Liz could now spend afternoons in the office and she basked in having evenings off.

She frowned again. She wouldn't have tonight off. She couldn't ask one of her employees to work on such short notice; all of them had children. Evening work meant extra child-care expense. Besides, Cain's house was back to being her assignment. After he'd been angry that she'd sent someone else after the waffle debacle, she'd taken the job back herself.

She sighed. She'd have to go to his house tonight.

But maybe that was good?

If nothing else, she had her perspective back. They were divorced, not trying to reconcile, and she had something to tell him. Alone in his house tonight, they could be honest with each other.

A mixture of fear and relief poured through her. Though telling him about the miscarriage would be difficult, it had to be done. He deserved to know.

She finished her paperwork around five and raced home to shower and change to have dinner with Ellie. She didn't mention that she had to work that night—

Or the odd tone in Ava's voice—

Or her realization that they hadn't gotten *one* re-
ferral from Cain—

Or that this might be the night she told Cain the
secret she'd kept from him.

All of that would put Ellie on edge. Or cause her to
make one of her powerful wishes. Instead, Liz listened
to Ellie chatter about the Happy Maids employees.
From the sparkle in Ellie's amber eyes it was clear she
enjoyed being everyone's supervisor. Not in a lord-it-
over-her-friends way. But in almost a motherly way.
Which made Liz laugh and actually took her mind off
Cain. Ellie was twenty-two. Most of the women she
now supervised were in their thirties or forties, some
even in their fifties. Yet Ellie clucked over them like a
mother hen. It was endearing.

Because they talked about work most of the meal,
Liz paid for dinner, calling it a business expense, and
parted company with Ellie on the sidewalk in front of
the restaurant. When she slid behind the steering wheel
of her car and saw the clock on the dashboard her mouth
fell open. It was nearly nine. No time to go home and
change into a Happy Maids uniform.

She glanced down at her simple tank top and jeans.
This would do. No matter how messy his house, she
couldn't damage a tank top and jeans.

Worry over being late blanked out all of her other
concerns about this job until she pulled into Cain's
empty driveway. Ava had been correct. Cain's guests
hadn't lingered. But suddenly she didn't want to see
him. She really wasn't ready with the "right words" to
tell them about their baby. She wasn't in the mood to
"play" friends, either, or to fight their attraction. Their

marriage might be over, but the attraction hadn't gone. And that's what made their situation so difficult.

If they weren't so attracted to each other there would be no question that their relationship was over and neither of them wanted to reopen it. But because of their damned unpredictable attraction, she had to worry about how *she* would react around him. Not that she wanted to sleep with him, but he'd seduced her before. And they were about to spend hours alone. If she was lucky, Cain would already be in the shower.

She swallowed. Best not to think about the shower.

But as she stepped out of her car into the muggy night, she realized it was much better to think of him being away from her, upstairs in his room, ignoring her as she cleaned, rather than close enough to touch, close enough to tempt, close enough to be tempted.

Cain watched her get out of her car and start up the driveway and opened the front door for her. "Come in this way."

She stepped into the echoing foyer with a tight, professional smile.

She was wary of him. Well, good. He was wary of her, of what was happening between them. It was bad enough to be attracted to someone he couldn't have. Now he was melting around her, doing her bidding when she looked at him with her big green eyes. He'd already decided the cure for his behavior around her was to treat her like an ex-wife. But he knew so little about her—except what he knew from their marriage—that he wasn't quite sure how to do that, either.

When he'd finally figured out they needed to get

to know each other as the people they were now, he'd had Ava call with the request that Liz clean up after his dinner party. Maybe a little time spent alone would give them a chance to interact and she'd tell him enough about herself that he'd see her as a new person, or at least see her in a different light so he'd stop seeing the woman he'd loved every time he looked at her.

"Most of the mess is in the kitchen," he said, motioning for her to walk ahead of him. He didn't realize until she was already in front of him that that provided him with a terrific view of her backside and he nearly groaned, watching her jean-clad hips sway as she walked. This was why the part of him that wanted her back kept surfacing, taking control. Tonight the businessman had to wrestle control away.

"And the dining room." He said that as they entered his formal dining room and the cluttered table greeted them.

"I thought you were eating outside?"

"My bragging might have forced me to prove myself to the partners by being the chef for the steaks, but it was a formal meeting."

"Okay." She still wouldn't meet his gaze. "This isn't a big deal. You go ahead to your office or wherever. I can handle it. I've been here enough that I know where to put everything."

He shook his head. If they were going to be around each other the next few weeks, they had to get to know each other as new people. Otherwise, they'd always relate to each other as the people they knew from their doomed marriage.

"It's late. If you do this alone, it could take hours. I'll help so you can be out of here before midnight."

The expression on her face clearly said she wanted to argue, but in the end, she turned and walked to the far side of the table, away from him. "Suit yourself."

She began stacking plates and gathering silverware at the head of the table. Cain did the same at the opposite end.

Though she hadn't argued with his decision to help her, she made it clear that she wasn't in the mood to talk. They worked in silence save for the clink and clatter of silverware and plates then he realized something amazing. She might be wary of him, but she wasn't afraid of his fancy silverware anymore. Wasn't afraid of chipping the china or breaking the crystal as she had been when they were married.

Funny that she had to leave him, become a maid, to grow accustomed to his things, his lifestyle.

"It seems weird to see how comfortable you are with the china."

She peeked up at him. "Until you said that, I'd forgotten how *uncomfortable* I had been around expensive things." She shrugged. "I was always afraid I'd break them. Now I can twirl them in the air and catch them behind my back with one hand."

He laughed, hoping to lighten the mood. "A demonstration's not really necessary."

She picked up a stack of dishes and headed for the kitchen. He grabbed some of the empty wineglasses and followed her. If discussing his china was what it took to get her comfortable enough to open up, then he wasn't letting this conversation die. "I never did understand why you were so afraid."

"I'd never been around nice things."

"Really?" He shook his head in disbelief. "Liz, your

job took you all over the place. You yourself told me that you had to wine and dine clients."

"In restaurants." She slid the glasses he handed her into the dishwasher. "It's one thing to go to a restaurant where somebody serves you and quite another to be the one in charge."

"You wouldn't hesitate now."

"No. I wouldn't. I love crystal and china and fancy silver."

The way he was watching her made Liz self-conscious, so embarrassed by her past that she felt the need to brag a little.

"I'm actually the person in charge of A Friend Indeed's annual fund-raiser." Her attention on placing dishes in the dishwasher, she added, "When we were married, I couldn't plan a simple Christmas party, now I'm in charge of a huge ball."

"There's a ball?"

Too late she realized her mistake. Though she wanted him to know about her accomplishments, she wasn't sure she wanted him at the ball, watching her, comparing her to the past. As coordinator for the event, she'd be nervous enough without him being there.

"It's no big deal," she said, brushing it off as insignificant. "Just Ayleen's way of getting her rich friends together to thank them for the donations she'll wheedle out of them before the end of the evening."

She straightened away from the dishwasher and headed for the dining room and the rest of the dirty dishes.

He followed her. "I know some people who could also contribute." He stopped in front of the table she was clearing and caught her gaze. "Can I get a couple of invitations to this ball or is it closed?"

Liz stifled a groan, as his dark eyes held hers. There was no way out of this.

"As someone working for the group, you're automatically invited. You won't get an invitation. Ayleen will simply expect you to be there."

But he would get invitations to Joni's barbecue and Matt's Christmas party. As long as he volunteered for A Friend Indeed, he'd be connected to her. She had to get beyond her fear that he would be watching her, evaluating her, remembering how she used to be.

The room became silent except for the clang of utensils as Liz gathered them. Cain joined in the gathering again. He didn't say anything, until they returned to the kitchen.

"Are you going to be uncomfortable having me there?"

She busied herself with the dishwasher to cover the fact that she winced. "No."

"Really? Because you seem a little standoffish. Weird. As if you're not happy that I want to go."

Because her back was to him, she squeezed her eyes shut. Memories of similar functions they'd attended during their marriage came tumbling back. Their compatibility in bed was only equaled by how incompatible they'd been at his events. A Friend Indeed's ball would be the first time he'd see her in his world since their divorce. She'd failed miserably when she was his wife. Now he'd see her in a gown, hosting the kind of event she'd refused to host for him.

"This *is* making you nervous." He paused, probably waiting for her to deny that. When she didn't he said, "Why?"

She desperately wanted to lie. To pretend nothing was wrong. But that was what had gotten her into trouble with him the first time around. She hadn't told him the truth about herself. She let him believe she was something she wasn't.

She sucked in a breath for courage and faced him. "Because I'll know you'll be watching me. Looking for the difference in how I am now and how I was when we were married."

He chuckled. "I've already noticed the differences."

"All the differences? I don't think so."

"So tell me."

"Maybe I don't want to be reminded of the past."

"Maybe if you told me about your past, you wouldn't be so afraid. If what you're fearing is my reaction, if you tell me, we'll get it out of the way and you won't have anything to fear anymore."

He wasn't exactly right, but he had made a point without realizing it. Maybe if she told him the truth about her humble beginnings and saw his disappointment, she could deal with it once and for all.

She returned to the dining room and walked around the table, gathering napkins as she spoke, so she wouldn't have to look at him.

"When I was growing up my mom just barely made enough for us to scrape by. I'd never even eaten in a restaurant other than fast food before I left home for university. I met you only one year out of school. And though by then I'd been wining and dining clients, traveling and seeing how the other half lived, actually being dumped into your lifestyle was culture shock to me."

"I got that—a little late, unfortunately—but I got it. We were working around it, but you never seemed to adapt."

"That's because there's something else. Something that you don't know."

Also gathering things from the table, he stopped, peered over at her.

Glad for the distance between them, the buffer of space, she sucked in a fortifying breath. "I…um…my parents' divorce was not a happy one."

"Very few divorces are."

"Actually my mom, sisters and I ran away from my dad." She sucked in another breath. "He was abusive."

"He hit you?" Anger vibrated through his words, as if he'd demand payback if she admitted it was true.

"Yes. But he mostly hit my mom. We left in the night—without telling him we were going—because a charity like A Friend Indeed had a home for us hundreds of miles away in Philadelphia. We changed our names so my dad couldn't find us."

He sat on one of the chairs surrounding the table. "Oh." Processing that, he said nothing for a second then suddenly glanced up at her. "You're not Liz Harper?"

"I am now. My name was legally changed over a decade ago when we left New York."

"Wow." He rubbed his hand along the back of his neck. "I'm sorry."

"It's certainly not your fault that my father was what he was or that I lived most of my life in poverty, always on the outside looking in, or that I didn't have the class or the experiences to simply blend into your life."

"That's why you're so attached to A Friend Indeed."

She nodded. "Yes."

A few seconds passed in silence. Liz hadn't expected him to say anything sympathetic. That simply wasn't

Cain. But saying nothing at all was worse than a flippant reply. She felt the sting of his unspoken rejection. She wasn't good enough for him. She'd always known it.

"Why didn't you tell me before?"

She snorted a laugh. "Tell my perfect, handsome, wealthy husband who seemed to know everything that I was a clueless runaway? For as much as I loved you, I never felt I deserved you."

He smiled ruefully. "I used to think the same thing about you."

Disbelief stole her breath. Was he kidding her? She'd been the one with the past worth hiding. He'd been nothing but perfect. Maybe too perfect. "Really?"

"I would think why does this beautiful woman stay with me, when I'm an emotional cripple." He combed his fingers through his hair as if torn between the whole truth and just enough to satisfy her openmouthed curiosity. Finally he said, "The guilt of my brother's death paralyzed me. Even now, it sometimes sneaks up on me. Reminding me that if I'd left a minute sooner or a few seconds later, Tom would still be alive."

"The kid who hit you ran a red light. The accident wasn't your fault."

"Logically, I know that. But something deep inside won't let me believe it." He shook his head and laughed miserably. "I'm a fixer, remember. Even after Tom's death, it was me Dad turned to for help running the business and eventually finding a replacement he could trust with his company when he wanted to retire. Yet, I couldn't fix that accident. I couldn't change any of it."

"No one could."

He snorted a laugh. "No kidding."

A few more seconds passed in silence. Fear bubbled in her blood. She had no idea why he'd confided in her, but she could see the result of it. She longed to hug him. To comfort him. But if she did that and they fell into bed, what good would that do but take them right back to where they had been? Solving all their problems with sex.

She grabbed her handful of napkins and walked them to the laundry room, realizing that rather than hug him, rather than comfort him, what she should be doing is airing all their issues. This conversation had been a great beginning, and this was probably the best opportunity she'd ever get to slide their final heartbreak into a discussion.

She readied herself, quickly assembling the right words to tell him about their baby as she stepped out of the pantry into the kitchen again.

Cain stood by the dishwasher, arranging the final glasses on the top row. She took a deep breath, but before she could open her mouth, he said, "Do you know you're the only person I've ever talked about my brother's accident with?"

"You haven't talked with your family?"

He shrugged and closed the dishwasher door. Walking to the center island, he said, "We talk about Tom, but we don't talk about his accident. We talk about the fact that he's dead, but we never say it was my fault. My family has a wonderful way of being able to skirt things. To talk about what's palatable and avoid what's not."

Though he tried to speak lightly, she heard the pain in his voice, the pain in his words, the need to release his feelings just by getting some of this out in the open.

This was not the time to tell him about their baby. Not when he was so torn up about the accident. He couldn't handle it right now. Her brain told her to move on. She couldn't stand here and listen, couldn't let him confide, not even as a friend.

But her heart remembered the three sad, awful years after the accident and desperately wanted to see him set free.

"Do you want to talk about it now?"

He tossed a dishtowel to the center island. "What would I say?"

She caught his gaze. "I don't know. What would you say?"

"Maybe that I'm sorry?"

"Do you really think you need to say you're sorry for an accident?"

He smiled ruefully. "I guess that's the rub. I feel guilty about something that wasn't my fault. Something I can't change. Something I couldn't have fixed no matter how old, or smart or experienced I was."

"That's probably what's driving the fixer in you crazy."

"Yeah."

"It's not your fault. You can't be sorry." She shook her head. "No. You *can* be sorry your brother is gone. You can be sorry for the loss. But you can't take the blame for an accident."

"I know." He rubbed his hand along the back of his neck. "That was weird."

"Talking about it?"

"No, admitting out loud for the first time that it wasn't my fault. That I can't take the blame." He shook his head. "Wow. It's like it's the first time that's really sunk in."

He smiled at her, a relieved smile so genuine that she

knew she'd done the right thing in encouraging him to talk.

The silence in the room nudged her again, hinting that she could now tell him about their baby, but something about the relieved expression on his face stopped her. He'd just absolved himself from a burden of guilt he never should have taken up. What if she told him about her miscarriage and instead of being sad, he got angry with himself all over again?

She swallowed, as repressed memories of the days before she left him popped up in her brain. All these years, she'd thought she'd kept her secret to protect herself. Now, she remembered that she'd also kept it to protect him. He had a talent for absorbing blame that wasn't really his.

If she told him now, with the conversation about his brother still lingering in the air, he could tumble right back to the place he'd just escaped. Surely he deserved a few days of peace? And surely in those days she could think of a way to tell him that would help him to accept, as she had, that there was no one to blame.

"We're just about finished here." She ambled to the dining room table again and brought back salt-and-pepper shakers. "I'll wash the tablecloth and wait for the dishwasher, but you don't have to hang around. I brought a book to read while I wait. Why don't you go do whatever you'd normally do?"

"I should pack the contracts we signed tonight in my briefcase."

"Okay. You go do that." She smiled at him. "I'll see you Friday morning."

He turned in the doorway. "I'm not supposed to be here when you come to the house, remember?"

She held his gaze. "I could come early enough to get a cup of coffee."

Surprise flitted across his face. "Really?" Then he grimaced. "I'm leaving town tomorrow morning. I won't be back until Friday night. But I'll see you on Saturday."

Another weekend of working with him without being able to tell him might be for the best. A little distance between tonight's acceptance that he couldn't take blame for his brother's accident and the revelation of a tragedy he didn't even know had happened wouldn't be a bad thing.

"Okay."

He turned to leave again then paused, as if he didn't want to leave her, and she realized she'd given him the wrong impression when she'd suggested they have coffee Friday morning. She'd suggested it to give herself a chance to tell him her secret, not because she wanted to spend time with him. But he didn't know that.

She turned away, a silent encouragement for him to move on. When she turned around again, he was gone.

CHAPTER SEVEN

THE FOLLOWING SATURDAY, Cain was on the roof of Amanda's house with a small crew of his best, most discreet workers. Even before Cain arrived, Liz had taken Amanda and her children to breakfast, then shopping, then to the beach. If he didn't know how well-timed this roof event had to be, he might have thought she was avoiding him.

Regret surged through him as he climbed down the ladder. He'd been so caught up in the fact that their talk had allowed him to pierce through the layer of guilt that had held him captive, that he'd nearly forgotten what she'd told him about her dad.

She'd been abused. She'd been raised in poverty. She'd run away, gotten herself educated in spite of her humble beginnings, and then she'd met him.

Their relationship could have gone one of two ways. He could have brought her into his world, shown her his lifestyle and gradually helped her acclimate. Instead, he'd fallen victim to the grief of his brother's death and missed the obvious.

He wanted to be angry with himself, but he couldn't. Just as he couldn't bear the burden of guilt over his brother's death, he couldn't blame himself for having missed the obvious. Blaming himself for things he couldn't change was over. But so was the chance to "fix" their marriage.

Somehow or another, that conversation over his dirty dishes had shown him that he and Liz weren't destined for a second chance. He could say that without the typical sadness over the loss of what might have been because he'd decided they hadn't known each other well enough the first time around to have anything to fix. What they really needed to do was start over.

He went through the back door into Amanda's kitchen, got a drink of water and then headed upstairs to assess what was left to be done, still thinking about him and Liz. The question was…what did start over mean? Start over to become friends? Or start over to become lovers? A couple? A *married* couple?

He'd been considering them coworkers, learning to get along as friends for the sake of their project. But after the way she'd led him out of his guilt on Wednesday night, his feelings for her had shifted in an unexpected way. He supposed this was the emotion a man experienced when he found a woman who understood him, one he'd consider making his wife. The first time around his idea of a wife had been shallow. He'd wanted a beautiful hostess and someone to warm his bed. He'd never thought he'd need a confidante and friend more.

Now he knew just how wrong he'd been.

And now he saw just how right Liz would have been for him, if they'd only opened up to each other the first time around.

So should he expand his idea from experimenting

with getting to know each other in order to become friends, to experimenting with getting to know each other to see if they actually were compatible? Not in the shallow ways, but in the real ways that counted.

Just the thought sent his head reeling. He didn't want to go back to what they'd had before…but a whole new relationship? The very idea filled him with a funny, fuzzy feeling. Though he didn't have a lot of experience with this particular emotion…he thought it just might be hope.

They couldn't fix their past. But what if they could have a future?

Shaking his head at the wonder of it all, Cain ducked into the first bedroom, the room with the most ceiling damage. He pulled a small notebook and pen from his shirt pocket and began making notes of things he would do the next day, Sunday. His crew would have the new roof far enough along that he could fix this ceiling and then the room could be painted. Because Amanda couldn't be there when any work crew was on site—to keep her identity safe—Liz would paint this room herself. The following weekend he and Billy could get to work on the baseboards and trim.

Proud of himself, Cain left the first room and walked into the second. This room still needed the works: ceiling, paint job, trim. He ducked out and into the bathroom, which was old-fashioned, but in good repair because he had fixed both the commode and shower the first week he'd been here. He dipped out and headed for the biggest bedroom, the one Amanda was using.

He stepped inside, only to find Liz stuffing a pillow into a bright red pillowcase.

"What are you doing here?"

Hand to her heart, she whipped around. "What are you doing down here! You're supposed to be on the roof."

"I'm making a list of things that need to be done tomorrow and next weekend."

"I'm surprising Amanda. I dropped her and her kids off at the beach, telling them I'd be back around six."

He leaned against the doorjamb. This room hadn't sustained any damage because of the bad roof. At some point during the week, Liz and Amanda had already painted the ceiling and walls. At the bottom of the bed were packages of new sheets and a red print comforter. Strewn across a mirror vanity were new curtains—red-and-gold striped that matched the colors in the comforter—waiting to be installed.

"By giving her a whole new bedroom?"

"Having a bedroom that's a comfortable retreat is a simple pleasure." Shaking a second pillow into a pillowcase, she smiled. "Women like simple pleasures. Bubble baths. A fresh cup of coffee. A good book."

"And a pretty bedroom."

She nodded. "And before you ask, Amanda's favorite color is red. I'm not going overboard."

"I'm glad because another person might consider this whole system a bit bright."

"This from a man with a black satin bedspread."

He laughed. "Point taken."

"How's the roof going?"

"It'll be done tomorrow night. That's the good thing about these houses. Small, uncomplicated roofs."

"Good."

With the pillows now on the bed and the fitted sheet in place, Liz grabbed the flat sheet, unfurling it over the bed.

Cain strode over and caught the side opposite her. "Here. Let me help."

"Thanks."

"You're welcome." He paused then added, "You know I'm really proud of you, right?"

"You don't have to say that."

"I think I do. Wednesday night, we sort of skipped from your childhood to my brother's death and never got back to it."

"There's no need."

"I think there is." He hesitated. In for a penny, in for a pound. "I'd like to know more." He shook his head. "No. That's not right. You said it's not something you want to talk about." In three years of living together, he'd bet she'd shown him signs of her troubles, but he'd never seen. He regretted now that he'd never seen her pain. Deeply. Wholeheartedly. If he'd noticed, he could have asked her about it at any time in their marriage. Now he knew she wanted it to be put behind her. If he really wanted a clean slate, he had to accept what she wanted, too.

"What I'm trying to say is that I want you to know that I get it. I understand. And maybe I'm sorry."

He still wasn't sure what he intended to do. If he should trust that funny feeling in the pit of his stomach that told him he should pursue this. Mostly because she was so different now that he had to treat her differently. She had goals and dreams. The first time they'd met he'd pulled her away from everything she had and everything she wanted. He wouldn't do that to her this time.

And maybe that was the real test of whether or not they belonged together. If he could coexist without taking over, and if she could keep her independence without letting him overpower her, then maybe they did belong together.

He nearly snorted with derision. That was a tall order for a man accustomed to being the boss and a woman so obviously eager to please.

"You don't have to be sorry."

"Well, I am. I'm sorry I didn't put two and two together. I'm sorry I made things worse."

They didn't speak while finishing the bed. Liz couldn't have spoken if she'd tried. There was a lump in her throat so thick she couldn't have gotten words past it.

When the bed was all set up, he said, "I better get back to the roof."

Liz nodded, smiling as much as she could, and he left the room. She watched him go then forced her attention on the bed she'd just made. She'd missed another really good opportunity to tell him. But his apology about her situation with her dad had left her reeling. She hadn't wanted to be overly emotional when she told him about their lost child. She wanted to be strong. So he could be sad. She wanted to keep the focus of the discussion on the loss being a loss…not someone's fault.

Still, she'd better pick a time…and soon. With two honest discussions under their belts, he'd wonder why she'd kept her most important secret to herself when she'd had opportunities to tell him.

The following weekend and the weekend after, Liz found herself working primarily with Amanda. With the roof done, Amanda and Billy didn't need to be off premises, and both were eager to get back on the job. Cain and Billy did the "man's work" as Billy called it, and Amanda and Liz painted and then made lunches. There was never a time when she and Cain were alone.

Their final Sunday of work, with the roof replaced, the rooms painted, the plumbing working at peak efficiency, and shiny new baseboard and crown molding accenting each room, Amanda had wanted to make a big celebration dinner, but Cain had a conference call and Liz had begged off in favor of a cold shower. She kissed Amanda, Joy and Billy's cheeks as Cain shook hands and gave hugs, then both headed for their vehicles.

"That was amazing," Cain said when they were far enough from Amanda's house that she couldn't hear.

Liz blew out a breath of relief. "Dear God, yes. Finishing is amazing!"

He shook his head. "No. I'm talking about actually doing something for someone." He sighed, stopping at the door to his truck. "You know that I give hundreds of thousands of dollars away a year, so you know I'm not a slouch. But giving is one thing. Working to help make a real person's life better is entirely different."

"No kidding!"

"I don't think you're hearing what I'm telling you. I feel terrific."

She laughed. "You've got charity worker's high."

He shook his head again. "No. It's more than that. I feel like I've found my new calling."

Shielding her eyes from the sun, she peeked up at him, finally getting what he was telling her. "Really?"

"Yes."

"You know A Friend Indeed has other houses."

"Yes."

"You can call Ayleen and I'm sure she'll let you fix any one of them you want."

He caught her gaze. "Will you help?"

Her heart stopped. Spend another several weeks with him? "I don't know." She pulled in a breath. When he looked at her with those serious eyes of his, she couldn't think of saying no. Especially since he'd been so happy lately. And especially since she still had something to tell him and needed to be around him.

But she didn't really want to connect their lives, and working together on another project more or less made them a team.

"Okay, while you think about that, answer this. I'm considering hiring Billy to be my assistant on these jobs. I know I'll have to clear it with Ayleen, but before I talk to her I'd like a little background. Just enough that I don't push any wrong buttons."

"As long as you don't hit his mother, I think you'll be fine."

"That bad, huh?"

Liz sighed. "I think the real problem might be getting him to accept a job."

"Really? Why?"

"He might think it's charity."

"I never thought of that."

"He's got a lot of pride."

Cain snorted a laugh. "No kidding. But we made headway working together." He grinned at her. "I think he likes me."

Liz rolled her eyes. "He admires you."

"So I'll use that. I'll tell him he's getting a chance to work with the big dog. Learn the secrets of my success."

She laughed and an odd warmth enveloped her. Talking with him now was like talking with Ellie. Casual. Easy. Maybe they really had become friends?

"Hey, you never know. It might work."

She grimaced. "I'm sure it will work." She finished the walk to her car. She didn't mind being friends with him, but she also didn't want to risk the feeling going any further.

As she opened the door, Cain called after her, "So, are you going to help me?"

That was the rub. If she agreed to work with him, they really would become friends. And she'd probably have plenty of time not only to tell him her secret, but also to help him adjust to it. On the flip side, if things didn't go well, she'd have plenty of time to see him angry, to watch him mourn, if he didn't handle the news well.

"I'm going to think about it."

Liz slid into her car and drove away. Cain opened his truck door. He'd expected her to be happier that he wanted to work on more houses. But he supposed in a way he understood why she wasn't. The very reason he wanted her to work with him—to be together, to spend time together so they could get to know each other and see if they shouldn't start over again—might be the reason she didn't want to work with him. Their marriage had been an abysmal failure. She didn't want to be reminded and she didn't want to go back.

If he was considering "fixing" their marriage, he'd be as negative as she was. But he didn't want to fix their marriage. He wanted them to start over again.

Unfortunately, he wasn't entirely sure how.

Tuesday, Cain spoke with Ayleen and got approval to hire Billy. Actually, he got gushing glowing praise on the job he had done and his generosity in taking Billy under his wing. Then he got the address of the next house he was to repair and the suggestion that he might want to start that Saturday.

So he drove to Amanda's and offered Billy a job, which Billy happily accepted, especially after Cain mentioned his salary.

High on the success of the first part of his plan, Cain called Liz the minute he returned to his house.

She answered on the first ring. "Happy Maids."

"You really should have a personal cell phone."

"Can't afford it. What do you want, Cain?"

"Is that any way to talk to the man who's offering you a ride to our job site on Saturday? I'm already stopping for Billy—one more will fit into the truck."

"You got Billy to take a job?"

"I made him an offer he couldn't refuse."

"That's great! Amanda will be so thrilled."

"I'm glad to be able to do it." He paused. "So what do you say? Want a ride?"

"I haven't even agreed to work with you yet."

He could have threatened her with calling Ayleen and forced her hand. He could have said, "Please," and maybe melted her the way she could melt him. Instead he said nothing, letting the decision be her own, following his own directive that this relationship would be totally different. Fresh. New.

"Okay. But I'll meet you there." Her answer was cool, businesslike, but he didn't care. They'd had a crappy marriage. He'd hurt her. But more than that, he'd pulled her away from her dreams. He had to accept that she'd be wary of him. Then he had to prove to her she had no reason to be. They were starting over.

Peggy Morris had chosen not to be home when Cain and company did the work on her house. Liz had said she would get the keys and be there when Cain and Billy arrived. As Cain opened the back door into the kitchen, she turned from the sink. When she saw the picnic basket Billy carried, she grinned.

"Your mom's a saint."

Billy frowned. "Why?"

"For making lunch."

"I made that," Cain said. "Well, actually, I had Ava call a deli and place an order. I've got sandwiches, soda, bottled water, dessert… The cheesecake you like."

She groaned. "Oh, Cain! I can't have cheesecake! I'll be big as a house."

He laughed. She might have groaned about the cheesecake, but she accepted that he'd brought lunch. It was a good start. "You've lost weight since we were married."

Billy glanced from Cain to Liz. "You two were married?"

Cain said, "Yes."

Liz said, "A long time ago."

Billy shook his head. "You don't look like married people to me."

Liz walked over and put her hand on Billy's forearm. "Your parents' situation wasn't normal, Billy."

"Yeah, but even my friends' parents argue all the time. You two get along." He looked from Cain to Liz again. "So why'd you get divorced?"

"Long story," Liz said.

"I was too busy," Cain countered.

Before Billy could say anything more about them, Liz turned him in the direction of the door again. "You don't need to know about this. It's ancient history, and we do need to get started on what we came here to do." She pointed at the door. "I'm guessing Cain's got about ten cans of paint in his truck. Let's go get them."

The three of them made a good team. Liz jumped into the truck bed and handed paint gallons, brushes, trays and other equipment to Cain and Billy who carted everything into the garage.

When the supplies were on the garage floor, Cain took charge again. "We're starting at this house because essentially everything is in good repair. When Ayleen brought me over this week to check things out, I noticed a few of the walls and ceilings need to be mended and there's also some work in the bathroom." He pointed at a new shower head and some unidentifiable plumbing equipment in another package. "I'll do all that. You guys can paint. I thought we'd start upstairs and work our way downstairs."

Liz said, "Okay."

Billy said, "I already know how to paint. I want to help with the repair work."

"The thing about construction is that you have to do whatever needs to be done. You don't get to pick your job." He handed Billy two gallons of beige paint. "Eventually you'll demonstrate that you have a strength or two like electrical or plumbing, and you'll be considered the expert and get to do those jobs whenever they come up. But if there's no electrical or plumbing, you'll paint."

Billy grumbled, but Cain pretended not to notice. Hiding a smile, Liz picked up some paint trays, brushes and rollers and followed Billy to the door into the kitchen.

He waited until Billy was through the door before he called her back. "Liz?"

She turned, her eyes wide and round, as if afraid of what he might say.

He wanted to tell her thanks. He wanted to say she looked pretty that morning. Because she appeared to be afraid of him and his motives, he handed the blue tape to her. "You're not a good enough painter to forget the blue tape."

She didn't have a free hand, so he tossed it onto a paint tray, then turned and picked up the bag of plaster.

Liz spent an enjoyable morning painting with Billy. A few times Cain came into the room and either pulled Billy to show him something about the repair work he was doing on the ceiling or in the bathroom, or to praise them for the good job they were doing. Billy blossomed under Cain's attention. He even chattered to Liz about the toilet tank "guts" exchange that Cain had explained to him.

"Because it's normal for commodes to need these kinds of repairs," Billy repeated Cain's comments verbatim. "My mom might need me to do that one day."

Though Liz was tempted to laugh, she held it back. "That's right. If you learn enough with Cain, you'll be able to fix things as they break at home."

"I know," Billy said seriously, sounding proud and responsible.

Liz ruffled his hair. "Get your paintbrush. We've got hours of this ahead of us."

Lunch was fun and relaxing. Billy had a million questions for Cain and he happily answered them. Having completed the repair work to the walls and ceilings, Cain joined the painting in the afternoon.

At five, Liz suggested they begin cleaning up.

"I could go for another hour or two, how about you, Billy?"

"I'm cool."

Liz shook her head. "The family has to come home sometime. Because Peggy is new and doesn't know any of us, Ayleen doesn't want her to find us here when she returns."

"Oops." Cain laughed. "Forgot."

Leaving the paint and supplies in the garage, Cain and Billy piled into his truck again. Liz walked to her car.

"See you tomorrow?"

She faced the truck. "Yeah."

Cain grinned at her. "Okay."

She climbed into her car with the same strange feeling she'd had at Amanda's about Cain being normal. Wondering if he was working to make her a friend or trying to ease her back into a relationship. But this time it was slightly different. Dealing with him today had been like dealing with a new friend. A *new* friend. Which was odd.

She knew their discussion about his brother had released him from the burden of guilt that had held him back emotionally. He was happy now. Easygoing. Which was probably why he seemed like a new person to her. She was also grateful that she had helped him. But something new was entering their equation. A question. A problem.

What if she told him about their baby and it threw him into a tailspin again?

She turned and watched his truck as it roared down the road. Billy sat in the passenger's side, his elbow out the open window. Cain sat in the driver's side, his elbow out the open window. They could be friends. Older and younger brother.

The truck turned right and disappeared down the street. Liz watched after it. He couldn't fake what he felt for Billy. The boy was just a tad too inquisitive for an impatient man like Cain to fake patience. He was the happiest she'd ever seen him. And her secret could ruin that.

The next morning Cain arrived at the house with Billy in tow and another picnic basket stuffed with food. Eager for lunch, Billy went straight to work. He'd become so good at painting and had such a steady hand that Cain suggested he paint the line bordering the ceiling and around the windows and trim.

Proud of himself, Billy continued to blossom under the praise.

But Liz found herself watching Cain, watching his patience with Billy, watching his commitment to doing a good job for A Friend Indeed, watching the way he treated her. Not as an ex-wife, not as a woman he was pursuing, but as a coworker.

In a lot of ways that was weird.

"Get the lead out, Harper. If you keep repainting the same wall, we'll be here again next weekend."

"Got it. Sorry."

"If you're tired, take a break."

She faced him. "A break? What's a break? Billy, do you know what a break is?"

"Not hardly."

She laughed and went back to painting, but Cain sighed. "All right. We'll all take ten minutes then we have to get back to it."

Liz didn't need to be told twice. After using the

bathroom, she jogged down the stairs and into the garage, where Cain had stored a cooler with bottled water and soft drinks. She took a can of diet cola, snapped open the lid and drank.

"Sorry about that."

Lowering the can from her mouth, she turned and saw Cain walking into the garage. "You don't have to go overboard with being nice."

"I'm not."

"Sure you are. I'll bet you wouldn't apologize to your workers if you got so wrapped up in a job you forgot to give them a break."

"Probably not."

"So why treat me and Billy any differently?"

"Maybe because I'm having trouble finding a happy medium."

"Billy's a good kid who needs to be in the real world. And that might include a boss who forgets to give him a break."

"I'm not having trouble figuring out how to deal with Billy."

Right. She got it. She was the problem. Their feelings around each other had gone up and down, back and forth and sideways. Plus they had a past. Even as objective as she tried to be, sometimes that past snuck up on her.

"Maybe that's because we shouldn't be working together."

Just when she thought he'd admit he'd made a mistake in asking for her help, he surprised her. "We both like Billy. We both recognize that if somebody doesn't grab hold of him right now God only knows what he'll get into." He caught her gaze. "We can do this, Liz. We can help him. Save him. Don't you even want to try?"

She swallowed. "Actually, I do." And for the first time since she'd seen him standing in only a towel in his kitchen, she wanted to tell *him* she was proud of *him*. She wanted to say it so much that she suddenly understood what he'd been going through every time he'd seen one of the changes she'd made since their marriage.

The feeling was nearly overwhelming.

"You know I'll help Billy. I'll do everything I can."

He smiled at her, a smile so warm and open, she could only stare at him. The spark was back in his dark brown eyes. His hair fell boyishly to his forehead. But that smile. Oh, that smile. She would have done anything to see that smile three years ago. It seemed to say that he was different. Happy. Easy to be around. If they didn't have a past, if she didn't have a secret, Cain would be the man she would actually consider giving her heart to.

But they did have a past. And she did have a secret.

She chugged her soda and headed into the house just as Billy came out.

"Hey! I didn't even get a drink."

"Go ahead and get one. I'm ready to get back to work, so I'm going in. You and Cain take all the time you need."

CHAPTER EIGHT

CAIN JUMPED INTO HIS Porsche and punched the address on the invitation in his hand into his GPS unit. He'd been invited to a party being hosted by one of the women who'd been helped by A Friend Indeed. In a few minutes, he found himself driving down the street of the middle-class, blue-collar neighborhood.

He hadn't wanted to attend this party. But it had been a real stretch for him to volunteer to help with the Friend Indeed houses and an even bigger stretch to have taken Billy under his wing and those things had worked out amazingly well. So attending an event for the families involved with the charity was simply another level of change for him. Especially since it would involve chitchat. No bankers or businessmen to schmooze. No business talk tonight. Somehow or other he'd have to be…well, normal.

But he'd decided to once again push beyond his own inadequacies to attend tonight because he couldn't stop thinking about something Liz had told him. When he'd first arrived at Amanda's, Liz had instructed him to accept anything any client offered because this might be the first time in a long time they'd had something to offer. He'd finally wrapped his head around just how demoralized and demeaned these women had been and then his thoughts had segued to the fact that Liz and her family had been abused.

Liz had been a child in a family just like this one. Alone. Scared. Usually hungry. He couldn't bear the thought.

But that also meant he couldn't refuse an invitation to anything connected to Liz. He didn't want her to feel rejected by him, or that somehow she and her friends weren't good enough. They were. He was the socially awkward one. So to protect her, here he was, driving in an unfamiliar section of the city, about to attend a gathering with people he didn't know.

He parked on the street and headed up the sidewalk to Joni Custer's house. As he climbed the stairs to the front door, he held back a wince of pain. He'd been so busy proving himself to Liz and enjoying doing the work he loved—the work that had nudged him in the direction of success and riches—that he'd forgotten he wasn't eighteen anymore. Billy was probably stronger. And maybe he should be the one hefting boxes of hardwood, while Cain stuck to measuring and fitting.

He found the bell and within two seconds, the bright red front door opened. Liz stood on the other side. Dressed in shorts and a halter top, she looked amazing. Comfortable. Confident. Relaxed.

Their gazes caught and she smiled sheepishly. His heart did a cartwheel. She was smiling at him now, like a real person, not a person she was forced to socialize with, not a person she had to pretend to like. Her smile was genuine.

"Come on. Everybody's outside on the patio." She

took a look at his attire and winced. "Somebody should have told you dress was informal."

Cain immediately reached for his tie. Walking into the foyer, he yanked it off and stuffed it in his jacket pocket. "I can make do." He removed his jacket and tossed it over a hook on a coat tree in the foyer. Following Liz to a sliding glass door at the back of the house, he rolled up the sleeves of his white shirt. "See, now I'm dressed appropriately."

"Well, not exactly appropriately." She turned and gave him another smile. "But better."

"How about a little background before I go out there into a sea of people I don't know."

"Joni is one of the first women we helped. Every year she hosts a barbecue. Most of the people attending are also A Friend Indeed women, but some are parents and friends of the clients." She hooked her arm in the crook of his elbow and headed for the door again. "I'll introduce you around, but then you're on your own."

It felt so good to have her at his side that it disappointed him that she wouldn't stay with him, but he understood. If they had just met, they'd still be in a friend stage, not behaving like a couple. He had to accept that.

"I appreciate the introductions."

She hesitated another few seconds at the door. "You might get a critique or two of the work you've done."

"Hey, you helped!" He opened the sliding glass door. "If I'm going down in flames, you're going with me."

She laughed and the second they stepped onto the stone floor of the small patio, Liz said, "Hey, everybody, this is Cain. He's the new board member who's been fixing up houses."

A general round of approval rippled through the crowd.

Liz leaned in and whispered, "Get ready. Any second now you'll be surrounded."

Her warning didn't penetrate. He was too busy analyzing whether it was good or bad that she hadn't introduced him as her ex-husband. On the one hand it did point to the fact that she saw their association as being a new one. On the other, she could be embarrassed about having been married to him. So it took him by surprise when a middle-aged man approached him and extended his hand for shaking.

"You did Amanda's house?"

"That was mostly painting," Cain said, snatching Liz's hand, holding her in place when it appeared she would desert him. "And Liz and I were equal partners on that one."

"Don't be so modest," Ayleen said, ambling up to them. "I hear the whole house is to die for."

"It is." Amanda walked over. She unexpectedly hugged Cain. "Thanks again."

Embarrassment flooded him at her praise. What he'd done was so simple, so easy for him. Yet it had meant the world to Amanda. "I guess that means you like the house?"

"Like is too simple of a word," she said with a laugh.

Liz shook her hand free of his, as if eager to get away. "How about if I get us a drink? What would you like?"

Not quite sure what to say, Cain raised his eyebrows in question. "What do they have?"

"What if I get us both a cola?"

"Sounds great."

The second Liz left, he began fielding questions

about the work he'd done on Amanda's house and the four houses he still planned to repair.

Eventually he and the middle-aged man who introduced himself as Bob, Joni's dad, wandered over to the grill.

"This is my grandson, Tony." Bob introduced Cain to the man flipping burgers.

Cain caught a flash of yellow out of his peripheral vision before a tall blonde grabbed his forearm and yanked him away from the grill. "Sorry, guys. But he's mine for a few minutes." She smiled at him. "I'm Ellie. My friends call me Magic."

"Magic? Like Magic Johnson, the basketball player?"

"No, magic as in my wishes generally come true and I can also pretty much figure out somebody's deal in a short conversation."

"You're going to interrogate me, aren't you?"

"I know who you are."

"Who I am?"

"You're Liz's ex. She hasn't said anything, but for her to be introducing you around, I'm guessing she likes you again."

He paused. His heart skipped a beat. Her wariness around him took on new meaning. He'd been so careful to behave only as a friend that she might not understand his feelings for her now ran much deeper. She might think he didn't like her "that" way anymore. But he did. And if she wanted more, so did he.

"Really?"

Ellie sighed. "Really. Come on. Let's cut the bull. We both know you're cute. We both know she loved you. Now you're back and she's falling for you. If she's holding back, I'm guessing it's only because she thinks you don't want her."

Cain couldn't help it; he smiled.

Ellie shook her head with a sigh. "Don't be smug. Or too sure of yourself. As her friend, I'm going to make it my business to be certain you don't hurt her again."

"You don't have to make it your business. You have my word."

She studied his face. "Odd as this is going to sound, I believe you."

Liz walked over with two cans of cola. "Ellie! What are you doing?"

"Checking him out," Ellie said without an ounce of shame in her voice. "I'm going to help Joni with the buns and salads."

Liz faced him with a grimace. "Sorry about that."

"Is she really magic?"

Liz laughed. "Did she tell you that?"

"Yes."

"Then she likes you and that's a big plus."

Liz casually turned to walk away, but Cain caught her arm. "So these people are your friends?"

"Yes."

He expected her to elaborate, but she didn't. She eased her arm out of his grasp and walked away. Ten minutes ago, that would have upset him. Now, Ellie's words repeated in his head. "If she's holding back I'm guessing it's only because she thinks you don't want her."

He glanced around and frowned. They were with her friends. He couldn't make a move of any kind here. That much *he* was sure of. But soon, very soon, he was going to have to do something to test Ellie's theory.

Cain went back to the group of men at the grill and in seconds he felt odd. Not exactly uncomfortable. Not exactly confused. But baffled, as if something important sat on the edge of his brain trying to surface but it couldn't.

The conversation of the men around him turned to children, house payments and job difficulties. He couldn't identify with anything they were discussing. He didn't have kids or a mortgage or job difficulties. So, he didn't say a word, simply listened, putting things in context by remembering the things he'd learned working with Billy and for Amanda, and then he suddenly understood why he felt so weird.

It wasn't because Liz's magical friend had basically told him that Liz cared for him. It was because Liz had left him alone with her friends. Alone. Not monitoring what he said. Not anxious or fearful that he'd inadvertently insult someone.

She trusted him.

She *trusted* him.

Just the thought humbled him. But also sort of proved out Ellie's suspicion that Liz liked him again as more than a friend. A woman didn't trust the people she loved to just anyone.

When the burgers were grilled to perfection, Cain scooped them up with a huge metal spatula and piled them on a plate held by Bob. When everything was on the table, he took a seat at the picnic table where Liz sat. He didn't sit beside her. He didn't want to scare her, but he did like being around her. And Ellie's comment that Liz was falling for him again was beginning to settle in, to give him confidence, to make him think that maybe it was time to let her know he was feeling the same way she was.

Not that it was time to get back together, but to start over.

The group at each table included adults of all ages and varieties and their children. They ate burgers, discussing football and fishing, and when everyone had eaten their fill, they played volleyball—in spite of Cain's Italian loafers. When the sun set, the kids disappeared to tell ghost stories in the dark, humid night and the adults congregated around the tables again, talking about everything from raising kids to the economy.

All in all it was a very relaxing evening, but an informative one, as well. Liz fit with these people. Easily. Happily.

And he had, too.

It was time for him to get their relationship on track. And since they were doing things differently this time around, he wouldn't slyly seduce her. He intended to actually tell her he wanted to be more than her friend, ask her if she agreed. To give her choices. To give her time.

Exactly the opposite of what he'd done when he met her six years ago.

The back door slid open. A little kid of about six yelled, "Hey! There's a jacket in here that's buzzing."

Everybody laughed.

An older girl raced up behind the kid. "Somebody's cell phone is vibrating. It's in the pocket of a jacket hanging on the coat tree."

Cain rose. He'd been so caught up in being with Liz that he'd forgotten his cell phone, hadn't cared if he missed a call. "I think that's mine." He glanced at Joni with a smile. "It's time for me to be going anyway. Thank you very much for inviting me."

Joni rose. "Thank you for coming. It was nice to meet the guy who's stirred up so much gossip!"

Not exactly sure how to take that, Cain faced Liz, who also rose. "She means about fixing the houses." She slid her hand in the crook of his elbow. "I'll walk you to the door."

Liz waited as Cain said his good-nights. Together they walked into the house and to the foyer. He lifted his suit jacket from the coat tree and the phone buzzed again. He silenced it without even looking at caller ID.

She nearly shook her head in wonder. She'd been worried about how he'd handle this party, how he'd get along with her friends, and she needn't have given it a second thought.

He opened the front door. "Walk me to my car?"

Her breath stuttered in her chest. If they hadn't had such a nice evening, she might have thought this was her perfect opportunity to tell him about their baby. But they had had a nice evening. A quiet, comfortable, relaxing time. She'd seen how hard he worked to get along with her friends. And she'd appreciated that. Her sad revelation was for another time.

She pulled her keys from her pocket. "How about if you walk *me* to *my* car?"

He smiled. "Sure. I just thought you'd be going back in."

"Nope."

"You know Ellie's going to give you the third degree. Might as well get it over with tonight."

"Not necessary. She'll call me before I even get home."

He laughed. Her chest constricted with happiness as

unexpected feelings rippled through her. She hadn't fully admitted to herself how important it was to her that he like her friends. But it had been. Seeing him interacting with the Friend Indeed people had filled her with pride. She couldn't remember a time when he'd ever been this relaxed and she knew she'd had something to do with that. She'd helped him get beyond his guilt and helped him acclimate at A Friend Indeed, and in the end he'd become the man she'd always known he could be. Warm. Caring. Wonderful.

When they reached her atrocious little green car, she turned and faced him. Their gazes met and clung and she suddenly realized asking him to walk her to her car might have seemed like an invitation for him to kiss her good-night.

Her heart stilled. Her breathing stalled in her chest. Part of her screamed for her to grab the door handle and get the hell out of here. The other part was melting into soft putty. She'd loved this man with her whole heart and soul. He'd suffered the torment of the damned and she'd had to stand by helplessly. Now he was back. Almost normal, but better.

Was it so wrong to want one little kiss?

As his head slowly descended, she had a thousand chances to change her mind. A million cautions pirouetted through her brain. Every nerve ending in her body flickered with something that felt very much like fear.

But when their lips met, it was like coming home. The years melted away and he was the Cain she'd fallen in love with. Cain before he'd been burdened by guilt over his brother's death or the drive to succeed to bury that guilt.

The Cain she knew loved her.

He was *her* Cain.

Her lips came to life slowly beneath his. His hands slid to her upper arms, to her back and down her spine. She stepped closer, nestling against him. For the three years of their marriage she'd longed for this feeling. For the three years they'd been separated, she'd tried to forget this feeling. The warmth, the connection, the spark of need that ignited in her and heated her blood. Nobody had ever made her feel what Cain made her feel.

And she was finally discovering part of the reason was that she didn't want anybody else to make her feel what Cain could. She wanted Cain.

He pulled away slowly. She blinked up at him.

"Good night."

His voice was a soft whisper in the warm summer night. Her lips curved upward slowly. A kiss. Just a kiss. He hadn't pushed for more, hadn't asked her to follow him home, or if he could follow her. He'd simply wanted a kiss.

"Good night."

"I'll call you."

"Okay."

She opened her car door and slid inside. He stepped back, out of the way, as she pulled her gearshift into Drive and eased out into the night.

A little voice inside her head told her not to be so happy, because she hadn't yet been totally honest with him.

But she would be.

Soon.

For now though she wanted to bask in the warmth that flooded her because he'd kissed her.

* * *

Cain couldn't remember ever feeling so good or so hopeful about his life. It wasn't simply because Liz had feelings for him and had admitted them in the way she kissed him. He was also a changed man. He hadn't pretended to like her friends. He liked her friends. He hadn't been bored, nervous, or eager to get away to get back to work. Somehow or another over the past weeks, his longing to make up to Liz for their horrible marriage had reordered his priorities. He'd done what he felt he needed to do to pay penance for their bad marriage and as a result learned to work with Billy and for a cause that genuinely needed him.

And when the dust settled, he was changed. When he looked ahead to their future, he could see them making it work this time.

Driving home with the top down, thinking about some of the brighter days in their marriage, he almost didn't hear his cell phone ring. He'd shifted it from vibrate to ring when he directed the last call to voice mail as he'd walked Liz to her car. Though it had taken a few rings, eventually the low sound penetrated his consciousness and he grabbed the phone. Somebody had been trying to get a hold of him for the past hour, but he hadn't even cared enough to check caller ID.

If that didn't prove he'd changed, nothing did.

He glanced at the small screen and saw his sister's phone number.

His sister? What would be so important that she'd call at least three times on a Sunday night? He frowned and clicked the button to answer.

"What's up, sis?"

"Cain. Thank God you finally answered. Dad's on

his way to the hospital. Mom thinks he had a heart attack. It's pretty bad."

All the good feelings welled in his belly turned into a rock of dread. Even if the words hadn't penetrated, the shiver in his sister's voice had.

"I'm on my way."

Without another thought, he pressed speed dial for Ava. Her voice groggy with sleep, she said, "Cain?"

"Sorry to wake you. My dad had a heart attack. I need to get to Kansas tonight. Can you wake Dale?" he asked, referring to his pilot.

"I'm on it," Ava said sounding awake and alert. "You just get yourself to the airport."

CHAPTER NINE

Liz's cell phone was ringing when she awoke the next morning. She reached over and pawed the bedside table to snag it. When she saw the name on caller ID, her breath stuttered out.

Cain.

He'd kissed her the night before. She'd wanted him to. Her insides tightened at the memory. She'd always loved him and now he was behaving as if he loved her, too. Doing things for her. Caring about the cause she cared about. Easing his way into her life.

Part of her wanted it. All of it. The attention, the affection, the connection. The other part of her was scared to death. They'd made a mistake before.

Her phone rang again and she pressed the button to answer. Her voice was soft and uncertain when she said, "Good morning, Cain."

"Good morning."

His greeting was rough, tired, as if he hadn't slept all night. And not for good reasons.

She scrambled up in bed. "What's wrong?"

"My dad had a heart attack yesterday. I'm in Kansas."

She flopped back onto her pillow. "Oh, God. I'm so sorry. Is there anything I can do?"

"No, I just—" He paused. "I just—"

He paused again and Liz squeezed her eyes shut. She got it. He'd called her for support, but he couldn't say it. Didn't know how. He'd never asked anyone for support or help before.

Tears filled her eyes and her heart clenched. She'd longed for him to reach out to her in the three years of their marriage, but he hadn't been able to. Now, after coming to terms with his brother's death, after spending some time with her, he was finally turning to her.

How could she possibly not respond to that?

"Would you like me to fly to Kansas?"

He sucked in a breath. "No. You have a business to run and things here are out of our control. There's nothing you could do."

"I could hold your hand."

She said the words softly and wasn't surprised when he hesitated before he said, "Right now I'm holding my mother's hand."

"She needs you, Cain." And he hadn't thought twice about flying out to be with her. At his core, he'd always loved his family. He simply felt he'd let them down. "Is there anything I can do for you here?"

"You could call Ava, let her know there's no news but that I arrived safely."

She smiled. That little kindness was also something she wouldn't have expected from him three years ago— or three weeks ago.

"I'll be glad to." She paused then said, "If you'll call me any time there's news, I'll call her and keep her posted."

"Okay."

"Okay." She wanted to tell him she loved him. The words sat on her tongue aching to jump off. He needed to hear it. She longed to say it. But what would happen when his dad was better and he came home? Would those three little words cause awkwardness, or push them beyond where they should be in this relationship they seemed to be building? Would it cause another mistake? Especially since love hadn't been enough the first time.

"I'll call you."

"Lucky for you you only have to remember one cell number."

He laughed. "Goodbye, Liz."

"Goodbye." She disconnected the call then sat staring at the phone. She'd said and done all the right things. She'd been supportive. He'd accepted her support. But they hadn't gone too far.

But he'd called *her*. Not his assistant. He'd been vulnerable with her in a way he'd never been before. He'd even asked her to make his phone call to Ava for him.

He was definitely different.

And she had a lot of thinking to do.

At noon, Ellie dropped into the Happy Maids' office with iced tea and sandwiches. "So dish! What happened?"

Liz looked up from the spreadsheet she was reading, as Ellie set the iced tea and sandwiches on her desk. "What happened when?"

"Last night. With your ex. I know you told me he was withdrawn after his brother's death, but it looks like he's getting over it and…" she nudged Liz across the desk. "He wants you back. Why else would a man play volleyball in those shoes he had on?"

Liz pulled in a big breath. "That's actually the problem. I think he does want us to get back together."

Ellie sat. "You say that as if it's bad."

"It was a crappy marriage. We both walked away hurt."

"Because he was closed off after his brother's death," Ellie insisted as she opened the bag and pulled out the sandwiches.

Accepting hers from Ellie, Liz said, "There's a lot more to it than that. I didn't fit in with the businessmen and their wives that he socialized with. I couldn't plan his parties." Even as she said the words, Liz realized that would no longer be true. Just as she'd explained to Cain as they were cleaning up after his dinner party, she had grown. Changed. "And he had a tendency to disappear when he had an important project. I spent a lot of those three years alone."

"Things would be different this time," Ellie said before she bit into her sandwich. "Even a person without magic could see that. He's different. Involved. Interested." She peered across the desk at Liz. "And you're different."

"Which sort of makes my point. We're so different that we'd actually have to get to know each other all over again."

"But that's good," Ellie said with a laugh. "Since the two people you were couldn't exactly make a marriage work before." She patted Liz's hand. "Trust me. Needing to get to know each other all over again is a good thing."

"The only thing we have in common is sex."

Ellie laughed. Then she said, "And A Friend Indeed. He's really involved and he wants to stay involved."

"Yeah, but I think he only went to work for A Friend Indeed to get to me."

"At first, maybe. But I watched him last night. He was sincere in getting to know our people. He's actually mentoring Billy. He's volunteered to do more work. This guy is in for the long haul."

Until the first crisis with his own company came along. Until a business acquaintance was more important than Billy. Until she was back in his bed and he considered that to be enough time spent with her.

She squeezed her eyes shut. There were just too many variables.

Cain called her every day, and every day she phoned Ava. "He's coming home on Friday morning," she told Ava the following Monday morning. "His dad is recovering well from the surgery, but he wants to stay the extra four days to be sure. His mother is calm. His sister is there for both of them."

The relief was evident in Ava's voice when she said, "That's great." She paused then asked, "Did he say if he's coming to work on Friday?"

"He didn't say."

"I'll have things ready just in case."

"Great."

"Great."

There was an awkward silence before Liz said, "Goodbye, then."

But instead of saying goodbye, Ava said, "He doesn't really turn to people, you know?"

Not quite sure what Ava was driving at, Liz said simply, "I know."

"So it's kind of significant that he turned to you."

Liz swallowed. Now she understood. The fact that

Cain had Liz touch base with his PA for him proved that Cain and Liz had a connection. Ava was probing and hinting right now because she didn't want to see Cain hurt.

"I'll call you if he calls again," Liz said lightly, trying to get off the phone without the serious discussion Ava wanted to have. Then she said goodbye, hung up the phone and put her head in her hands.

No one knew better than Liz that it was significant that Cain had reached out to her. But she couldn't just jump off the deep end and let herself fall head over heels in love. She had to be careful. She had to be smart. Somehow or other *he* had to prove that if she let herself fall in love with him, things really would be different this time.

Cain called Liz with a glowing report of his dad's prognosis when he returned on Friday. It was already noon, so she'd long ago finished cleaning his house and was onto her second house of the day. He'd asked her to come over, but Friday was the one day that she had an entire eight hours' worth of houses to clean. She begged off and he accepted her refusal easily, saying he was going to take a dip in his pool before he checked in with Ava.

"I'll see you tomorrow morning, then."

"Fran Watson's house?"

"Yes. That's the house I talked about with Ayleen."

She hadn't thought he'd jump into A Friend Indeed work so quickly, except she knew the physical activity relaxed him. So the next morning she woke early, put on her jeans and tank top and headed for Fran Watson's house.

Because the entire house needed new floors, Liz

expected to see rolls of discounted carpeting and padding extending from the back of Cain's truck when she pulled into the driveway. At the very most, inexpensive tile or linoleum. Instead, she found Cain and Billy unloading boxes of oak flooring.

"Oh, Cain! This is too much."

"Not really." He heaved a box out of the truck. Though Liz tried not to look, she couldn't help herself. His muscles shifted and moved beneath his T-shirt, reminding her of times they'd played volleyball by the ocean, laughing, having a good time.

She turned away. She had to stop noticing things, remembering things and begin to look in earnest for some kind of proof that these changes in him were permanent. That he wouldn't hurt her or desert her after he married her. That he really wanted a second chance.

He headed for the kitchen where he and Billy began stacking boxes of flooring. When he returned outside, he wiped sweat off his neck with a red handkerchief.

Expecting him to say something about his dad or to be uncomfortable about the fact that the last time they'd seen each other, he'd kissed her, Liz was surprised when he said, "I got the hardwood at a discount supply store."

She almost couldn't believe this was the same man who had called her every day with reports on his dad, the guy who'd wanted to spend Friday afternoon with her. He seemed so distant, so cool.

Of course, they were working—and Billy was only a few feet away in the kitchen.

"Enough for the whole house?"

"I'm going to do the kitchen in a tile of some sort. If you've got kids in a kitchen, it's best to stay away

from wood. Then I'm putting carpet in the bedrooms."
He caught her gaze. "Personally, I like the soft feeling
of carpet when I first roll out of bed."

Unwanted memories surfaced again. He'd always
loved soft carpet, soft towels, soft pajamas. Especially
hers. He'd said that was part of why he liked her. She
didn't just wear soft clothes. *She* was incredibly soft.
The softest woman he'd ever held. Even years later, she
could remember the warmth of happiness from his
compliment. And a glance in Cain's eyes told her that
was why he'd said it.

Billy walked by with a box of wood on his shoulder.
"I think we should listen to him. He's pretty smart."

Cain winced at the praise, but Liz laughed, grateful
Billy had brought them back where they belonged.

When the kitchen door closed behind Billy, she
turned to Cain. "I think he's officially your number-one
fan."

"I just don't want him to be too big of a fan. One
mistake and I can undo every good thing we've accomplished by being friends."

"Just keep teaching him and you'll be fine." She
glanced in the back of the truck, at the stacks of boxes
of wood and the table saw. "What am I going to do?"

"I pretty much figure you'll be our cutter."

She studied the wicked-looking blade on the table
saw then gaped at him. "I'm going to use *that*?"

"I need Billy's strength for the rubber mallet. I'm going
to be the one on the nail gun. That leaves the saw for you."

"Oh, good grief!"

"You can do it. It's not nearly as complicated as it
looks."

As it turned out, most of the morning was spent

ripping out the old flooring in their target rooms, and carting it to the Dumpster Cain had arranged to have in Fran's backyard. He'd brought safety glasses, gloves and all the equipment they'd need, plus lunch, because Fran also didn't want to be in the house while they worked.

"How did you have the time to get all this together?"

"I didn't stay at work yesterday. I handled the important messages, then told Ava to arrange for the lunch and the things we'd need like safety glasses, then I headed to the building supply store."

"You did this yesterday?"

"Yes."

She wanted to ask, "After spending an entire week out of the office, you weren't clamoring to get back to work?" But she didn't. His actions spoke louder than any words he could have said.

When they began installing the new floors, Liz did some of the cutting, but Billy did his share, too. He'd paid attention as Cain showed Liz how to use the saw and easily stepped into the role. He and Cain worked like a team that had been together for decades, not a few weeks, and Liz marveled at their connection. She marveled at Cain's easy patience with the boy, and even the way he tempered his reactions to her around Billy.

There was no mention of the kiss. No mention of the way he'd called her for support. But there was something about the way he looked at her that said more than words could that his feelings for her had grown, sharpened. When their hands accidentally brushed, he would let his fingers linger, as if he wanted the contact but knew it wasn't the place or time.

At the end of the day, he and Billy gathered the saw

and tools for installing the floors and stowed them in his truck. "One more day and the hardwood's in. Next week we lay carpet. The week after, we get the linoleum in the kitchen. Piece of cake."

As he said all that, he punched notes into his BlackBerry. Probably a summary for Ayleen of what they'd accomplished that day.

He jumped into the truck. On the passenger's side, Billy followed suit. With a flick of a key, his truck's engine roared to life.

Liz stepped back, out of his way, then she ambled to her car and slid inside. When Cain's truck rolled out of the driveway and into the street, she laid her head on her steering wheel in dismay.

She finally understood why he hadn't made a big deal out of calling her or even out of kissing her the night of Joni's barbecue. This life they were building had become normal to him. Working with her on the Friend Indeed houses, mentoring Billy, calling her to talk about his family, even kissing her had become routine for him. He was different, eased into an entirely different way to live, and he was easing her in, too. And the next time they were alone she had no doubt he'd suggest a reconciliation.

She lifted her head and started her car. She hadn't forgotten that she had something she needed to tell him. She'd been waiting for the right time. But she finally saw the right time wasn't going to magically materialize. And even if it did, he might take hold of the conversation and she'd lose the chance to tell him about their baby.

She had to visit him, at home, and get the final piece of their past out in the open.

CHAPTER TEN

MONDAY MORNING, when Ava paged Cain on the
intercom to tell him he had a call from Liz, he dropped
to his desk chair and grabbed the phone. "Liz?"

"You know your assistant hates me, right?"

"Ava? She doesn't hate anybody." He paused. "But
I'm glad you called."

She sighed. "You don't even know why I'm calling."

He was hoping that she'd missed him. Hoping she
wanted to see him outside of work or A Friend Indeed.
He'd settle for her simply wanting to talk to him. "I'm
hoping you wanted to talk to me."

"I do. But privately. Would you have a few minutes
to see me tonight?"

Privately? He fell back in his chair in disbelief. Then
he scrambled up again. "Sure."

"I'll be over around six. Right after work."

"Great."

He hung up the phone. "Ava! I'm going to need a bottle
of champagne and some fresh flowers for the house."

She walked to his office door and leaned against the
jamb. "And why would you need that?"

"I'm having a guest tonight."

Her eyes narrowed. "The Happy Maids woman?"

Ah. So Liz wasn't so far off the mark after all. Ava didn't like her. "Am I sensing a bit of a problem?"

"Cain, you're a rich guy. You don't like little people, remember? It amazed me that you were working for A Friend Indeed, then I remembered how pretty Liz Harper is."

"Why do you care?"

"I worry about you because you're doing so many things out of character lately that you're scaring me." Sounding very much like his mother, she pushed away from the doorjamb and came into the room. "How do you know she's not after your money?"

"Because she refused alimony when we divorced."

Ava looked aghast. "She's your ex-wife."

"I probably should have told you that before this."

Ava studied him with narrowed eyes. "Getting involved with an ex is never a good idea."

He forced his attention back to the work on his desk. "I don't want to get involved with my ex." He *didn't* want to get involved with his *ex*. The old relationship hadn't worked. He wanted something new. Something better. He wanted something with the new Liz.

"Then why the champagne and flowers?"

Trying to ignore her, he tapped his pen on his desk. He and Ava had never really had a personal conversation. Even though she'd handled every nitpicky need in his life and knew him as much as anybody could, she'd kept the line of propriety with him. He couldn't believe she was walking over it now.

She took a few more steps into the room. "Cain, I know you well enough to know that you're up to something. Why not just tell me? Maybe I can help?"

Help? He wasn't the kind of man to confide about things like relationships with anyone let alone someone he worked with. But he'd ruined his marriage by being clueless. And right now he might be making progress with Liz, but he knew one wrong word could ruin everything.

Maybe he could use some help?

He *did* trust Ava. Plus, he would do anything, even ask for help, to figure out the best way to start over again with Liz.

"I don't want to get involved with my ex-wife because I want us to start over again."

"There's a difference?"

"Liz is different." He leaned back in his chair and tossed his pen to his desk. "I'm very different. I want our relationship to be different."

Ava walked closer to the desk. "You're serious."

"Never more serious. She's the only woman I've ever really loved. Our marriage got screwed up when my brother died." He wouldn't tell her the whole story. Just enough that she'd understand Liz wasn't at fault in their bad marriage. "I withdrew and I basically left her alone. I wasn't surprised when she left. She's one of the most kind, most honest, most wonderful people I've ever met. Another woman would have been gone after six months. She stayed three long years. And I hurt her." He pulled in a breath. "She shouldn't want me back."

"But you think she does?"

"I think she still loves me."

"Wow."

"So now I want her back and I have no idea how to go about getting her back."

"You're sure this is the right thing?"

"Absolutely."

"You're not going to hurt her again?"

Cain laughed. Leave it to Ava to so quickly take Liz's side now that she knew Cain had been at fault.

"I swear."

"Okay, then for starters, I wouldn't do the things you did the last time around."

"That's the problem. The last time I wined and dined her. Swept her off her feet." He half smiled at the memory. "If I don't wine and dine her—" He caught Ava's gaze. "How is she going to know I'm interested?"

"Lots of ways. But you don't want to use champagne and flowers. That would be too much like the past. Plus she's a businesswoman now." Her face scrunched as she thought for a second, then she said, "What time is she coming?"

"Six. Right after work."

"Feed her dinner." She sat on the seat in front of Cain's desk. "Trust a working woman on this one. Be practical."

"I've spent the past few weeks being practical. Pretending we were work buddies at A Friend Indeed." He wouldn't mention the kiss after the barbecue. The sweet memory might linger in his mind, but spending the following two weeks in Kansas had wiped away any opportunity he might have had to talk about it or expand on it with Liz. When he returned home, they'd had to pretend to be just friends in front of Billy. Private time was at a premium and he didn't want to waste it.

"This might be my only chance to be romantic."

"I didn't say you couldn't be romantic. I just said be practical first. Feed her. Have a normal conversation. Then do whatever it is you want to do romantically."

Cain's mouth twisted with a chagrined smile. What he wanted to do and what he had finally figured out was appropriate for a first date were two totally different things. Still, this might be his only shot. He had to play by the rules.

"All right. I'll try it your way."

Ava rose. "We should talk more often. Makes me feel like you're almost human."

He laughed. "Trust me. I'm fully human." Otherwise, Liz wouldn't have been able to break his heart the last time around. He also wouldn't be worried that she could very well break it this time, too.

At a quarter to six that night, with steaks sizzling on the grill and his refrigerator stocked with beer, Ava's words repeated themselves in Cain's head. The first time around he'd done his damnedest to impress Liz. He hadn't been practical at all. His head had been in the clouds. This time around he would be better, smarter.

The doorbell sounded just as the steaks were ready to come off the grill. He raced through his downstairs, opened the door and pulled her inside. "Steaks have to come off the grill. Follow me."

"I didn't want you to cook dinner!"

"I like to grill." He did and she knew that, so that eased them past hurdle one.

She followed him through the downstairs into the kitchen and toward the French doors to the patio. "I still didn't want you to cook for me. I can't stay that long."

"You can stay long enough to eat one measly steak."

He said the words stepping out onto the cool stone floor of his patio.

Liz paused on the threshold. "This is beautiful."

He glanced around at the yellow chaise lounges, the sunlight glistening off the blue water in the huge pool and the big umbrella table with the white linen tablecloth rustling in the breeze coming off the water just past his backyard. He hardly noticed how nice it was. With the exception of grilling and sometimes using the pool, he was never out here. In the past six years, he hadn't merely worked too much, he missed too much. He didn't enjoy what he had. Or the people in his life.

Maybe that's what Ava meant when she told him to be practical. To be normal.

"There's beer in the fridge."

She stopped midstep. "Beer?"

"Yes. Get me one and one for yourself, while I get these steaks off."

"Sure."

By the time she returned, he had the steaks on two plates, along with foil-wrapped potatoes and veggies, both of which he'd also cooked on the grill.

Studying the food he'd prepared, she handed him a beer. "This looks great."

He shrugged and motioned for her to take a seat. "All easy to do on a grill."

"I'm impressed."

He sat across from her. "I don't want you to be impressed. I want you to eat."

She unwrapped her potato and reached for the butter and sour cream. "I think you really were serious about seeing me put on some weight."

He laughed. "I like you just the way you are." His compliment didn't surprise him as it popped out of his mouth. Ava wanted him to behave normally, which he took to mean behave as his real self, and that was how he felt. But the compliment embarrassed Liz. Her cheeks reddened endearingly.

He wanted to tell her how beautiful she was but Ava's words rang in his head again. *Be practical.* He hadn't been practical the first time and as a result they'd never gotten to know each other. They'd each married a stranger.

"So tell me about your family."

She peeked up at him. "I did, remember?"

"You told me about your dad…about your past. I'm interested in your family now. You said you had sisters."

She licked her lips, stalling, obviously thinking about whether or not she should speak, what she should say, if she should say anything at all. Cain's heart nearly stopped. This was it, the big test of whether or not she was interested in a real relationship, and she was hesitating over the easy questions.

Could he have read this whole situation wrong? The kiss before he left for Kansas? The lifeline she'd been while his father was sick? The heated looks and lingering touches at the Friend Indeed houses?

"My mom works as a nurse."

Relief poured through him. "No kidding?" Feigning nonchalance he didn't feel, he unwrapped the foil around his veggies. He had to be comfortable if he wanted her to be comfortable. "What about your sisters? What do they do?"

"My older sister is a physician's assistant. My younger sister is a pharmaceutical sales rep."

"Interesting. Everybody's in medicine in some way." He took a bite of broccoli.

Liz cut a strip off her steak. "Except me."

"You're still helping people."

"Yeah, but my degree's in business. I didn't get the nerves of steel my mother had. I couldn't have gone into medicine. I'm the family rebel."

"Me, too. My dad owned a chain of hardware stores. And here I am in Miami, running three companies that use hardware but aren't in the hardware business."

"I always wondered why you didn't just stay in Kansas and join the family business."

"When it was time for me to go to school, the stores hit a rough patch. That's why I put myself through university." He shook his head. "But what a backhanded lucky break. It led me to the work I love."

"You *were* lucky."

The second the words were out of her mouth, Liz regretted them. Cain might have been lucky in business but he hadn't been lucky in life. He'd suffered a horrible tragedy in the loss of his brother, particularly since he'd been the driver of the car. Their marriage had failed. Now she was here to tell him of another heartbreak. The conversation had been going in the absolute right direction until she'd made her stupid comment about him being lucky.

"I was lucky, but not entirely. Once I figured out what I wanted to do with my life I had to work hard to make it happen."

She nearly breathed a sigh of relief that he hadn't taken her comment the wrong way and challenged it as he could have. "True."

He slid his hand across the table. "And that's why I'm glad you wanted to talk tonight." He pulled in a breath, reached for her fingers. Before Liz could stop him he had his hand wrapped around hers. "I know I'm going to say this badly, but I can't go on the way we have been over the past few weeks." He caught her stunned gaze. "I don't want a reconciliation. Neither one of us wants to go back to what we had." He brought her fingers to his lips and kissed them. "But there's no law that says we can't start over. We're both different—"

Liz's breath froze in her lungs. She was too late! She loved him and now he was falling for her. She'd thought she'd fallen first and maybe too fast because Cain was so different that it was easy for her to see that and respond to it. But he was right with her. Falling as fast and as hard as she had been. Now she had to scramble to set things right.

Only with effort did she find the air and ability to speak. "Oh, Cain, we can't pretend we don't have a past."

"Sure we can."

"We can't!" She sucked in a breath, calmed herself. For weeks she'd been waiting for the right time to tell him her secret. She'd hesitated when she should have simply been brave and told him. She couldn't let another opportunity pass. "Cain, I can't forget the past and neither can you. We have to deal with it. I left you because I had a miscarriage. I needed help. Real help to get beyond it."

His face shifted from happy to shocked. "You were pregnant?"

"Yes."

"And you didn't tell me?" He let go of her hand and combed his fingers through his hair.

"I *couldn't* tell you—"

Music suddenly poured from Liz's cell phone. She

pulled it from her jeans pocket, hoping that a glance at caller ID would allow her to ignore it. When she saw it was Ayleen, she almost groaned. She couldn't ignore a call from A Friend Indeed.

She glanced at Cain in apology, but opened her phone and answered. "Hey, Ayleen. What's up?"

"We got an emergency call tonight. Is the old Rogerson place clean?"

An emergency meant a woman had suddenly run from her husband or boyfriend. She could be hurt. Mentally and physically. She could have kids with her.

Liz sat up, coming to attention, breaking eye contact with Cain. "Yes. It's ready."

Ayleen breathed a sigh of relief. "Great. Can you be there to meet the family?"

"Absolutely." Once again, she didn't hesitate but she caught Cain's gaze. "I can be there in a half an hour."

"No rush. The family's in transit. Their estimated arrival time is forty minutes."

"Ten minutes to spare." Ten minutes to talk Cain through this. "I'll call you later, after they're settled." She snapped her phone closed. Her gaze still clinging to Cain's, she said, "I'm sorry."

"For a miscarriage that wasn't your fault? For not telling me you were pregnant? Or for leaving me now before I can even wrap my head around it?"

"For all three."

He rubbed his hand across the back of his neck, and turned away. Fear trickled down her spine. Not for herself, for him. She didn't want him to blame himself. Or be angry with himself.

"I know you have questions. I'm not sure I can answer them all, but I'll try."

He faced her again. "You know what? I get it." He shrugged. "We were both in a bad place. You did what you had to do. I'm stunned about losing a baby, but I can deal with that."

Her phone rang. She longed to ignore it, but knew what happened when A Friend Indeed was in crisis mode. The troops rallied. They called each other, making arrangements for what each would do. She couldn't ignore a call.

She flipped open her phone. "Hello."

"It's me, Ellie. Who's getting the groceries for the Rogerson house? You or me?"

"Could you do it?"

"Sure. See you, boss."

Warring needs tore her apart as she closed her phone. She wanted to be here for Cain, but he seemed to be handling this well. Three years had passed. Though she was sure he'd mourn the loss, it wasn't the same as actually going through it.

And the woman racing to the Friend Indeed house needed her. This was what she was trained to do.

Before she could speak, Cain did. "Go. I'm fine."

Liz studied his face and he smiled weakly. "Seriously, I'm fine. I'll call you."

His smile, though shaky, reassured her.

She rose. Her voice carried a gentle warning when she said, "If you don't call me, I'm calling you."

He smiled again. This time stronger. "Okay."

She turned and walked back into the house, through the downstairs and to the front door. On her way to her car she stopped and glanced back.

He'd taken that so well that maybe, just maybe, they really could have the new beginning he wanted.

CHAPTER ELEVEN

WALKING INTO THE SHOWER the following Saturday, Cain
cursed himself. He'd hardly slept since Monday night,
and, when he had, he'd dreamed about things that made
him crazy. The smoothness of Liz's perfect pink skin. The
way her green eyes smoldered with need in the throes of
passion. The feeling of her teeth scraping along his chest.

He shouldn't want her. *Shouldn't*. He was smarter
than to want somebody who didn't want him.

She'd been so hesitant about spending time with
him, to befriend him, to even consider anything romantic between them, yet he'd been oblivious to what her
behavior was telling him. Just as he had been in their
marriage. Now that he knew the real reason she'd left
him, her not wanting anything to do with him made
perfect sense.

He ducked his head under the spray, trying to rid
himself of the overwhelming shame that wanted to
strangle him, but he couldn't. After his three years of
guilt over his brother's death, he knew he couldn't
assume responsibility for something that had been out
of his control. And if her secret had simply been a
matter of a miscarriage, he probably could have ab-

solved himself. But how could he forgive himself for being so self-absorbed that his wife couldn't tell him she was pregnant? How could he forgive himself when her telling him about their baby might have been the thing that brought him back to life, bridged their marital gap, kept them together?

Stepping out of the shower, he grabbed a towel, telling himself to stop thinking about it. Running it over and over and over in his head wouldn't change anything. But memories of those final few months together had taken on new meaning and they haunted him.

And he could not—he would not—forgive himself.

At Amanda's house, Cain told Billy to take his time, hoping to delay seeing Liz. He hadn't called her as he told her he would but she also hadn't called him. He suspected she'd been busy with the new family moving into the Friend Indeed house. And for that he was grateful. He'd wanted to be alone. He didn't want to talk this out with her. Worse, he didn't want her to tell him it was "okay" that he hadn't been there for her. It wasn't "okay." It was abysmal—sinful—that he'd been so oblivious that his wife had to suffer in silence.

But the bad thing about avoiding her all week was that Billy would now witness their first meeting since she told him about their baby.

He pulled his truck into Fran's empty driveway. "No Liz," he mumbled, hardly realizing he was talking.

Billy pushed open the truck door. "Isn't there some kind of big party tonight?"

Cain turned to Billy. "Yes." How could he have forgotten? "A Friend Indeed's fund-raiser." On top of the new family that had moved in on Monday night, Liz had probably been occupied all week with last-minute details for the ball.

Billy jumped out of the truck. "And she's the boss of the whole deal, right?"

Cain nodded.

"So she's not going to be here." Billy slammed his door closed.

Cain's entire body sagged with relief. Until he remembered that he'd see her that night at the ball—

Unless he didn't go.

All things considered, that might be the right thing to do. Not for himself, but for her. This was her big night. He didn't want to ruin it. And seeing him sure as hell could ruin it for her. He'd been a nightmare husband. And when they'd "met" again in his kitchen when she came to work as his maid, she hadn't wanted to be around him. Yet he'd forced himself back into her life. He couldn't even imagine the pressure she'd endured for the weeks they'd worked together, the weeks he'd insinuated himself into A Friend Indeed. Not going would be a kindness to her.

For the next eight hours, he kept himself busy so he didn't have to think about Liz or the fund-raiser ball or their God-awful marriage. But at the end of the day he remembered that he'd promised Ayleen he would mingle with the guests, talking about the work he'd done, hoping to inspire other contractors and business owners to get involved in a more personal way. So if he didn't show, Ayleen would get upset and then Liz would worry about him.

He didn't want Liz to have to worry about him anymore. He wasn't her burden. He'd fulfill his responsibility and go to the ball, but he'd let her alone.

* * *

Liz had spent all day at the home of Mr. and Mrs. Leonard Brill, the couple who had volunteered their mansion for the ball for A Friend Indeed. After seeing to all the last-minute deliveries and details, she'd even dressed in one of their myriad spare bedrooms.

The event itself wasn't huge. Only a hundred people were attending. That was why the Brill mansion was the perfect choice. It was big enough to be luxurious, but not so large that the fund-raiser lost its air of intimacy. But the ball didn't need to be immense. All the people invited were big contributors. Liz expected to beat last year's donations by a wide margin, especially with the new guests Cain invited.

Walking into the empty ballroom ten minutes before the guests were due to arrive, she pressed her hand to her stomach. *Cain.* Just thinking his name gave her butterflies. He hadn't called her as he had promised, but she'd been overwhelmed with the ball, the new family in the Rogerson house and Happy Maids. He probably knew that and didn't want to add any more stress to her week.

But she remembered the expression on his face when she left, the calm way he'd taken the explanation of why she'd ended their marriage, and she not only knew she'd done the right thing by telling him, she also knew they were going to be okay.

Maybe better than okay.

"You look fabulous!" Wearing a peach sequined gown Ayleen floated across the empty dance floor to Liz, who pirouetted in her red strapless gown.

"Wow." Ellie joined them. "You two are going to be the talk of the town."

Liz laughed at Ellie, who looked like a vision in her

aqua halter-top gown, her blond hair spilling around her in a riot of curls. "I think *you're* going to be the talk of the town."

She laughed. "Maybe we should all just settle for making our special men drool."

"My husband's past drooling," Alyeen said with a laugh, but just as quickly she frowned and her eyes narrowed at Liz. "I know Ellie is dating that lifeguard, but I've heard nothing about a special man in *your* life."

Liz felt her face redden and suspected it was probably as bright as her dress.

"Oh, come on!" Ellie chided. "Tell her about Cain."

Ayleen's eyebrows rose. "Our Cain?"

Ellie leaned in conspiratorially. "He was Liz's Cain long before he was A Friend Indeed's. He's her ex."

Ayleen's mouth dropped open. "No kidding."

"And I have a feeling," Ellie singsonged, "that they're not going to be exes long."

"Is that true?" Ayleen asked, facing Liz.

Liz sighed. "I have no idea."

Ellie playfully slapped her forearm. "You need to be more confident. That man loves you. I can see it in his face."

"But we have issues."

"Oh, pish posh!" Ayleen said. "Do you love him?"

"I don't ever think I ever stopped." As the words came out of her mouth, Liz realized how true they were. That was why she'd been so afraid to tell him about the miscarriage. She didn't want to hurt him or lose him. Which was why she was so grateful he'd reacted as well as he had to the news. She loved him. She always had and now that her secret had been confessed, they could finally move on with their lives.

"Then trust our magic friend. If she says he loves you, he loves you." She patted her hand. "You need to relax."

Cain strode up the stone sidewalk to the elaborate entrance of the Brill mansion. Twin fountains on both sides of the walk were lit by blue-and-gold lights. At the top of ten wide stone steps, columns welcomed guests to a cut-glass front door.

He could see why A Friend Indeed had chosen the Brill residence for their ball. It was one of Miami's most beautiful mansions. Plus, it was small enough to create an intimate atmosphere for guests. The kind of atmosphere that would allow Ayleen to personally walk among the guests and gather checks. Cain himself had an obscenely large check in his pocket. He wanted Liz to succeed.

Liz.

He could picture her now, excited about being pregnant and not being able to tell him. Then devastated by the loss and not being able to depend on him.

He cursed himself in his head for remembering, just as Leonard opened the front door.

"Cain! Welcome."

Cain pasted on a smile and stepped into the foyer. "Good evening, Mr. Brill."

"Call me Leonard, please," the older, gray-haired gentleman said as he directed Cain to the right. "Everyone's in the ballroom."

Nerves jangled through Cain as he entered the grand room. His eyes instantly scanned the crowd milling around the room, looking at artwork that had been donated for a silent auction that was also part of the event. A string quartet played in a corner as a dance band set up across the room.

He didn't see Liz, but he knew she was here and his heart began to hammer in anticipation. He shook his head. He had to get over this. Let her go. Let her find somebody worthy of her love.

Plus, he had a job at this fund-raiser. Ayleen had assigned him the task of walking around, talking about what he'd done for the houses so he could generate support and bigger contributions.

But only ten minutes into a conversation with a potential contributor he spotted Liz. As he spoke to Brad Coleman, his eyes had been surreptitiously scanning the room and he saw her standing with a small group of women, engaged in lively conversation.

He'd missed seeing her before because her beautiful black hair wasn't cascading over her shoulders, in a bouncy ponytail or even pulled back into a Happy Maids bun. It had been swept up into an elegant hairdo that gave her the look of a princess or aristocrat.

He let his eyes move lower and his breath whooshed from his lungs. Her dress was red—strapless—and didn't so much cling to her curves as gently caress them. He swallowed hard just as she turned and noticed him. She smiled hesitantly and his heart swelled with something that felt very much like love. But he stopped that, too.

He didn't deserve her. He never had.

"Why didn't you tell me that you and Liz had been married?"

Cain spun around and saw that Brad had deserted him and Ayleen had taken his place.

"It didn't seem relevant."

She laughed. "Men. You never know what's relevant."

Since he was the one so distant his own wife couldn't tell him she was pregnant, Cain couldn't argue that.

"She looks very beautiful tonight, doesn't she?"

Cain's gaze followed the direction of Ayleen's. Taking in the way her gown clung to her curves, and the sparkle in her brilliant green eyes, his blood raced in his veins, but his chest tightened in sadness. He had to walk away from her. Give her a chance for a real life.

"Yes. She is beautiful."

"You should ask her to dance."

"I don't think so. In fact," he said, reaching into his jacket pocket and producing his check, "I'll just give this to you."

Ayleen glanced at the check, then up at him. "This is the second time you've tried to give A Friend Indeed a check without going through the proper channels."

"I thought you were the proper channel."

"And I thought you'd want to give it to your ex-wife, so she could be impressed and proud of you."

He reared back as if she'd physically slapped him. If there were two things Liz should never be of him, they were proud or impressed.

He pressed the check into Ayleen's hand. "You take it."

She studied his face. "So you don't have to speak with her?" She smiled ruefully. "Cain, this is wrong. She's excited to see you tonight and you're running?"

"Believe me. This is for her benefit, not mine." He lifted his eyes and luckily saw one of the guests he'd had Ayleen invite. "And before you ask why, I see one of my contributors." He slid away. "I'll see you later."

* * *

Liz shifted through the crowd, pausing to speak with people, asking if there was anything anyone needed, wishing everyone a good time. The dance band had been playing for about an hour. Dancers swayed and gyrated around the room. The silent auction proceeded as planned. Still, she walked around, introduced herself, saw to every tiny detail.

After another hour of pretending it didn't matter that Cain had ignored her when she'd smiled at him, she couldn't lie to herself anymore. He'd chosen not to speak with her. He hadn't said hello. Hadn't even returned her smile.

Pulling in a breath, she greeted a passing couple who praised her for the beautiful ball. But questions about why Cain wouldn't talk to her raced through her head. What if Cain hadn't taken her news as well as he'd seemed to? What if he'd been pretending? Or what if he was angry with her for not telling him she was pregnant?

It could be any of those things or all of them. She longed to find him and simply ask him, but she had a job to do. As if to punctuate that thought, a woman caught her hand and asked her a question about the auction. An elderly gentleman handed her a check. She couldn't walk two feet without someone stopping her.

The band took a break and the auction results were announced by Ayleen, with Liz by her side on the small elevated platform that acted as a stage for the band.

"Those are our winners," Ayleen finally said, having given the final name on the list of those who'd won the bids. "You know where the checks go," she added with a laugh. "Thank you very much for your participation in this event. A Friend Indeed couldn't exist without you and on behalf of the women we've helped, I thank you."

The group broke into a quiet round of applause and after a reasonable time Ayleen raised her hand to stop them.

"I'd also like to thank Liz Harper for all of her hard work, not just on this ball but also for the group on a daily basis."

The crowd applauded again.

When they were through, Ayleen said, "And special thanks to Cain Nestor. He's been renovating the houses. Donating both his time and the materials to make the homes of our women some of the prettiest houses in their neighborhoods."

The crowd erupted in spontaneous, thunderous applause, and Liz felt such a stirring of pride for Cain, tears came to her eyes. He never saw what a wonderful person he was. But she did. And she'd made another huge mistake with him. She should have told him about their baby sooner.

Lost in her thoughts, she wasn't prepared when Ayleen caught her hand and pulled her forward, toward the microphone again.

"What most of you don't know though is that Liz has been helping Cain. At first she acted as A Friend Indeed's liaison, but then she picked up a paintbrush and threw herself into the work, too. Cain and Liz are an unbeatable team."

She hugged Liz in thanks then turned away, scanning the room. "Cain? Where are you? How about if you and Liz get the next set of the dancing started, so everyone can see who you are?"

Liz's mouth fell open in dismay. Ayleen had probably

noticed Cain hadn't even spoken to her and was playing matchmaker. She didn't know Cain was upset about their child and he didn't want to talk with her. Liz had only figured it out herself. But there was nothing she could do to get out of this without embarrassing herself or Cain.

With her heart hammering in her chest, Liz looked down off the makeshift stage and searched the crowd for Cain. She found him in the back in a corner, watching her. Their gazes locked. She waited for him to look away. He didn't. She told herself to look away and couldn't. He walked out of the crowd to her.

Cain swallowed the last of the champagne in his glass and dropped it on the tray of a passing waiter. He wouldn't embarrass Liz by publicly refusing to dance with her. But he also knew this was as good of a time as any to get their relationship on track. She didn't want a second chance with him. He didn't deserve one. But they both worked for A Friend Indeed. So they had to spend time together. They couldn't ignore each other forever.

The whole room stilled as he and Liz met in the center of the dance floor. He pulled her into his arms, and the band began to play a waltz. Forcing himself to focus on the music, he tried to ignore her sweet scent, but it swirled around them like the notes of the song, tempting him. Especially when she melted against him. Not in surrender, but in acknowledgment. They would always have chemistry. But sometimes that wasn't enough.

He wasn't enough. She was worthy of someone much, much better.

The music vibrated around them as other dancers

eased onto the floor. In minutes they were surrounded by a happy crowd. Not the center of attention, anymore. Not even on anyone's radar. He could slip away.

Just as he was ready to excuse himself and end the dance, she pulled back. Her shiny green eyes searched his.

"Are you okay?"

"I'm fine." He said the words casually then twirled her around to emphasize his lightness. He'd never make her feel responsible for him again.

She pulled back again. "But you're angry with me."

He laughed. "No, Liz. If there's one thing I'm not, it's angry with you."

"You have every right to be. I should have told you about our baby sooner."

The hurt in her voice skipped across his nerves like shards of glass. As if it wasn't bad enough he had to walk away from her, she was taking it all wrong.

"And I'm sorry. I'm very, very sorry."

He nearly squeezed his eyes shut in misery. He was the one who hadn't been there for her. Yet she was apologizing to him?

He stopped dancing, tugged his hand away from hers. "Stop."

"No. You told me on Monday night that you wanted to start over. I think we could—"

Other dancers nearly bumped into them. He caught her by the waist and hauled her against him, spinning them into the crowd again. "Don't say it," he said, nearly breathless from her nearness. They couldn't go on like this. And he'd made it worse by mentioning starting over before he knew just how bad he'd been as a husband. Now, in her innate fairness, or maybe because she was so kind, she was willing to try again. But he couldn't do that to her.

And if the only way to get her away from him, off the notion that somehow they belonged together, was to hurt her, then maybe one final hurt added to his long list of sins wouldn't matter.

"I made a mistake the other night when I mentioned reconciling. I was a lousy husband. You never should have married me. It's time we moved on. Time we let go. Time *you* let go."

With that he released her. The horrified expression on her face cut to his heart, but he ignored it, turned and walked off the dance floor. Letting her go was for the best. Even if it did break his heart.

Stunned, Liz turned and scanned the great room, until she found Ellie. She raced over. "I have to go."

Ellie's face fell. "What?"

"I'm sorry," she said, pulling Ellie with her as she ran through the foyer to the front door. "Everything's done, except the final goodbye and thank-you. Ayleen has already done the official thank-you. All you need to say is thank you and good night. Can you do that?"

Ellie said, "Sure, but—"

Liz didn't give her the chance to finish. She raced out the door and down the stone steps. The tinkling of the fountains followed her and the silver moon lit the way as she raced down the driveway to her car. The only thing missing from the scene was a pair of glass slippers.

Because like Cinderella, she'd lost her prince.

Again.

The old Cain was back. And the worst of it was Liz

had brought him back. He'd pretended to take the news of their baby well, but the truth was he'd tumbled back into the horrible place where he'd lived the three years of their marriage. There had been no help for it. She couldn't have entered into a relationship with a secret hanging over them.

But she'd hurt him. More this time than she had by walking away from their marriage without a word.

He'd never forgive her.

She'd never forgive herself.

Balling up the skirt of her gown, she slid into her car and a horrible thought struck her. They had to work together in the morning. After the way he'd rejected her, dismissed her, she had to go to Fran's house in the morning and pretend nothing had happened.

CHAPTER TWELVE

THE NEXT MORNING, Cain nearly called Ayleen and begged off his work on Fran's house. He hadn't wanted to hurt Liz, but he'd had to to force her to get on with her life. So he didn't really want to spend eight hours with her, seeing her hurt, knowing he'd hurt her and knowing he really would spend the rest of his days without the one woman he wanted in his life. All because he could never see her needs. She might be right for him, but he most certainly wasn't right for her and he had to let her go.

But in the end he conceded that bailing on Fran's house wasn't the thing to do. He had made a commitment to A Friend Indeed. Fran shouldn't have to wait for her house to be finished because he and Liz shouldn't be working together.

He rolled his truck to a stop in front of Fran's garage but didn't immediately open his truck door. Stuck in his thoughts, he stared at the empty space beside his truck.

"She'll be here," Billy said, undoubtedly assuming Cain was wondering where Liz was. "She never lets anybody down. Just ask my mom."

The kid's voice held the oddest note of both trust in

Liz and scorn. It might have been simple teenage angst or it could have been that something had happened that morning to make him angry. Cain couldn't tell. Sooner or later, he'd get it out of him, but right now Cain's mind was still on Liz. About how his next step would have to be getting her off his work crew.

He shoved his truck door open and jumped out just as her little green car chugged into the driveway. He rushed back to his truck bed and immediately reached for the cooler and picnic basket. Intense and primal, the desire rose in him to get away before the need to talk to her, to touch her, became a hungry beast he couldn't control. He would have done anything, given anything, if there would have been a way they could start over, but they couldn't. He wouldn't do that to her. He would not ruin her life a second time.

Stepping out of her car, Liz saw the picnic basket and smiled shakily. "You brought lunch again."

He almost groaned. Even sweet Liz shouldn't be able to forgive him for how he'd rejected her the night before. Yet, here she was trying to get along, giving him the damned benefit of the doubt.

"Yes. I brought lunch." He turned away, taking the cooler and stowing it in the garage before he hauled the picnic basket into the kitchen.

Following him, she said, "What are we doing today?"

"We're finishing the carpet in the bedrooms." And it wasn't a three-person job. He and Billy had handled it alone the day before. This was his out, his way to save her, his way to save himself from the misery of being within arm's distance of the woman he'd always loved, but never deserved.

He faced her. "This is actually a two-person job. Billy and I can handle it. I know you're probably tired from all the work you did for the ball yesterday." Casually, as if nothing were wrong, he leaned against the counter. "So why don't you go on home?"

She took a step back. "You want me to leave?"

"Yes." The wounded look in her eyes made him long to tell her he was sorry that he hadn't been there for her. To tell her how much he wished he could make all his misdeeds up to her. To tell her he wished there was a way they didn't have to give up on their relationship.

But he couldn't do that. The only honorable thing for him to do would be to sacrifice his own needs, so that she'd find someone who really would love her.

She stared at him, as if waiting for him to change his mind. As the clock above the sink ticked off the seconds, her eyes filled with tears. Without a word, she turned and raced out the door before Cain could even say goodbye.

Billy shook his head in wonder. "Are you nuts?"

Before he could stop himself, Cain said, "Trust me. This is for her own good."

It might have been for her good, but the sadness that shivered through him told Cain that he wouldn't ever get over this. Forcing her to find a better man was the best thing for her, but it was the worst that could happen to him.

In her office that morning and afternoon, Liz kept herself so busy catching up on the work she'd ignored while she worked on the ball that she didn't have time to think about Cain.

She knew telling him about their lost baby had

caused him to close himself off. But this time he didn't seem to be closing himself off from the world. Only from her.

She refused to let herself think about any of it, and instead worked diligently in her office until it was dark. Then she walked to her car, head high, breaths deep and strong. She'd lost him twice now. But this time she'd lost him honestly. She'd lost him because she wouldn't start a relationship while hiding a secret. She'd done the right thing. She'd simply gotten the wrong result.

And now she would deal with it.

In her condo, she tossed her keys to the table by the door and reached for the hem of her T-shirt as she walked back to the shower. She might have lost him honestly but she'd still lost him, and it hurt so much even the soothing spray of her shower didn't help. She'd lost Cain's love, the affection she craved from him, but more than that she would have to live with the knowledge that he would torment himself for the rest of his life.

She knew he was a good man. If only he could forgive himself and live life in the now, he could be free. But he couldn't, not even for her. Not even for *them*.

After her shower, she wrapped herself in a robe and headed out to the kitchen to make herself some cocoa. She reached into the cupboard for a mug just as her cell phone rang. For the second time in as many weeks, she wished she could ignore it. She wanted to weep, not for herself but for Cain. For as much as it hurt her to lose him, she knew he suffered the torment of the damned. He'd never be happy.

But as an integral part of a charity that didn't sleep, she couldn't ignore any call. She reached over and picked up her phone. Seeing that the caller was Amanda, she said, "Hey, Amanda. What's up?"

"Liz! Liz! Billy is gone!"

"What do you mean gone?"

"We had a fight this morning that we didn't get to finish because Cain came to get him for work. When he got home this afternoon he tried to act as if nothing happened, but I picked up right where we left off." Amanda burst into tears. "I'm so sorry. I was so stupid. But I'm so afraid he'll turn out like his dad that I go overboard. And now he's gone. He just walked out, slamming the door. Before I could go after him he was gone. I didn't even see if he turned right or left. It was like he disappeared." She took a shuddering breath. "I've looked everywhere I know to look. He's no-where."

Liz's own breath stuttered in her chest. Fear for Billy overwhelmed her. "Don't worry. We'll find him."

"How? I've looked everywhere. And it's too soon to call the police. They make you wait twenty-four hours." She made a gurgling sound in her throat. "By the time twenty-four hours pass, anything could happen!"

"Okay, I'm calling Cain—" She made the offer without thinking. Even Amanda was surprised.

"Cain?"

"They talk a lot as they're working, Amanda. There's a good chance he'll know where Billy is."

Amanda breathed a sigh of relief. "Okay."

But Liz's breath froze when she realized what she'd done. Now she had to call Cain. "You sit tight. I'll call you back as soon as I talk to him."

"Okay."

Liz clicked off and immediately dialed Cain's cell

phone. She wouldn't let herself think about the fact that he hated her now. Wouldn't let herself consider that he might ignore her plea for help.

"Liz?"

Relieved that he'd answered, Liz leaned against her counter and said simply, "Billy's gone."

"Gone?"

"He had a fight with Amanda. She says she knows she pushed a bit too hard, and he flew out of the house and was gone before she could even see what direction he ran in."

A few seconds passed in silence before Cain said, "Look, Liz, I'm going to be honest. I think I know where Billy is, but you can't come with me."

"Like hell I can't!" He might have been able to kick her off the job site that morning, but Billy was her responsibility, and she wasn't letting Cain push her out of finding him.

"I think he's gone to his father's. If he has, this could be dangerous."

"I get that. But I'm trained for this! *You* aren't. If either one of us goes, it should be me."

There was a long pause. Finally Cain blew his breath out on a sigh. "I can't let you go alone, so we have to go together. Be ready when I get to your apartment." He stopped. "Where is your apartment?"

She gave him the address and, as he clicked off, she raced into her bedroom and pulled on jeans and a tank top. By the time he arrived in front of her building, she was already on the sidewalk.

She jumped into his Porsche and he raced away. The humid Miami air swirled around her as they roared down the street. With Cain's attention on driving, Liz glanced around at the car she'd loved when they were married. Memories of driving down this very highway in this very car, six years ago, before all their troubles, assailed her. They were so sweet and so poignant that part of her longed to pretend that everything was okay between them.

But that was their biggest problem. When things weren't working out, they'd tried to pretend they were. She was done with that and Cain was, too. She had to accept that they were over.

Cain tried not to think about Liz sitting next to him as he drove to Billy's old house, the house he and Amanda had lived in with an abusive father. He prayed that Billy hadn't been so angry with his mom that he told his father the location of their safe house. If they didn't get to Billy on time, Billy's dad could be on his way to Amanda's before they could warn her.

He pressed his gas pedal to the floor. Billy's dad lived far enough away that Billy would have had to take a bus. Cain didn't know the schedule, but he prayed Billy hadn't been lucky enough to walk out onto the street and hop on a bus. If he'd had to wait that bought him and Liz time to get to him. So there was still hope. Slim hope. But hope.

Nearing Billy's old neighborhood, Cain also prayed that if Billy had made it to his dad's and had had the gumption to refuse to tell his dad where his mom and sister were that his dad hadn't taken his fists to him.

A sick feeling rose up in him. There were too many ways this night could end badly.

Because he didn't have an exact address, Cain

slowed his car. When he did, he heard Liz suck in a breath.

He automatically reached for her hand. "Don't worry. We'll do this."

The feeling of her hand in his brought an ache to his chest. He knew he shouldn't have touched her. But she looked so sad and he was so scared that it came automatically to him. She smiled at him across the console and his heart constricted. He'd give anything to deserve the trust she had in him.

He glanced away, at the area around them.

"Billy talked about a bar that was two buildings down from his house and going to the convenience store across the street." Cain let his Porsche roll along slowly as he and Liz scanned the area.

"There's the bar," Liz shouted, pointing. "And the convenience store."

"And Billy," Cain said, pointing at the kid sitting on the curb in front of a little blue house.

He found a parking space, and they pushed their way out of the car and raced up to Billy.

"Hey, Liz." Billy's eyes roved from Liz to Cain. "Hey, Cain."

"Hey." The kid's mood was sad more than upset, so Cain took a cue from him. Not caring about his gray trousers, he casually sat on the curb beside Billy. Liz sat on the other side. "Your mom is worried."

He snorted a laugh. "My mom is always worried."

"Looks like she's got good reason this time," Liz said, turning and gesturing at the house behind them. "Is that your old place?"

Billy nodded.

"Dad not home?"

"He might be. I don't know."

Cain sat back, letting Liz take the lead in the conversation. She was the one who had been trained for this.

"You didn't go in?"

"I sorta feel like I'm doing that cutting off my nose to spite my face thing my mom talks about."

Cain chuckled and Liz out-and-out laughed. He could hear the relief in her voice. He felt it, too. Billy had run, but he couldn't take the final steps. He probably liked his new life. Even if his old life sometimes seemed like a way out of his troubles, he really didn't want to go back.

"Yeah. That's probably accurate." She waited a few seconds then said, "Do you want to talk about it?"

Billy shrugged. "Same old stuff."

"I'm not familiar with the stuff, so you'll have to fill me in."

"She's afraid of everything."

Liz's eyebrows rose. "She has good reason, Billy."

"I'm not my dad and I'm tired of paying for his mistakes."

Cain got a sudden inspiration and before Liz could reply, he said, "How does she make you pay?"

"She yells at me. I have a curfew."

"That's not paying for your dad's mistakes, Billy. That's her guiding you, looking out for your welfare, being a mom."

Billy looked at him sharply. "No one else I know has a curfew."

"Maybe that's why half your friends are in trouble." Cain sighed and shifted on the curb, glancing at Liz who only gave him a look with her eyes that encouraged him to continue.

"Look, trust isn't handed out like hall passes in school. You have to earn it."

Unexpectedly, he thought of Liz, of all the ways he'd failed her and yet she trusted him. She trusted him when he didn't trust himself. Liz had always believed in him. Even when he let her down, she believed he'd do the right thing the next time.

Hooking his thumb toward the house behind them, he said, "Earning trust isn't easy, but running back to the past isn't the alternative. It's just a way of staying right where you are. Never learning from your mistakes. Never having what you want." A strange feeling bubbled up in him as he said that. As if he wasn't talking to Billy but to himself.

He cleared his throat. "But that means you're going to have to do a thing or two to earn your mom's trust."

"Like what?"

"Like not arguing about the curfew and coming in on time. Like telling her where you're going." He gave Billy a friendly nudge with his shoulder. "Like getting your grades up in school."

Billy snorted a laugh.

"So it sounds as if you agree that there's room for improvement."

"I guess."

Cain clasped his hand on Billy's shoulder. "Let's get you back to your mom."

Billy rose. "Okay."

Liz rose, too.

"But first let's go across the street and get a gallon of ice cream. What kind does your mom like?"

Billy blinked. "Chocolate. Why?"

"It never hurts to bring a present when you've made a mistake."

* * *

When Liz, Cain and Billy walked in the kitchen door of Amanda's house, Amanda burst into tears.

Billy held out a brown bag to his mom. "I'm sorry, Mom. I shouldn't have been mad. I know all your rules are to protect me. I'll do better."

Amanda took the bag and set it on the table without looking at it so she could grab Billy in a hug. Sobbing out her fear, she clung to him and wept.

Liz caught Cain's gaze and motioned that they should leave. He hesitated, but she headed for the door and he followed her.

The strangest feelings assaulted him. By punishing himself for something so far in the past he couldn't change it, he wasn't moving on. And he also wasn't learning any lessons. He was losing the one thing he'd always wanted—Liz. She was never the one to condemn him. He continually condemned himself. What if she was correct. What if—for once in his life—he gave himself a break?

She stepped out onto the sidewalk, walked to the driveway and got into his car.

Their car.

He squeezed his eyes shut and pressed his lips together. She wanted to forgive him. Was it so wrong to want to forgive himself?

CHAPTER THIRTEEN

THE NEXT MORNING, Liz lay on her sofa, wrapped in a blanket, drinking hot cocoa, even though the temperature outside had long ago passed eighty.

She had awakened so sad and lonely, after a sleepless night, that she considered it a real coup that she'd made it to the couch. She'd seen the best of Cain the night before when he'd talked Billy into going home and even paid for the ice cream to take to his mother. Yet she knew he didn't see any goodness in himself. And because of that he couldn't forgive himself for the mistakes in their marriage. And because he couldn't forgive himself, he was letting her go. Freeing her.

She loved him with her whole heart and soul but if he didn't want her, then maybe it was time she got the message? She couldn't go on always being alone. Ellie dated. Her friends had gotten married. Yet she was still mourning a marriage that was over.

A soft rap on her door got her head off the back of the sofa. She didn't intend to answer it, but the knock sounded again. This time stronger.

Whoever it was wasn't going away, so she might as well answer. Rising from the sofa, she wrapped herself in her security blanket. When she reached the door, she tugged the soft fleece more securely around herself before she grabbed the knob and opened the door.

Cain smiled at her. "You know, last night when I got home I thought about the things I said when I was counseling Billy, and it occurred to me that I was actually pretty good at talking to people." He pulled in a breath. "Everybody but you."

She snorted a laugh.

"So I'm going to give this a shot. This past week, I've hated myself for being such a terrible husband to you."

"Oh, Cain!"

"Let me finish. I really let you down and I had every right to be angry with myself. But I also can't wallow in that."

Hope filled Liz's heart. Could he really be saying what she thought he was saying? She opened the door a little wider and invited him inside. "Why don't we have this discussion inside?"

He walked into her small living room. His eyes took note of the neat and tidy room. He smiled sheepishly at her. "How am I doing so far?"

She laughed. Please, please, please let him be headed in the direction that she thought he was headed. "So far you're doing fairly well."

"Okay, then." He drew in a breath and caught her gaze. "I love you and I want to remarry you. I can't change who I was. But I sure as hell don't intend to be that guy anymore."

"Now you're doing fabulously."

This time he laughed. "I was so miserable, so angry with myself, until I remembered what I said to Billy.

Suddenly I realized that just like him I had a chance to move on, but I wouldn't if I didn't stop reaching back to the past. Punishing myself. Wallowing in grief."

"Cain, what I told you wasn't easy news," she whispered, so hopeful her voice rattled with it. "I think you deserved a week of confusion."

"I don't want to lose you because of things that happened in the past. We're different. Different enough that this time we can work this out."

"I think so."

"Good. Because I've got some plans." He tugged on her hand, bringing her against him.

Liz smiled up at him. He gazed down at her. And as always happened when they truly looked at each other, the unhappy six years between his brother's death and the present melted away. He looked young and happy, as he had on the flight from Dallas. His eyes had lost the dull regret they'd worn all through their marriage. He really was *her* Cain.

She couldn't pull her gaze away. Not even when his head began to lower and she knew—absolutely knew in her woman's heart—he was going to kiss her.

His lips met hers as a soft brush. It felt so good to be kissed by him, touched by him, that she kissed him back. For three years of being married to him she'd longed for this. Not the passion they'd had in their six-month long-distance relationship. They'd never lost that. But they had lost the need to be together, to connect. They lost happy, joyful, thankful-to-have-each-other kisses. And that's what this was. A happy kiss. An I'm-glad-I-know-you kiss.

He pulled away slowly. "I swear I will never hurt you again."

"I know." Tears flooded her eyes but she blinked them away. This was not the time for tears. Not even happy tears. "So where do you think we should start with this new relationship of ours?"

"At the beginning." He turned her in the direction of her bedroom. "How about if I make you something to eat while you get dressed? Then we can go out on the boat for a while? Just like normal people dating."

"Dating?"

"It's a little something people who like each other do to see if they should be married or not. It's a step we seemed to have missed."

She laughed. "All right."

He made lunch. Cheese sandwiches and soup. She changed into shorts and a tank top and they went out on the ocean for the rest of the day. The next weekend and every weekend after that for the next six months, they worked on A Friend Indeed houses during the day and attended Cain's myriad social engagements at night. They spent Christmas with her mother and sisters in Philadelphia and New Year's with his parents in Kansas.

When they returned on January second, he lured her back down the hall to his office and sat her on the edge of his desk.

Laughing, she waited while he opened the bottom drawer of his desk and pulled out a jeweler's box. "Open it."

Obedient, but cautious since he'd already given her a Christmas present, she lifted the lid on the little box and her eyes widened. The diamond on the engagement ring inside was huge.

"This is too big!"

He laughed. "In the crowd we run in five carats is about average size."

"The crowd *we* run in is very different from the crowd *you* ran in. We have all kinds of friends now. But I like the ring." She peeked at him. "I'm going to keep it."

"Is that a yes?"

"I don't recall you actually asking me a question."

He got down on one knee and caught her fingers. "Will you marry me?"

Unable to believe this was really happening, she pressed her lips together to keep herself from crying before she said, "On two conditions."

"I'm listening."

"We have a real wedding."

He nodded his agreement.

"And we stay who we are."

He grinned. "I sort of like who we are."

She laughed. Her heart sang with joy that communication could be so easy between them. That they could say so much with so few words, and that they really were getting a second chance.

"Then you are one lucky guy."

He stood up, bent down and kissed her. "You better believe it."

He broke the kiss and Liz noticed an odd-shaped manila envelope stuffed with bubble wrap in the drawer. She kicked it with the toe of her sandal. "What's that?"

"I don't know."

Cain sat on his desk chair and reached down to lift out the fat envelope. He pulled out the bubble wrap and unwound it.

"That's gotta be from your dad. He's the only person I know who goes overboard with bubble wrap."

Cain laughed, but when he finished unwinding, he found the family photo his dad had sent him the weekend Liz had come back into his life.

"What is it?"

He inclined his head, waiting for sadness to overwhelm him. It didn't. "It's my family's last picture together."

She plucked it from his hands. "Very nice. But your sister looks like a reject from a punk band."

He laughed. "I know."

She turned and set the photo in front of his desk blotter. "I think it should go right here. Right where you can see it every day and be thankful you have such a great family."

Cain smiled. She'd turned his life around in the past few months. She'd brought him out of his shell, got him working for a charity and made him happy when he wasn't really sure he could ever be happy again.

How could he argue with success? Especially when she'd said she'd marry him. Again.

"I think you're right."

EPILOGUE

CAIN AND LIZ'S WEDDING DAY the following June turned out to be one of the hottest in Miami's history, making Liz incredibly glad she'd chosen a strapless gown.

On the edge of a canal, in the backyard of the Brill mansion, they toasted their future among family and friends this time. Liz's mom and sisters finally met Cain's parents and sister. The two families blended together as if they'd known each other forever.

Cain's parents were overjoyed that he'd gotten involved in A Friend Indeed and loved that the board of directors from the group *and* many of the women the charity had helped attended the wedding.

Though Liz's mom was happy to see Liz remarrying the man she'd always loved, she was more proud of her daughter's successful business. Her sisters were bridesmaids with Ellie and Amanda. Billy, the surprise best man, lived up to the role with a funny and sentimental toast to the two people who helped him grow from a boy with little to no prospects for the future to a guy who now believed the sky was the limit.

When it was finally time, Cain whisked Liz away. Driving with the top down in "their" beloved Porsche, he took a few turns and got them on the road to his house.

"Why are we going back to the house?"

"It's a surprise."

Wind blowing her veil in a stream behind her, she laughed. "Do we have time for this?"

"It's not like the pilot's going to leave without us, since he has no other passengers." He snuck a glance at her. "Plus, I sign his paycheck."

"True enough." She laughed again and within minutes they were at Cain's front door.

"Is this surprise bigger than a bread box?" she asked as he opened the door and led her inside.

"You'll see." He directed her up the steps.

Raising her full tulle skirt, she raced ahead eager to see what he'd done. "I knew there was a reason you only wanted to sleep at my condo these past few weeks."

"Here I thought I'd pulled a fast one on you."

She turned around and placed a smacking kiss on his lips. "Not hardly."

He laughed and pointed her in the direction of one of his empty bedrooms. He opened the door for her and let her walk inside.

"Oh, Cain!" Staring at the beautiful nursery she could hardly take it all in. "Did you do this?"

"I hired a designer."

"It's gorgeous." She faced him. "But we're not... well, you know. We're not pregnant."

He pulled her into his arms. "I know. I just don't ever want there to be any doubt in your mind again that I'm with you this time. A hundred percent. I want little girls with your eyes and little boys to take fishing."

He kissed her and what started off as something slow and dreamy quickly became hot and steamy.

Just when she thought he'd lower them to the floor, he whispered in her ear, "We have a perfectly good shower in the master suite. We can kill two birds with one stone."

"Two birds?"

"Yeah, we can make love and take a shower before we change into clothes to wear on the trip to Europe."

"I thought we were supposed to change on the plane."

He nibbled her neck. "Plans change."

"And Dale won't mind?"

"Dale is a very patient, understanding man."

He swept her off her feet and carried her to their bedroom, while she undid his tie. He set her down and she tossed his tie to the dresser, as he unzipped her dress. It puddled on the floor and she stepped out of it.

She stood before him in her white lace bra and panties and he sucked in a breath. "You're beautiful."

She kissed him before undoing the buttons of his shirt. "You're not so bad yourself."

He finished undressing and carried her to the shower.

And Dale the pilot got comfortable on the sofa in the office in the hangar housing Cain's private plane, smiling because he had a sneaking feeling he knew why his boss and his new bride had been delayed.

MAID FOR THE
SINGLE DAD

BY
SUSAN MEIER

CHAPTER ONE

ELLIE SWANSON had not signed up for this.

Yes, she'd agreed to run Happy Maids while her boss, Liz Harper Nestor, took a well-deserved honeymoon after remarrying her gorgeous ex-husband, Cain. And, yes, she was perfectly capable of supervising the fourteen or so employees on Happy Maids's payroll for the four weeks Liz would be in Paris. But she wasn't authorized to make a change in the company's business plan, as the man across the desk wanted her to.

"I'm a friend of Cain's."

Of course he was. Tall and slender with perfect blue eyes and black hair cut short and businesslike, Mac Carmichael wore his tailored navy blue suit with the casual ease of a man accustomed to handmade suits, fine wines and people taking his orders. Just like Cain.

"And he told me his wife's company was the best in town."

"But we're a weekly cleaning service. We don't place maids in clients' homes."

"You should."

A bead of sweat rolled down Ellie's back. The air-conditioning had broken the day Liz left. But Ellie could handle the heat and humidity of June in Miami. What she couldn't abide was failure. Her first day on the job and already she was turning away a client. An important client. A client who could not only tell Cain that Happy Maids hadn't come through for him; he could also tell all his wealthy friends—the very people Liz would be marketing to when she returned.

Ellie leaned back on the chair, tapping a pencil on the desk blotter. "Explain again what you're looking for."

"My maid quit unexpectedly. I need to hire a temporary replacement while I interview for another one."

"I can send someone to your house a few times a week to clean," she said hopefully.

He shook his head. "I have a daughter and a son. They need breakfast every morning."

"Then I'll be happy to send someone every day at seven."

"Lacy gets up at five."

"Then I'll have someone at four."

"I work some nights."

Ellie gaped at him. "You want the maid to be a nanny too?"

He caught her gaze. His sinfully blue eyes held hers and she fought the urge to swallow as pinpricks of attraction sparkled along her nerve endings.

"And live in."

She gasped. "Live in?"

"I also pay very well."

Ah, the magic words. A victim of domestic violence herself, Liz had gotten involved with A Friend Indeed, a charity that helped women transition out of their abusive homes and into new lives. It was a natural fit that Liz should begin employing the women from A Friend Indeed until they got on their feet. Ellie had actually been the first employee Liz had hired after they met at the charity. The company needed every job—especially the good paying ones—to provide work for all the women who wanted help.

Mac rose from his seat. "Look, if your firm can't handle it, I'll be on my way."

He turned to the door.

Stop him!

She bounced out of her chair. "Wait."

He faced her again. This time she did swallow. His eyes reminded her of the ocean in the dead of summer, calm and deep and perfect blue. His dark hair gleamed in the sunlight pouring in from the window to his right. High cheekbones angled to blissfully full lips, the kind that made most women take a second glance and wonder what it would be like to kiss him. It should have been pure pleasure to look at him. Instead, the scowl on his face caused Ellie to doubt the intuition that guided her life.

"Yes?"

"I—" Why had her intuition told her to stop him? She didn't have anybody who could work as a maid/nanny. Most of Liz's employees had kids of their own and homes to get back to every night. They couldn't live in. And that's what he needed.

"I—um—maybe we can work something out."

His scowl grew even darker. "I don't work things out."

No kidding. She didn't need intuition to tell her that.

"I want someone today."

Don't let him go.

She groaned inwardly, wondering why her sixth sense was so insistent on this. But accustomed to listening to the intuition that had saved her life, she couldn't ignore it.

"I'll do it."

His scowl shifted into a look of confusion. "You?"

"I know I'm behind the desk today, but I'm only filling in for Cain's wife, Liz. She runs the business herself, but this month she's on her honeymoon. I'm more than capable of cooking, cleaning and caring for children."

His eyes held hers for another second or two. Then his gaze dipped from her face to her pretty red dress, and Ellie suddenly regretted her decision to wear something as exposing as the short strapless creation made more for having lunch with friends on a sunny sidewalk café than working in an office. But not having air-conditioning had made the choice for her. How was she supposed to know a client would show up?

He smiled and all the air whooshed out of Ellie's lungs. The temperature in her blood rose to an almost unbearable level. She could have melted where she stood. If this guy lived up north, snowflakes wouldn't stand a chance against that smile.

"We have air-conditioning, so you might want to change into jeans and a T-shirt." He took a business card out of his jacket pocket, scribbled on the back and handed it to her. "That's my home address. I'll meet you there in an hour." Then he turned and walked out the door.

Ellie collapsed on the office chair. Damn it! What had she gotten herself into? Now she not only had all of Liz's work, she also had a full-time job. More than full-time! She had to live in!

With a sigh of frustration at herself, she lifted the receiver of the phone on the desk and quickly dialed the number for Cain's personal assistant, Ava.

"Are you busy?"

"Hey, good morning, Magic. How's your first day going?"

"Abysmally. Don't call me Magic anymore. I think my intuition is on the fritz."

Ava laughed.

"I'm serious. Some guy came in here this morning, demanding a full-time maid and nanny—someone to live in—and I volunteered to take the job."

"Yourself?"

Angling her elbow on the desk, Ellie cradled her chin on her palm. "Yes."

"Oh, that's so not like you!"

"I know. But he's a friend of Cain's and I worried about disappointing him. My intuition got all jumbled while he was here and before I knew it I was taking the job myself." She winced. "I was thinking maybe you could find an agency that can get him a real temporary maid, then call him back and tell him I made a mistake."

"All right. I'll handle it. Give me his name."

Ellie flipped the card over. "Mac Carmichael."

"Oh, damn."

Oh, damn?

"Oh, damn what?"

"Ellie, you're stuck. He is a major pain in the butt, so not even finding him a real full-time maid would fix this. He'd never change a deal he's already made. But he's also somebody Cain's been courting for years."

"Courting?"

"His family owns hotels all over the world. Cain's been trying to get in on the construction end. This might be a test for Cain."

Ellie lowered her forehead to her palm. "Which is probably why my intuition wouldn't let me tell him no."

"I'm guessing," Ava agreed. "Okay, here's what we'll do. It doesn't matter where I work, so I'll forward my calls to the Happy Maids office and handle your phone and walk-ins during the day. Then we'll spend an hour or so together every night doing the day's paperwork."

"You'd do that for me?"

"Of course! This isn't just Happy Maids on the line. It's also Cain's business and I'm Cain's assistant. I have to do whatever needs to be done. Beside, I like you."

Ellie laughed. "Okay."

"Okay? Miss Magic, it will be more than okay. We will make it great. You'll do such a good job for Mac that you'll earn all kinds of brownie points for Liz and Happy Maids, and you might just get Cain the 'in' with Carmichael Incorporated that he's been lobbying for for years."

Ellie sat up. "Yeah. You're right. This is a good thing."

"This is potentially a very good thing," Ava agreed. "And I will do anything at all you need me to do."

"Handling the office during the day should be all the help I need."

"I'll be over in an hour."

"Bring a key because I have to leave right now. Mr. Carmichael wants me at his house in—" she glanced down at the card again "—Coral Gables in an hour, and I need to pack a bag if I'm going to be living there."

"You better get a move on."

"Okay. And Ava?"

"Yes."

Ellie winced. "You might want to stop on your way and buy a tank top and shorts."

Ava laughed. "How about if I just call an HVAC repairman?"

"That'll do it, too. I'll see you tonight."

Mac Carmichael raced his Bentley along the winding streets of Coral Gables and onto his driveway. He stopped at the gate, punched a code into the box on the left, opening the gate, and then roared up the stone drive to the side of his huge house. The garage door opened with another press of a button and he zipped inside. As the door closed behind him, he hopped out of his car, walked through the garage, into the butler's pantry then into the huge gourmet kitchen.

His blond-haired six-year-old daughter, Lacy, sat at the long weathered-wood table by the French doors, coloring. Nine-month-old son Henry sat in a highchair beside her. His former nanny and current next-door neighbor, Mrs. Pomeroy, wiped baby food off his mouth with a wet cloth.

"How did it go?"

He sighed. "Well, I found someone."

"Great."

"I'm not sure. She's—" Tall and blond and so good-looking he damned near turned around and sought out another agency. "Well, she seems a little spacey."

Eighty-year-old Elmira Pomeroy laughed. "Spacey? Is she a drinker?"

"No, she's just—" inappropriately dressed, too pretty for words "—kind of odd."

"Are you sure you want her around your kids?"

"She's not *that* kind of odd. Besides, I don't have a choice. I need total and complete privacy. I can't risk hiring a big impersonal firm or someone who doesn't need me enough to keep her silence."

"You think she's made the connection yet that if she does well her boss's husband could make millions?"

He tossed his suit coat over the back of a chair. "I'm hoping. If she hasn't yet, one call to anybody in Cain's office will get her the info. That should be the carrot on the stick that keeps her here long enough for me to find someone." He leaned in over Lacy. "Hey, baby. What are you doing?"

She gave him a patient look. "Coloring."

"Why don't you put on your swimsuit and we'll take a dip while Mrs. Pomeroy is still here for Henry."

Her heart-shaped face wreathed in smiles. Her blue eyes danced with delight. "Okay!"

She raced from the room and Mac pulled Henry from his highchair. "And how are you today?"

Blond-haired, blue-eyed Henry slapped a chubby fist on his father's cheek.

"Feisty, I see."

"You better believe he's been feisty." Mrs. Pomeroy took his bottle from the warmer and tested the temperature. "I'm not sure if he tired himself out enough that he'll fall asleep immediately after he drinks this or if he's too wound up to sleep at all."

"If you have any problems, come and get me from the pool."

Mrs. Pomeroy's wrinkled face fell in sympathetic lines. "No. You take the time with Lacy. You both could use a few minutes of fun."

"I'm fine. I don't want to shirk my responsibility to the kids."

"You're a good dad."

He pulled in a breath and turned away, trying to make light of her compliment. "I only do what any father should do."

That was why it never would have even crossed his mind to desert his children the way their mother had. He couldn't believe any person would be so narcissistic that she'd abandon her kids just because a second child had been inconvenient to her career. Pamela had been so angry to be pregnant again when she'd read the results of her early pregnancy test that she'd packed a bag, left him and filed for divorce within days. She returned to Hollywood, California, where she immediately resurrected her movie career.

Nine months later, she handed Henry over to Mac. She visited once a month, saying it was difficult to fly across the country anymore than that. But on her last visit she told Mac she might not be able to visit in July. The movie she had made while pregnant with Henry was being released and she would be making the rounds of talk shows promoting it. Mac tried not to panic, but he couldn't help it. If anybody asked Pamela about her divorce or her kids, he had absolutely no idea what she'd say. But he did know that if she mentioned their names, he and the kids would become fodder for the paparazzi.

He'd lived his entire life with bodyguards, alarm systems and armor-plated limos. He'd thought he knew how it felt to live under lock and key, but that was nothing compared to living in a fishbowl. As the ex-husband of a movie star with custody of that movie star's kids, protection and visibility had risen to a whole new level. Not only were his kids targets for kidnappers and extortionists because of his money, but their mother's career could put their faces on the front page of every tabloid in the world. He'd had to go to extreme measures to protect them, and even with those measures in place he wasn't quite sure they were safe.

"You're thinking about that crappy wife of yours again aren't you?"

"No."

Mrs. P. laughed. "Right. You always scowl before a morning of fun with your daughter in the pool." Satisfied with the temperature of the milk in Henry's bottle, she took Henry from Mac's arms. "You know what you need? A good woman to replace the crappy one."

Mac laughed. "It will be a cold frosty day in hell before I trust another woman."

Mrs. P. harrumphed as she headed for the door. "Don't let one bad apple spoil the whole bunch."

Lacy skipped into the room dressed in a bright blue one-piece swimsuit. Mac lifted her into his arms. It was very easy for Mrs. P. to spout quaint sayings, quite another for Mac to heed their advice. Pamela had broken Lacy's heart when she left. Henry would know a mother who only popped in when the spirit moved her. Mac couldn't risk the hearts of his children a second time.

Ellie debated sliding into one of her Happy Maids uniforms. Nothing said hired help better than a bright yellow ruffled apron and a hairnet. But Mac had suggested she wear jeans and she wasn't taking any chances. If she had to endure being a full-time maid, then she intended for Cain to get the recommendation into Carmichael Incorporated. The best way to do that would be to follow Mac's instructions to the letter.

She slowed her car as she wound through the streets of Coral Gables, looking for the address scrawled on the back of the business card. Finally finding the property, she turned onto the driveway only to come face-to-face with an iron gate. She rolled down her car window, pressed a button marked "visitors" on a small stand just within reach of her car and watched as a camera zoomed in on her. She expected a voice to come through the little box, asking for identification. Instead, within seconds, the gate opened.

Good grief. How rich was this guy?

Slowly maneuvering up the wide stone driveway that was a beautiful yellow, not brick-red or brown or even gray, but beautiful butterscotch-yellow, Ellie swiveled her head from side-to-side, taking in the landscaping. Trees stood behind the black iron fence that surrounded the huge front yard, increasing the privacy. Flower gardens filled with red, yellow and orange hibiscus sprang up in no particular order, brightening the green grass with splashes of color. But it was the house that caused her mouth to fall open. Butterscotch-yellow stucco, with rich cocoa-brown trim and columns that rose to the flat roof overhang, and a sparkling glass front door, the house was unlike anything she'd seen before.

She followed the stone driveway around to the side where she found cocoa-brown garage doors and a less auspicious entryway than the front door. She parked her car and got out.

Oppressive heat and humidity buffeted her, making her tank top and jeans feel like a snowmobile suit. The sounds of someone splashing in a pool caught her attention and she walked around back and stopped. Her mouth gaped.

Rows of wide, flat steps made of the same butterscotch-colored stone as in the driveway led from a wall of French doors in the back of the house to an in-ground pool. Shiny butterscotch-colored tiles intermingled with blue and beige tiles, rimming the pool and also creating a walkway that led to a patio of the same stone as the stairs. Behind the patio was a huge gazebo—big enough for a party, not merely a yard decoration—and beyond the grassy backyard was the canal where a bright white yacht was docked.

"Ellie?"

She glanced at the pool again. Mac Carmichael was swimming with a little girl of around six, probably his daughter.

She edged toward them. Trying to sound confident, she said, "Hi."

The little blonde wearing water wings waved shyly.

Mac wiped both hands down his face and headed for the ladder in the shallow water on the far side of the pool. "I'll be right with you."

She wanted to say, "Take your time," or "Don't get out on my account. I'll find my way to the kitchen," but the sight of Mac pulling himself onto the ladder stopped her cold. His dark swimming trunks clung wetly to his firm behind. Water pulled them down, causing them to slip as he climbed the ladder. By the time he got out of the pool his trunks clung precariously to his lean hips. He walked to a beige-and-white-flowered chaise and grabbed a huge towel.

"You got here quickly."

She stared. With the blue skies of Florida as a backdrop, his eyes turned a color closer to topaz. Water ran in rivulets down the black hair on his chest. His still-dripping swimming trunks hung on to his hips for dear life.

"I…um…" She cleared her throat as attraction rumbled through her. It had been so long that she'd been overwhelmingly attracted to a man that she'd missed the symptoms. But here they were. Sweaty palms. Stuttering heart. Inability to form a coherent sentence.

Now she knew why her intuition wouldn't let her allow Mac to leave the Happy Maids office. It wasn't because of Cain. It was because she was attracted to Mac.

Telling herself not to panic, she could handle one little attraction, she smiled. Her intuition might have brought her here for a frivolous reason, but once Ava had told her about Cain wanting an "in" with Mac, she knew she couldn't back out. Liz had saved her when she desperately needed someone. Now she finally had a chance to repay the favor. This was a mission. "I just had to run home to put on jeans and pack a bag."

He motioned to the steps. "You go on up. It's too hot for you to stand out here in this heat in those jeans. As soon as I get Lacy from the pool I'll be in."

This time she could say, "No hurry. I'll be fine," because she seriously needed a minute alone to compose herself. How did one man get so lucky as to not only be rich and live in a house that took her breath away, but also be so good-looking he rivaled the pristine Florida sky?

"Just go up the stairs and turn left, into the kitchen. We'll be there in a minute."

She nodded and started up the steps, feeling as if she were walking the stairs to a museum or some other prestigious building rather than someone's residence. Of course, she wasn't exactly well versed in what a "normal" home should look like. She'd grown up in foster homes until she was seventeen when she ran away. Then she'd slept on the streets and fought tooth and nail just to find something to eat each day until she met Sam. She'd stayed with him, enduring increasing verbal and emotional abuse until the night the abuse became physical. Then she'd run. A Friend Indeed couldn't take her in because they were a charity chartered to care for women with children, but Liz had offered her her couch and ultimately a job. After four years with Happy Maids, interacting with Liz and the friends she'd made through A Friend Indeed, she was only now coming to understand what normal relationships were.

So, she could forgive herself for being a tad awestruck by this house. She might clean for Miami's elite but this guy was in a class by himself, and from the outside, his house absolutely looked like a museum.

Pushing open the second door of the four French doors lining the back wall of the house, she found herself standing between a huge kitchen on the left and a comfy family room on the right. Decorated with an overstuffed brown leather sofa and chairs with shiny cherrywood end tables and a huge flat-screen TV between bookcases that ran along the entire back wall, that part of the open floor plan appeared to be where the family did most of their living.

That she liked.

But only a few steps into the kitchen, she swallowed hard. The stove had eight burners. The refrigerator was actually hidden behind panels of the same cherrywood as the cabinets. Copper pots and pans hung from a rack above the stove. Pale salmon-colored granite countertops accented the rich cabinets. A sink with a tall copper faucet sat in the middle of the center island and another sat in a counter along a far wall. Crystal gleamed behind the glass doors of all the cabinets on the right wall.

She looked around in awe. She'd been in kitchens almost as elaborate as this one. She did, after all, clean for some fairly wealthy people. But men in Mac's caliber weren't wealthy. They were beyond wealthy. They didn't hire weekly cleaning services. They had full-time employees and gourmet kitchens big enough to cook food for parties attended by hundreds of people. As a Happy Maid she only cleaned, didn't cook for any of her clients.

She glanced around again, her mouth slightly open, fear tightening her chest.

She grabbed the cell phone she had stashed in her jeans pocket and hit a speed dial number.

"Ava, I think I'm gonna need a cook book."

CHAPTER TWO

A FEW minutes later, Mac and Lacy entered the kitchen. "Lacy, this is Ellie."

Ellie smiled at the wet-haired little girl wrapped in a bright blue towel. "Nice to meet you."

Lacy glanced down shyly. "Nice to meet you too."

"Ellie's going to be staying with us while we look for a replacement for Mrs. Devlin."

Lacy nodded.

"So why don't you go upstairs and change out of your swimsuit?"

"I could help her," Ellie suggested, eager to do a good job more than to get out of the kitchen. She no longer had a problem being alone with Mac. He was definitely good-looking, and everything female inside of her had absolutely taken notice of his ropey muscles and firm butt in his swim trunks. But being attracted to him was wildly inappropriate. People in his tax bracket didn't mingle with the help. And people in her tax bracket would be foolish to drool or harbor crushes. She'd be safe with him.

Mac shook his head. "Lacy's fine on her own. I'd like to show you to your room and talk about the job a bit while Henry's still napping."

"Henry is your son?"

"Yes." Mac winced. "He's only nine months old. I hope that's not a problem."

Spending a few weeks with a baby a problem? Ellie nearly laughed. She didn't have brothers and sisters. The foster homes she'd lived in only took children, not babies. And after Sam she'd vowed she'd never have another "serious" relationship, which put kids out of reach for her. She'd babysat a time or two for new mothers who lived in A Friend Indeed houses, so she knew how to care for a baby. But she'd never be a mother herself. Having such a lovely block of time with a baby would be pure joy.

"Actually, it's kind of a thrill for me to take care of a baby."

Her words appeared to startle Mac. His face bloomed with happy surprise. His eyes gleamed. His lips bowed upward, into a breathtaking smile. It was so appealing, so genuine, so gorgeous, she was sure it could move mountains. The air thinned in her lungs and for a few seconds she struggled for breath, but she'd already recognized this attraction would come to nothing. He was her employer and she was his employee. That was that. Even if she had to pretend to cough to recoup her air supply every time he smiled at her, he'd never have a clue that he took her breath away.

"Is your bag in the trunk?"

"Yes."

"We'll get that first then I'll show you to your quarters."

"Great." She headed for the door and he followed her. Confused that he was coming with her, she stopped. "I only have one small suitcase. I can get it."

Mac shook his head. "My mother would shoot me for making a lady carry her own bag."

His courtesy caught her off guard. Employers were not supposed to help their employees. Or even be overly nice to them for that matter. And she didn't want him to. She wanted their relationship to be as professional as possible. Decorum was what would keep her safe. She hadn't slept alone in a house with a man since Sam and part of her would be shimmying with fear except this wasn't a personal relationship. It was a professional relationship. And as long as they both abided by that, she'd be fine.

"The bag won't weigh any more than the laundry baskets I'll be carrying down the stairs to the washer."

"Washer and dryer are upstairs." He headed to the left. "Besides, this will be a good opportunity for me to familiarize you with this part of the house."

Relieved that the trip to her car had more of a purpose than just a courtesy—which was inappropriate—she nodded and he led her through the butler's pantry. The cupboards were the same rich cherrywood as the kitchen. The countertops the same salmon-colored granite. When he reached the door at the back, he opened it and motioned for her to precede him.

Stepping into the garage, she took note of the four cars—a Bentley, a Corvette, a black Suburban and a Mercedes—and could have happily swooned. But she knew better. Just as she couldn't even once let her attraction to her new employer show, it was bad form to admire his possessions.

He stepped in front of her again to quickly open the door. Her beat-up compact car came into view. He said nothing—commenting on her possessions would have been bad form for *him*—and waited while she hit the button on her key fob and popped the trunk.

Without a word, he pulled out her suitcase. Because he still wore his swimming trunks she could see the muscles of his arm bunch and his chest ripple with the simple movement. She averted her eyes instead of reacting, firmly putting herself in "household employee" mode where she belonged.

Retracing their steps, she reached the garage entry first and pulled open the door for him.

"Your suitcase weighs about two pounds. I could have gotten the door."

"I know."

Still, she hustled to get ahead of him to open the door to the butler's pantry. She knew her place and she fully intended to stay in it.

Seeing her stilted smile, a shiver of something worked its way through Mac. He'd grown up around servants and knew that technically Ellie should have gotten her own bag. He also knew she felt duty-bound to open the door for him. Yet, when she mentioned going out to her car an odd stirring of unease started in his stomach and worked its way to his chest. He couldn't let her carry her own bag. It felt ungentlemanly.

He chalked it up to their unusual meeting. He hadn't met her as a household employee, but as a woman who was currently running the company he'd needed to cajole into his employ. So he wasn't seeing her as an employee first, but a woman. An equal. Though that wasn't exactly good, he could control that. He could even shift their positions back to employer and employee.

Just as soon as he got her settled.

After all, he had sort of manipulated her into taking a job she hadn't wanted. And he wasn't being forthright even now. When he discovered Pamela's new movie was to be released next month, he'd bought the empty house next to Mrs. Pomeroy and put it in the name of one of his family's smaller corporations so he and his kids could disappear.

Ellie didn't know any of that. She didn't need the information, but more than that her being in the dark was another layer of protection for Mac. As long as she didn't know anything, she couldn't accidentally talk to a reporter in disguise as a grocery bagger.

He was keeping her in the dark, forcing her into a job she normally wouldn't have done. A little social nicety wasn't out of line.

In the kitchen, she faced him with a pretty smile. Her full lips turned upward. Her amber eyes sparkled. The blond hair that floated around her head to her shoulders gave her the look of an angel.

"Where to?"

Okay. Maybe this attraction would be a little harder to handle than he'd imagined. She was pretty and sweet. Agreeable. Genuine. She looked like a woman who couldn't tell a lie if her life depended on it, like somebody he could trust with his life. He wanted to melt into a puddle at her feet, to tell her his secrets, ask for her help protecting his kids.

He almost snorted a laugh. Right. With the exception of Mrs. Pomeroy, the last woman he trusted ran out on those same kids. He already knew his instincts about women were way off-kilter. He didn't need another experiment with a woman to prove it.

"Turn right and go up the back stairs."

She frowned. "I don't have quarters near the kitchen?"

"Since you'll be the one waking with Henry in the middle of the night, you need to be close to him."

She hesitated. He couldn't figure out why she'd want to be by the kitchen. She was far too thin to be a midnight snacker. She could want assurance that she wouldn't disturb him when she woke to make Lacy's breakfast—

Or maybe she wanted private space? Damn. He'd forgotten about that. She wasn't normally a live-in employee. She probably didn't know how she'd get downtime.

"When I'm home, I care for the kids. With the exception of getting up with Henry for his 2:00 a.m. feeding when I go back to work. That will be your domain. So you can go to your room any time you're not busy. You can watch TV all you want. You have use of the pool, and you can also leave when I'm here if your work is all caught up."

She nodded, but didn't look reassured. Still, she started up the stairs.

Averting his eyes to resist the temptation of watching her bottom as she walked the thin flight of steps, Mac said, "First door on the right is yours."

She tossed a shaky smile over her shoulder. "So I'm right by the stairway?"

He almost laughed. It sounded as if she wanted assurance that she could make a quick getaway. "Yes. You're right by the stairway."

She breathed a sigh of relief and his brow furrowed. Maybe he hadn't been so far off the mark about the quick getaway? Or at least the possibility of one. She wasn't normally a live-in worker. If assurance that she had an escape route pleased her, then who was he to argue?

In the upstairs hall, she turned right and entered the suite. But she stopped so quickly Mac almost ran into her back.

Hesitantly stepping into the room, she smoothed her hand along the arm of a simple yellow sofa that sat beside a matching chair and in front of a wide-screen TV. Her head turned from side to side as she walked to the door that led to the bedroom. Then she gasped.

"This is gorgeous."

He ambled up beside her and glanced into the room which, he supposed, was pretty with its black four-poster bed and pale gold spread and matching curtains.

"It's a bit of a perk since our maid also has to be a nanny."

This time when she faced him her angelic smile had been replaced by one of sheer joy. Her amber eyes were so brilliant they virtually shone.

"Maybe I should take this job permanently," she said with a laugh.

Bowled over by the power in her smile, he nearly said, "That's a great idea." Luckily he stopped himself. First, he was too darned attracted to her to keep her forever. Second, she was a stranger hinting for a full-time position caring for his kids. He knew all the employees of Happy Maids were bonded, which meant they'd passed routine background checks, but he'd still ordered his security team to do a full background check on Ellie after she'd agreed to take the job. Within twenty minutes Mac knew she'd never been in jail, never been arrested, never even had an unpaid parking ticket. Which meant his children were somewhat safe with her.

But he still didn't feel he knew enough to be comfortable leaving her alone with his kids. Lacy and Henry were everything to him. He wouldn't trust them with just anybody. He'd ordered his security team to keep looking into her past. By this time tomorrow, he hoped to know everything there was to know about Ellie Swanson. If he found anything at all in the report he didn't like he might actually be asking her to leave, not inviting her to stay permanently.

He walked over to the door leading to the nursery. "Henry's in here."

She followed him into the huge room decorated with rainbows and unicorns, white rockers and fuzzy lime-green throw rugs. Henry stirred. Mac leaned in to check on him and Ellie leaned in, too.

She whispered, "Oh, we're going to wake him?"

Her breath fanned across his cheek. The scent of her cologne wafted to him. Her upper arm brushed against his. He swallowed and decided he'd better speed up his search for a permanent maid. He'd never been more aware of a woman. Let alone someone who was technically help.

But he hadn't met her as help and she didn't behave like help. And if he didn't soon establish a boss/housekeeper relationship between them, this attraction could be trouble. He could embarrass her, or worse, embarrass himself. Then her entire stay would be awkward.

Henry woke and let out a little cry to awaken his voice before he shrieked in earnest. Mac hoisted the baby into his arms before he terrified his new nanny.

To his surprise, though, she laughed. "Oh, gosh, he's cute." She tweaked his cheek. "And listen to those lungs! You're going to be a rock star someday, aren't you, little pumpkin!"

Henry stopped crying and peered at her curiously.

It appeared Mac wasn't the only Carmichael male who was being thrown off-kilter by this woman's looks and far too casual behavior.

"Henry, this is Ellie. She's going to be caring for you when Daddy can't. Ellie, this is Henry."

"Can I hold him?"

"Sure."

She took the baby from his arms with the ease of someone accustomed to holding a baby.

"Hey, sweetie," she said, bouncing him a bit. But Henry only continued to stare.

I'm right with you, kid. She's so beautiful I could stare at her all day too, Mac thought, taking a step back out of range of her cologne. He walked to the changing table and retrieved a diaper and other necessary items to clean up the baby before putting him into a new outfit. "Bring him here. I'm sure he needs to be changed."

Ellie smiled at him. "I can handle this. You go and do whatever you would usually be doing right now."

"No."

"No?" She took a few steps closer to the changing table. "I thought I was here to care for your kids?"

"Yes, you are. But," he said, keeping his gaze and attention on Henry as he removed his diaper, "as I've already mentioned, I'll care for the children while I'm here."

"Okay."

She didn't sound at all understanding of his position that he'd be caring for his own kids. But Mac didn't feel the need to explain that he had to make up for his ex-wife's neglect by being available to his kids as much as he could be. Through his peripheral vision he saw that she stood off to the side, watching him, making Mac nervous until he realized she was waiting for instructions.

Mac glanced up at her. "Why don't you go to your room and unpack your bag? When I'm done with Henry, I'll give you the rest of the tour of the house."

Ten minutes later, Mac knocked on her bedroom door and stepped inside, a clean and happy Henry on his arm.

Closing the closet door where she'd stowed her suitcase, Ellie faced him. "Ready for the tour?"

"Yes." Mac led her out of her suite and to the right. He pointed at the door beside the nursery door. "This leads to my suite."

"Okay."

She didn't like the warmth that bubbled in her middle with the realization that their bedrooms were so close. Fear or apprehension wouldn't have surprised her. But anticipation? That was ridiculous and wrong. She'd sworn off men forever. The proximity of their bedrooms shouldn't matter. Plus, her suite had its own bathroom. She wouldn't be venturing into the hall in her nightclothes or wrapped in a towel before or after a shower—neither would he. She had nothing to fear and nothing to worry about—except maybe this crazy attraction which seemed to have a life of its own.

Mac opened the next door. With a motion of his hand he invited her to peek into the pink-and-white room. "And this is Lacy's room. Also close enough for you to hear her if something happens."

Glad to have her mind moving off his master suite and to the kids, Ellie said, "Good."

Walking again, they passed eye-popping red statues and etchings done in cocoa-brown ink. Behind a curving cherrywood staircase, a wall of windows displayed a panoramic view of the canal. Sharp, contemporary accent chairs with chrome arms and legs and nubby yellow fabric backs and seats sat by tall, thin chrome lamps. The floor was a warm honey-colored hardwood. Once again she thought of a museum.

"These two doors," Mac said, pointing to the right and then the left, "lead to two guest suites."

They turned a corner. Mac pointed at two doors on opposite sides of the hall. "Two more guest suites."

"Of course."

"I don't have guests often," Mac continued, leading her down the hall. Over his shoulder, blue-eyed Henry grinned toothlessly at Ellie.

She smiled and waved.

"And won't be having any guests at all until I've hired a permanent maid." He paused at a set of double doors. After shifting Henry on his forearm, he opened them, revealing a laundry room complete with a bright red washer and dryer, a folding table, carts, baskets and cherrywood cabinets that she assumed held laundry detergent and the like.

Smiling her professional household employee smile, Ellie said, "Okay."

"You can easily gather everyone's laundry, wash it, dry it, press it in here and return it to the proper room."

With that he closed the doors and directed her back down another hall.

"As you can see, we're making a full circle. These steps," Mac said as they approached the set of back stairs, "are the same ones we used to get up here."

They started down the wooden steps and at the bottom turned left to enter the kitchen.

"We have a very simple floor plan."

Glancing around the kitchen, Ellie said, "Yes."

"Okay, now for the first floor."

Mac led her out of the kitchen, down a short hall and turned right into a room that had to be the playroom. The back wall held cherrywood bookcases and built-in cupboards, probably for storing toys, and a wide-screen TV. A thick brown-and-red print rug sat in the middle of the hardwood floor. Otherwise, the room was without furniture. Unless you counted the bright blue plastic table and chairs with accompanying yellow plastic dishes and cups where Lacy sat—probably having an imaginary tea party—and the beige plastic stove, refrigerator and sink that Ellie recognized from her last trip to a toy store.

Looking up from her tea party, Lacy said, "Hi, Daddy."

"Hi, sweetie. You remember Ellie."

She nodded enthusiastically, her fine blond hair bobbed around her.

"Hi, Lacy. I like your playroom."

Lacy only grinned and nodded again.

Mac walked over to his daughter, who tugged on his pant leg to get his attention.

"Daddy, I'm hungry."

Though Lacy tried to whisper, her voice came out loud and clear.

"Okay." Mac faced Ellie. "Can we finish our tour later?"

She nodded. "Sure."

Mac said, "Great," and headed for the doorway on the right. "Let's go make something for lunch."

Lacy's face brightened as Ellie's stomach fell to the floor. She hadn't had time to get the cookbook yet! What would she do if Mac asked for something Ellie had no idea how to prepare?

Before she could panic Lacy said, "Can we have peanut butter sandwiches and ice cream?"

Walking into the hall, Mac laughed. "We'll negotiate the ice cream after you've eaten the sandwich."

Still carrying Henry, Mac left the room with happy Lacy skipping behind him. Ellie took a minute to breathe a sigh of relief before she bounded out of the room. She caught up with them in the kitchen.

Sliding Henry into a highchair, Mac said, "Now that I think about it, Ellie, you could actually finish the tour of the rest of the house by yourself. Dining room and living room are at the front of the house. Over there is the family room." He pointed at the area beside the kitchen with the leather furniture and big-screen TV. "My office is above the garage, but there's no reason for you to go there."

He straightened away from the highchair. "While I feed the kids, you can make a list of what needs to be done cleaningwise. Then when the children and I are done, you can clean the kitchen and get started with supper."

"Okay."

He smiled patiently. "Okay."

Not exactly sure what happened with lunch and feeling oddly dismissed, Ellie turned and walked out of the kitchen. It wasn't that she had a burning need to make peanut butter sandwiches. She felt unnecessary. He'd insisted that she start today, yet she wasn't doing any of the things he'd hired her to do. No. He wouldn't *let* her do any of the things he'd hired her to do.

Her intuition tried to tell her that something was wrong with this situation, but she ignored it, as she intended to do for the rest of her stay here. After all, her intuition had already steered her wrong about taking this job. She wasn't letting it in on any more decision making.

And she certainly wasn't about to let it spark her imagination. That would only result in her becoming too curious about this man and his adorable children and asking some very inappropriate questions. Like what kind of woman would leave such wonderful kids and such a handsome, courteous husband?

Unless Mac had only been putting on a good front for her?

Because he had custody of his kids she automatically assumed he was a good man.

But what if he wasn't?

What if he had his kids because he was an overbearing rich guy who threw his weight around to get everything he wanted?

What if she was about to spend the next several weeks living with another man like Sam?

CHAPTER THREE

AFTER lunch, Mac took the kids out on his yacht for the afternoon. Standing in the kitchen in front of the French doors, Ellie watched the boat pull away from the dock, grateful for a few minutes to herself.

She had silenced her concerns that Mac might be like Sam by reminding herself of two things. First, she didn't know Mac. She shouldn't jump to conclusions. And second, Mac genuinely seemed to like his kids, to like spending time with them. So what if he'd nudged her out of lunch and really wasn't letting her be the nanny? He might have done it unconsciously. She had no idea how long he'd been without a maid and nanny. But it could have been long enough that caring for his kids was now second nature. And if Ellie didn't soon stop acting like a high-strung spinster, suspicious of every man she met, she'd lose this job, and Cain and Liz would be the ones to suffer.

Her cell phone rang. She looked down and saw Ava's number in caller ID.

"Hey."

"Hey! I'm at the gate. Now what?"

Ellie glanced around. Not only did she not know how to open the gate, but Mac wasn't here to show her. She couldn't even attempt to please this privileged family on her limited knowledge of cooking. She had to get that cookbook. "I don't know. I don't know how to open the gate and I can't ask Mac because he just took the kids out on his boat."

"Well, all I have is the cookbook. Why don't you come to me and I'll pass it through the gate to you?"

Ellie sighed with relief. "Good idea."

Feeling like a criminal, she snuck out the front door of the echoing mansion, raced down the front yard and reached through the gate bars to get the cookbook from Ava.

"Thanks."

Cain Nestor's fifty-five-year-old assistant peered over her black frame glasses at Ellie. "Tell me I'll be able to get through the gate tonight when we have to debrief about Happy Maids."

"You will. I swear," Ellie said, walking backward up the grassy front yard to return to the house.

"Good. I'll see you tonight," Ava called, but Ellie was already running toward the door. Cookbook under her arm, she tiptoed up the silent hall to the kitchen even though she knew she was alone in the house. Mac had said he and his children would be gone the entire afternoon, yet she still felt as if she was doing something wrong.

But she wasn't. *She could cook.* She simply hadn't memorized recipes for anything beyond burgers and spaghetti. All she had to do was find a recipe, prepare the food, and serve it like a good maid, then Cain and Liz would both get the recommendations they needed.

Sitting at the weathered table by the French doors, she took the cookbook out of the plastic bookstore bag. *Easy Main Dishes in Under An Hour.* Ellie laughed. Ava was nothing if not perceptive! This should be a cinch.

She perused the recipes, with one eye on the canal so she would see the Carmichael family if they returned unexpectedly. Spotting a recipe she liked—penne pasta with portabella mushrooms and red and yellow peppers—she took the book with her as she walked around the kitchen, checking for supplies.

The well-stocked refrigerator had both red and yellow peppers and portabella mushrooms. The cabinet held penne pasta. Next she found the ingredients for the Alfredo sauce. Interestingly, in the last cabinet on the row closest to the door leading to the stairway, she also found the controls for the gate, including a small computer monitor that displayed the feed from the video camera. One button said "Open gate." One said "Close gate." A system couldn't get any simpler than that.

Because the meal would only take an hour to prepare, she decided to do laundry and some light cleaning while Mac and the kids were out on the ocean.

She found baskets of dirty clothes in each of the kids' bathrooms, but she stopped at the master suite. Mac hadn't even opened the door to let her peek in as he'd done with Lacy's room. A bedroom was such a private space, it felt like an invasion to even look inside. Forget about walking in. She'd feel like an interloper. She'd already had to talk herself out of being suspicious of this guy. She didn't want to give her free-wheeling imagination any more grist for the mill!

Maybe tomorrow she'd be adjusted enough to collect his laundry, but she'd handled enough for today.

After sorting the kids' clothes, she put a load into the washer then returned downstairs, this time using the fancy curved cherrywood stairway.

She walked past the living room with shiny marble floor, heavy tapestry drapes and ultra-modern furniture with glass tables. Not exactly her taste, but in keeping with the rest of the museum-like décor. The room wasn't even in need of a light dusting. So she checked the dining room, playroom, sitting room and den and found them all in the same spotless condition. She walked to the kitchen where she grabbed the notepad on which she'd made the list of everything that needed to be done as Mac had suggested, and began arranging things in the best order for cleaning. Whether the rooms "needed" dusting or not, she would begin a rotation that maintained the spotless condition of this home.

By the time the yacht returned, she had a schedule developed that would assure the entire house would be kept spotless, the laundry would be done and three meals would be prepared.

Chopping the peppers, she watched out the window as Mac carried Henry on his arm and led his daughter up the dock to the backyard and toward the house. She fought the suspicion again that something was wrong with this picture because she didn't know what it was. It wasn't something she could see or something she'd heard, only a sense she had. If she just had something substantial to base the feeling on, she'd know how to handle it. Instead, she had only an unhappy imagination that was making her crazy.

Annoyed with herself for not dropping this, she waited for them to enter the kitchen, but after fifteen minutes she realized they had probably come in through another door. Two seconds later, Mac walked into the kitchen wearing jeans and a T-shirt.

"Everything okay?"

Trying to behave like a normal maid, not an overly suspicious idiot, she smiled shakily at him. "Great. I spent the afternoon creating a cleaning schedule, so I can hit the ground running tomorrow."

"There's no rush." Mac opened the refrigerator and snagged an apple. "The place is immaculate. It can go a day

or two without being dusted. I want you to get accustomed
to the house and the cleaning end of things these next few
days so that when I go back to work, the kids can be your
priority." He caught her gaze. "I also want this time for the
kids to get accustomed to seeing you around the house. To
get to know you before you're their primary caregiver."

Okay. See? He had a good explanation for having her
around the kids, but not actually interacting with them.
He was giving her time to get accustomed to the house and
giving the kids time to get accustomed to her. That
made more sense than to think something was wrong with
him.

"I'll be fine with the kids." That she could say with
complete confidence. "Helping some friends—" She
almost said the women living in A Friend Indeed houses,
but thought the better of it. She didn't really know Mac
and most of the charity's work was confidential to protect
the identities of the women seeking shelter. "I've babysat,
played board games and gone to the beach more times than
I can count."

He crunched a bite of the apple, chewed then swallowed
and said, "Great." He paused for a second before he added,
"This job won't last long. My assistant is working with two
employment agencies now, looking for a replacement for
Mrs. Devlin. She'll do initial interviews. I'll do the second
interview."

"So you should have a replacement in three weeks?"
Ellie asked hopefully.

He winced. "More like four."

Liz's entire honeymoon.

"I'm sorry that I sort of strong-armed you into this. But
my kids are important to me and I don't want just anybody
around them."

Surprised, but pleased that he'd apologized—once again confirming that he was a nice guy and she had to stop looking for bad things about him—she nodded. "I get that. We'll be fine."

"And there's one other thing I forgot to mention. I'd prefer that you not tell anyone where you're working."

She winced. "I'm sorry but I already told Ava. She's helping me with Happy Maids. But you don't have to worry," she hastily added, not wanting to anger him unnecessarily. "Ava works for Cain. He owns five businesses. She knows how to be discreet."

"Okay." He turned to leave the room, but suddenly faced her again. "What are you making for dinner?"

"Penne pasta with red and yellow peppers." She glanced up at him. "I never asked what time you'd like to eat."

"I eat with Lacy, which means we always eat before six."

"Okay." That gave her forty minutes. "I better get a move on then."

Henry's soft cries poured from the baby monitor and Ellie froze. Already her impulse was to drop everything and rush to get the baby when he cried. But she waited to see what Mac wanted her to do.

He said, "I'll get him," and headed for the back stairway. "As I said, when I'm here, I take care of the kids."

This time his doing her job didn't bother her. He'd explained that he wanted her to get accustomed to things… the house, the cleaning schedule… All that was good. It even made more sense from the perspective of his wanting to give the kids a chance to get accustomed to her.

She had nothing to worry about.

She gathered the items from the recipe and began preparing the sauce. Her eyes on the list of ingredients, she measured and poured milk, cheese and butter into the pan. Stirring the sauce as it heated, she tried to keep her mind on her cooking, but couldn't.

The instincts she kept trying to ignore tiptoed into her conscious, whispering that Mac wasn't being nice. He was keeping his kids away from her because he didn't really trust her. Sure, he'd apologized about strong-arming her, and, yes, he had a good explanation about why he was doing her job…but there was something in the air in this house. Something that didn't quite fit.

Something…

The sauce in the pot bubbled over and Ellie jumped back out of the way with a squeak as she snapped off the gas burner.

She heard the sound of Mac racing down the stairs and quickly placed her body in front of the stove to hide the mess.

"Everything okay?" he asked, walking into the kitchen with Henry on his arm.

"Great."

"I thought I heard a squeal."

The odd feeling returned again. He had every right to investigate a squeal, but the tone of his voice just didn't sit right.

Of course, she might be overanalyzing because she was nervous about having just burned a big part of his dinner!

"I… Um…" She swallowed to gather her courage. "My sauce just boiled over."

"Oh. Okay, if everything's under control the kids and I are going to take a short walk."

He took it so casually that Ellie blinked in surprise as Mac turned away. Sam would have screamed at her for hours for ruining dinner, proving Mac wasn't a full-fledged grouch or even really a control freak. So what the heck was going on here?

As Mac called, "Lacy!" Ellie noticed Henry had on a straw hat and a lightweight one-piece pajama that covered his entire body to protect him from the sun. Ellie didn't criticize Mac's diligence. But it did further the theory that he was very protective of his children and she'd better do the absolute best job she could do when she was alone with them—

Ah! Now she got it.

The parents of the kids she typically babysat for trusted her. This guy didn't know her. So how could he trust her? He couldn't! That was why he seemed to be keeping the kids from her. Until he got to know her he'd probably huddle over Henry and Lacy rather than let her alone with them…and probably also question her every move. His distrust could even be the "odd" thing she sensed in the air of this house.

Lacy ran into the room. She also wore a straw hat to protect her from the sun. "I'm ready, Daddy."

Mac said, "Let's go." Then he and the kids trooped out of the kitchen.

Ellie spun around and looked at the milk-covered burner on the stove with a groan. She grabbed her cell phone from her jeans pocket.

"Ava, can you get a jar of store-bought Alfredo sauce here in twenty minutes?"

Ava laughed. "Ellie, you're going to wear me out."

"This time I can let you in the gate."

"Great. I'll fill you in on the Happy Maids stuff while I'm there."

Twenty minutes later, Ava arrived with two jars of Alfredo sauce and the maids' time sheets to be signed for payroll. As Ellie poured the penne pasta, portabella mushrooms and red and yellow peppers into a casserole dish and then covered them with Alfredo sauce and popped them into the oven, Ava briefed her on Happy Maids' day.

"Nothing out of the ordinary happened. The houses were cleaned as scheduled. The Maids have their jobs for tomorrow."

"Thanks, Ava."

"You're welcome. Now, I have to get home. I'll see you tomorrow afternoon around this time." Ava headed for the butler's pantry, but stopped and grinned at Ellie. "Don't hesitate to call me if you need something."

Ellie shook her head in dismay. "I'm sorry but this guy is a serious control freak." She'd finally decided to label him a control freak, if only because distrust was such an ugly word and she didn't want Ava to realize she was uncomfortable. She might want Ellie to leave and she couldn't. Cain and Liz needed for her to do a good job. "I didn't dare risk a mistake."

Ava laughed. "I was teasing. I don't mind you calling me for help. You're doing this as much for my boss as for yours. So we're in this together."

With that Ellie scooted out through the butler's pantry and garage, leaving Ellie to prepare a salad in the twenty minutes it would take to heat the pasta and sauce.

She was just pulling dinner from the oven when Mac and the kids returned.

She greeted them with a smile. "You're right on time."

"Great. We're starving." He ambled to the door. "You may serve us in the formal dining room."

Ellie smiled, breathing a silent sigh of relief that he'd told her what to do and quickly set the table. As she did that, Mac grabbed a jar of baby food, a baby dish and a tiny spoon.

She served the food while Mac fed Henry.

"That'll be all, Ellie."

Ellie nodded in acknowledgement and scurried back into the kitchen. But she opened the swinging door a crack and peeked into the dining room. Watching the happy little family, she amended her opinion of Mac once again. It seemed wrong to call him a control freak when he was looking out for his kids. In some circles that would make him a good dad.

Still, there was the matter of the missing wife. She couldn't reconcile herself to thinking that any woman would give full custody of two adorable children to her husband. Had there been a custody battle? Were these two kids scarred for life?

Of course, his wife could be—Ellie swallowed—dead. Oh, dear. That would certainly raise a whole different set of issues! Including the curiosity of why he hadn't told Ellie, if only to explain whether or not the kids were still dealing with that.

No. He would have told her if his wife were dead. As diligent as he was, he'd want her to be prepared about everything to do with his kids. His wife had to have left.

But where was she? And why had *she* gone, leaving her kids behind?

Telling herself it was none of her business and that she could handle not knowing for one month if it meant that Liz got the recommendations she needed and Cain got the contracts he wanted, Liz began scrubbing pots and wiping the kitchen counters.

When the Carmichaels were finished eating, Mac leaned into the kitchen. "We're done. Lacy and I will be upstairs getting Henry ready for bed."

"Okay."

"Once you've cleaned up, you're done for the day. You may do whatever you wish. It's still hot out, so you might want to take a dip in the pool. The kids and I are in for the night, so it's all yours if you wish. Good night, Ellie."

He pulled out of the room without waiting for her reply and Ellie leaned against the counter with a sigh of relief.

Day one down!

After clearing the dining room and popping the dishes into the dishwasher, Ellie went to her room.

She wouldn't mind a swim, but she hadn't brought a suit. Plus, she needed to get up early the next morning. She set her alarm for four, so that she'd be ready for Lacy whatever time she awoke, then did a quick pirouette in the massive bedroom she'd be staying in for the next month. Her boss's life might be a bit of a mystery. She might wonder what happened to the kids' mom. And she absolutely *had* to get better at cooking. But spending a month in this suite could almost make up for that. It was the lap of luxury.

Running her hand up one of the black posts of the four-poster bed, she noticed the gold decorative rings at the top and sighed dreamily. What must it be like to have so much money that you could have *everything* you wanted, exactly as you wanted it?

Lifting her makeup bag from the black mirrored dresser, she turned and walked into the bathroom. Again, she stopped and stared in awe. Brown travertine tiles on the floor matched the brown tiles in the shower and surrounding the spa tub. This bathroom was as big as the kitchen in her and her roommate Mitzi's apartment.

She set the makeup case on the counter of the double sink with black-and-gold granite countertops, then stripped to make good use of the spa tub. After a nice long soak, she stepped into lightweight pajamas, applied face cream and crawled into bed with a book. Cool silk sheets greeted her and she groaned. There was a definite difference between cleaning someone's house once a week and staying in that house—even if it was as hired help. She certainly hoped she didn't get used to this!

She read until about ten, then turned out the light of the brushed gold lamp on the bedside table and immediately fell asleep.

What seemed like only minutes later Henry's loud crying woke her. Slightly disoriented, she bolted up in bed, wondering what the sound was. But the second burst of crying brought her to full alertness and got her to her feet.

"Henry!" she cried, not even sure if the little boy could hear her. "I'm coming, sweetie!"

Intending to change his diaper and take him downstairs while she warmed a bottle, she ran into the room. As her door opened on the left side of the nursery, Mac's door on the right side of the nursery also opened. Both flew into the room and stopped dead in their tracks.

Her pajamas, though lightweight, were covering. *His* chest was bare above low-riding bottoms. His dark hair was mussed. His eyelids drooped sexily and his brilliant blue eyes were glazed over. He had the sleepy look of a man who cuddled after sex.

The very fact that that popped into her mind shocked her. She couldn't speak. She couldn't move. She'd seen him in swimming trunks that afternoon, but with her brain jumping to inappropriate places and both of them soft and warm from sleep, everything about the moment felt different.

His gaze fell from her pajama top to her bare feet. As it leisurely crawled back up her body again, the haze in his eyes disappeared. She stifled a shiver. The way he had looked at her stole her breath. Not awake enough to monitor his reaction, he'd taken inventory from the top of her head to the tips of her toes and back up again, very obviously liking what he saw.

Their gazes caught and the light in his eyes intensified, sharpened.

Ellie swallowed, told herself to speak and speak now, but nothing came out.

Then Henry screamed.

"I'm sorry, buddy," Mac said, breaking eye contact to race to the crib. He hoisted the little boy into his arms. It fleetingly occurred to Ellie that he was adorable with his son, especially when the baby so eagerly wrapped his chubby arms around his dad's neck, but the ripple of the muscles of his biceps and back as he cuddled Henry caused her heart to stutter in her chest and warmth to pool in her middle.

She took a step back. This attraction was ridiculous. As her boss, he was off-limits for too many reasons to count. But even if he was interested in her, she didn't want to be attracted to him! He was her boss. Cain and Liz needed for her to do a good job. And by God, she would.

She walked over to the crib. "I'll go downstairs and get the bottle."

He peeked over at her. Gooseflesh sprinkled over her entire body. She tried to remind herself that Cain and Liz were depending on her, and that meant she had to behave in a professional manner, but her gaze stayed locked with Mac's.

What was wrong with her? Her intuition was scrambling. Her hormones had executed a coup. And her brain seemed to have gone on vacation.

Finally Mac said, "I'll get it."

Ellie took a breath. "No. That's okay. You change him. I'll get the bottle." She had to get out of this room! "By the time I return, you'll be ready for it so you can feed him."

He nodded, and she walked toward the nursery door, but at the last second she changed her mind and headed for the door of her suite. She closed it behind her then walked through her sitting room to get to the hall. It wasn't that she didn't want him seeing her things. She hadn't scattered her things about. She was a tidy person. It was more that there was something about both of them sleeping so close, with only a nursery to separate them. Something intimate was happening between them and she didn't want him thinking about her any more than she wanted to be thinking about him.

But she would.

Damn it. She knew she would.

What was it about this guy that drew her? Sure, he had beautiful blue eyes. Yes, he was perfect physically with his well-defined muscles that rippled when he moved, and shiny black hair that looked silky smooth and made her itch to run her fingers through it.

But he was…unattainable!

And she didn't know him. Rich people always had secrets in their closets and this guy's very demeanor screamed trouble.

Plus, she didn't want a relationship. Damn it. One day in his company and she'd almost forgotten every lesson she'd learned with Sam!

At the refrigerator, she put her attention on preparing Henry's bottle. Her mind back where it belonged, she got one of the pre-poured bottles of milk from the refrigerator. She heated it to room temperature as she'd been taught by several of the mothers at A Friend Indeed and returned to Henry's room.

Mac sat on the rocking chair with Henry on his lap, his towhead nestled against his daddy's chest. Ellie's heart squeezed.

Fuzzy feminine feelings rose up in her and she suddenly understood why Mac was so appealing to her. No matter what his secrets, he truly loved his kids and somehow or another that hit her right in the maternal instincts. She'd always wanted children and if she'd met someone normal before she'd met Sam her life probably would have been very different.

"Here," she whispered, handing Mac the bottle.

He glanced up at her. Their gazes caught for only a second, but it was long enough for Ellie to feel the sizzle again, reminding her that this attraction wasn't one-side. And *that* was the problem.

"Thanks."

She took a step back. "You're welcome."

Then she turned and all but ran back to her suite.

Even if an employer felt an attraction for the help, most wouldn't let it show. Mac hadn't let it show all day. But being half-asleep, his guard had been down. Nine chances out of ten, he wouldn't even acknowledge this in the morning.

But what if he did?

What if he liked her?

What if living with him for a month was enough that their barriers broke down?

He already had her stuttering and staring. If he made a pass at her, could she resist him?

And what if she didn't?

No one knew better than Ellie that there were consequences to relationships.

Especially relationships with bosses.

CHAPTER FOUR

ELLIE awakened at four, dressed in a clean pair of jeans and yawned her way to the kitchen. To her amazement six-year-old Lacy was waiting for her.

"Lacy?"

From her position on one of the chairs at the table, she peeked at Ellie. "Sorry."

"Oh, that's okay, honey," Ellie said, walking over to the table where the little girl sat. She stooped down to make herself eye-level. "I'm just a little concerned about you being up by yourself."

Lacy leaned her elbow on the table and angled her chin on her fist. She wore pale blue pajamas covered in tiny pink hearts. The color brought out the blue in her eyes and made her wispy pale hair seem even more golden. "I just sit here until somebody gets up."

"Really?"

"Yes. She does. She's fine."

Ellie spun around to face the door when Mac spoke. He stood on the threshold, not in last night's pajama bottoms, but in a pair of sweatpants and a baggy T-shirt. Barefoot, he ambled into the kitchen.

"She likes an egg for breakfast, toast and some blueberries."

"And a glass of milk," Lacy added with a grin.

Staring at Mac, Ellie told her heart to settle down and her hormones to please take a vacation, but neither listened. Her heart tumbled in her chest and adrenaline surged through her blood. The man was just too good-looking. And he was dedicated to his kids. She'd never met a man who changed diapers and awakened at four without complaint. Yet she still felt something was off.

Suddenly the entire situation began to make sense. He was a great dad, seemingly a good person, and he was gorgeous…so she was attracted to him. But her experience with men wasn't good. So while her hormones were loping off the charts, her common sense was trying to find things wrong with him.

He wasn't a mystery. She was the one with the problem. Or maybe their attraction was the problem.

Still, she was the help and nothing more. From the nonchalant way he drifted into the kitchen and ambled to the table where Lacy sat, Ellie knew he had absolutely no interest in following up on the attraction he felt to her. After all, it was only physical. They hadn't spoken beyond the work required for this job. What they felt for each other couldn't be anything other than a healthy case of sexual attraction.

A good relationship required so much more. Shared interests. Mutual likes and dislikes. Even a shared background would be nice. Her background was so different from his that they probably didn't even share one similar childhood memory! She didn't even need to remember all the other reasons they were wrong for each other. With pasts as different as theirs, none of that mattered.

Reminded of her place, Ellie said, "We're fine here, Mr. Carmichael. You can go back to bed."

Mac gave her a puzzled frown. "Mr. Carmichael?"

Ellie winced. "You never did tell me what to call you."

"I'm Mac." He paused significantly. "*Everyone* calls me Mac."

"Okay, Mac," she said, trying out the name and finding it was much easier to call him by his first name than it should be given that she was his maid. "I'll take care of Lacy's breakfast. You can go on back to bed."

"I'm home. I take care of the kids when I'm home. Remember?"

"Yes, but it's so early."

"So why don't *you* go back to bed?"

She pressed her had to her chest. "Me?"

"There's no point in both of us being up at four."

He wasn't angry and what he said made sense. Now that she'd totally squelched her instincts, the entire situation made perfect sense. She took a step backward, toward the door. "Okay, then. I guess I will go back to bed."

She turned to leave the kitchen, but Mac stopped her. "Ellie?"

She faced him. "Yes?"

"I don't always get up with her. When I'm working I usually sleep through her early-morning-wake-up days. So I appreciate that you're okay with this."

She couldn't believe she'd let her intuition talk her into thinking there was something wrong here. Yes, she might not know where the kids' mom was, but Mac was a normal man. A good dad. A good guy. She had been wrong to be suspicious of him.

She smiled her best professional, I'm-your-maid smile. "You're welcome."

She left the room, glad that everything was handled amicably. But halfway up the stairs she stopped as another question confronted her. Why would a six-year-old get up at four o'clock—or close—every day?

She squeezed her eyes shut. Mac might be an okay guy, but she couldn't dismiss her suspicions so easily. No matter how or why Lacy's mom had left, losing her mom had affected her. Without knowing the truth, Ellie could make a million mistakes with that little girl.

Three hours later, with Lacy fed and back to bed for a morning nap, Mac headed for his office, then realized he couldn't go there because it was too far away. He changed directions and headed for the master suite. Halfway down the hall, his cell phone rang. He glanced at caller ID and saw it was his investigator, and not a moment too soon.

"Hey, Phil."

"Hey, Mac. I've got some news on your new girl."

Mac opened the door to his suite, stepped inside and closed the door behind himself. "Spill."

"Well, she's from Wisconsin."

Walking to one of the two white chairs in front of the never used fireplace, Mac laughed. "You say that as if it's bad, but this is Florida. Lots of us are Northern transplants."

"It's not the part about coming from up north that's bad. Your new housekeeper was a foster child."

That stopped him. "Oh. Why is that bad?"

"It isn't. I mean, it doesn't positively indicate bad things. Lots of foster kids grow up to be perfectly normal. But that's not the end of the story on your temporary maid. She ran away at age seventeen. Didn't finish high school."

"How does a seventeen-year-old support herself in a strange city without an education?"

"That's just it. The possibilities that come to mind aren't good ones. If she worked on the street or under the table, from here on out it's going to be harder and harder to find information."

"I don't care. Whatever it costs, you fill in the blanks of her past."

"Not only is that going to be expensive, but also it will take days."

"Again, I don't care. This woman is going to be caring for my kids. I want to know everything about her."

Phil said, "Will do, boss."

Blowing his breath out on a sigh, Mac disconnected the call and leaned back in his chair. Being attracted to an employee was bad enough; being attracted to someone he didn't know—at all—who had missing pieces of her past was downright foolhardy.

In fact, he'd have to watch her very, very carefully over the next few days as his security team continued their investigation. If she made one move he didn't like, he'd have to let her go. He wasn't worried about the silver or the artwork or even money she might find. He was concerned for his kids. God only knew what Ellie had done in the years after she ran away from home. Without a high school education, as a runaway on the streets, she could have been a thief...or worse.

After doing some cleaning, Ellie once again took out her cookbook and cruised the well-stocked Carmichael cupboards. She found the ingredients for many of the recipes, but she also found boxes of ready-to-cook hamburger dishes, noodle entrées and macaroni and cheese. Maybe the Carmichael pallet wasn't so sophisticated after all? Mac did have a six-year-old, and children did like to eat food they saw on TV. So maybe the thing to do would be prepare simple lunches of the prepackaged foods and cook more elaborate—more nutritious—suppers?

Satisfied with that decision, she headed to her room for a half-hour break before she had to return to the kitchen and prepare lunch. After turning on the television to listen to the day's news, she began taking inventory of the clothes she'd brought. Knowing she'd be here at least a month, she realized the few jeans, shorts and tops she'd packed wouldn't be enough. Especially if she needed to take the children somewhere that required more than casual clothes.

But that was fine. She could go back to her apartment and get more clothes once she had a handle on what kinds of things she'd be doing. In fact, with the temperature as warm as it had been, she might want to make a run back to her apartment for a bathing suit.

At eleven-thirty, she scampered downstairs to prepare a box of the macaroni and cheese she'd found. But when she made the turn to get into the kitchen she found Lacy already at the weathered table and Mac standing at the counter slathering peanut butter on bread.

"I was just about to make macaroni."

Lacy's face lit up, but Mac said, "We're fine."

"I know you wanted me to spend these first few days getting oriented, but I'm all set now. Ready to handle this job completely. I can make today's lunch."

"I've got lunch, Ms. Swanson."

Finding it curious that he wanted her to call him Mac, yet he had just called her Ms. Swanson, she ambled over to the counter. "Peanut butter sandwiches again?"

"Lacy likes peanut butter."

"I like macaroni too," Lacy said hopefully.

"I'll make that tomorrow," Mac said, dropping another slice of peanut butter bread onto the paper plate and walking it to the table. Lacy frowned and sent Ellie a pleading look.

Ellie half smiled at Lacy. This was it. One of those tests household employees were forced to use. If she pushed him and he barked, she'd know to back off and never push him again. But if she pushed him and he relented, then she'd know there were things about which he could be reasonable.

"It really is no trouble for me to make a box of macaroni."

Mac said, "We're fine—" at the same time that Lacy said, "Please."

The pleading in Lacy's voice, sent Ellie into action. Surely he couldn't resist his daughter? She headed for the stove. "Seriously, Mac. It's no trouble."

Mac pressed his lips together as if to prevent himself from saying something he'd regret. After a few seconds he quietly said, "That's all Ms. Swanson. You may finish your cleaning or take your break. Whatever is on your schedule now. But Lacy and I don't require your services."

Wide-eyed Lacy immediately glanced down at her sandwich. Ellie swallowed and took a step back. She'd just learned two things. He didn't relent, but also this was a man who didn't need to yell to let everybody know he was furious.

Ellie took another step back and prudently said, "I'll be upstairs cleaning."

"Thank you."

Sucking in another breath, Ellie ran upstairs. It had been foolish to anger him—doubly foolish for *him* to get angry over something so trite. But she'd had to push to see how far she could push. Now she knew. Clearly, she'd overstepped her boundaries. And though Mac's volume had been civil, his tone had told her he wasn't pleased.

She wouldn't care if this were just a matter of her job security. As far as she was concerned she could leave tomorrow. But this wasn't about her. This was about Liz and Cain. Liz getting referrals and Cain getting his "in" with Carmichael Incorporated. Surely, she couldn't have blown it over trying to make macaroni?

Not about to go to her room where she'd pace and chastise herself for being stupid, Ellie headed for the laundry room. She set the washer to begin filling, then retrieved the baskets of dirty clothes from the kids' rooms. Seeing that she didn't really have enough for a load, she frowned.

The obvious thing to do would be go into Mac's room and get his dirty clothes to round out the loads. She narrowed her eyes, considering that, and realized that she didn't feel as uncomfortable going into his room today as she had yesterday. All those feelings of attraction she'd been feeling had been snuffed out by the way he'd just treated her.

She almost laughed. Nobody liked being reprimanded, but Mac's behavior might have actually made her time here more tolerable. She wouldn't have to worry about wayward hormones around him anymore.

Her head high, she strode to the master suite door, twisted the knob and marched inside.

A sitting room greeted her. Comfortable white leather chairs sat atop a yellow-, green- and cream-colored Oriental rug on the honey-brown hardwood floors, creating a conversation grouping in front of a fireplace that Ellie would bet had never been used. The room was spotless. There wasn't even a book on the table between the two chairs. It was almost as if no one had ever set foot in this room.

She frowned. Maybe no one had? There were plenty of other places in this house for Mac to read or watch TV. He probably only used this suite to—she swallowed—sleep. In pajama bottoms, with his chest bare and his muscles exposed.

Damn it! She wasn't supposed to be attracted to him.

She gingerly made her way to the bedroom and was surprised when she stepped inside. While her room had a gorgeous black four-poster bed with elaborate bedspread and matching drapes, this room had a simple wooden bed. A queen-size at best. The spread was an almost ugly red-and-yellow print that matched the equally ugly drapes. The area rug beneath the bed was a tortured brown.

She walked to the center of the room and turned in a circle. If she were rich, she'd sue the person who designed this room. As ugly as it was, she was almost afraid to go into the bathroom. But that was where the clothes basket was. In a tidy little cupboard beneath the sink. At least that was where the kids' had been.

With a deep breath for courage, she walked into the bathroom and blinked. It was huge and gorgeous. Turning in a circle again, she took in the shower, complete with an enormous showerhead and six body jets. As in her bathroom, there was a spa tub. An open door in the back of the room revealed a walk-in closet.

Okay. So the house itself wasn't ugly, but Mac's ex-wife's tastes left a lot to be desired.

As she thought the last, she heard the click of the doorknob to the suite and she froze. Oh, great! Here she was standing in the bathroom of his suite like an idiot, obviously snooping! If he hadn't fired her before, he'd probably fire her now. She shot for the cupboard beneath the double sink, hoping she'd find the laundry basket there. As she opened the door, brown wicker greeted her and she just barely had time to yank it out before he walked in.

"Oh, Mr.—Mac." She lowered her head and started for the door. "Just collecting the laundry."

"Actually, I've been looking for you."

She swallowed and glanced up, meeting his gaze. "You have?"

He nodded. "I know you're not a professional nanny. I know you're not even a real maid. But when I give an order you are not to contradict me."

"I didn't realize making peanut butter sandwiches was an order."

Damn it! Why had she said that? Why hadn't she simply said, "Yes, sir," and gotten the hell out of here!

His eyes narrowed at her. "Anything I say and do in this house—especially if it pertains to my children—is an order. Do you understand that?"

This time she did say, "Yes, sir." She actually got halfway to the bedroom door, before something inside her rose up and she couldn't stop herself from turning around. Mac stood by the ugly, ugly, ugly bed. He was gruff. His house was a museum. His daughter was adorable, but subdued. She got up at four o'clock in the morning because she couldn't sleep. Probably because she was nervous. Probably because her dad was so…unbendable.

"All she wanted was a little macaroni."

Mac gaped at her. "Are you questioning me?"

Feeling a strong need to help Lacy, she lifted her chin. "Maybe I'm confused because I'm not a full-time employee," she said, trying to soften the blow. "Maybe I'm confused because I'm also not a parent. But I can't see what difference it would have made to let her eat a little macaroni. She's a kid. She was hungry."

Mac sucked in a breath. Once again Ellie got the impression he was controlling his temper. Fear flooded her. She knew better than to anger a man. Yet, here she was arguing about macaroni. No, she was arguing for Lacy. The kid was a kid, yet in two days Ellie had only seen her playing once. She hadn't been able to choose her own lunch. Something was wrong here!

Finally Mac slowly said, "I was feeding her. And I'll make her macaroni tomorrow."

"But she wanted macaroni today."

Mac squeezed his eyes shut. "Miss Swanson, go do the laundry."

An odd sense of empowerment swelled in Ellie. He was furious with her for questioning him. Yet, he hadn't made a move toward her. He hadn't even yelled.

Still, she wouldn't push her luck.

That afternoon while both kids were napping, Mac paced his office. Nobody—*nobody*—questioned him, yet Ellie hadn't hesitated. He should be furious. He should have instantly fired her for insubordination. Instead, he'd felt a stirring of guilt for denying Lacy what she wanted for lunch and unexpected appreciation that Ellie had a soft spot for his daughter. His appreciation actually got worse when she turned around before leaving and questioned him one more time.

Lacy was a little girl whose mother had abandoned her. Her nanny had refused to move to Coral Gables when they'd run here before Pamela's new movie could be released. She had no aunts and uncles or cousins because Mac was an only child. Her grandparents were jetsetters.

Even Mac felt for her. He'd lived that himself. An only child, dependent upon nannies for support and love. But at least he'd had one stable, consistent nanny. Mrs.

Pomeroy. She was more of a grandmother to him than his grandmother had been. Their bond was so strong that he'd bought her the house in Coral Gables as a retirement gift. It was also why he'd called her when he'd made the decision to hide while Pamela resurrected her career, and Mrs. Pomeroy had suggested he buy the house next to hers. She was here for support, to love his kids, and could even babysit for short spans. But she was eighty years old now. She couldn't be his children's nanny. Not even for three or four weeks while he looked for a new one.

So he knew the value of having a loving nanny. A consistent, stable nanny. If Ellie Swanson checked out, he'd be tempted to offer her anything she wanted to be Lacy and Henry's nanny permanently.

Except for his damned attraction to her.

There they'd stood, in his ugly bedroom—he certainly hoped the people who'd owned the house before him hadn't paid the decorator well—with Ellie being insubordinate, and all he could think of was how close they were to the bed.

It was ridiculous. He didn't know the woman. He could embarrass her or cause her to leave if he made a pass at her. Yet, the pull of attraction he felt to her was so strong, he'd forgotten every one of those good reasons he was supposed to keep his relationship with her purely professional.

He opened his cell phone and checked one more time for messages. If Phil would just get back to him and tell him one way or another about Ellie, then Mac could act. He could either fire her or feel comfortable leaving her alone with his kids and go back to work so he wouldn't have to be around her so much.

But there was no cell phone message from Phil. No incoming call. He was on his own with Ellie Swanson until Phil dug around enough that he was satisfied he knew everything about Ellie's past and could make a recommendation.

CHAPTER FIVE

AT TWO o'clock, Mac came into the kitchen with Lacy and Henry. Ellie looked up from the cookbook she was scouring for recipes.

"I'm taking the kids next door to visit Mrs. Pomeroy."

She frowned at him. "Your neighbor?"

"Yes. She's an old family friend."

Lacy sheepishly said, "I like her."

"Well, of course, you do, sweetie," Ellie said, stooping down to Lacy's level. "You're one of life's very special children who loves everybody."

The little girl grinned happily and Ellie's heart swelled. Lacy was so adorable, and her dad such a grouch, that Ellie had to fight the urge to pull her into her arms and hug her.

Mac directed Lacy away from Ellie toward the hall behind the kitchen. Earlier that day, Ellie had found a side door that led to a walkway that went to the fence and a gate that led to the next house over. So she knew where they were going.

Walking toward the door, he said, "We'll be back before dinner." Then he paused and faced Ellie again. "I'll be grilling hot dogs for supper." He cleared his throat. "And you can…um…make some of that macaroni for us too."

Ellie's mouth fell open in surprise. Their gazes caught and a lightning bolt of electricity sizzled through her. She reminded herself that he was a grouch. She told herself he was out of her league. She reiterated her life plan—that her intuition was always wrong about men, so she was better off staying away from relationships. Yet here she was attracted to a grouchy employer, a man too rich for her, who probably wanted to fire her for questioning him.

But at least he didn't have a temper.

She groaned inwardly as Mac and the kids left the kitchen. Then she slammed the cookbook on the table. It was one thing to be softening her feelings about him as a boss. But finding reasons it was okay to like him—that was wrong! Was she nuts? Seriously? Did she need another lesson about how she always chose the wrong men to be attracted to?

Apparently.

Annoyed with herself, she jogged up the staircase. Mac's bedroom hadn't been a disaster, but it was on her rotation for cleaning. It was better to wipe down the showers and tubs every day than to wait until an employer noticed soap scum. So she headed for the laundry room, where she'd also found cleaning supplies for the upstairs, and went into Mac's room.

The ugly bedroom reminded her that she and Mac were totally different. Scrubbing toilets helped her to remember who she was and where she was and why she shouldn't be attracted to him. By the time she was done in the bathroom she felt much better. Normal. Like a woman who earned her living by the sweat of her brow, who, in spite of her positive attitude, would never set herself up for the embarrassment of falling for an employer and being...well, patted on the head and told she wasn't good enough.

No. No. She knew how the world ran. She wouldn't be bucking that particular system.

Satisfied, she took a dust cloth over the furniture in Mac's room, once again noticing how hideous it was. In a giddy moment, she wondered if poor taste was why he'd dumped his ex-wife, then she spun around, curious. There was not one sign that a woman had ever shared this suite. In fact, that thought actually made sense of the ugly room. Lots of men didn't have any idea how to decorate. If Mac had chosen these things himself, without the assistance of a wife or decorator, then the man wasn't totally gifted after all. He might be rich, good-looking and successful, but he couldn't color coordinate. Plus, if he'd completely redone this bedroom that explained why there wasn't a trace of his ex.

Of course, she hadn't looked in the closet. Surely there was at least a picture.

That roused her curiosity enough that she left her dust cloth on the dresser and tiptoed to the closet. Opening the door, she gasped. The thing was bigger than her apartment! She walked inside, running her hand along the hundreds of dark suits that hung in two long rows. Open shelving held more casual clothing. A back cabinet contained at least five hundred ties. Twenty-three pairs of assorted black shoes lined one row of a three-row shoe rack. The other rows held numerous tennis shoes, different colored dock shoes, various and sundry brown shoes, and ten pairs of navy shoes.

She snooped around, even peeking behind the suits for a door or a box that might contain a few things left behind by his wife. But she found nothing.

Feeling like a fool for being so curious and also realizing that if Mac came in it would appear as if she was casing the joint to rob him, she quickly scrambled out of the closet, grabbed her dust cloth on the way out of the bedroom, stored her cleaning supplies in the laundry room and headed downstairs again.

Through the wall of windows behind the stairway, she saw Mac and the kids returning from their afternoon with the neighbor, and she picked up her pace so she could beat them to the kitchen. The safety zone. The place he expected her to be.

But they didn't come into the kitchen. Using one of the many doors in the house that she couldn't see from behind the stove, they'd entered and probably gone to the playroom or maybe upstairs for the kids' naps.

Walking to the cabinet to retrieve two boxes of macaroni, she shook her head in wonder. Her heart squeezed at the thought that he loved his kids so much he wanted to be their primary caregiver. Her brain was suspicious, thought he was overprotective and worried that he would smother his kids when they got older.

She blew her breath out. Her past too frequently caused her to worry too much about people she didn't know. But maybe that was the real bottom line? She always jumped to conclusions about people she didn't know, speculated about their lives, wondered about their behaviors. But as soon as she got to know someone her confusion stopped. So maybe what she needed to do was get to know Mac?

That made her wince. There were only two problems with that. First, he didn't seem to want her around. Second, she was fighting an attraction for him. She tapped her finger on her cheek. The truth was she'd never met a man she couldn't talk herself out of being attracted to once she spent some alone time with him. It wasn't that she found faults or flaws; it was simply easier to categorize someone as only a friend once she got to know him.

Her phone buzzed and she pulled it from her jeans pocket.

"Hey, Ava."

"Hey, Ellie. What time do you want me over tonight? In time to bring something for dinner?"

"Mac's grilling."

"Oh. That's interesting."

Though she understood Ava's curiosity, Ellie didn't comment. That was one thing she'd always understood. When employed to walk through someone's house, dust their personal things, wash their clothes, a maid could not comment on what she saw. Instead, she said, "How about eight o'clock? Dinner will be over and Mac should be busy upstairs putting the kids to bed."

"Sounds great."

Plus, Ellie was considering spending time with Mac. The best thing to do would be to insinuate herself into dinner somehow. With the worry of Ava popping in at any minute now gone, Ellie could relax and do that. Then this time tomorrow she wouldn't feel any attraction to Mac and she and Mac would probably get along much better.

Mac hadn't needed her help getting the kids or the hot dogs out to the grill that had been set up in a gazebo just beyond the patio. The patio itself had two love-seat-sized sofas with thickly padded seats and glass tables. But the gazebo appeared to have been furnished with the kids in mind. Four-foot walls kept the little ones inside, but also hid the big gas grill and the practical plastic furniture more suitable to children's needs. Comfortable dark-colored chaise lounges created a seating arrangement to the right of the eating area. A leather wet bar probably served the needs of both the gazebo and the patio.

Ellie saw all that when she brought the macaroni and cheese to the table.

"Set it here," Mac said, pointing to one of the huge side arms of the grill, then he went back to tending the sizzling hot dogs, dismissing her.

Ellie's brain scrambled around for a reason to stay. Mac had secured Henry in a highchair and settled Lacy with a coloring book at the comfortable-looking heavy plastic table. There was nothing for her to do. No reason to stay.

But she couldn't leave. This relaxed atmosphere was the perfect place for her and Mac to begin to get to know each other so their relationship would be less strained. Yet she couldn't think of a way to detain herself.

"Everything okay?" Mac asked.

Ellie looked over at him. Think, she told herself. But gazing into his blue eyes, her brain shut down and her hormones kicked in. She wanted to smile, to flirt, to put her arms around his neck and coax him into admitting there was something between them.

Good grief! Why was her imagination so vivid with him? Especially when that was exactly the problem! She *did* want to flirt with him. They had to get to know each other in a more professional way, maybe even become friends, so these crazy feelings inspired by their chemistry would evaporate like the insubstantial vapor they were.

She took a breath. "I thought maybe I could help with the grilling."

"I'm fine."

"Then maybe I could entertain Lacy and Henry while you're busy."

He shot her a look of such distrust that Ellie actually stepped back.

"No."

"I'm really good with kids—"

"You're dismissed, Miss Swanson. May I suggest you tend to your own duties while you have sufficient time to get the housecleaning end of your job in order."

She swallowed. She wanted to call him a pain in the butt, a grouch, a horrible father. But because she was an employee, she couldn't say any of those. Plus, he wasn't a horrible father. If anything, he tried too hard to be a good father and ended up being an overprotective father... She frowned. He'd said he was caring for Lacy and Henry because he was giving her and the kids time to get adjusted to each other. But what if he just plain didn't trust her with his kids?

The thought almost made her gasp. She'd actually considered this already, but had forgotten about it because their damned attraction was so strong it usually pushed every other thought aside.

But she got it now. His secondary purpose for his caring for the kids truly might be to give her and Lacy and Henry time to get adjusted, but the main reason was that he didn't trust her.

"He's a blooming control freak."

Ellie had gone over everything she'd done for Mac and the kids and knew, absolutely knew, the problem was not hers. She'd been helpful, patient, kind, honest, trustworthy. If he still didn't trust her, then *he* had the problem. And because she wasn't telling Ava anything about his kids, his preferences of underwear, even what he stocked in the fridge, she didn't feel she was breaking a confidence.

Particularly since she needed Ava's help understanding him or she'd never last the entire month she'd promised to handle this assignment.

Ava strolled to the weathered table, dropping a stack of files at a place in front of a chair. "Most rich men are control freaks. Cain can be pretty darned demanding himself."

Ellie shook her head, taking the seat beside Ava at the table. "Demanding is one thing. Surrounding your children to keep them from your new nanny is another."

Ava peered over at Ellie. "Why hire a nanny if you won't let your kids near her?"

"Exactly my point."

"That doesn't make any sense."

"Especially since he'll never trust me if he doesn't let me spend time with the kids."

Walking to the kitchen for an apple after putting the kids to bed, Mac heard Ellie's voice. Though he couldn't make out what she'd said, he very clearly heard her speaking and stopped. Was she talking to herself?

"He cooks for them, gets up with Henry at night and Lacy in the morning. He entertains them before he puts them down for their naps and bathes them before bedtime—"

Mac froze. The tone of her voice quite clearly said she was not only displeased with his overbearing behavior about his kids, she was also suspicious.

That wasn't good. Suspicious people went snooping. She wouldn't find anything in this house. But if she got curious enough to go on the Internet, she'd not only discover his ex-wife's identity beyond Mrs. Carmichael, but she'd also realize why Mac was so protective. What she wouldn't guess, though, was that he was still in the process of investigating *her* while his children became accustomed to seeing her in their home, so they'd be comfortable when he went back to work.

Phil probably only needed another day or two. The question was did Phil have that long before Ellie began an investigation of her own?

"He… He…"

"He what?"

Mac's jaw dropped. The voice that nudged Ellie along was new. It took several seconds for that to fully penetrate when it did his feet took on a life of their own and he propelled himself through the swinging door into the kitchen She'd let a stranger into his house!

A short, dark-haired woman with black frame glasses sat beside Ellie at the table by the French doors.

"Who is this!"

Ellie's faced turned white in horror. "She's Cain's assistant, Ava."

"And how did she get in?"

Ellie rose. "I let her in. I told you that while Liz is on vacation I have to run Happy Maids. Ava's been doing the office work during the day, but at night I have to approve hours, shift changes and assignments."

Mac tried to stem the roar of his blood through his veins but he couldn't. This was exactly the kind of mistake that could give away his location.

"Yes, and I also told you that you could leave the house when I'm with the kids."

"But…"

"But what?" he thundered, so afraid for his kids and their sanity that he lost control of his temper. Lacy already didn't sleep through the night. He didn't want her life to become a circus. "You haven't had the kids at all. I told you that the housework was secondary. Why, exactly, couldn't you leave?"

Her already white face paled again. "I'm sorry. You're right. I should have gone to Ava, not had her come to me."

Her apology stopped him cold. He didn't know why he expected her to argue, but when she didn't his anger deflated and he stood there like an idiot. Embarrassed because he'd yelled.

He rubbed his hand along the back of his neck. "I'm sorry that I lost my temper."

"Thank you. But in fairness, you never told me Ava couldn't come in."

He pulled in a breath, counted to ten, then said, "Okay. That was my mistake." He'd thought telling her that she couldn't let anyone know where she was working covered that, but then again by the time he'd set down that stipulation she'd already told her helper at Happy Maids about her assignment. So maybe she felt this woman was grandfathered in or something?

"But I really don't want outsiders in the house. I understand your responsibilities to your boss's company, but I also want my house rules kept. Plus, you're free to leave anytime you don't have charge of the kids. Tomorrow," he said, pointing at Ellie, "you go to her—" he pointed at Ava "—for this meeting."

With that he walked out of the kitchen, his heart pounding and his head beginning to ache. This had been a terrible plan. Hiding in plain sight had sounded so good when Mrs. Pomeroy suggested it, but it was failing. He couldn't use a typical maid company. He'd hired a woman who needed more training and guidance than he had time to give. And that woman was probably growing tired of breaking rules she didn't even know existed.

Still, he didn't blame himself. He blamed the circumstance. His options had been limited.

Walking along the marble floor Mac headed to the main stairway. The cell phone in his pocket rang and he grabbed it. *Phil.* Thank God. He didn't know what he'd do if he had to fire Ellie. He'd used his only option for secrecy when he'd found her. But he did know that one way or another something had to give.

"Can you talk?"

"I'm on my way to my room." He couldn't even go to his office because he had to be available in case Lacy or Henry woke. It was no wonder he was off his game. "So you talk for the two minutes it will take me to get there."

"Okay." Phil paused and Mac heard the sound of his indrawn breath as if what he had to say wasn't good. "I don't know if you're going to like this or not."

"Just spill it. This situation has to change. Even if what you tell me is bad, it only means I start over."

"Okay. Ellie Swanson was a foster kid who ran away. South to Florida where it's warm."

"All of which I know."

"She actually got a job in a pizza shop that was part of a big chain of shops that was growing with leaps and bounds in the South Florida area."

"Oh." So she hadn't spent a lot of time on the streets. That relieved Mac. He hated thinking of her cold and hungry. Which didn't just puzzle him; it angered him. The very fact that he cared about her showed he was beginning to like her and he didn't want to like her. She was insubordinate, pretty, funny…all kinds of things that could be trouble. He wanted her to be a normal employee.

"Yeah. All that's good," Phil said as Mac reached his bedroom.

He walked inside, closed the door behind him and flopped into one of the white leather chairs in the sitting room in front of the bedroom. "So what's bad?"

"I did some digging. Real digging. Talked to friends, employees of the pizza shop who'd been around awhile, neighborhood people, and discovered that the owner of the chain of shops took a special liking to Ellie."

Mac sat up on his chair. "What do you mean 'special liking'?"

"They dated and eventually moved in together."

"Oh." Technically that had no bearing on her ability to be a nanny, so Mac wasn't happy when the news squeezed his heart. It could mean that he was jealous, but since he didn't know her well enough to be jealous, that left option two. He knew what happened when starstruck employees dated bosses who had money and power.

"One employee…a Jeanie Blair…said that Sam Kenward hung around the shop where Ellie worked for a few weeks chatting her up, flirting, being really good to her. He asked her out and he continued to be good to her. Then they moved in together and within a few weeks, Ellie became withdrawn."

Mac sat back in his chair again. "Damn."

"She lived with him for a year. Nobody ever saw a mark on her, but it was fairly common knowledge that he verbally abused her."

Mac pressed a finger to his forehead.

"The reigning rumor is that he hit her once and only once, and she left him."

"Good for her."

"Yeah," Phil agreed wholeheartedly. "She came out of it really well. I don't have specifics on what happened. She never came back to the pizza shop where she worked or contacted her friends."

"Probably because whatever shelter she went to told her that if she contacted anyone they could slip her location to the pizza shop owner."

"Precisely. Anyway, she appears again in employment records when she got a job working for Liz Harper at Happy Maids." Phil chuckled. "From the looks of things she was Harper's first employee."

Which was why Liz trusted her to run her company while she was away.

"I talked with a few of the ladies at Happy Maids and every one of them adores her. They call her Magic."

Mac laughed. "Magic?"

"Yeah, something about her intuition. Anyway her co-workers would trust her with their lives. They call her fierce. They adore her. She babysits for most of them."

Bracing his elbow on the arm of his chair, Mac leaned his face into his hand. "Thanks, Phil."

"So are you keeping her?"

"Actually, I feel like I owe her about eight apologies."

"You've been a real pain in the butt with her, haven't you?"

"Yeah."

"So fix it."

Only someone Mac had known for most of his life could be so bold with him, which was why Mac laughed. "Crawl back under your rock, Phil."

"Call me when you need me."

"I always do." Not because Phil was an employee, because he was an old friend. Phil knew how difficult Mac's life was and knew to keep his secrets. He was discreet when he investigated, and people like Ellie would never know Phil had been investigating them. He might have questioned Ellie's friends and coworkers, but he'd undoubtedly used a great ruse to get information. Her coworkers probably wouldn't even have realized they'd been questioned. Phil was that good.

Mac hung up the phone, paced to his bedroom and opened the drapes to look out at the water. As Phil had said, he had a right to be careful about his kids, but he might have pushed things a bit too far with Ellie. Worse, he'd yelled at her. Sure, he'd backed off once he realized he hadn't told her she couldn't let anyone into his house. But he'd yelled at a maid who'd had a difficult enough life.

Plus, he was attracted to a woman who'd lived the worst-case scenario of getting involved with a boss. He'd have to be a hundred times more sensitive in her presence. He couldn't even say one inappropriate word.

And he somehow had to make this up to her.

CHAPTER SIX

"GOOD morning, Ellie."

Surprised by Mac's unexpectedly happy greeting, Ellie stepped into the kitchen. "Good morning."

"I'm going into the office today."

Though Ellie's mouth dropped open in shock, she noticed that he was wearing a suit and tie. As always, Henry sat in his highchair, beating a rattle on the tray. Lacy sat beside Mac at the table, sneaking shy peeks at Ellie.

"The children are all yours."

That took her shock to astonishment and she had to stifle the urge to say, "Really?" Instead, she said, "Great."

Mac rose, kissed Henry's cheek, then Lacy's, and headed for the door. "I'll see you guys tonight around six." He paused and faced Ellie again. When their eyes met, something new shifted through her. He looked at her totally differently than he had just the day before. It was as if in the past twelve hours something had happened that caused him to trust her.

"I'd like dinner on the table at six when I get home. Lacy can't wait much longer than that to eat. Feel free to give her a decent-sized snack when she wakes up from her afternoon nap."

Then he was off. Ellie got a cup of coffee from the pot that had been brewed and ambled to the table. Dropping to a chair she said, "Well, guys, it looks like we're on our own." She glanced at Lacy. "What would you like to do today?"

Lacy didn't hesitate. "Swim."

"We can do that in the morning. Then this afternoon, what do you say we have a picnic?"

Lacy gasped and put her chubby little hands over her mouth. "A picnic!"

"In the yard."

Lacy bounced out of her seat. "All right!"

She was so excited that Ellie said a silent prayer that she hadn't accidentally stepped over any boundaries. Because the truth was she was as excited as Lacy. She had a month to do all the things she'd always wanted to do with a child. She didn't want to waste a moment.

When Mac came home at three o'clock that afternoon and couldn't find either his children or his nanny, panic filled him. He raced through the house, checking empty rooms and finally saw them when he ran to the French doors to see if they were in the pool.

They weren't in the pool. They were under a tree. In fact, he might not have seen them at all, except something shiny caught the sun and reflected a flash of light strong enough to be noticed.

His loafers made a soft tapping sound as he ran down the stone stairway, then grew silent as he walked across the grass. But he stopped suddenly. Close enough to see Ellie and the kids, but not so close that he'd interrupted them, he gaped at the scene in front of him.

Over shorts and a T-shirt, Lacy wore one of the pretend princess dresses his mother had bought her for her birthday and—he wasn't sure—but he thought his maid was wearing a sheet draped around her and then gathered at the waist to look like a ball gown. Sitting in his baby seat at the edge of the blanket, Henry giggled nonstop, as if thoroughly enjoying the whole thing.

The glimmer of light that had caught his attention came from a mirror Lacy held.

"It's mirror, mirror on the wall, who's the fairest one of all?"

Lacy frowned at Ellie. "What does that mean?"

"Well, the wicked queen was asking the mirror who was the prettiest."

"Why?"

"Because she was jealous of Snow White…a beautiful princess…and she worried that someday everyone would love Snow White more than they loved her." Ellie leaned in closer as if to tell Lacy a secret. "But the truth was the wicked queen wasn't really loved by her subjects."

Lacy's eyes rounded. "Why not?"

"Because she was mean. Snow White was very, very good."

"Oh."

"And do you know what that means?"

Lacy shook her head, sending her soft blond locks bouncing.

"It means that real beauty comes from inside. From how you behave and how you treat people. Not from how you look or what you wear."

Lacy nodded.

"But you'll never have to worry about that," Ellie said, pouring something from a plastic teapot into one of the matching little plastic cups. "You're a very good little girl."

Lacy nodded enthusiastically. "Daddy calls me a princess."

Ellie laughed.

Taking the teacup from Ellie, Lacy asked, "What was the other story?"

"Cinderella?"

"Yes. I like that one better."

"I like that one better too."

Twin arrows lanced Mac's heart. The first arrow was pain. He couldn't believe his ex-wife had never told their daughter simple fairy tales. The second arrow was gratitude. Even after the shabby way he'd treated Ellie the past few days, she wasn't angry or upset. And she was treating his children better than their own mother had.

"What's going on here?" he asked, announcing his presence as he walked over to the blanket spread out on the thick grass.

"We're having a tea party!" Lacy said, springing to her feet. "Do you want some tea?"

"It's actually fruit punch." Ellie picked up one of the tiny cups and poured about two tablespoons of fruit punch into it before handing it to him.

"Thanks." Awkwardness filled him. Not because he'd just lowered himself to a blanket while still dressed in the suit and tie he'd worn to the office. But because he'd so horribly misjudged this woman. She'd had a difficult life. The kind of life he only read about in news magazines. Yet here she sat, playing with his daughter, treating her like a friend or a daughter rather than someone she was employed to care for.

"How did your day go?" He asked the question of Ellie, but Lacy bounced with enthusiasm and joy.

"We swam. We ate pickles. And Ellie told me stories."

"So I heard." He ruffled Lacy's hair. How did a man thank someone for making his child feel normal? He caught Ellie's gaze and she smiled at him as if what she'd done for Lacy had been no big deal.

His heart swelled with something he didn't even dare try to identify. His entire purpose for living was now tied up with these kids. And he suddenly realized that they were his vulnerability. All a woman really had to do was mother his kids and he'd be putty in her hands.

But that was the problem. Pamela's beauty had turned him into a blathering idiot when he'd met her. He'd learned his lesson about getting so wrapped up in one or two of a woman's good traits that he missed the bad ones and found himself tied to the wrong woman forever—if only because of their kids.

He wouldn't put himself through that again. Because of the kids he had to be doubly careful. It didn't matter that the "good" trait of Ellie's that seemed to be snagging his heart was her kindness to his kids. A vulnerability was a vulnerability. A way for Ellie to get power he didn't want her to have. He was too careful to create the same problem twice.

He rose from the blanket. "What do you say we have some Daddy time? You guys stay with Ellie while I change out of my suit, then I'll meet you in the playroom. We'll play that video game you like while Ellie makes dinner."

Lacy bounced up and down. "Okay! This is the best day of my life."

Sadly, Mac knew she was correct. He also knew that even though he would judiciously squelch any and all romantic notions he might get about his temporary housekeeper, he did owe her for everything she'd done for him. Thanks to her, he now had a very good idea of what he'd look for when he began interviewing a new maid/nanny. But more than that, he appreciated how good she was to the kids. Yet, he'd misjudged her.

How did a man make up for any of that?

Halfway up the yard, close to the shimmering pool, he stopped and faced her again. She and Lacy were gathering the tea set and blanket as Henry gurgled happily. "Ellie?"

She stopped. "Yes?"

"Your friend, Ava, can come to the house anytime. I'm sorry I was a little harsh last night. I'm overprotective of the kids, but for good reason."

"Okay."

He turned and headed for the French doors again. Oddly, for the first time in about eight years, he felt his world righting.

The rest of the week passed in a blur for Ellie. Mac worked every day but Sunday. He planned to take the kids out on the ocean for a few hours on Sunday morning and they would spend the afternoon with Mrs. Pomeroy. He suggested that Ellie take the day…really take the day…leave the house, go to her own apartment to check on things, have lunch with friends, even sleep in her own bed and come back early Monday morning.

Ellie didn't need to be told twice. Though she had access to a washer and dryer she hated being in the same clothes all the time. Plus she missed sleeping on her own pillow. She spent the day running around, visiting her friends from A Friend Indeed, doing some shopping and packing a second suitcase.

She returned to Mac's house Monday morning, second suitcase in hand and pillow under her arm. Stepping into the kitchen, she saw Lacy at the table and Mac standing at the counter, holding Henry. She dropped her suitcase to the floor and set her pillow on an available counter.

"Here, let me take him."

Mac didn't hesitate. With another dad, a woman might suspect he was eager to get rid of his slobbering son. But Mac being so quick to give the baby to her was a show of trust. Happiness swelled inside her and the oddest thought occurred to her. If she didn't like her Happy Maids job so much, she really would consider taking this one permanently.

He handed the bubbly baby boy to her. Their arms and hands brushed in the transition and a sprinkle of awareness twinkled through her, reminding her of why she couldn't take this job permanently. Not only did she owe her loyalties to Liz, but also she was attracted to Mac. Lately, with him treating her well, the physical attraction had morphed into a full-blown attraction. She wasn't merely responding to his looks. She liked him.

The second Henry was in her arms, he slapped her, bringing her back to reality.

Mac winced. "I seriously think that means he missed you."

She kissed the baby's cheek. "Well, I missed him." The realization caused her breath to catch. She *had* missed Henry. She'd missed Lacy. She'd missed Mac. She'd been away only twenty-four hours, yet she'd missed this little family. They were definitely staking a claim on her heart. And if she didn't get a hold of these feelings she'd be sad when she left.

Because she would leave. She had to leave. She couldn't risk another mistake with a man that ended in disaster.

Mac ate his breakfast while Ellie fed Henry and chatted with Lacy. Both kids kissed him goodbye, then Lacy spouted a list of things she'd like to do that day. While Henry napped, Ellie and Lacy colored and Lacy filled her in on what they'd done the day Ellie had been away. After that they swam and ate lunch then Lacy and Henry took an afternoon nap, giving Ellie time to take inventory of the house.

The place wasn't any worse for her being away. Mac was very disciplined about replacing toys and tossing dirty clothes into the basket. She ran two loads of laundry, dusted and vacuumed the floors. By the time she was done both kids were awake and ready for a snack.

She fed Henry first then as Lacy ate her fruit and crackers, Ellie began dinner. Just as she was opening the freezer, her cell phone rang.

"Hey, Ava. What's up?"

"Would you mind if I came over a little early today?"

"No. Early's fine."

"Like about four?"

She glanced at the clock on the wall. "Are you at the gate?"

Ava laughed. "Close. But not there yet. I figured I'd call to see if there was anything you needed me to bring you."

"Actually, I forgot to get something out of the freezer for dinner." She winced. "If you really want to help me out, you could stop at Fredrick's and get me some spaghetti sauce and meatballs."

"Sure. Not a problem. See you in about half an hour."

"Great."

True to her word, Ava arrived in a half an hour. She set the steaming container of spaghetti sauce and meatballs on the counter and said hello to Lacy. "Hey, pumpkin."

"Hey, Miss Ava," Lacy said, using the name Ellie had suggested she use when Ava had visited the week before.

"What are you coloring?" Ava asked, sliding onto a seat beside Lacy after giving Ellie the report on the Happy Maids employees' hours and the schedule to sign off on.

"It's Cinderella."

"She's beautiful. Purple is a good color for her."

"Ellie says purple is for royalty."

"Ellie is right," Ava agreed with a laugh.

Ellie handed the signed papers to Ava. "So what's up tonight that you had to come early?"

Ava winced. "Would you believe I have a date?"

"Oh my gosh!" Ellie laughed with glee.

Lacy said, "What's a date?"

"It's when the prince comes to the princess's house, picks her up and takes her to dinner," Ellie explained, using language Lacy could understand.

Lacy's eyes widened. "Wow."

"Yeah, wow is right." Ava rose from her chair. "It's been thirty years since I went on a date. I can't believe I'm going on one now."

"You'll be fine," Ellie said, stifling a laugh. "It's about time you got back into the real world. Your husband's been gone ten years. I can't believe you waited this long to even date."

"Call me picky." Ava organized her papers and turned to go, but she stopped and faced Ellie again. "And you'd do well to follow my example. I've never heard you talk about going on a date."

"I date."

Lacy's eyes widened even further. "You do?"

Ava frowned. "You do?"

"Yes. I've gone out with Norm and Gerry, two of the volunteers from A Friend Indeed."

"Norm and Gerry? Good grief, Ellie! Norm still lives with his mom and if Gerry steps away from his computer long enough to go on a date I doubt that—"

She stopped as Mac stepped into the room.

"Hey, don't stop talking on my account."

Ellie sent Ava a pleading look. Ava's eyes narrowed shrewdly. "I was just on my way out the door."

Lacy said, "Miss Ava has a date."

Mac laughed.

Her gaze on Ellie, Ava said, "Yeah, I've gotta scoot. But we will continue this discussion later. Especially since you and I have to figure out a place to hold the Labor Day picnic for A Friend Indeed." She glanced at Lacy then Mac, letting Ellie know exactly why she wasn't pursuing Ellie's non-dating status. "I'll see you tomorrow."

Grateful Ava had taken the hint and didn't say any more, Ellie spun on Mac. "You're home early."

"And you're using sauce from Fredrick's."

She grimaced. "And meatballs. I forgot to take hamburger out of the freezer. Fredrick's food is always great. I thought if I tossed a salad and added freshly made spaghetti everybody would be happy."

Mac grabbed an apple from the refrigerator and headed out of the kitchen. "That's fine. When you buy things like that just remember to keep the slip from the store. My accountant will reimburse you. I'll be in my office on a conference call. I should be done by six."

"Great."

Ellie breathed a sigh of relief when he was gone. Lacy went back to coloring. Henry slapped his chubby fist on the highchair tray.

Everything was back to normal except the beating of Ellie's heart. Mac always looked ridiculously sexy in his suits and ties, but today the blue shirt he'd worn had picked

up the color of his eyes and he looked amazing. With thing
so comfortable and companionable between them she'c
nearly told him that. But she couldn't. Though she wasn`
his permanent housekeeper, she was here in a housekeeping capacity. Forget about the fact that she was befriending
his children and getting along with him. She was still a
servant and she was going to have to do something abou
this crush of hers.

That night Mac waited until the kids were in bed before he
began searching for Ellie. He hoped she hadn't decided to
retreat to her room and was glad when he found her sitting
on one of the two chaise lounges by the pool.

"Can we talk for a second?"

He asked his question before he walked around the
chaise and saw she wasn't sitting in shorts and a T-shirt
having a glass of tea to unwind for the day. She wore a re
one-piece bathing suit. Her damp, curling hair indicated
she'd been in the pool. And the contented expression or
her face reminded him of the expression of a woman after
a particularly satisfying love-making session.

He swallowed as visions of satin sheets and palming
smooth naked skin filled his brain. But before he coulc
stutter and stammer or even run the hell away, Ellie glancec
up from the book she was reading. "Sure. What do you
want to talk about?"

Her bathing suit, though a sensual red that revealed the
swell of her breasts, was very demure. So why it sent his
pulse scrambling, Mac couldn't say. Still, he'd be a blathering idiot to ask her to slip into her cover-up. Instead, he
locked his gaze on her face. "You're really doing a grea
job with the kids."

"Thank you."

"Actually, the reason I came looking for you is that I wanted to thank you for taking such good care of them."

Ellie laughed. "I am the nanny."

He shook his head. "You'd be surprised how many nannies think that just being in the same room with their charges is sufficient." He drew in a breath, sneaked another peek at her swimsuit—the way the taut red material caressed her curves, particularly accenting her tiny waist—then forced his mind back on his purpose for being outside with her.

"You play with the kids. You're especially good for Lacy. I appreciate that."

She ducked her head. "Well, you're welcome."

Mac took a deep breath. Oh, Lord. He hoped he hadn't embarrassed her by looking at her. He was such an idiot. But in his defense she was so beautiful it was damned difficult not to stare.

But he was here on a mission. He'd only used wanting to thank her for taking such good care of his kids as his conversational in. Now that he'd gotten his full report from Phil, it was awkward knowing things about her that she didn't realize he'd been told. Somehow or another he had to get her to tell him about being a foster child, about leaving an abusive relationship, and her close friendship with Liz Harper, so he didn't have to worry that he'd slip up and reveal that he knew any or all of it someday.

He lowered himself to the chaise beside hers. Sitting sideways, so his feet were on the decorative tiles that made up the seating area around the pool, he dropped his clasped hands into the space between his knees. Focused on what he had to say, he ignored the tingling of his fingers. This close to her, every inch of his body jumped to red alert, but his fingers itched to touch her. And that was wrong. And he was an adult. He could ignore one simple attraction.

"You know, we've never really talked."

She peeked at him. "About what?"

"About…you know…about your past."

The confused expression on her face told him this wasn't going well at all. His attraction was making him sound like a starstruck teenager finally alone with his first crush. Which was ridiculous. He was a grown man who had been married. Hell, now that he was free again, he could have his pick of women. Why this one made him stutter was beyond him.

"Like an interview?"

He sucked in a breath and expelled it quickly. "More like a conversation."

She sat up, shifting to sit sideways on her chaise, facing him. The knees of her perfect legs angled only inches away from his. They were so close he could touch her accidentally, satisfy his curiosity about whether her skin was as soft as it looked. But that would be wrong. Wrong. Wrong. Wrong.

"You mean like you would fill me in on a bit of your past and I'd fill you in on a bit of mine?"

Thank God she was thinking like a normal, rational human being and kept the conversation going where he wanted it to go. He could handle telling her a bit of his past. After all, she probably should know some of it in order to properly care for the children.

"Yeah. We should share information about our pasts."

"Okay. I'm really curious about the kids' mom." She grimaced. "Not curious in a gossipy way. But curious in a way that helps me to care for them. I don't want to accidentally say something I shouldn't."

Damn.

He'd hoped she'd start off by talking about herself. Instead she'd led with a question about him. This was what he got for being tongue-tied and stupid just because she was wearing a bathing suit.

"The children's mom left me because having a second child made her career difficult."

Ellie gaped in horror. "Are you kidding?"

His sentiment exactly. "She left when she got pregnant, using the pregnancy months to reestablish herself so that when Henry was born, she could hand him off to me and jump back in again."

"I don't care how liberated you rich people are—that stinks."

He couldn't agree more. Oddly, talking about Pamela had given him back perspective about being attracted to Ellie. He knew the consequences of falling too hard for someone. He had to keep this professional. He couldn't talk in great detail about his ex-wife with a servant. He'd stick with the information she needed to know to do her job. "She visits the kids about once a month—"

Ellie bounced from her chaise indignantly. "Once a month!"

"And I spend the next week answering questions from Lacy. Consider yourself lucky that she's cancelled her visit for July or you would be too."

"How nice of her to let you know in advance," Ellie said sarcastically.

Mac laughed. "I'm sorry. Normally I don't find anything humorous about this situation. But your reaction is a bit funny."

She paced to the pool then back to the side-by-side chaise lounges. Looking down at Mac, she said, "I volunteer for a charity called A Friend Indeed. We work with women with children who are forced to leave abusive homes. I've seen the trauma of a child who misses a parent—even when that parent is abusive. Considering her probable feeling of abandonment, Lacy's fairly well-adjusted."

Finally! The conversation had shifted, and in a brilliant way. Though talking about Lacy, she'd thrown in some pertinent information about herself. Now he could get everything out that he already knew and he could stop tiptoeing around her.

"Well, her mom's been gone eighteen months. Time is healing the wound, helping her adjust," he said, then instantly turned the discussion back to Ellie. "So tell me about this charity. I don't think I've ever heard of them."

"That's because the work they do is confidential."

"I understand. Everything you tell me will be kept in strictest confidence. What, exactly, do they do?"

The mental debate she held about whether to trust him changed her expression at least twice. Finally, he said, "My family's charitable foundation is always looking for worthwhile causes, charities that actually go in the trenches and help people. We know how to be discreet." He caught her gaze. "And we can be very generous. It might be beneficial to A Friend Indeed for you to tell me about them."

Obviously seeing his point, she sucked in a breath and began to pace alongside the pool again. "The charity purchases homes and places abused women in them."

"That's wonderful. How do the women who need help find them?"

"Social Services doesn't exactly recommend a woman leave her husband, but they do provide information about A Friend Indeed to women with kids in high-risk situations."

He frowned. That was the second time she'd mentioned women with children. He knew Ellie had gone to A Friend

Indeed for help. Did this mean she had a child? By forcing her into working for him, was he keeping her away from her own kids?

"How did you get involved with them?"

"I found them." She stopped pacing and faced him, as if suddenly realizing he'd led her to talk about herself, maybe even a part of her past that she wanted to keep hidden.

Feeling the game was up, he smiled sheepishly. "I told you about my wife."

"Because I'm caring for your children. I need to know."

"I'm employing you. Trusting you with those same children. I'd like to know about you."

She licked her lips, drawing Mac's attention to them. Full and smooth, they all but begged a man to kiss her. Now that he'd gotten control of himself, he wouldn't let himself stare too long or want too much, but he couldn't believe a man would be so foolish as to have her and then mistreat her.

"I was…or wanted to be helped by A Friend Indeed." She walked away again, toward the pool, keeping her back to him. "But the night I ran, when I got to the charity, they told me they only take women with kids. Liz happened to be with Ayleen, the group's leader, that night, and she offered me her couch."

That answered his question about her having kids and also explained her fierce loyalty to Cain Nestor's wife.

"And she hired you?"

Ellie nodded then turned suddenly. "So what does your wife do for a living that's so important that she can only see her kids once a month?"

He stifled a sigh. She wasn't going to tell him about the pizza shop owner. Wasn't going to share her fears or the struggle to get back to a good place in life. And both of those were too personal for him to push her into talking about them.

Of course, maybe if he answered a few more questions about Pamela, Ellie would answer a few more personal questions about her life.

He caught her gaze. "It's not what she does. It's where she lives. California."

Ellie's pretty mouth dropped open. "California!" She blinked a few times then she said, "Oh, my gosh! She's on TV or something, isn't she?"

"Or something."

His vague answer brought a spark of fire to Ellie's amber eyes. "Oh, I get it. I can tell you about me, but you're not going to give me any more information than you have to."

He was tempted to debate that. Not only had he revealed much, much more than she had, but also she hadn't really told him about herself. Thanks to Phil, he knew there was more. *Lots* more. But he also understood what she was saying. Her admissions were difficult. His was merely embarrassing. Sad for his children, but not gut-wrenching, the way hers had been. He had to tell her everything, make himself vulnerable, if he wanted her to share with him.

"Okay. She was a movie star. She's trying to edge her way into a comeback." He rose from his chaise and walked over to her. "Nothing seriously awful happened in our marriage. We fell out of love. She wanted her career back. She deserted her kids. But she didn't abuse them. She isn't one of Satan's minions. She's a selfish, narcissistic pain in the ass, but we survived her leaving. My big secret and the reason I don't talk about this is that we're sort of in hiding."

"Sort of?"

He got close enough to smell her soft scent, tempting fate because they were in one of those odd positions of life. They were too attracted to be friends, but he had to trust her and she had to trust him if this situation was to work. They were both pushing. And his admissions, though less serious, weren't any easier than hers. So why not get a tiny reward? Why not step close to the fire?

"Mrs. Pomeroy was my nanny. She called me when this house came on the market and suggested that we hide in plain sight. Our neighbors know who we are. But when Pamela's movie comes out next month, the paparazzi who come looking for us will go first to the family mansion in Atlanta. By the time they realize we're not there and investigate where we've moved, the noise Pamela tries to create might be over. If it's not, we'll move again."

Her big brown eyes captured his, holding his gaze. She studied him, as if trying to figure out if he were being honest. A few seconds stretched into a minute, and before common sense had time to remind him that they couldn't be this close for this long without resurrecting their chemistry, suddenly the air between them crackled with life and energy. His blood heated. His fingers itched to sink into her curling hair. His mouth longed to taste her. And though he knew nothing could ever come of this, he once again stepped closer to the fire.

Ellie took a step back, away from the powerful pull of him. She longed to run her fingers through his hair, touch his cheek, kiss his wonderful mouth. She told herself that he was off-limits. Yet for some reason or another, her body wasn't listening to her common sense tonight.

She took another step back. "Your ex-wife is Pamela Rose?"

He nodded.

"Wow." She wasn't surprised by the fact that his ex-wife had been a starlet. He was the kind of guy who'd attract a starlet. What wowed her was that she was here—in his company, living in a mansion. Sometimes she forgot just how rich and powerful he was. And he was confiding in her.

"Now, do you see why we're in hiding?"

"I guess."

He chuckled. "You guess?"

"Come on, Mac. A rich guy like you has to have an army of public relations people at your disposal. Surely, they could dispel a few rumors."

"I'm not worried about rumors. I'm worried about pictures. Because of my family's money, I grew up with bodyguards, silent alarms and restrictions on where I could go and what I could do. But I still had a measure of privacy. Once I married Pam, everything changed. When your picture gets on the front page of enough tabloids, people start to recognize you. I don't want that to happen to my kids. So I have to keep them away from the paparazzi, so they're not recognizable, because that makes them targets for extortionists and kidnappers."

She'd never thought of that. If no one knew what Mac's kids looked like, they could walk the streets or go to the beach, without anyone suspecting who they were and seeing potential ransom amounts instead of two beautiful children.

"True."

"Which is why I don't want the kids off the grounds."

She shook her head. "But that's exactly the opposite of what you're trying to accomplish."

"Not really."

"Yes. *Really.* You're supposed to be hiding in plain sight but in case you haven't noticed, you're a prisoner in your own house."

"It's the price we pay for my stupidity in making such a poor choice for a mate."

Her heart thumped at his admission that he'd made a bad choice in his first marriage. He really wasn't in love with his ex-wife anymore. And he really was attracted to her. So much so that he couldn't keep his eyes off her. They held her gaze when she stood close, followed her when she paced. And now he was confiding in her. Part of her longed to step closer to take what it seemed he was trying to offer. The other part knew they were a bad match. This very conversation proved it. He was a man who felt he needed to hide. She was a woman who'd only recently learned how to live without hiding.

She stepped away from him and focused on the kids. She knew what it was like to be a prisoner. She also knew that she'd gone overboard before Liz had talked her into getting out into the world beyond simply working. It had taken Liz an entire year to lure her into restaurants and help her to make friends at A Friend Indeed. And her life was better, richer for it.

She'd spent a lot of unnecessary time in her self-imposed prison. And perhaps he and his kids were too.

"I think you're crazy. Hiding in plain sight means you move to a place where no one expects you to be so that when they hear your name, even if they recognize it, they don't connect you to the 'billionaire' Mac Carmichael because they expect the billionaire Mac Carmichael to be under lock and key, and certainly not out and about in their neighborhood."

"That's ridiculous."

"Really? Because the way I see it, if there have never been pictures of your kids, the average person couldn't possibly know who they are. It's not like they wear a sign that says, 'My dad's a billionaire'."

He laughed, so Ellie pressed her point home. "Even *your* face isn't that recognizable. Everyone knows who you are when you're connected to your companies, like giving a press conference. But put on a pair of shorts and a fishing hat and walk into the mall and I'll bet nobody knows you."

At first Mac laughed, then he realized she wasn't kidding and his laughter stopped. "You're serious?"

"Yes. As long as no one knows what your kids look like there's no reason to hide them."

He shook his head. "Going out hoping that no one knows who we are would be a dangerous way to live. All it takes is one person to recognize even one of us for pictures to be taken and the entire world to know."

"I doubt it. Most people don't read *Forbes* or *Fortune*. And those are the only places your name and picture appear regularly."

"Right. The second I pull out a credit card the clerk knows my name."

"And you think a clerk at the mall is going to know who Mac Carmichael is?" She laughed gaily. "Come on. You're only famous in your own circle. Store clerks won't know you. Neither will the kid at the food court."

He frowned, seeing her point.

Her eyes sparkled with mischief when she caught his gaze. "Let's do an experiment. Let's take the kids to the mall tomorrow night. We'll go to a fast food restaurant and walk through a few stores. Lacy will probably die of happiness and you'll see that you don't have to be a prisoner."

With her voice light with merriment and her eyes shining, it was so tempting to Mac to lean into her, brush a kiss across her lips, tease her into taking his side. So he stepped back, away from temptation, into his comfort zone.

Obviously thinking he'd stepped away because he disagreed, she caught his arm. "Please. Even if you never want to do it again, do it once. For Lacy. She'd love this."

A storm of electricity burst through him, like lightning penetrating thick storm clouds. He stared into her wise brown eyes and didn't see the corresponding attraction he knew she felt. Instead, her earnest expression told him she really was bartering for the day out for his daughter. Appreciation rose up in him, battling the sexual needs coursing through him. He had a choice: say he'd think about it and run like hell to get away from temptation. Or stay. Take the conversation away from Lacy and to him. What he wanted from her. What he needed. What it could mean for them, if he were that free. That trusting.

He swallowed as intimate pictures formed in his brain, surprising him with their simplicity and intensity. He wanted this woman in a way he hadn't wanted a woman in a long, long time. Not just sexually, but intimately. There was definitely a difference. A frightening difference.

She gasped as if suddenly thinking of something. "You've probably never been to the mall." She laughed merrily. "Trust me. Lacy will love it. And I swear I'll guide you along the whole way."

Trust her. That was the problem. He wanted to trust her. But he knew he couldn't. At least not with his heart. But maybe the best way to get over his desire would be to get to know her as a normal person. Take her up on her offer with Lacy. Not to acquiesce to what she wanted, but to put her into the position of nanny more firmly. Surely he could risk one day. Especially if he stationed bodyguards in the mall.

"Should I come home early for this?"

Her eyes lit with joy. "Really? You're going to do it?"

"Sure."

"You don't have to come home early. Just be ready to put on a pair of jeans and a T-shirt when you get home." She headed for the house but faced him again and smiled. "And we'll take the suburban. That's the car that will attract the least attention."

"If we really wanted to blend, we should take yours."

That seemed to tickle her and she laughed with delight. "You probably couldn't fit into the front seat."

Then she turned and walked up the stairs, into the house. Mac lowered himself to one of the chaise lounges. He couldn't believe he'd just agreed to a trip to the mall, but he had. Partially because she was right: Lacy would love it. Partially because it was simply fun to see Ellie so happy, so full of life. She was the kind of woman who would make a happy home. The kind of woman any man would want for a wife.

He ran his hand down his face again, wishing he'd met her before his ex-wife had destroyed his faith in people.

And before a former boss had destroyed hers.

CHAPTER SEVEN

SITTING in the driver's seat of the suburban, wearing a yellow fishing hat, one of his golf shirts and cutoff jean shorts, Mac felt like a damned fool.

"This is a stupid idea."

Ellie peeked over at him and, God help him, she couldn't stop her eyes from wandering up to the yellow hat. She giggled.

He scowled. "A *very* stupid idea."

"Not really."

Her voice was soft and placating, causing him to suspect she was lying. But she smiled, and even in the semi-dark garage, the car seemed to light up.

"The purpose of the hat is for you to blend in."

"By looking like an idiot?"

"You look like an average guy going to the mall with his kids."

"Average guys don't wear stupid hats and look ridiculous."

"Of course they do." She peeked over at him again. "How long has it been since you've been in the real world? Men wear baseball caps backwards and knit hats in the summer. Hats are the big way men make their fashion statements."

He snatched the offending yellow hat off his head. "Rappers wear knit caps and goofballs wear their baseball caps backwards. Mostly to cover bald spots. But my hair is perfectly fine as it is."

In the booster seat in the back Lacy giggled. "Not really, Daddy."

He looked in the mirror. The hat had reshaped his hair so that portions were sticking out at odd angles. He flattened it down with his hand. "There. Now, let's go."

He'd be canceling this trip right now if Lacy's eyes hadn't lit with absolute astonishment when Ellie announced that they were going to the mall. Hell, why not get to the real bottom line? They wouldn't be going to the mall at all if he didn't feel like hell for treating Ellie harshly when she'd already had a difficult enough life.

He was a goofball. And maybe he *should* put on the yellow hat.

Mostly because he knew this wasn't the end of it. He might not let Ellie taunt him into another foolish trip, but he would sometimes buckle under about stupid things for Lacy. She was a kid and he wanted her to have some semblance of a life. He most certainly wanted her to have fun. And going to the mall with her dad—as long as she stayed with her dad—wouldn't be dangerous. Particularly since he had called Phil and company and told them to be at the mall at seven o'clock. They weren't to wear dark suits with their shoulder harnesses exposed so everyone around could see they had a gun, but were to blend in.

He glanced at the offending yellow hat on the compartment between him and Ellie. If hats were a way to blend, then Phil should be the one wearing this one.

"The first thing we're going to do is go to the food court," Ellie said, turning on the front seat of the Suburban so she could speak to Lacy and Henry.

Mac hid a grin. He had to admit he loved the way she kept Henry in the loop. The baby probably didn't understand much beyond Daddy, eat and nap, but when Ellie spoke he stared at her with rapt fascination.

"We'll eat a hamburger and fries and then I understand there are three children's stores on the first level."

Lacy gasped. "Can I get a princess dress?"

Ellie glanced at him and he caught Lacy's gaze in the rearview mirror. "Let's wait and see what's in the store."

"Ah, Dad!"

"Princess dresses are typically found in toy stores," Ellie jumped in, saving him. "They aren't normal clothes. They're special. When you put on a princess dress your imagination soars and you become anyone you want. At school, you have to be yourself so that you remember everything you learn and some of the things we might buy tonight would be for school."

Lacy nodded sagely as Mac drove them to the mall. Hundreds of multicolored cars were parked in long, rather organized rows. At first glance, he didn't see an empty space. And he hadn't instructed Phil to arrange for one.

Of course, that would have defeated the purpose of the entire trip. If a bodyguard arranges with mall management to have orange cones in a front row spot until you arrive so you can be hustled in, everybody pretty much knows you're somebody important. Pamela had loved that.

But this trip was about seeing if they could blend, seeing if they could every once in a while take Lacy out into the world and let her observe how real people lived. It was about seeing if maybe—if they kept her profile low-key enough and if he secretly placed bodyguards inconspicuously around her—maybe she could go to the mall with her friends when she was in her teens.

"Where to?"

"Just drive around until we find an open space."

He nodded and they circled the mall twice, not finding a space close enough that they didn't have to walk a distance to get into an entrance. By the fourth pass, he decided he would carry Lacy and Ellie could carry Henry, because they weren't going to find a closer spot.

They stepped into the noisy mall and Ellie directed him to the right. "It's a bit of a walk, but the food court is this way."

Mac couldn't help it; his head twisted from side to side, taking in the people as well as the building. Ellie was right. Real people did sometimes dress like goofballs. The atmosphere was almost like that of a carnival. They found the food court where Mac took a quick look around and saw Phil and three of his employees milling about. Phil wore a suit, but it was older and he let his jacket hang off the back of a white plastic chair where he sat eating a hamburger. Two of the other guards wore jeans and T-shirts. The third guy wore shorts and by damned if he wasn't wearing a khaki fishing hat.

Okay, so maybe Ellie hadn't been too far off the mark about the ugly hat.

Lacy ordered something called a "happy meal" and Mac and Ellie ordered salads. Then Ellie added a small order of fries for Henry.

Though he'd never been to a mall, Mac had eaten fast food before. He hadn't been particularly impressed, but for some reason or another, the scents from the food in this mall were amazing. Everything smelled delicious. When his stomach rumbled, he quickly added two hamburgers to his salad.

When they were finished eating, Ellie directed them to the three stores stocked with children's clothing. Lacy ran in, her mouth open with shock, her face registering pure, unadulterated feminine pleasure.

He leaned over to Ellie and said, "This is going to cost me a pretty penny."

Ellie gaped in horror. "No! You don't let her buy everything she wants. You tell her she can have two things."

Mac frowned. "Two things? There are hundreds of things in here."

"And she'll never possibly be able to use them all. She already has a closet full of clothes. Plus, if you buy her everything she wants, she'll have too much to appreciate it."

"But she's never shopped on her own before."

"Which makes this a perfect time for her to learn to shop with care. Not to be greedy. To appreciate what she has."

"She's only six."

Ellie shook her head and laughed. "Yes. Old enough to understand the lesson and young enough that you can still have the hope that the lesson will stick."

Mac pulled in a doubtful breath. "Okay. We'll play it your way."

He turned to catch up with Lacy, who was skipping up the aisle of the colorful specialty shop, but Ellie caught his arm. Pinpricks of awareness raced to his shoulder, across his chest and down to his stomach. She looked beautiful in her light blue T-shirt and white shorts. Her legs were long and tan, her golden hair bouncy and shiny.

"She'll thank you for this when she's older. She won't see the world as a place to take. And if we carry this lesson a bit further we might also teach her that she should also give, not always get."

He caught the gaze of his housekeeper, knowing she'd been a foster kid, knowing someone had abused her, knowing she'd worked her way from nothing and still she had the common sense and intelligence of a true lady.

Something warm squeezed his heart. Not only was she a lady, but she wanted his daughter to be a lady too. That was all any father really wanted. A daughter who appreciated what she had, gave as much as she got and acted like a lady.

"Have I told you thank you for the suggestion to come to the mall?"

"Mostly you groused about the hat."

"Well, thank you." A sudden instinct to lean in and kiss her rose up in him. It was so strong that if they hadn't been in a public place he sincerely doubted he would have been able to resist it.

But they were in a public place and she was his employee. And she'd been abused by a former boss. She'd trusted an employer and he'd hurt her in the worst possible way. No matter what Mac wanted, no matter how tempted, no matter how much he told himself he would be different, he couldn't forget her needs, her fear. He had to squelch any romantic urges.

After ten minutes of Lacy rummaging through the racks, Ellie broke the news that she could choose two things.

Lacy turned her pretty blue eyes up to her father. "Can't I have more?"

"Why do you need more?" Mac asked, taking his cue from Ellie who had told him that Lacy probably wouldn't use everything she'd want to buy.

"Because they're all so pretty."

"And you already have lots of pretty clothes."

She stuck out her lower lip. "But I want these!"

Mac's heart rate sped up. His soul filled with remorse. He wanted to give Lacy everything she wanted. He knew it was wrong. He knew everything Ellie said was right. But, damn it, Lacy was his little girl. He was rich. She *should* have everything she wanted!

"Lacy?" Ellie called to the little girl who looked on the verge of tears. "You don't want to buy everything here. You might not want to buy anything here at all. We have two other stores to go to. What if the dresses in those stores are prettier?"

Lacy's face transformed from sulking to confusion. "There are more stores?"

"Three. Remember?" She put her hand on Lacy's shoulder and guided her out of the store. "You don't simply want to buy everything. You want to buy the best, the prettiest. In the next store, I'll show you how to look for something that suits the color of your eyes. We're also going to think about where you'll wear what you buy. You may see that you actually have nowhere to wear some things." She shrugged. "So there's no point to buying them."

Lacy's face brightened with understanding. "Okay."

She skipped toward the entrance where two of Phil's guys sat on a bench pretending to be holding a conversation. Knowing Lacy was safe, Mac turned to Ellie. "There's some secret woman code in what you told her, right?"

She laughed. "No. Just common sense."

They trooped to the second store. Lacy checked out the racks in a more judicious way. Mac had taken the baby so Ellie could help her, and he strolled down a nearby aisle.

He'd never considered the time or money that went into purchasing things for his children. Mrs. Devlin had done all that. But now he didn't have a nanny and he seriously wondered if there weren't things he should be buying.

After a few minutes, they found the third store. Lacy and Ellie went their way and Mac walked the aisles, looking at clothes for Henry, wondering if he needed new things and even what size he wore. Lacy chose a pair of capris with a new blouse and a brightly colored sundress.

"Two outfits," Ellie explained, telling Mac with her expression that he shouldn't question that.

"That's great. They're very… pretty," he said at the last second because he wasn't sure what to say.

Ellie laughed. "We might want to pick up a pack or two of diapers," she said as they approached the checkout lane.

Mac pulled in a breath. "I wondered. We've been without a nanny for a while. You've worked for us almost two weeks and Mrs. Devlin left the week before that. Even if we had a stockpile of diapers, Henry has to be going through them fairly quickly."

Ellie chose the diapers and put them on the counter with Lacy's things.

"Does he need any clothes?"

Ellie shook her head. "No, he's fine for a few months. Then you may have to shop."

"By then I hope to have a real nanny."

A shadow passed over Ellie's face and Mac instantly regretted his comment. "I didn't mean to sound as if we'll be relieved when you go. It's more about getting our lives back to normal."

She glanced away. "I understand."

But he didn't think she did understand. Her voice was soft, sad, as if she was accustomed to being unwanted, asked to leave. She turned and walked out of the store, Lacy chattering happily on her heels.

Mac hung back, cursing in his head for his stupidity. He didn't want her to leave. He wanted to keep her. But how

could he? How could he ask her to give up a life she was
building as an executive in a new company to become his
permanent nanny? Worse, if she stayed too long, he knew
he wouldn't be able to resist her. Some moonlit night or
sunny afternoon he'd kiss her…and he'd be no better than
the boss who seduced her and then abused her.

So she couldn't stay.

But he also wouldn't let her spend the night feeling
badly. As soon as the kids were in bed, Mac intended to
explain how much he appreciated her, how much he wished
he could keep her and maybe even why he couldn't.

CHAPTER EIGHT

AFTER Mac had put the kids to bed, Ellie stepped out of the French doors onto the steps that would take her to the gazebo. She wasn't sure what she was doing. She had no idea what she would say. But even though they'd had a great trip to the mall, she'd seen the bodyguards. She'd also sensed Mac's fear. He might have taken Lacy and Henry out that night, but she sincerely doubted he'd do it again.

The thought that he couldn't see that they didn't have to live in a prison wouldn't let her alone. She had lived that prison. Plus, she was trained to help women transition out of abusive homes, and everything about this family reminded her of the families she dealt with at A Friend Indeed. She'd be shirking her duties as A Friend Indeed volunteer if she didn't try to help him.

She tripped down the yellow steps and strolled past the pool. Cool night air swirled around her, indicating that a storm was probably rolling in.

Passing the patio beyond the pool, she walked along the stone path to the gazebo where she paused just in front of the two steps that would take her inside, to where Mac sat.

When she entered the gazebo he'd either think it was a coincidence that they'd gone to the same place, or he'd know she'd watched him come out here and followed him.

Which was bad on so many levels. The only way she could comfort herself was to remind herself that she was trained to help spouses transition out of bad relationships. And if he needed her...

She took the two steps up into the gazebo.

Soft music greeted her. She didn't recognize it. It wasn't pop or rock or even a well-known classical song. Soft and mellow, it reminded her of a blues melody.

"Hey."

He glanced up at her and rose from the chaise lounge. "Hey."

Showing him the baby monitor, she said, "I brought this so we could have a few minutes to talk."

His eyes narrowed. "You want to talk?"

She nodded.

"So do I."

"Then it looks like we're on the same wavelength. You go first."

"No. You go first."

"All right. I thought the trip to the mall went very well tonight, but I sense that you weren't comfortable and you might not do it again."

"Ellie, this isn't a matter of me being uncomfortable. It's a matter of safety."

"I understand that, but you can't keep your kids in a bubble forever."

"I won't."

She laughed lightly. "You'll try."

"Of course, I'll try. I'm a father. It's what we do."

"But without a mom to argue the other side for your kids, you're always going to win."

This time he laughed. "Actually, that's what I wanted to talk about with you."

"Really?"

"Yes. Tonight when I mentioned getting a permanent nanny, you seemed to get really sad. I wanted you to know that if you truly wanted the job, I'd hire you in a heartbeat. Nobody's ever been as kind to Lacy. She adores you."

Ellie fought the tears that wanted to form in her eyes. Lacy was such an adorable little girl that Ellie couldn't believe a mother could abandon her. But soon Ellie would also abandon her. "I like her too."

"But?"

"But I have a job that I love."

He smiled ruefully. "That's exactly what I told myself when I saw the sad expression come to your face. You might love my kids, but you also love your Happy Maids job. And you're working your way up the corporate ladder. You're getting experience in management that will lead to security."

She straightened her shoulders, obviously proud of her accomplishments. "I am."

"So you need to stay where you are."

She nodded. "Yes."

"Which means someday I won't be your boss."

She frowned, wondering what the heck that had to do with anything. She raised her eyes until she could meet his gaze. When she did she saw the same curiosity in his expression that she felt twinkle through her every time they got close enough to touch. The sensation got worse every day because every day they seemed to grow closer emotionally.

He'd held his curiosity at bay because of their employment situation, but tonight they'd basically set it in stone that soon she wouldn't be his employee.

She swallowed. She'd never thought of that and from the look on his face he hadn't either—until tonight. Tonight with a gentle rumble of thunder mixing and mingling with the soft music filling the gazebo, and a sweet-scented breeze wafting around them, they'd made the connection that they didn't have to ignore their attraction.

The music shifted from a spirited blues song to something soft and wistful and he stepped toward her. "I can't remember the last time I danced. I'm very adept at dodging would-be partners at charity events. But tonight is different. Tonight I'm in the mood." He caught her gaze. "Want to dance?"

His blue eyes were soft and honest and though she knew it was foolish considering that she was still in his employ, still living under his roof, something inside her couldn't say no. She wanted this. She wanted to feel his arms around her, his chest pressed against hers, his chin resting on the top of her head. Nothing would come of it. At least not while she was in his employ. She was very strong when it came to holding the line in her relationships. Plus, he was as taken as she was by their attraction, but she had seen him pull back several times. Surely, she could trust him to pull back again, if things got too heated.

She smiled and held out her hand. He pulled her into his embrace and the whole world softened. It was everything she could do not to close her eyes and melt against him.

He nudged her a little closer.

The muscles she held so stiffly ached in protest, so she relaxed a bit.

He pulled her closer still.

And her body relented. Doing what her head had been so determined to stop, she melted against him.

"That's nice."

"Yes." Her voice was nothing but a thready whisper that wove into the sweet music drifting around them. The remnants of distant thunder continued to grumble overhead, matching the muted warnings whispering through her brain. *Be careful. Be careful. Be careful.*

But the warnings were soft, and as she swayed to the song, nestled against a man she was coming to care for, they grew quieter and quieter, mitigated by the other side of the argument running through her brain. Mac wasn't a man who would hurt her. She'd seen his worst when he discovered Ava in his kitchen. He'd also apologized, not rationalized that no matter what her explanation she was somehow at fault, as Sam would have done.

Thinking about Sam sent a burst of fear skittering through her, but as quickly as it manifested, it shimmied into nothing. Sam and Mac were nothing alike. In fact, she'd venture to say they were polar opposites.

Oddly, that realization scared her even more. The defenses that had been protecting her, the fears that saved her from another mistake, were being silenced around Mac. Her instincts were screaming that that was because Mac was a good man. But was he? How could she say for sure when she'd only known him a few weeks?

Suddenly Ellie realized they were no longer dancing. The music still drifted around them but they stood perfectly still. Her hand tucked in his. His arm comfortable at her waist. Their chests a breath away from each other. Their eyes locked.

"I won't hurt you."

Had he read her mind? Was she that transparent?

She whispered, "I know."

"So don't be afraid."

"I'm trying."

"That's all I ask."

She expected him to pull her close again. Instead, he leaned down and brushed his lips across hers. A light, wistful sweep of his mouth against hers. A promise more than a real kiss.

Mac stepped back, releasing her. "You might want to go back inside now."

She continued to hold his gaze. Sincerity and stability were the two most important things to her right now and his perfect blue eyes were telling her she could trust him.

Then his gaze dropped to her mouth and as seconds ticked away, the expression in his eyes shifted from soft to sexually charged. He was a good man, but he was also a man who wanted her.

Her heart stuttered in her chest. She wasn't sure how to deal with that or even if she could. Part of her simply wanted to relent and do what they both wanted to do. The other part was afraid. She'd been burned once. No matter how many times she told herself he was different, he wouldn't hurt her, she knew her instincts about men had been wrong before. They'd told her she could trust Sam. She knew she had to be strong, smart.

And the smart thing right now would be to follow his suggestion and leave.

She turned and ran out of the gazebo, up the soft grass, along the cool tiles and up the stone stairs to the kitchen. In her room, she stood by the window, staring out at the gazebo, knowing he sat in there alone.

Mac fell into the chaise lounge again. He squeezed his eyes shut, trying not to think of that kiss. Unfortunately, when he shoved his mind off the kiss it jumped to Ellie being abused. When he shifted his mind off that, he envisioned her younger, alone and frightened on the streets, running from a foster home. He couldn't handle the thought of Ellie being alone. He tried not to imagine how it felt to live on the streets as Phil had said she had done. He tried to ignore the swell of protectiveness that rose up in him.

Especially when a soft voice reminded him that he'd opened a door tonight that he probably shouldn't have opened. She'd already escaped several bad situations, and if he got involved with her he would be taking her directly into another. She wouldn't be on the streets or living with an abusive man, but she'd be locked in what she so clearly described as a private prison. If what he felt for her blossomed into love and they married, she'd live here, behind a gate. If she did leave the house, she'd be surrounded by bodyguards.

He cursed and began to pace. What was wrong with him? He knew better than to start something with her. She was too sweet, too innocent. He should have kept his hands off her. Not because she wasn't pretty enough or even because she wasn't special, but because she *was* special. Honest. Genuine. His life would crush her—or at the very least crush her spirit.

But what if it didn't? What if beneath all that sweetness was a layer of steel? What if her life had made her strong? And what if she chose him? What if she entered this life of his with her eyes wide-open? Ready to handle whatever came their way. Ready to mother his kids and love him.

Thunder rumbled closer this time, as if reminding him that wishful thinking was dangerous.

The only way she could come into his life, eyes open, fully prepared, would be if he really did let her choose. If he backed off and let her make the next move.

CHAPTER NINE

AFTER a nearly sleepless night, Ellie woke at four. Refusing to let herself think about what had happened in the gazebo, she sauntered downstairs, but Lacy wasn't at the weathered table. So she made a pot of coffee and sipped at three cups, waiting to make Lacy's breakfast, but to her complete joy Henry's six-thirty wake-up call came before Lacy woke.

Finally, closer to seven, the little girl tripped into the kitchen, rubbing her eyes sleepily. "Hi."

"Hey, pumpkin." Ellie juggled Henry on her lap. "You must be really hungry after that long sleep."

"Yeah." Bear under her arm, Lacy ambled to the table.

"Who had a really long sleep?" Mac walked into the room, dressed, as always, in a dark suit. Today he wore a white shirt and aqua tie. He couldn't have been more handsome to Ellie if he'd tried.

Then she remembered he'd kissed her.

She caught his gaze and for several seconds they simply stared at each other. So much had happened between them the night before and yet nothing had really happened. He'd brushed his lips across hers. That was all. It hardly counted as a kiss.

So why was her heart beating erratically at just the memory? Why did her breath shiver through her chest? Why couldn't she look away?

"Lacy had a really long sleep," she said, working to make her voice sound normal. "She just woke up."

Mac's gaze swung to his daughter. "Really?"

She grinned at him and nodded.

He strode to the table. "Well, that's cause for celebration." He glanced at his watch as if gauging the time he had and turned to Ellie. "Can you make pancakes?"

Glad to have both of their minds off that kiss, Ellie happily said, "Absolutely."

Henry screeched.

Mac took him from Ellie's lap. "I haven't forgotten you." He kissed his cheek noisily. "Has he eaten yet?"

"Yes. Henry woke a little before Lacy did. I bathed him and fed him." She surreptitiously caught Mac's gaze again. "So you're safe."

Mac laughed and hugged his son.

Something warm and soft floated through Ellie. She didn't have to worry that he'd ravish her in front of his kids. He was a dad and though he liked Ellie, there was propriety to consider. She also didn't have to worry that he'd treat her any differently. In fact, they were behaving as they always did. Except today she wasn't on the outside looking in. That kiss the night before had brought her into the world she'd only been working in yesterday. Today she was part of the family. A *normal* family. Everything she'd always dreamed of. Everything other people had but she'd always believed was just beyond her reach was suddenly hers.

Tears filled her eyes and she turned away, busying herself with the pancakes as Mac entertained the children.

That was foolish, dangerous thinking. This wasn't hers. It wasn't her life. She wasn't even really their maid. She was a stand-in. Temporary help.

But what about that kiss?

Beating the pancake batter, she squeezed her eyes shut. It wasn't really a kiss. It was only a brush.

No. It was more like a question.

Is this right?

Do you want this?

The tears filling her eyes threatened to spill over. Did she want this? Of course, she wanted this. That wasn't the question. The question was…was it right? Would she get hurt?

Didn't she always get her hopes up and get hurt?

Yes.

That was why she was strong. Why she looked before she leaped.

She sucked in a breath, forced her tears to stop, made the pancakes and served them to this happy little family the way a good maid was supposed to. Though she knew Mac wouldn't have protested if she'd served herself a pancake and sat at the table with him and his children, she resisted temptation. She was too smart to wish for something she couldn't have.

She helped Henry wave goodbye to Mac as he left for work then dressed Lacy in something pretty. And fought not to think about how well she fit, how much her intuition screamed that she belonged here.

When Ava arrived that afternoon, Lacy and Henry were napping. The kitchen was quiet enough that the instincts and urges tormenting Ellie couldn't be quieted. To get her mind off her own troubles, she focused on Ava's date.

"So how'd it go?"

"It was fun." She peeked up from the pages she was separating for Ellie's signature. "We're going out again over the weekend."

"Really?" Ellie kept her voice light and found she actually did feel better forgetting about herself and talking about Ava.

Ava's face reddened endearingly. "Mark is a very nice man."

Ellie rolled her eyes. "That's all you can say? That he's nice? You're such a romantic."

"And since when are you an expert on romance?"

Since the night before.

Since she'd been kissed with tenderness and honesty that zapped her fear and made her yearn for things she'd long ago forgotten she wanted.

Since she'd felt sexual heat that hinted at pleasure far beyond what she'd ever experienced.

Since she honest to God wondered if she wasn't falling in love.

The thought nearly suffocated her. In love? Oh, Lord! How could she fall in love with a man she couldn't have?

"You're right. I'm not the one to give romantic advice."

Ava sighed. "Ellie! I was teasing."

"I know, but I'm still not the one to be giving advice."

Ava laughed. "Good grief, girl! You are *Magic*. You are the advice giver." She glanced around the kitchen. "What the heck is happening to you here?"

Ellie pulled in a breath. "I'm losing touch with reality."

"Since when did you deal in reality?"

"Since my intuition went on the fritz."

"I find it hard to believe that your intuition is on the fritz. Why would the woman who's been right on the money with every premonition she's had suddenly decide she had no more intuition?"

"Because I'm always wrong when it comes to myself and men."

"Really?"

"Yes! That's how I know the weird vibes I've been getting here have to be wrong."

"What vibes?"

Ellie debated telling Ava the truth. She was going crazy with sadness one minute and going crazy wishing for things she was sure she couldn't have the next. But the worst were the times when she genuinely believed she could have everything she wanted from this little family, if she'd just say the word. If that was true, and she walked away, let fear control her, then Sam was winning. Ruining her life when he wasn't even around.

Ava was older, wiser, able to discern things. Maybe instead of intuition she needed real advice from someone with experience?

"All right. You asked for it. I'll tell you. My intuition keeps telling me Mac is the man of my dreams. The love of my life."

Ava gaped at her. "No kidding. He's quite a catch. I'd be tempted to take that premonition and run with it."

"This from the woman who hasn't dated in thirty years."

"My situation was different. I was married for twenty years before my husband died. I had known what it was like to be blissfully in love. I'd had children. I'd built a very satisfying life. I already had my good memories. I didn't fear another relationship. I wasn't sure I wanted one." She caught Ellie's hand. "You, on the other hand, are afraid."

"You're damned right I'm afraid."

"Mac is, by all accounts, a wonderful guy. Even you've told me that."

"He is."

"And does he feel the same way about you?"

Ellie whispered, "He kissed me last night."

"Ah." Ava squeezed Ellie's hand. "I don't think there's any reason to be afraid, but if you are, there's a simple cure. Take this slowly. Get to know him. And everything will turn out fine."

"Right."

"You don't sound so sure."

"I have my reasons."

Ava's face fell in concern. "Like what?"

"For one, his ex-wife is a movie star! How could I possibly believe I'm in his league? What if I'm setting myself up for a colossal fall just because my instincts really want for me to belong here?"

"So in other words, you're afraid because your intuition is telling you you belong here and you're questioning it?"

Ellie took a breath. "I've spent my whole life listening to my intuition, and in this house it's seriously on the fritz. I feel lost not being able to trust it."

"Well, if you don't trust your intuition, there's another way to analyze this. Think about what you would listen to if you didn't have intuition."

Ellie frowned. "What else is there?"

"Your head and your heart. What do they say?"

"Well, my head knows that he's a fabulous dad, a good man."

"And your heart?"

"My heart thinks he's wonderful."

"Oh, my dear, Ellie." Ava rose from the kitchen table. 'You've already made up your mind. Now you just have to get over your fear, and the best way is what I've already said. Get to know him. Take your time."

"What if he goes faster than I can handle?"

"Then you just pretend he's one of the Happy Maids' employees who won't listen to your instructions."

Ellie laughed. "Are you telling me to fire him?"

"No. I'm telling you to stand your ground."

Ellie rolled her eyes. "Right."

"I am right. That *is* what you need to do. When he gives you work instructions you have to listen. But when the mood turns romantic, you're in charge. If he goes too fast, pull away...walk away." Ava patted Ellie's hand one more time for good measure. "Trust me. You'll know what to do."

"I hope you're right."

"Right about what?"

Both Ava and Ellie spun to face the butler's pantry as Mac walked through into the kitchen.

"I...um..." Ellie stammered, unable to think of anything to say.

Luckily, Ava picked up the ball. "Ellie and I are in charge of a Labor Day picnic for the woman at a charity we work for. I told her we wouldn't have to worry about finding a place even though it's late and everything's already booked."

"That's why I hope she's right," Ellie jumped in, glad for Ava's perfect cover story. "We don't want to have to cancel the picnic just because we were a little slow on the uptake."

Mac set his briefcase on the counter. "How many attendees?"

"Counting workers, we have about thirty."

"This place can accommodate thirty people."

Ava's eyes widened in surprise. Ellie gasped. "You'd let us have a picnic here?"

"Sure. I have a pool, a big yard and a gazebo with a huge grill. I think this place is perfect for a picnic."

Ellie shook her head in dismay. "We can make quite a mess."

"I'll hire Happy Maids to do the clean up the next day."

Ava pulled a pen from her purse and a small notebook. "Sounds good to me. I'll call Ayleen and tell her we can stop looking. We're having our Labor Day picnic here." She smiled at Ellie.

Ellie faced Mac, so flabbergasted by his generosity she was surprised she could speak. "Thanks. You don't know how much we appreciate this."

He waved his hand dismissively. "I think that gazebo was built for parties, yet I've only grilled hot dogs for the kids. It'll be good to see the house get some use."

"True," Ellie agreed, loving the fact that he was coming out of his shell because of her.

"Besides, Lacy will enjoy it."

"Exactly. Plus, we won't be here all day. Most of the guests will arrive around four. We usually clear out around nine or ten," Ava said, obviously not about to let Mac change his mind. She faced Ellie again. "I'll see you tomorrow."

Ellie walked on air the rest of the afternoon as Mac worked in his office. He let her serve dinner and clean up while he played with the kids, and took charge of getting Lacy and Henry ready for bed. He even stepped back when she came into the bedroom to kiss Lacy good-night. Then he said good-night to her and headed for his own room without so much as a hint that he might kiss her.

Relief rippled through her. Then she wondered why. She wanted this. She wanted to be romantically involved with him. She knew Mac was a good man. His light kiss might have been his way of telling her he wouldn't push. And tonight's behavior might have been his way of reinforcing that. So, why was she so worried?

She made her way to her suite, undressed and got into bed. Thoughts of Mac again filled her head. And she did something she hadn't done in years. She discounted her intuition and really thought about him. She thought about his life, his bad marriage, the way he behaved with his kids. She thought about how he'd strong-armed her into taking this job then apologized. She considered how well he treated her and even how he'd changed his mind about letting Ava come to the house as a show of trust.

That was the one that pushed her over the top. He wasn't just fair; he treated her like an equal. Even though she was his employee and he didn't owe her any explanations or apologies, he admitted his mistake in yelling at her, and eventually gave her her own way on the situation, telling her Ava could come to the house to do the daily reports for Happy Maids.

Sam would have never done that.

For a few seconds she also thought about Sam, but they were very important seconds. Not because she once again realized how different Mac was than Sam, but because she realized how different *she* was.

It might have taken her three years to get beyond the emotional hurts enough that she could mature into the person she was supposed to be, but she'd done it. Thanks to Liz. Thanks to A Friend Indeed. She was normal. Finally.

The next morning she awoke feeling totally different. She was a strong, vital woman, who had gotten beyond a bad past. She was different. She was ready.

This time when Mac came into the kitchen and asked for French toast as a way to celebrate Lacy's second day of sleeping until almost seven, she didn't wonder about her place in his home. She didn't burst into tears with fear over losing this little family. She told herself she had choices. She'd take them one at a time and see where they led.

She set the plate of French toast on the table, along with syrup and fresh fruit.

Mac glanced up at her, his blue eyes soft and apprecia-tive. "Thanks."

"You're welcome." She turned to go, but stopped herself and pivoted around again. "You know what? I'm kind of hungry myself."

She took a plate from the stack Mac had brought to the table. She'd thought it was a mistake that he'd brought three plates, but what if it wasn't? What if he wanted her to have breakfast with them?

"I think I'll have some French toast, too."

Lacy said, "All right!" as Ellie sat, snagged two slices of French toast and slathered them with syrup.

"I'm taking the helicopter to Atlanta this morning," Mac said, for the first time ever telling her his plans for the day, really making her feel like part of the family.

Instead of second guessing why he'd done that, instead of panicking over what she "should" say, Ellie simply said the first thing that popped into her head. "That sounds like fun."

"Well, it is and it isn't. I have to attend a meeting of the executive board."

"Who's on your executive board?" Ellie asked, taking Ava's advice that she needed to get to know him. This was his world. The more she knew, the more she'd be able to ascertain if she wanted to be in it.

"My parents retired last year and we replaced them with two cousins." He grinned at her. "You'd be proud of us. One's a woman."

"I'm not that much of a feminist."

"No, but you like to make sure the men in your life aren't chauvinists."

Because it was true, she couldn't deny it. But his observation lightened her heart as much as the third plate had. He was noticing her. Thinking about her. He wasn't going into this mindlessly, either.

After another fifteen minutes of eating and chatting, Mac rose from the table. "Okay. I've got to go now." He kissed Lacy, kissed Henry and faced Ellie, who had risen from the table when he had.

Her heart thundered in her chest. Would he kiss her? First the baby, then the child, then his...girlfriend? Good Lord, she didn't even know how to categorize herself.

But he didn't kiss her. He didn't even make a move to get any closer. He simply smiled. "I'll see you tonight. If all goes well, I won't be late. If I'm not here before six, have dinner with Lacy."

"Okay."

He held her gaze a few seconds longer. He wanted to kiss her, she could see it in his eyes. But he wasn't making any kind of move and she couldn't tell if she was supposed to. And even if he was waiting for some kind of sign from her, what kind of sign would she give him?

She had absolutely no idea. Worse, she'd be mortified if she guessed wrong. So she stepped away. "If you're late, Lacy and I will eat without you."

When he left, Ellie collapsed on her chair. Lacy said, "Are we going to swim before it gets too hot?" bringing Ellie back to the real world.

But she was grateful to be back. As Ava had said, she did need time to adjust. Time to get to know him. Time to adjust to this relationship. And smaller steps were better.

Mac arrived home exhausted. His two cousins were idiots. They were only on the executive board thanks to the good will of Mac's parents, yet they had attacked him, attacked his business practices, attacked his overprotective attitude with their employees, especially abroad, insinuating that the money spent on security was wasted.

The money they spent on security was a pittance compared to some of their other expenses. And his cousins' attacking that small sum only proved how little they knew about running a business.

He'd called his parents, asked them to remove the cousins, but they'd refused, telling Mac he would have to help them learn the ropes. They were family and Carmichael Incorporated was run by family. Because Mac was their only child, if something happened to him, someone in the family had to be properly trained to take over.

Fabulous. So now he had months if not years of tolerating their attitude, while trying to show them the important things they should be focused on.

He walked through the butler's pantry into the kitchen, expecting to see Lacy at the table or Ellie bustling around, only to find the room was empty. He looked at his watch and groaned. It was nearly ten. Lacy should be sound asleep. Ellie was probably in her room.

Disappointed, he dropped his briefcase on the table and went in search of leftovers. He found roast beef and mashed potatoes and carrots and took them to the counter. He got a plate so he could divvy out a portion and microwave it, just as Ellie raced into the room.

"I'm sorry! I'll get that," she said, scrambling to the counter and bumping him out of the way.

He bumped her back. "I'm fine."

She tried to take the spoon from his hand. "I know. But this is my job."

Resisting the urge to laugh, he held on to the spoon. "It's nearly ten. Your workday is done."

Looking confused, she said, "Okay," and stepped out of his way, but she didn't leave the room.

Mac's heart rate sped up. Maybe she didn't want to leave the room? That morning she'd had breakfast with them and chatted with him about his day.

Maybe he could entice her into staying while he ate. There was nothing worse than eating dinner alone, but more than that, he enjoyed her company. Plus, it was another step toward them getting to know each other. Another step toward her, hopefully, making a romantic move.

"My cousins turned out to be pains in the butt."

A laugh escaped her. "Really?"

He winced. "Maybe I shouldn't call them pains as much as I should say they don't have any experience."

"So they asked a lot of questions."

He slid his supper into the microwave. "All the wrong questions. Which means that maybe my parents promoted them prematurely."

"Ouch."

He set the timer and shrugged out of his suit jacket and hung it across the back of an available chair before leaning against the countertop. "I asked them to remove them from the board and they asked me to train them."

She casually took a seat at the table. "And what did you say?"

"I said I'd train them."

"That's very nice of you."

The microwave buzzer beeped and he turned to retrieve his dinner. "Not really. It's what my parents want and I always try to please them."

She laughed. "So you're not the family rebel?"

He set his dish down at the place across from her. "No. Just your garden variety family grouch."

She chortled merrily. "You're not a grouch. You just like things done a certain way. Ava tells me Cain is the same way."

He filled his fork with mashed potatoes. "Have you heard from the newlyweds?"

"Ava got a call last week. I think they're ignoring us."

"Wonder why?"

Ellie laughed again and Mac's fork stopped halfway to his mouth. He loved to hear her laugh, but he loved even better that he was the one making her laugh. He shoved the mashed potatoes into his mouth to cover the fact that he was staring at her. When the buttery mixture hit his tongue, he groaned in ecstasy.

"These are fabulous."

"I know! I love them. The secret is tons of butter."

"Whatever the secret, I'm glad you know it."

"Me too."

The conversation died, and silence stretched out. Mac could have thought of a hundred questions to ask, a hundred things to say, but he was hungry. Besides, he wanted her to be a part of this learning process. He wanted her to talk to him, not just answer his questions.

She drew an imaginary line on the table, focusing her attention on that, Mac believed, so she didn't have to look at him when she said, "I missed out on things like family recipes, holiday traditions, so I sort of make up my own."

"Nothing wrong with that."

She glanced up at him. "Really?"

"I think it's a great idea. My family has traditions like going to the Bahamas for Christmas. But I'd rather have an old fashioned Christmas...up north. Maybe in Vermont." He caught her gaze. "Someday I'm going to do that for my kids."

She smiled at him. "That's very nice."

"And a little selfish. I'd like to spend Christmas somewhere that it snows. I want to see snow-covered lights twinkling on Christmas trees."

"I grew up in Wisconsin." She turned her attention to the table again. He wondered if she was debating what to tell him, how much to tell him, and silently begged her to tell him everything.

"I've seen lots of snow."

When she fell silent he decided to nudge her. She'd told him the beginnings of plenty of things, enough that he could question her without her realizing he already knew most of what she would say. "What happened to your parents?"

"I don't know. The story is my mom left me in the vestibule of a church. No one knew who she was. So, obviously, no one knows who my dad is either." She caught his gaze. "Everybody thought I'd be adopted...since I was only about six weeks when I was dropped. But somehow or another I fell through the cracks."

He almost cursed. Her story should have saddened him; instead he was angry. He knew the pain of being abandoned if only because he'd watched Lacy live through it. But Lacy had him and Mrs. Pomeroy. Ellie had had no one. Everybody had let her down.

Again, the intense urge to protect her rose up in him. But he squelched it. She didn't want protecting. She wanted normalcy. And, for them, normalcy was acting on the sexual attraction that pulsed between them. If he really wanted to do the right thing for her, he would create such a wonderful future for her that she'd never again think about the past.

That almost caused him to drop his fork. Already he was thinking about a future with her. He wasn't sure if they were right for each other. But he did know it felt right. He absolutely couldn't say that he loved her. But he did know he was falling.

Still, it all hinged on her and he couldn't rush her. This had to be done on her timetable. Unless she told him she wanted a future with him, he couldn't make assumptions.

He finished his dinner and helped her clear the kitchen. When she turned to go up the stairs, he debated walking with her. He was bone tired and ready for bed, but he didn't want to scare her or push her.

At the same time, he needed to behave normally and he was tired. He should be on his way to bed. Maybe the thing to do would be stop overthinking and simply do what came naturally?

"I'm coming too."

They walked up the stairs together silently. At the top of the steps, instead of opening her door, or even grabbing the knob, Ellie simply stopped.

Mac froze. Was this the sign he kept looking for from her? She'd obviously waited up for him…but she could have waited up to fulfill her responsibility as his maid by warming his dinner. Even her talking to him while he ate could be ascribed to her only wanting to do her job by needing to wait to clean up the kitchen after he was done eating.

Damn. He had forgotten how nerve-racking dating could be.

She pulled in a breath. Mac struggled not to watch her chest rise and fall with it.

"So, I'll see you in the morning."

"Yeah."

She put her hand on the knob, turned it slowly, but still didn't make any move to go inside.

But just when Mac got the courage to take a step toward her, she turned and disappeared behind the door.

Damn it. This was not going to be easy.

"Maybe he doesn't like me?"

Ava laughed. "Just because he didn't kiss you good-night?"

"The mood was set. The time was right. Yet he backed away."

Ava harrumphed as she rose from the table and gathered the papers Ellie had just signed. "He's a wealthy man, potentially falling in love with his maid…plus, he had a fairly crappy marriage. You don't think he has a right to be cautious?"

Ellie grimaced. "I see your point."

"Or maybe he's waiting for you?"

"For me? For me to what?"

"For you to kiss him this time."

"Oh, no. No. No. No. I have to be sure this is what he wants and the only way I know that is if he makes all the moves."

"Well, he's been burned once. So he wouldn't want to enter into a relationship that he wasn't at least reasonably sure of. Plus, you're the help. Technically, you're a sexual harassment suit waiting to happen." She headed for the butler's panty. "You can't just come right out and say, 'I won't sue you if you kiss me,' but I'm guessing you're going to have to give him some kind of sign."

With that Ava opened the garage door. She said, "See you tomorrow," and was gone.

Ellie sat at the table pondering what Ava had said. She'd already realized she'd have to give him some kind of sign. But kiss him? That was too scary for her to contemplate. What would she do? Stand on her tiptoes and just press her lips to his? That would take so long that he'd realize her intention and have time enough to back away if she'd read this whole situation wrong.

Oh, God! That would be so embarrassing!

She wouldn't risk it.

She had to think of a way to get her point across without actually saying or doing anything.

Yeah. Like that would be possible!

Still, she was a creative woman. Surely, she could think of a way to say, "I think I'm falling in love with you" without actually saying those very words.

Perusing the cookbook Ava had given her, she found a recipe for lemon garlic chicken and remembered how much he'd liked the roast beef. He hadn't kissed her after the roast beef, but they had had their most personal conversation as he'd eaten it. So maybe the way to a man's heart really was his stomach?

She cooked the chicken and almost made mashed potatoes, thinking she would go with her strong suit, but in the end decided that would be too obvious.

Of course, she also knew she was going to have to be somewhat obvious or he wouldn't get the message. She found candles and a lace tablecloth for the dining room table, but when she dimmed the lights and lit the candles, the scene was so romantic that she knew it would be weird with Lacy also sitting at the table.

Not exactly the right time for seduction.

She blew out the candles and carried them back into the kitchen so Mac wouldn't see them and wonder why they were on the table but not lit.

He arrived right on time, kissed the kids, changed his clothes and was at the table with Lacy the way he usually was a few minutes after six. Without waiting for an invitation, Ellie sat down at the place she'd set for herself across from Mac at the far end of the long table. They had a pleasant conversation with Lacy, who sat between them on the right.

But the very second Mac finished his chicken, he bounced from his seat, explaining that he had a conference call, and ducked out of helping with clean up.

Which, technically, was his right as boss.

She sighed and instructed Lacy to grab the napkins while she got the dishes. She and Mac's six-year-old daughter cleared the dining room and played Yahtzee while the dishwasher ran.

She got both Lacy and Henry ready for bed with no sign of Mac, then retired to her own room to come up with Plan B.

Unfortunately, she fell asleep before a Plan B could form. So she decided to stick with the one thing she knew consistently got Mac's attention. Food. Once again using a recipe she found in Ava's cookbook, she baked homemade muffins for breakfast. Lacy thought she'd died and gone to heaven. Mac, however, raced into the kitchen, telling Ellie and Lacy that he had another early-morning meeting and was out the door without even as much as a whiff of a muffin.

Disappointed, Ellie dropped to one of the kitchen chairs. The only explanation was that she'd totally misinterpreted everything. Obviously, Mac liked having a casual relationship with her. He wanted her to eat with them. He wanted the kids to be comfortable with her at the table.

But everything else must have been Ellie's imagination.

What about that kiss?

It hadn't been a kiss. It had been a brush. An accident. An accident.

And she had better let it go!

As was their custom, after breakfast, Ellie and Lacy put Henry down for a nap, then they changed into swimsuits and went to the pool. She and Lacy played for an hour then Lacy set up a tea party in the grass for her stuffed animals and dolls while Ellie stretched out on a chaise lounge to enjoy the sun.

Twenty minutes later, the sound of Mac's car roaring up the driveway interrupted their quiet morning. She sat up on the chaise as Lacy rose from her gathering of stuffed animals.

Mac appeared around the side of the house. "Hey, kitten," he said to Lacy.

"Hey, Daddy."

He turned his attention to Ellie. His mouth opened as if he were about to say hello, but his gaze fell to her swimsuit and whatever he was about to say was apparently forgotten.

He wasn't the first man to notice her figure, especially in the royal blue bikini, but he was the man she wanted to notice. And right now he was noticing.

Hope swelled inside her. Maybe the kiss hadn't been an accident?

"I forgot my briefcase."

He said the words, but he didn't make a move to go into the house and get the darned thing. Instead, he stood staring at her.

All right. She didn't need intuition to tell her he was attracted to her. But she'd known that. They'd been attracted since the day they'd met. What she wanted from him was for him to act on that attraction as he'd said he wanted to the night in the gazebo.

Of course, she really couldn't expect him to kiss her in front of his daughter.

She rose from the chaise and slipped into her white lace cover-up. With one hand on Lacy's shoulder, she guided all three of them up the steps.

Needing to get his attention and the conversation back to a safe place for Lacy's sake, she said, "You also left without breakfast."

They reached the French door and Mac opened it, allowing Ellie and Lacy to enter before him.

"I made muffins."

He stopped three steps into the kitchen. "Homemade muffins?"

She laughed. "Don't get too crazy with appreciation. The recipe was really simple."

"Can I take one with me? I really didn't have time for this trip. But I—I—really needed my briefcase."

She frowned, almost asked him why he hadn't sent someone to get his briefcase and suddenly understood.

He'd left so quickly that morning he hadn't had time to interact with either his kids or her. So he'd made an excuse to come home again.

It was the sweetest thing she'd ever seen a man do. Though she wouldn't press him to admit it, she did decide he deserved a reward.

"Sure. I'll wrap one for you while you get your briefcase."

Lacy hooked her arms around Mac's leg, proof that she had been missing him as Mac obviously suspected. He glanced down at her. "Maybe I can take five minutes to eat a muffin." He peeked over at Ellie. "Sit with us while I do?"

"Sure."

She set several muffins on a plate and took it to the table with three dessert dishes. Mac hoisted Lacy to a chair. He took his seat at the head of the table and smiled at Ellie as she took her seat opposite him.

Ellie's world righted again. And suddenly Plan B became abundantly clear.

Mac walked down the back stairs after tucking Lacy into bed that night. Ellie had kissed her good-night and scampered out of the room fairly quickly, so he wondered if there was something wrong. He wasn't surprised to find a note from her on the table in the kitchen, telling him that she needed to talk with him.

The fact that she asked to meet him in the gazebo was a bit puzzling, but not that she wanted to talk. He'd sensed for days that something was bothering her. He'd waited and waited and waited for a sign from her that she'd been okay with him kissing her. But though she'd eaten meals with him and the kids, other times she'd actually been more distant.

Walking down the stairs and past the pool to the grass, he racked his brain trying to think if he'd said something wrong, or even something too suggestive. But he couldn't think of anything.

Which was why he didn't notice that the gazebo was dark until he reached it. He climbed the two steps into the little room and saw the space was illuminated by only a few thin candles. Ellie stood behind the wet bar. Wearing a long dress made of material so insubstantial it basically floated around her, she walked out from behind the bar and handed him a glass of Scotch.

"Glenfiddich," she said, naming his favorite brand.

"How did you know?"

"The article when you were bachelor of the month is archived on the Single Girl Magazine Web site." She stepped close and smiled at him. "I like to be prepared."

So did he, and tonight he felt at a distinct disadvantage. Not only had she done a little research so she'd know his favorite drink, but also she wore the magnificent flowing dress, created, he was sure, to send a man's temperature into triple digits.

He caught her gaze. Was this the sign he'd been waiting for? "I'm underdressed."

"You're fine."

"You said you wanted to talk?"

"Yes." She turned away and walked to the far side of the gazebo. "You kissed me the other night."

Oh, God. This wasn't a sign. She was leaving. She might be dressed like a temptress, but she was such an innocent about some things she probably didn't realize the dress was seductive. She'd called him here for privacy so she could tell him she was leaving without the kids overhearing. The drink had been to soften the blow.

"And since then we've had a sort of different relationship."

"But not a bad one." He wasn't letting her go without a fight. The kids loved her. His feelings for her were growing with leaps and bounds. His gut was telling him they could have something wonderful. He'd be a fool to just let her quit.

She turned on a bubbly laugh. "I know. I've been very happy these past few days, being a part of things."

"Then why are you leaving?"

"Leaving?" She took a few steps toward him. "I'm not leaving."

"Then why are we here? Why are you softening me up with liquor?"

"Because I'm nervous and I wanted a way to give myself a little time before I told you…" She sucked in a long breath.

Mac stood staring at her, his muscles tight with the tension of anticipation, his breathing barely discernable.

"I trust you."

Another man probably would have wanted to hear something like "because I'm attracted to you." Or "I can't resist you." But Mac knew having Ellie say she trusted him was damned near a declaration of love.

He took two steps toward her. "Really?"

"I know that sounds silly."

He took another two steps, set his drink on the plastic table in the center of the gazebo. "No. You've told me you had a difficult life. But I've had a bad marriage. Trust is very important to both of us."

She took two steps toward him. "I think we want the same things."

"A home. Happy kids." He took another two steps. "Plus, we're attracted."

She laughed. "Yeah. There is that." The final two steps she took put her directly in front of him. His hands slid around her waist as hers slid around his neck.

This time when their lips met there was nothing tentative about the kiss. His mouth slanted against hers with the force of all the pent up sexual frustration he'd been feeling since she walked into his life. Arousal hit him in a dizzying wave of hunger for her. The need was so strong, so intense, he forced himself to pull back a bit, to gentle the press of his mouth on hers. But he wanted her. There was no denying that he wanted her. And, because the need was so strong and so sharp, not for the first time he worried that it was manipulating his common sense. He'd rushed things with Pamela and had been so wrong. Now he was rushing with Ellie. The only way this would work would be if they could take it slow.

Reluctantly, he pulled away completely.

She smiled at him. "Wow."

"Yeah, wow."

"We better watch how many times we do that or we'll get ahead of ourselves."

He rubbed his hand across the back of his neck. "I was just thinking the same thing."

"So we better take things slowly."

He marveled at her. How had he ever found someone this beautiful and this sweet? And this much on his wave length? Did he actually deserve her?

"Okay."

She blew out the first of the three candles and said, "Walk me back to the house?" as she walked to the second and third.

When the gazebo was totally dark, she strolled over to him and he caught her hand. "Sure."

He was absolutely positive he was the happiest man in the world, even with the little voice in the back of his head insisting something was wrong. With both of them in agreement that they should take this slowly, he couldn't see anything wrong with what they were doing. Yet, the little voice kept insisting that he was forgetting something.

Something important.

CHAPTER TEN

MAC didn't exactly stop looking for a nanny, but he didn't feel the pressure to get one immediately. He and Ellie took care of his children, not as a maid and her boss, but more like parents. Each night after they put the kids to bed, they spent romantic evenings in the gazebo or the pool, almost as if they were dating. Then he would kiss her good-night at her bedroom door.

Without any more discussion than the one they'd had in the gazebo, they took everything slowly. Kisses had grown into passionate interludes that didn't go beyond a certain point because he didn't want to rush her. He didn't want to be rushed. And the little voice that insisted there was something important about this relationship dimmed until it was gone.

June quickly became July. Newlyweds Cain and Liz came home. Mac didn't know how Ellie explained her work situation to her boss, but she had to have said something because Ellie continued to work for him and Ava stopped dropping by with Happy Maids sheets to be signed.

After the one trip to the mall, Ellie stopped trying to get Mac to loosen the reins on his security. Mac suspected she hadn't mentioned it again because she enjoyed being in their own little world, alone with only each other for company for the past few weeks while they explored their budding relationship. But one Thursday night in mid-July, Ellie suggested that they invite Cain and Liz for dinner the following night.

At first Mac balked at the idea of bringing strangers into his home when Phil and his crew wouldn't have enough time to investigate them. But with everything going so well for him and Ellie personally, he decided maybe she was right. He didn't want to live in a prison. He didn't want his kids living in a prison and most of all he didn't want to put Ellie in another prison.

That was the "thing he was forgetting" that had been nagging at him about starting a relationship with Ellie. She'd lived in a prison once. He couldn't put her in another. He had to get over his fears, and work himself and his family into the real world. Which meant he couldn't investigate every single person who came into his home. Trusting Ellie's word that Liz and Cain Nestor were good people had to be enough.

So he told her yes, she should invite the Nestors, and the next day he arrived home to a happy Lacy and Henry sitting in the gazebo while Ellie prepared the place for a barbeque.

"You have twenty minutes to get changed into shorts and a T-shirt," she said after placing a smacking kiss on his lips.

"So this dinner is informal?"

"Yes. I didn't want to exclude the kids. Though Ava is coming over at seven to read to them before putting them into bed, I want them to eat with us."

He loved that she thought of his kids. Not as a maid, not even as a nanny, but as someone who loved them. "Ava doesn't mind?"

Ellie laughed merrily. "Are you kidding? She misses the kids now that she doesn't have to come over every day."

The thought that an outsider, someone who didn't have to like his kids, was eager to babysit filled his heart with emotion he couldn't even describe it. Something was happening to him. Something significant. And it was all wrapped up in having Ellie in his life.

The Nestors arrived. Cain in khakis and a golf shirt and pretty brunette Liz in shorts and a T-shirt. Mac recognized Cain from a few casual meetings they'd had at parties and charitable events. Ellie and Liz kept the conversation lively through dinner and after they'd eaten barbequed ribs and scalloped potatoes, Ava arrived and shuttled the kids into the house. After an hour, Ava returned to the gazebo, baby monitor in hand, announcing the kids were both sleeping and Ellie volunteered to walk her to her car.

That was when Mac began to figure everything out. With another couple seated in the comfortable patio chairs in the seating arrangement of the gazebo, his children being cared for by a new friend, and a real relationship developing between him and a wonderful woman, Mac suddenly, unexpectedly, felt normal. He liked being able to trust. Especially Ellie. All this time he'd been working to help Ellie feel normal but he was the one who was changing, being introduced to a totally different way of life.

He glanced around his well-lit, but rather small property. This residence wasn't like the compound he and Pamela had lived in with his parents in Atlanta. This place was a home. Cain and Liz weren't like the stuffy society friends he'd rubbed elbows with his entire life. They were real people. Nice people. And Ellie wasn't anything like the women he typically dated. She was simply a happy, charming woman who enjoyed sharing his life. His life. His *real* life. Not a prison.

Swirling the Scotch in the glass in hand, Mac said, "So, Cain, I understand your company's been courting mine for about ten years."

As Mac expected he would, Cain laughed. "I wouldn't say ten years. Eight maybe."

Carrying the baby monitor, Ellie returned from the driveway.

"No talking business," she said, sitting beside Mac.

He unobtrusively took her hand. "All right. Ellie's right." He glanced at Cain again. "Call me this week."

Cain raised his glass as if in salute and said, "Will do."

Ellie bounced up from her seat. "Cain, it looks like you need another drink." She rounded the bar and lifted the bottle of vodka then frowned. "We're out of ice."

Mac rose. "I'll get it."

Ellie said, "Great," and busied herself behind the bar. She didn't seem to notice that Liz also rose and faced Mac.

"I'll help get the ice."

With his gaze locked with Liz's, Mac easily understood why she'd volunteered. She wanted to have a talk with him. He could have panicked, but his intentions toward Ellie were good. If Ellie's friend wanted to grill him or even just wanted a chance to talk to him privately, he could handle it.

He motioned toward the gazebo entrance. "After you."

They walked up the grassy backyard in silence. Mac suspected that Liz intended to get out of earshot before she said anything. When they reached the pool and she caught his forearm to get his attention, he wasn't surprised.

"Ellie's probably my favorite person in the world."

"Then we instantly agree on something."

"She's sweet and kind and would do anything for anybody."

"I know."

"And I'm going to be very angry if she gets hurt."

Mac laughed, leading her up the steps to the French doors. "I'm not going to hurt her." They reached the top, he opened the door for Liz and followed her inside his kitchen.

"Which means you know about her past?"

Mac pulled an ice bucket from the cabinet. "Bits and pieces."

"Has she told you about Sam?"

He headed for the refrigerator. "Some."

"But not everything?"

"Not yet."

Liz shook her head. "She really is taking this slowly."

Mac caught her gaze. "We both are."

"Okay."

Dumping two handfuls of ice into the bucket, Mac chuckled. "I take it I just got your blessing."

"Not even close. I don't know you. There's so little written about you that I'm not sure anybody knows you."

"Ellie's getting to know me."

"And that's what counts."

He gave her points for speaking her mind and also for being accepting when she didn't hear what she wanted to hear.

"But the thing is Sam really hurt her. She virtually went into hiding for a year after she…she…left him." Liz caught Mac's gaze. "She's too happy, too fun loving, too good with people to be afraid. If you hurt her, I will find you."

"I get it." There was nothing she could do to him, but he understood the sentiment. He loved that Ellie had good friends, strong relationships. It was part of what he wanted with her—part of what he loved about her.

He stopped halfway to the French door. Liz turned around and gave him a puzzled look. "What? Are we forgetting something?"

He rubbed his hand across the back of his neck. "No." He paused, dazed by the realization that he loved Ellie. He *loved* her.

He couldn't. Not that she wasn't wonderful. But he knew better. People who fell in love too fast made mistakes. He wanted to take this slowly. Hell, he'd just told Liz they were both taking it slowly. He *couldn't* love her.

Not yet.

He shook his head a bit to clear the haze then directed Liz toward the French door again. "I'm fine."

Ellie had known the minute she looked at Liz that she was pregnant. She knew it for certain when Liz turned down a glass of wine and asked for a cola with dinner. She hadn't mentioned it in the hope that Liz and Cain would make an announcement. But when they didn't, Ellie had a choice. Wait for Liz to tell her, or simply spill the beans.

The news was too exciting to try to hold back, and she also had to worry that she'd inadvertently let it slip to Ava one day, so she had to out them. When Liz and Mac returned with the bucket of ice, Ellie poured another round of drinks, including a soft drink for Liz.

As she passed the glasses around, she said, "I think I'd like to propose a toast."

Mac laughed. "Really?"

"Yes, to Cain and Liz and their new baby."

Ellie smiled, watching Cain's face fall comically, but Liz only shook her head. "Does anybody ever hide anything from you, Miss Magic?"

Taking her glass of wine to her seat beside Mac, Ellie laughed, but she didn't sit. Mac rose and so did Cain and Liz.

"To your new baby."

"To our baby," Liz and Cain agreed.

"So this is your first child?" Mac asked as they all took their seats.

"Actually, we were married before and had a miscarriage," Liz said quietly.

Before Ellie could come to his rescue, Mac said, "Oh, I'm sorry."

"It's okay," Liz said.

"We had an odd first marriage," Cain said, taking Liz's hand. "My brother died three weeks after we eloped. And for three years after that I was difficult to live with."

"But that's our past," Liz said, smiling at Cain. "And we focus on the future now."

"Having a child is a good way to get yourself in the moment," Mac said.

Knowing a discussion of kids could potentially turn on Mac, and that the last thing he'd want to explain was his situation with his ex-wife and their children, Ellie quickly said, "So, did you ever get the boat you were looking at, Cain?"

Cain launched into a discussion of a new sixty-footer he'd bought right after they returned from Paris, and Mac was more than happy to join in. They shifted from boats to fishing and from fishing to professional football and after an hour Liz yawned.

Cain was on his feet immediately. "You're ready for bed, aren't you?"

"I'm fine."

Understanding Cain's concerns and feeling them herself because of Liz's prior miscarriage, Ellie rose, too. "You're sleepy!"

As Cain pulled Liz to her feet, she yawned again. "I guess I am a bit tired."

"Then we'll say good-night," Cain said to both Ellie and Mac.

Mac said, "We'll walk you to your car."

They strolled up the yard, past the moonlight-dappled pool and to the driveway.

At Cain's car, Mac held out his hand to shake Cain's. "It was nice having you here. Call my direct number on Monday and arrange a lunch with my secretary."

"Thanks, but you know we didn't come here to finagle some business. We wanted to meet the guy who's finally winning Ellie's heart."

Liz slapped Cain's upper arm. "Cain!"

He winced. "Sorry. Was I not supposed to notice that they're living together?"

Liz groaned.

Ellie laughed. "We're not living together, living together. We just happen to live in the same house."

Cain raised his hands defensively. "Sorry. My bad."

The Nestors got into their Porsche. Liz waved goodbye. Cain tooted the horn once and drove out into the starry night.

Ellie stood on the driveway, watching them leave. Before she had a chance to think too much about how seeing Liz reminded her that she was abandoning the life she loved, Mac turned her around, led her into the house and followed her up the steps. When they reached her bedroom door, he walked up behind her, put his arms around her waist and kissed her neck. "We could be living together, living together, if you wanted to."

His smooth lips tickled her neck, but his eagerness to get her into bed tickled her even more. Oh, she was so tempted.

She turned in his arms and he kissed her. This time there was something different in his kiss. This time he didn't start slow and build them to a place where the only thing that existed was each other. This time, his mouth met hers greedily, and, oh, she desperately wanted to simply fall into the kiss. Lose herself in him. Lose herself in the people they were becoming, the life they were creating.

His hands roamed her back, down her bottom and up to her waist again. He seemed restless, hungry, as if only she could fill a void in his life and he was tired of waiting. She kissed him back, letting him know with her kiss that she felt the same way. But in the last second when she would have totally succumbed to the power of need, Mac pulled back.

He stared into her eyes for several seconds then he took a long breath and set her away from him.

"It's still too soon."

She nodded reluctantly. "I think so."

With that she quickly slipped behind her bedroom door. She wanted this so much and so did he that she knew they could very easily make a mistake.

It was better to wait.

Though it got harder and harder to leave Ellie at her bedroom door, the following Monday night Mac counted his blessings as he walked to his suite. It was good to live such a free life. His kids were happy. He was happy. Ellie was happy. They were being cautious, smart. Everything was good.

He wasn't even as concerned about the release of his ex-wife's picture as he had been. The plan was in place. He and the kids weren't at the family compound in Atlanta. They weren't exactly "hiding" but no one really knew where they were. Plus, he had discreet bodyguards and a state-of-the-art security system. He could give Ellie the reasonably normal life she wanted and have a reasonably normal life himself.

That part was perfect.

The only possible hitch was Pamela herself. Tonight she had her first interview scheduled to promote her movie on a late-night talk show. If she focused on her project, Mac, Ellie and the kids would breeze into the next phase of their lives. If she badmouthed him, gave the kids' names or worse held up their pictures on national television, then there would be trouble.

But he couldn't see any reason she'd bring up the kids. She had a movie to promote. Plus, she was trying to get back on track as a Hollywood sex symbol. Kids shouldn't even come up in her conversations.

He entered his suite and slumped into one of the white leather chairs in front of the big-screen TV. He didn't want to have to watch this. Phil had actually volunteered to view the show to see what Pamela would say, but Mac couldn't leave this to Phil. Yes, Phil knew the whole story. But Mac knew Pamela. He could spot one of her lead-ins to trouble a mile away.

He sat through fifteen minutes of monologue and a guest who'd wowed the world with a YouTube video and finally it came time for Pamela.

The host introduced her and she popped from behind a curtain, making her entrance funny. Her long sandy-brown hair swayed around her short sparkly black dress. Mac settled into the chair with a sigh. Ellie ran rings around Pamela any day of the week. He wouldn't deny that his ex-wife was beautiful, but even the way she mugged for the camera so clearly showed that deep down she was an actress, always working the room, always vying for everyone's attention. If she'd ever loved him, it had been only for what he could do for her. He had been a fool for not seeing it.

"So, you have a movie out?" the host said, leading Pam into the discussion that had gotten her onto the very popular show.

"Yes." Her face lit with excitement. "It's a story of a woman who gets involved with a charming man who seems perfect for her. But he's really a serial killer."

Pam again mugged for the camera. Mac rolled his eyes. Phil was right. He didn't need to watch this.

They talked for a few more minutes about the movie. Mac leaned an elbow on the arm of the white leather chair and propped up his head, enduring the inane chitchat.

He was just about to turn off the TV and go to bed when the talk show host said, "I understand you're divorced now."

Mac sat at attention as Pamela's pretty blue eyes drooped with sadness.

"Yes."

"Want to talk about that?"

She pulled in a breath as if considering it, and Mac said a silent prayer that she'd say no. She was on the show to talk about her movie, but Mac knew there was another side to fame. Part of getting people to go to her movies was getting people to like her. He couldn't see how she'd spin their divorce in her favor. The smart thing for her to do would be to simply avoid the topic. Or say something about being back on the market, looking for fun. She was, after all, supposed to be a sex symbol. She shouldn't want to talk about her failure.

He leaned forward, held his breath, said a prayer that she'd simply say no. *Say no. I don't want to talk about my divorce.*

"I loved my husband…"

He slumped back in his chair. *Yeah, right.*

"But sometimes things don't work out."

"Hey, look who you're talking to," the host said, pointing at his chest. "Divorced three times."

Her face fell into sympathetic lines. "Then you know the drill."

"Honey, I invented the drill."

The audience laughed.

Mac breathed a sigh of relief. This really was going okay.

"But I had no kids," the host said, "I understand there was an issue with yours."

Mac's face fell. An issue? What the hell was that supposed to mean?

Pam sat back, laid her hands demurely on her lap and looked for all the world like somebody who didn't want to talk about it. But Mac was familiar with this pose. This was her bid for sympathy pose.

Once again, he leaned forward and prepared himself for the worst.

Pam sighed. "I don't really like to talk about this."

Huh! He was right. She damn well better not want to talk about this. How could she spin giving up her own kids?

"But I don't have the kids." She glanced down at her hands again.

Mac stared at the screen. She was admitting she didn't have the kids?

"I was shocked when my husband took them from me."

What?

Damn her!

Memories of other lies, other deceit came tumbling back, suffocating him. Years of living with her selfishness, years of watching her ignore Lacy, years of feeling like a fool for falling for her so hard, so fast, years of regretting that he'd married her so quickly, all flashed in his head.

He grabbed his cell phone from his jeans pocket, and almost pushed the number for Phil until he realized he had nothing to say. This wasn't a security issue. This was a truth issue. He couldn't do a damned thing about her lie beyond suing her for slander, which would accomplish nothing.

"That is sad," the host said, bringing Mac's attention back to the TV.

"Yes, but I don't want to talk about it."

The host changed the subject and Mac sat back in his chair again, trying to calm himself down, trying to think logically.

All right. So she'd lied. She'd lied before. To him. To his face. At least this time he understood. She'd lied to protect her reputation. It would be foolish to try to do anything about it. Hell, it would be stupid to even get upset. He couldn't expect her to admit she'd walked out on her kids.

He sucked in a breath. He couldn't believe he hadn't seen her for what she was before he married her, but he'd been overwhelmed by her beauty. Almost the way he was being overwhelmed by Ellie's. He stopped his thoughts. There was no comparing Pam and Ellie. None. No way. No how. They were too different.

But *he* wasn't. He was the same guy. Prone to the same mistakes. No matter how slowly he thought he was going with Ellie, as Cain had said, they were living together. Already joining their lives. She'd given up the job she loved. He was letting her into his kids' lives.

What if he was making another mistake?

On a growl, he stopped that train of thought too, turned off the TV and went to his room, focusing on Pam, her deceit. The fallout from this might be a few questions from his friends. His parents might want him to sue her for slander. But he could handle them. His kids were safe. Hell, *he* was safe. She hadn't even used his name.

Life could go on.

And what a good life it might turn out to be.

Ellie liked him. She trusted him.

He trusted her.

The next morning he woke late and raced around to get dressed. Because of a board meeting, he barely had time for a cup of coffee, but when he walked into the kitchen and saw Ellie at the table sitting beside Lacy and feeding Henry, his heart turned over in his chest.

It seemed as if his entire world had righted itself the night before. His ex-wife, though she'd lied, hadn't done the damage she could have done. And the woman he was coming to adore was in his kitchen, smiling at him.

"Good morning."

Her voice was soft, sexy, and everything inside of Mac responded. He never thought he'd see the day when he'd really be free. It wasn't so much the worry of Pam and what she might do, but his own internal fears that had kept him trapped, but Ellie had opened the doors of his heart. She made him feel young, rational, handsome and worthy of love. After the number Pamela had done on him, he almost couldn't believe it.

He walked over to the table and bent down and kissed her. On the mouth, in front of the kids. Lacy giggled. But Mac's heart rate tripled, his pulse scrambled and everything inside him turned to gold.

When he pulled away, Ellie smiled up at him. "Now, that's a good morning."

Lacy laughed in earnest. "Daddy's Ellie's prince."

He held her gaze. He hoped he was her prince. Though she liked him and he liked her, there was so much they hadn't talked about. So much to get to know about each other.

But instead of being afraid, he was excited. Getting to know her would be wonderful.

He pulled away at the same time that his cell phone rang and the roar of cars bounding up his driveway filled the kitchen. He glanced at Ellie, whose eyes had gone round with confusion.

He grabbed his cell phone, saw it was Phil. "What's up?"

"Is everyone in the house?"

"We're all in the kitchen."

"Stay there. We're coming in."

"What's going on?"

"Just stay there. I'm two steps away from the garage."

Phil burst into the butler's pantry and was in the kitchen in seconds. He adjusted a microphone at his mouth. "All clear in the kitchen."

"Did we have a threat?"

Phil held up a hand as he apparently listened to someone speaking through the headset.

Lacy grabbed Mac's leg. Henry began to cry. Ellie jumped up and lifted him from the highchair.

Phil blew his breath out on a sigh. "I got the all clear from the guys outside, but you're all going to have to come outside while they search the rest of the house. Then I'm afraid you're going to have to leave."

Mac's face turned to stone. "Leave?"

"You got an e-mail threat this morning."

"What kind of threat?"

Phil glanced at Ellie and the kids just as one of Phil's top guys, Tom Zunich, stepped into the kitchen. "How about if we talk after Tom takes Ellie and the kids outside to one of our vans?"

Mac turned to Ellie. He knew Phil wouldn't ask him to leave the house if the threat to his life wasn't viable. He was keeping fury and terror at bay by only the barest thread. He needed to talk to Phil to sort this out and Phil was right: he didn't want Ellie and the kids to hear.

"Can you go with Tom?"

She didn't even hesitate. Holding his gaze, letting him know that the words of trust she'd spoken still held, she said, "Sure." She tugged Lacy's hand off Mac's leg. "Come on, sweetie."

Phil and Mac followed Tom and Ellie out of the house. But Tom led Ellie and the kids to a van, while Phil and Mac walked toward the grass.

The second Ellie and the kids were out of earshot, Mac spun on Phil. "What the hell is going on?"

"Did you watch your ex on TV last night?"

"Yes. She lied about the kids, but other than that I didn't hear anything worth worrying about."

"Her lie might have seemed small to you but one of her crazed fans doesn't like the fact that you took her children from her. The e-mail to your private account was very explicit. There will be a bomb. We don't know if it'll be in your house, your car or at Carmichael Incorporated headquarters, but she was serious."

Mac stifled a groan. "Pam didn't even mention my name. How the hell did somebody get to me so quickly?"

"It was common knowledge that your ex was married to you during the time she wasn't making movies. We don't know that the e-mailer found *this* house, but your corporate headquarters and family home are well-known. Plus, the skill level of this person is a variable. A really good hacker can find all of your family's properties."

"But Pam *lied*. She only said that I took the kids to protect her image."

"Yeah, well, she protected it so well that lots of people are standing up for her. You're a hot topic on Twitter. Her Facebook page has gone down twice from too many hits. Her fans are on her side. She was America's sweetheart and you took her kids."

He rubbed his hand across his forehead.

"And one of them was crazy enough to take action." Phil caught Mac's arm, making sure he had his undivided attention. "As a precaution, you can't take any of your cars. You can't go to any of your homes. You're going to have to check into a hotel until our bomb squad can sweep everything." He pulled his BlackBerry out of his jacket pocket. "I've taken the liberty of booking the penthouse suite for you at a hotel in Miami."

Mac smiled ruefully. "You're not going to tell me the name of the hotel?"

"Not until we get there."

The penthouse suite turned out to be the most beautiful place Ellie had ever seen. Green club chairs sat in front of a fireplace with a mahogany mantle trimmed in gold.

Gold and burgundy accent pillows dotted a sofa beside the chairs. An armoire hid a flat-screen TV. A mahogany dining room table was set up just beyond the seating arrangement. A kitchen sat behind that.

Gold trimmed mahogany doors led to three bedrooms. Heavy burgundy drapes on the wall of windows in the main seating area were open to reveal a breathtaking view of the ocean and a tropical storm that was moving in. The waves roared below them, reminding Ellie of Mac's mood.

After they put the children down for a nap, she sat beside him on the sofa.

She took his hand and said, "This too shall pass."

He snorted a laugh, bounced from the sofa and paced to the window. "Really?"

"I have some experience dealing with really bad exes."

He turned and faced her. "Don't tell me…from the A Friend Indeed people."

"And my own experience."

That seemed to stop him cold. He said nothing, merely waited.

She blew out a breath. "I lived with a guy named Sam who seemed like the most wonderful guy in the world until about three weeks after I moved in with him."

Mac took two steps toward the sofa. "Then?"

"Then he became verbally abusive." She shrugged. "At first I blamed it on bad days. Everybody has them. He was a small-business owner." She glanced up at Mac. "He owned four pizza places and sometimes they struggled. Plus, he wasn't as bad as one of the foster parents I'd had. So I figured I could deal with it."

Talking about it resurrected the fear she'd lived for three long years. It crawled along her spine like a living thing. She sucked in a deep breath, blew it out slowly.

"I was a homeless clerk in one of his shops. I didn't have any money. So when we began living together, I didn't bring anything to the table for him. Technically, I was another expense. He lived and died by the sales in each shop every week. His financial future was always on the line."

Mac dropped to one of the club chairs, put his elbow on the arm and his chin on his fist. His own troubles seemingly forgotten, he caught her gaze. "That's one of the risks of owning your own business."

"I know that now. But back then I was eighteen. I saw him as a knight in shining armor, facing battles every day that provided me with a home." She squeezed her eyes shut. "I believed a little too much in fairy tales."

"You were still a kid."

She met his gaze. "I was never a kid."

He shook his head sadly. "I know."

"Anyway, one day about twenty minutes before he should have come home from work, I had this really strong sense that I should toss all my clothes into a suitcase and run."

"The intuition that makes you Magic?"

She smiled ruefully. "Except I didn't run. I couldn't imagine why suddenly that day the intuition that kept telling me to stay, that he was providing me with a place that kept me warm and dry and I needed him, was now telling me to go. I thought I was just being weird."

She swallowed hard and suddenly felt as if she couldn't finish. Fear roamed through her, taking up residence in her stuttering heart, as memories tripped over themselves in her brain.

Mac quietly said, "So what happened?"

"He came home with a gun."

Mac sat up. "What?"

"He came home with a gun. Before I could run he caught my wrist and wouldn't let me go. He yanked me close and put the gun to my head and told me he was going to kill me then kill himself." She shook her head. "He was so out of it, talking about killing us in this romantic way that scared me so much I started to cry."

"My God."

"Crying saved me. It annoyed him and he shoved me away from him. He raised the gun and pointed it at me and I turned and ran. The first shot missed me. The second shot hit the door as it closed behind me." She peeked at Mac. "The rest is sort of a blur."

"I'm sorry."

"Yeah. I was sorry too. Sorry I didn't recognize the signs. Sorry I didn't try to get help…for both of us."

"It wasn't your fault."

She knew that. And, actually, telling Mac the story seemed to allow that truth to penetrate. It was as if telling him had resurrected the ghosts that haunted her, deconstructed them and took away their power to hurt her. She felt distanced from the story. She knew it had happened to her, but it didn't define her anymore. In fact, she felt so beyond that part of her life that she knew she had to tell him the rest.

"The worst part is when it's over. Wondering where he is, what he's doing… Whether or not he's going to find you."

Mac's fury with his ex-wife morphed into fury with Ellie's ex boyfriend. Now he understood why Liz Nestor had wanted to talk with him privately, why she wanted to be sure Mac wouldn't hurt Ellie. She'd been hurt enough already.

"Tell me more about what came after."

"About running and hiding? Living with Liz, fearing that I was dragging her into my mess? Only being able to clean houses of people who were out of town because I was so afraid I'd run into someone who remembered me from a pizza shop." She combed her fingers through her hair and rose from the sofa, walked to the wall of windows. "I was a mess."

"How long did it last?"

"Almost a year, then Liz talked me into coming on one of her assignments for A Friend Indeed. Sharing stories with the other women really helped me snap out of a lot of it." She stared out at the storm. Foamy white waves hit the shore. "But I still wouldn't risk running into anyone in any of the houses I cleaned." She faced Mac with a sad smile. "Liz was very patient."

"Liz is a good friend."

"I know."

"So it's really only been a little over a year or so that you've been out in the world?"

"Almost two." She caught his gaze. "I'm not proud of that."

"You shouldn't be ashamed either." Mac thought of himself, about how hard it had been to get over his anger with Pamela, and realized it had probably been a hundred times harder for Ellie to get over her past. Yet, here he was, dragging her into another relationship. Maybe one even more dangerous.

"You had a right to take all the time you needed to heal."

The penthouse elevator bell rang and the sound of footsteps on the marble foyer floor echoed into the living room. Mac tensed until Phil stepped into the room. "We're getting all clear messages from all of your properties. But I still don't feel comfortable with you going home."

"We're fine here until you say the word."

"And I also think it's time to discuss your new casual attitude," Phil added, glancing meaningfully at Ellie.

She blanched. "I wouldn't ever ask him to do something foolish! To take a risk with his kids!"

"No, but you don't seem to get it. The people who pursue people like Mac are nuts. They can conjure a vendetta out of a simple slight. Real or imagined."

"That's enough, Phil."

"I'm just saying—"

"We get it," Mac said, dismissing him.

With a shake of his head, Phil turned back to the foyer. Within seconds the sound of the elevator bell rippled through the room.

Mac turned to Ellie. "He's right, you know."

"Not always."

"No, but there is no foolproof way to tell when a threat is viable unless you investigate it and that means you can't go to the mall, pretending nothing's wrong. We get threats regularly. Just because of who we are. Now my wife's fans are adding trouble to the mix. Plus, there's all our foreign dealings. We're a target simply because we're global."

Ellie swallowed. "I understand."

He squeezed his eyes shut. "No. I don't think you do." His eyes popped open and he walked over to the wall of windows where she stood. The sea raged. Lightning lit the dark sky. Thunder rattled the windows. "This is my life."

He once again remembered the "something important" that had been nagging at him after the night she kissed him in the gazebo, the night he'd believed if they took this slowly they could make it work. His life was a prison and Ellie deserved better.

"I know."

With one finger on her chin, he tipped her face up until she met his eyes. "I can't change it."

With their gazes locked, she studied him for several seconds, but ultimately her eyes softened. "Okay."

"No, it's not okay." He shook his head. "You think you understand, but until you've lived it you can't understand and it's not right for me to ask you to live this way."

She stepped back. "What?"

"Ellie, you yourself just told me that you've only recently recovered from a really bad experience. My life is a potential smorgasbord of bad experiences. I won't put you through this. I won't steal your life again."

This time the fear that rose up in her was fresh, not remembered. She *loved* him. She knew the risks. She'd rather face them than spend the rest of her life without the one person she genuinely believed loved and understood her.

"I'm not a hothouse flower!"

"I never said you were. You're one of the strongest, smartest women I know. You're also the kindest. It would be selfish and wrong for me to keep you." He sucked in a breath, pulled his cell phone from his pocket and buzzed Phil.

"You may take Ms. Swanson to the Happy Maids' office. Put her into Liz Nestor's hands. Check out the situation to be sure it's safe and assign a bodyguard to her until this threat has passed."

Then he turned and left Ellie alone in the room to wait for Phil because he wasn't sure he was strong enough not to change his mind and beg her to stay.

CHAPTER ELEVEN

MAC and his children stayed at the hotel for an entire week. Mrs. Pomeroy was waiting at his house when they returned. She spent the night, but she wasn't a real nanny and Mac knew his time for procrastination had run out.

The next morning he strode off the elevator into his secluded office, carrying Henry in a baby carrier. Phil marched behind him, carrying Lacy.

"Ashley!"

His personal secretary appeared at the door. Five-nine, reed thin, with auburn hair and an ever present yellow pencil behind her ear, Ashley was a recent university graduate. "Yes, Mr. Carmichael—" She saw Lacy and Henry. "Oh."

"Has Mrs. Davis scheduled those nanny interviews today?"

Mac asked the question as the elevator opened on two of Phil's men. Wearing a dark suit, sunglasses and an ear bud communication device in his ear, Tom carried a playpen and Henry's diaper bag. Similarly dressed, Paul toted a bag of Lacy's toys.

Ashley watched as they set Mac's kids' things in the corner by his desk. Then she faced Mac with a smile. "You're going to have the nannies interact with the children."

He hadn't thought of that, but since they were here that was as good of an excuse as any for having his kids with him. "Yes. Are they scheduled?"

She glanced down at the calendar she held. "One for nine. One at ten-thirty. One at twelve." She closed the book. "Mrs. Davis gave you an hour and a half with each candidate."

Without removing his sunglasses, Tom quietly set up the playpen.

Lacy squirmed until Phil set her down on the floor. "Daddy, I want my doll."

He looked at Tom. "Doll?"

"In the car." He headed for the elevator. "I'm on my way."

Paul followed him. "We should have all the children's things up here in three or four trips, sir."

"That's fine."

Phil headed for the elevator too. "I'll help."

"Great." Mac looked at Ashley. "Have Mrs. Davis send the first candidate in when she arrives."

Ashley's cheeks turned pink. "It's a man."

"Great." Resisting the urge to squeeze his eyes shut, Mac instead reached for Lacy. After all, it didn't matter if it was a man or woman who cared for his kids as long as the candidate was competent.

Ashley raced out of the room. Mac lifted Lacy into his arms. "Tom will set up a place for you to play. You have to be quiet while daddy talks to nannies."

"I want Ellie."

Right.

He understood Lacy's feelings. He wanted Ellie too. Not because she was good with the kids, but because he missed her. He missed being normal. He missed having a real life. He missed having someone to talk to, someone who was interested in him as a person, not because he was rich. Someone who loved him.

Yeah, he wanted Ellie too. But he wasn't so selfish that he'd drag her into this life.

He walked Lacy to the small conference table in the back corner of his office. "I think this would be a great place for you to play."

"What about Henry?"

"He'll nap in the playpen."

As Mac said the last, Mrs. Davis, Mac's longtime administrative assistant, stepped into the room. Dressed impeccably in a navy blue suit, she led a short balding man into Mac's office. "This is James Collins."

Mac offered his hand for shaking. "Mr. Collins."

"Mr. Carmichael. I've heard so much about you."

Undoubtedly. Somehow or another the bomb threat had been leaked. Pamela played horrified actress, using the threat to get her face all over the papers. Mac had had no choice but to let her visit the kids, but he'd set the time and the place and his team had kept the press out. Her crazed fan had been arrested. And now life was going on.

Sort of. Without Ellie it was all kind of gray and lifeless.

Mac pointed toward his desk, indicating he and Collins should talk there. "You've heard so much about us, yet you still want to work for us?"

"Absolutely. In fact, I think I might be your best candidate. I've been in the Marines."

Mac took his seat behind the desk as Jim Collins sat on one of the chairs in front of the desk.

"You should know the children were madly in love with our last nanny."

"Can I ask why she left?"

He wanted to say no. He wanted to say he was afraid for her life, afraid that he'd ruin her life, afraid that he'd stifle her and she'd run…and hurt him a hundred times more than Pamela had. Instead, he glanced down at the résumé Mrs. Davis had surreptitiously set on his desk and said, "Personal reasons."

Ellie unlocked the door of the Happy Maids office and simply stood on the threshold for a good five minutes. Even though it had been a week, she couldn't believe she was here. It seemed surreal. At the oddest times memories would sneak up on her and stop her cold. A little over a week ago, she had been falling in love, mothering two wonderful children. Today she was alone again. Unwanted.

No, she thought, walking to the desk and tossing her purse into the bottom drawer on the right. Mac wanted her. He simply didn't trust her to be able to handle his life.

Tears filled her eyes and she cursed herself. Why was she crying? Hadn't she cried enough? Hadn't she learned a million times over that crying didn't help anything?

She sucked in a breath and stemmed her tears. She had learned that lesson. And she'd also learned that life went on.

She sat at the desk, confused about where to start, what to do. Oh, she loved this job, but it didn't feel like hers anymore. She almost called Ava then couldn't bring herself to do it. How would she explain? What would she say? Liz was home, working a very light schedule, dependent upon Ellie to keep things going, and by God she would.

She was stronger than anybody believed she was. She got over her fear when she left Sam. She'd get over the unbearable sadness of losing Mac.

Hopefully.

* * *

Jim Collins was a great guy and would probably make an outstanding nanny. He also came with the benefit of training in the security field. He'd been trained to handle kids in all the worst-case scenarios Mac envisioned. But the kids hadn't warmed to him. Oh, they liked him enough. Mac liked him. But something was missing.

Mac chalked it up to the fact that Jim was a professional bodyguard. And neither Mac nor his children could see past that. It was almost as if hiring Jim would be like saying they expected more trouble. Mac *did* anticipate trouble. But he also had Phil and his various teams. His hiring a nanny who was also a bodyguard would have driven Ellie crazy.

He told himself not to think about Ellie, to stop filtering his decisions through the question of what she'd do. Not only did he need to get over her, but also she had never once tried to contact him. Even Liz Nestor hadn't made good on her threat to "find" him if he hurt Ellie. So his only logical guess was Ellie was fine without him.

He thanked Jim for coming in and told him that they would get back to him.

The second interview went only slightly better than the first. Mrs. Regina Olson was a widow. She adored children, had raised three of her own, and needed the income. Only in her forties she expected to work until she was sixty-five and would have been blessedly pleased if she could work for the same family that entire time. Especially a family with two gorgeous children.

Unfortunately, she tweaked Lacy's cheeks and Lacy howled in pain. Mac knew Regina hadn't hurt Lacy, but Lacy had not appreciated the tweak. Panicked, Mrs. Olson insisted she hadn't tweaked that hard, but Lacy only cried all the more.

Ms. Nancy Turner was a tall blonde around Ellie's age. Lacy approached her carefully and stood by her chair while Mac tried to ask questions without calling attention to the fact that his six-year-old daughter was staring at her.

Finally, Mac said, "Lacy, come sit on Daddy's lap."

She walked around the desk slowly, backward, not taking her eyes off Nancy Turner.

"So you've been a nanny before?"

"I worked in New York City." She laughed lightly. "Last winter I decided I hated snow. *Really* hated snow," she emphasized, laughing again. "And here I am." She reached into her purse. "Mrs. Davis has my references, but here they are again."

She handed him a sheet with the names of two prominent Wall Street investors, both of whom were personal friends of Mac's. He could see why she'd wanted him to take special note of that.

"That's very good."

"Are you Ellie's sister?"

Nancy smiled at Lacy. "I don't have any sisters." Then she glanced at Mac. "Who is Ellie?"

"Ellie was our last nanny. You sort of look like her."

"I see."

"The children were quite fond of her."

"Of course." She gave Lacy a soft smile. "You can tell me all the things you liked about Ellie, all the things you liked to do with her and I'm sure we can do a lot of those things."

He tried to picture Nancy Turner with a sheet wrapped around her for a make-believe ball gown and couldn't. She looked enough like Ellie that she really could have been her sister. She also had a pleasant disposition, great references and seemed to genuinely like Lacy.

But there was something off. Something wrong.

Nancy unexpectedly rose. She extended her hand to shake Mac's. "I'm sorry, but I scheduled another interview for immediately after this one." She smiled engagingly. "Have to keep all my options open, you know."

Hoisting Lacy with him, Mac rose too. "Of course." He shifted Lacy to sit on his hip. "We'll call you when we've made a decision."

She smiled. "Thank you."

With that she turned and left. Lacy looked up at him and said, "What are options?"

"She wants to make sure she gets a job, so we're not the only people she's talking to."

Lacy simply said, "Oh," then scooted down and returned to the play area Phil had set up in the corner of his office.

Mac buzzed Mrs. Davis. She stepped into the room a few minutes later. "Hello, Lacy."

Lacy said, "Hello, Mrs. Davis."

Pride rose up in him at not just how polite Lacy was, but more than that how she was no longer shy, and Mac instantly remembered that he owed Ellie for that.

She'd told Lacy fairy tales, taught her to shop, told her the value of being good.

And he suddenly knew why none of the nannies had seemed right. None of them was Ellie.

But that was wrong. She didn't belong with them. She had a life. Mac had given it back to her. And she'd never tried to contact him. Not even through her friends. She hadn't really loved him. Didn't want him.

If it killed him to live without her, and it just might, he would.

Even if the next weeks were the hardest of his life, he would push through them.

* * *

The first Monday in September, Mac was at the end of his rope. Lacy was back to waking at four, but now she also refused breakfast. For some reason or another, today, she also didn't want lunch. At four, even knowing dinner wasn't until six, she refused a snack.

Mac had hired a fifty-something grandmother named Blanche to be the nanny. Though she wasn't Ellie, she was more than qualified to care for his kids. As Mac's phone rang, she stooped beside the table tempting Lacy with crackers.

"Please. We'll put cheese on them."

Mac extracted his ringing phone from his jean's pocket and barked, "Yes?"

"Mac?"

Hearing Phil's voice, Mac squeezed his eyes shut. He'd barked at the one person who consistently supported him. He had to get over losing Ellie or he'd alienate everybody in his world. "Sorry. What's up?"

"There's a van here. Woman inside says you told her she could have a picnic here with thirty of her friends. ID says she's Ava Munroe."

Mac's eyes popped open. "Oh, my gosh. What day is it?"

"Monday…Labor Day."

He groaned. "That's the A Friend Indeed group. I did tell them they could have a picnic here."

"Actually, I'm looking at the files in my laptop. You had me check them out a few months ago. And they all cleared. Every person on the guest list."

"And we haven't changed the list."

Mac heard Ava's unmistakable voice coming from somewhere near Phil and sucked in a breath.

"The only people I brought were those you cleared."

Every memory he had of Ava also included Ellie, and pain ricocheted through him. Weeks had passed and he was no closer to getting over her than he had been the day he asked her to leave.

Worse, today, the bomb threat that caused Mac to enact the protocols and procedures to keep him and his children safe seemed so far away. And nothing, absolutely nothing even slightly dangerous had happened in weeks. He and the kids were back to living in a prison and with thirty happy people sitting at his gate, thirty people about to have a picnic, oodles of kids who could potentially make his daughter happy, that prison suddenly seemed oh so unnecessary.

Still, he'd lost Ellie because of the danger in his world. Because he had to erect barriers. Because he couldn't be too careful. If he changed his mind now, if he loosened his restrictions, losing her would be for nothing.

"Tell Ava that I'm sorry. My staff should have called her and told her that with the new security procedures—"

"Give me that phone!"

Mac heard Ava's voice again. Two seconds later her voice, not Phil's, came through his cell phone. "Mac?"

"Hello, Ava."

"You cannot tell a woman with a vanload of kids that she can't use your pool. You promised."

"I know, but—"

"No buts! You *promised*. Besides, I miss your kids." Her voice softened. "Please? I'd love to see Lacy and Henry."

His gaze slid over to Lacy. She sat with her elbows on the table, her lips turned down in a frown, her eyes clouded in misery.

"I heard your guy say that he checked us out," Ava said, sounding angry now. "And there are six guards here. If you're really that afraid of us, leave while we're here and lock your house. All we need is your pool and gazebo anyway."

Realizing how ridiculous he seemed, Mac sighed. He did have six guards. And this was a charity. And it was Ava he was talking with, not Ellie.

He swallowed, wondering why he'd harbored the hope that she'd come. That he'd get to see her. At least he didn't have to worry that he'd see her and melt into a puddle of need at her feet.

"Okay."

Snapping his phone closed, he turned to see Blanche smiling at him. "Okay, what?"

"A friend works for a charity. I promised her that she and some of the kids from the charity could swim in the pool."

Lacy's eyes widened. "Ellie?"

"No, Ellie isn't coming, but Ava is."

Lacy's pretty face fell again. "Oh."

"Hey," Mac said, walking over to her. "You get to swim with some kids. They're going to barbecue. Ava specifically asked to see you."

Lacy nodded. Mac sucked in a breath. He knew exactly what Lacy was feeling but worse. She might adore Ellie, but Mac had loved her. He'd had the promise of a whole new life with her and he'd had to walk away from it.

The sound of cars pulling up the driveway filled the kitchen. The garage door opened and Phil walked up the butler's pantry. They exchanged a look and Mac turned to Blanche. "Why don't you take the kids upstairs? Lacy can get into her swimsuit."

When Blanche and the kids were gone, Phil said, "Seriously, Mac, they're fine. As Ava pointed out I have six guards. We'll be discreet. The kids will have a good time."

Mac said, "Okay," then dismissed Phil. He didn't really want to be a bad host, but, then again, he wasn't really the host of this party. A Friend Indeed was. He could disappear and let Blanche stay with Lacy at the pool.

Lacy came skipping into the kitchen with Blanche on her heels. She was happy because she was finally going to see people other than him and Henry. How could he not let her enjoy this?

He stooped to her height. "All set to have some fun?"

"Yes."

"I'm not going to swim, but I'll watch from the sidelines."

Lacy nodded eagerly and Mac rose and led them to the French doors.

They walked outside to a yard full of people. As Ava introduced Mac to a string of adults who carried coolers and bags of groceries past them to his gazebo, Lacy jumped into the pool with the kids who must have gone straight from the van to the water.

Their noisy laughter filled the air and something inside of Mac shifted, relaxed. He loved that his property was getting some real use. Loved that Lacy was finally smiling. He could handle this.

Then he saw Ellie.

Dressed in white shorts and a pink T-shirt, with her long blond hair floating around her, and wearing big black sunglasses, she made her way from the driveway, carrying a green cooler. She looked soft, happy, so touchable, so kissable.

When she reached him, she stopped. "Hey."

Desire stuttered through him. He couldn't see her eyes, but the smile she gave him was genuine and something tripped in his heart. He wanted to swing her into his arms and welcome her home, but he couldn't do that. He might have relaxed his regulations enough to keep a promise and let a charity hold a party on his grounds. But his life was a trap. A prison. She deserved better.

"Hey."

"So how have you been?"

Miserable. Sad. Lonely. Desperate for you.

"Okay."

"Me too."

She shuffled the cooler she was holding and Mac immediately took it from her hands. "Let me take that to the gazebo."

He expected her to argue, remembered the day she arrived when she'd told him she wanted to carry her own suitcase, but he wouldn't let her. Even then he'd known she was special.

They started walking toward the gazebo. "How are the kids doing?"

"Better."

She pulled the sunglasses down her nose and peeked over the top at him. "They were bad at some point?"

"They don't like the new situation."

"Really? I'm shocked."

He stopped. "Don't. Don't make fun of what I think I have to do."

"Is that what you think I'm doing?" She shook her head. "Don't be ridiculous. I know you need a certain amount of protection. The protection isn't the issue. It's how you handle it that is. You've got bodyguards. Big deal. Lots of people do. You have a fence. So what? Most people do. I'll bet you have alarms and cameras too. Again, what does it matter? A person can't go into a convenience store these days or stop at an ATM without getting his picture taken." She met his gaze. "Precautions aren't the issue. It's accepting them. And being realistic."

Her answer unexpectedly angered him and when she would have turned and walked away, he dropped the cooler and caught her arm. "And you're the expert?"

But rather than be angry that he'd confronted her, she smiled her brilliant smile again and Mac's heart melted. "I am. I had to learn how to stop being overprotective. How to live." She met his gaze with a world of love shining out of her eyes. "If you'd let me, I'd help you."

He swallowed. Everything inside of him screamed that he should take her help. Instead, he stood frozen. Torn between what was good for her and what was good for him.

She picked up the cooler. "In fact, I think you know that I could help you navigate this part of your life. I think the truth is you ran scared. Your ex-wife did such a number on you that you're afraid to try again. I think seeing her on TV reminded you of that, and the bomb scare gave you a legitimate excuse to push me away."

With that she walked away, disappearing into the gazebo, and though Mac wanted to sputter protests that she was wrong—he *was* protecting her from his life, not afraid—he glanced around, actually considering what she'd said. He had bodyguards. But they were discreet. His yard was fenced in. There were alarms and cameras everywhere. But, again, a person couldn't go to an ATM without getting his face on a camera.

Dear God. Was she right? Had he panicked not because of the bomb scare but because seeing Pamela scared him?

Was he punishing Ellie for sins Pamela had committed?

Ellie watched Mac walk away, back to the house, and her spirit deflated. She hadn't intended to harbor the hope that when he saw her he'd realize what he'd lost—what they'd lost—and change his mind.

But she had.

When that hope hadn't materialized, she'd tried shaming him into admitting he'd made a mistake. She'd prayed that his pride would bluster to the surface, and as he argued that he wasn't running scared he'd admit he loved her and wanted her back before his common sense could kick in.

That hadn't happened either.

Now he was leaving. He opened the French doors and in a few seconds was gone from sight. Ellie stared at the door.

She couldn't believe he'd forgotten everything they had. Yet, no matter how strong their feelings, they weren't strong enough for him to take a risk with her.

"Ms. Swanson?"

Ellie glanced to the right to see Phil standing at attention in front of her, wire in his ear, sunglasses reflecting her surprised expression back at her.

He caught her arm. "Would you come with me please?"

"He's kicking me off his property?" Ellie sputtered, remembering how Phil guided her out of the hotel.

Phil said nothing, simply directed her up the steps to the kitchen and from the kitchen back to a hall and from the hall up a set of stairs.

"Everybody at that party saw you take me," Ellie said. "In a few minutes everybody's going to wonder where I am—"

"Then let me suggest you hurry so you can get back out before they do."

Ellie whipped her head around to see Mac following them. "Why? What do you want?"

Mac laughed. "A little privacy."

As if he'd just heard a secret word or code, Phil dropped her arm and walked away. Mac opened the door to an office and motioned her inside.

"After you."

Her heart stuttered then leaped into overdrive. Privacy could mean that he'd thought about what she'd said and agreed with her and didn't want to kiss her in front of thirty strangers. Still, she wouldn't let herself get her hopes up. Not only had he passed on two really good opportunities to tell her he was sorry out by the pool, but his methods for getting her into his house were a bit high-handed.

"You can't keep me here."

"That's been my point all along with us." He sucked in a breath, closing the door behind them. "I wanted to keep you here." He rubbed his hand along the back of his neck. "Hell, I did a great job of actually keeping you here for over two months."

Her eyes narrowed. "What are you saying?"

"I'm saying that you're right. I panicked."

He looked too calm, too normal, to be accepting what she'd said. "Panicked?"

"As long as we were playing boss and maid, I sort of had you locked in."

She frowned. "You let me leave anytime I wanted to. How did you have me locked in?"

"Because I knew you'd come back." He sighed heavily. "But when we really got serious and my life sort of imploded, I realized I loved you and there was absolutely no reason for you to stay."

She gaped at him. "You think I had more reason to stay as a maid than a woman who loved you?"

"So I asked you to leave before you could leave me."

"You are a silly man."

Suddenly Mac's face changed. His expression shifted. His eyes narrowed. "Did you just say you loved me?"

"Of course, I did."

"But you hardly had time to know me. I have a crazy ex-wife, two kids who need a mother, a house that will probably be perpetually surrounded by bodyguards."

"Which makes you really lucky that you found someone who can handle it."

He rubbed his hand along the back of his neck. "Are you sure you know what you're getting yourself into?"

She shook her head. "You have really got to work on your romantic lines. Right about now, you should be saying, 'I love you too' and sweeping me off my feet."

He quietly said, "I love you too." Then he smiled. "I really love you. I really missed you."

"Better."

He took a step toward her. "I want to kiss you senseless."

She took a step toward him. "I'm listening."

"And make love until we're exhausted."

She laughed. "With two kids who are going to be wearing us out every day, that's not very ambitious."

He put his arms around her waist and she raised his to his neck. "Ah, but those two kids have a grandmother in Atlanta who wants to take them for two weeks in November."

"Sounds like a honeymoon."

He kissed her. "Exactly."

They stared into each other's eyes for several seconds, then his head lowered slowly and he kissed her again. His lips caressed hers with a tenderness that told her a million times over how much he had missed her.

When the kiss ended, he bumped his forehead to hers. "I'm sorry."

"For?"

"For taking so long to think it all through."

"That's okay. That only makes you human."

"You see, that's one of the things I love about you. You let me be me."

She smiled into his eyes. "And you let me be me."

He laughed. There was a light tap at the door and Phil said, "Everything okay in there?"

Mac opened his mouth, but Ellie pressed a finger to his lips. "Let me handle this one." She glanced over Mac's shoulder at the door. "Get lost, Phil."

A loud clearing of Phil's throat let them know he hadn't gotten lost. "Excuse me?"

"You heard the lady. She said, get lost, Phil."

"But—"

Ellie laughed and said, "Go check the perimeter."

"Very good, sir… Um, ma'am."

They waited a few seconds and when Phil didn't say anything else, they broke into gales of laughter.

Mac hugged her and said, "I think you're going to be very good at this."

"There are a lot of other things that I'm actually a lot better at." She pressed a kiss to his neck, then ran her tongue to his ear and whispered a delightful suggestion.

Mac pulled away. "Here? Now?"

The anticipation in his voice made her laugh again. "This might be the one perk of having a live-in nanny and six bodyguards. Not to mention a yard full of friends. I'm pretty sure they can occupy the kids for an hour."

Mac laughed, scooped her off her feet and headed for the master suite.

She stopped him. "I'm guessing one of the guest rooms is prettier than your master suite."

He considered that. "Probably."

"I don't want the first time we make love to be in that ugly red-and-gold thing you call a bedroom."

He changed directions. "Agreed."

Ellie smiled. They did agree. About nearly everything. And disagreed about enough to keep life interesting.

That was the real bottom line. She'd love this guy for the rest of her life because she knew there'd never be a dull moment.

MAID IN MONTANA

BY
SUSAN MEIER

CHAPTER ONE

JEB WORTHINGTON watched the aging sport utility vehicle chug up the tree-lined road leading to his ranch. He pulled on his horse's reins, stopping Jezebel, and reached for his small binoculars.

Yep. Just as he suspected. His new housekeeper, Sophie Penazzi, had arrived.

Adjusting the glasses, he watched her get out of the car, taking in her straight, shoulder-length brown hair that, if he remembered correctly, was a color almost identical to the dark brown of her eyes.

She stretched, working the kinks out of her back and shoulders from the long drive. The smooth, even tan of her skin brought visions of her in a bikini, rushing into the crashing waves of the Pacific, surfboard under her arm. It didn't surprise him that he'd envision her that way. Not only did her résumé list her home as Malibu, but also there was a part of him that would pay very good money to see her perfect bottom in a bikini.

He dropped the glasses to his thigh. Those were exactly the kinds of things he could not—*would not*—think about his new housekeeper. He'd lost the last one because she'd made a pass at him and he'd fired her. But instead of admitting she'd been let go because she'd tried to use her position as a springboard to becoming mistress of the house, Maria had promptly gone into town and trashed his reputation, claiming she'd quit because he was a grouch, too difficult to work for. The only way he'd recoup his standing with the locals would be to be nice to this new housekeeper, proving Maria had lied.

But being nice came with trouble of its own. Or maybe better said: Being nice to a live-in employee came with rules of its own. A line had to be drawn. He didn't want to be accused of sexual harassment or even flirting. And he wouldn't. He'd find a middle ground.

He nudged Jezebel, urging her to increase her pace.

Sophie bent into the rear compartment of her SUV. After setting several suitcases on the ground behind her vehicle, she lifted out an odd looking thing covered in net, at least four feet long and flat as a pancake. From the brackets on the side, he suspected that whatever it was, it was folded up. God only knew what it became when she unfolded it.

Once again, he nudged Jezebel, this time increasing her walk to a trot.

Adjusting the glasses so he could watch her as he rode, he saw Sophie slam the rear hatch, open the back door and bend inside.

There was more?

She pulled out a small seat and what looked to be a cooler and Jeb took Jezebel to a full gallop. What the hell was this woman doing? Planning to take over a wing of his house? Sure, she had to live with him, but he remembered telling her that her quarters were a bedroom, sitting room and a bathroom. She didn't get to spread out all over his home.

He galloped past the outbuildings and barn, slowing Jezebel when they neared the driveway and taking her down to a walk when they reached the pavement.

Obviously hearing the clip-clop of Jez's approach, Sophie turned around. Shading her eyes with her hand, she looked up at him and called, "Hey! Good morning."

Her bright brown eyes shone with joy, accenting her pert little nose, wide smile and nicely defined chin. He should have kept his eyes on her face, but the blue top clinging to her breasts and the jeans outlining her perfect bottom drew his gaze downward until he'd taken in every feminine inch of her.

Irritated with himself, he nearly cursed. Why had he hired someone so cute?

A glance at her mountain of gear only increased his ire. Obviously she was all wrong for this job. He reined Jez a few feet ahead of the car, and growled, "What are you—"

Too late. Sophie ducked into her back seat again and Jeb stopped talking. Not only was she providing him with a jaw-dropping view of her backside, but also there was little sense talking when his conversation partner couldn't hear him.

He waited patiently, ready to ask her just how much junk she thought she could get into a small suite of rooms, but when she pulled out of the back seat, baby in her arms, the words he'd intended to say fell out of his head. He was—for the first time ever—speechless.

She smiled at him. "I'm sorry. What did you say?"

He stared at her. Then the baby. The kid was small, but chubby. Healthy. With pink cheeks and a thatch of thick black hair that poked out in all directions.

The only thing that came out of his mouth was, "What are you doing?"

She frowned. "You said move in. Today. So I can start working tomorrow. Did I misread your instructions?"

"Apparently! Since I don't remember telling you to bring a baby!"

"Oh!" She laughed. "This is my son. Brady." She kissed the little boy's cheek. "Say hello, Brady."

The baby cooed and gooed and Jeb's heart stuttered in his chest. Willing back the swell of emotions that threatened to overtake him, he simply said, "You can't have a baby here."

Sophie kissed the baby's cheek again. "Why not? The agency said it wasn't a problem."

"The employment agency told you that you could bring him?"

"Yes, when they explained that this job was for a live-in housekeeper, I told them about Brady and they said it was no problem for me to bring him."

"I gave them the exact opposite instruction! I said, *no kids*." Somebody's head was going to roll.

"What difference does it make?" she asked cheerfully before she ran her fingers through her baby's unruly dark hair, trying to tame it. "I'm not working 24/7. Only eight or ten hours a day. And not all back-to-back hours. You said that on my interview. Since my work requires feeding you supper…which takes us past a five o'clock quitting time, especially cleaning up the dining room and kitchen after you eat, you said my days are pretty much my own. I can organize them any way I want. And that means I have plenty of time to care for Brady."

"I can't have a baby here!"

Her expression hardened. Her shiny brown eyes turned into laser beams of steely determination. The laughter was gone from her voice when she said, "Mr. Worthington, obviously there was a mess-up at the agency, but that doesn't mean we can't make the best of it."

Jezebel danced from foot to foot. A clear sign that Jeb's agitation was transmitting itself to her. He took a breath and spoke more calmly. "I don't want to make the best of it. I have clients coming—"

Jezebel danced around some more. Jeb tugged lightly on the reins, knowing he had to get her to the stable before he could finish this conversation. "Don't move. I'll be back."

He rode Jezebel into the stable, slid off the saddle and tossed the reins to a hand who was mucking stalls. "Take care of her."

With the anger in his belly churning into hurricane force, he strode outside again and to the driveway. Sophie Penazzi stood beside her vehicle, her child sitting in the plastic basket thing, her arms crossed on her chest.

"I want a thousand dollars to pay for the cost of this trip."

He stopped a few feet in front of her. "A thousand dollars?"

"It should be three. I let my apartment go." Her voice

wobbled, but she paused, drew in a breath and very strongly said, "I paid to put my things in storage. I also have the expenses of traveling here. It's cost me a lot to take this job, and if I'm not staying, then I want to be reimbursed." She caught his gaze. "Now."

"We have an employment agreement. You're staying," Jeb said, holding his temper in check by only a thin thread. He pointed at the baby in the basket-carrier thing. "He's not."

"And where is he supposed to go?"

"That's not my problem."

She pulled her employment agreement from her pocket. "It might be the agency's mistake that they told me it was okay to bring my son, but this is *your* agreement and I don't recall anywhere in here that says I can't bring a child. If you won't let me keep him, you're in breach…" She paused, smiled. "All you have to do is give me a check for a thousand dollars and I'm out of here."

Jeb was just about to remind her that since the agency made the mistake they were responsible to reimburse the money she spent, until she said the magic words…

"And you can find yourself another housekeeper."

All the wind evaporated from his angry sails. He *couldn't* find himself another housekeeper. Thanks to Maria, the women in town wouldn't work for him and none of the other California candidates he'd inter-viewed had been suitable. She was the only person he considered qualified. If she left, he started at square one and it would take him months to find someone willing to work for him. He didn't have months. He had poten-tial clients coming to see the ranch in three weeks.

He took a pace back. "Haul your gear inside. I'll send Slim out to show you to your quarters." He turned to leave, but spun to face her again.

"And keep him," he said, pointing at the happy baby, "out of my sight."

He pivoted toward the house and strode to his office, all but hyperventilating from fury. He *couldn't* live with a baby for the entire year of her employment agreement. And if money could get her to leave, he would happily pay it. Just as soon as his potential clients were gone, he'd give her the damned thousand dollars and she could leave.

But that meant he had only three weeks to find a replacement. He fell into the tall-backed chair, grabbed the phone receiver and punched in the number of the employment agency from memory.

"A baby!" he sputtered. His thoughts were so angry he couldn't merely think them; he spoke out loud. "What kind of woman brings a baby to a job?"

"The kind forced to live somewhere for a year."

Seeing Slim standing in the doorway of his office, Jeb slammed the receiver in the phone cradle again. A bear of a man, with shoulders as wide as the doorway, Jim Cavanaugh was one of those people whose childhood nickname no longer fit, but who couldn't seem to get rid of it.

"Don't take her side."

"I'm not taking her side. I'm just stating a fact. The agency told her it was okay for her to bring her child. And since she and the kid are here, what harm can it do to give her a chance?"

What harm? Slim, of all people, should know exactly

why he didn't want a baby around. "I'm hiring somebody else."

Slim planted his hands on his hips. "Oh, really? Where
do you propose to find someone? Are you going to trust
the agency that already got your instructions wrong with
Sophie? Or are you going to try the girls in town again?"

Jeb scowled.

"Look, Jeb. I'm not the kind to state the obvious, but
you have to keep her."

Jeb picked up a pencil and tapped it on the mouse
pad beside his computer keyboard. "Fine. Whatever.
She's got three weeks."

"Just long enough to get the house clean for your
clients? You're all heart."

"Don't push it, Slim."

Slim left the room, annoyed that the surfer girl
wasn't getting much of a chance to prove herself, but
Jeb didn't care. He picked up the phone again. Too
much was at stake for him to deviate from his plan.
Having a baby around might seem insignificant, but Jeb
had seen many a little thing topple big plans. There was
no way he'd risk his future—his home—when it had
taken him so long to get one.

He'd spent his childhood hopping from one tropical
paradise to another with his wealthy jet-setter parents.
His first year at university he thought he should feel
"settled"—since he was actually staying in one place
for nine consecutive months—but he didn't. Eventually
he realized "home" was more than a house or a place
to consistently lay his head. For the next two years he'd
longed for the sense of direction, sense of purpose,
sense of identity that the other students had.

Then he had gotten an apartment off campus, next door to two very determined brothers. Ranchers. People of substance. People with roots and identity. People whose great-great-grandparents had settled in Montana and who knew that a hundred years from now their property would still be Langford land.

With too much money and very little meaning to his life, Jeb wanted so much to be one of them that he'd married their sister Laine, and bought the ranch he now lived on, prepared to fulfill his adopted destiny of handing his ranch down from one generation of Worthingtons to the next… Until he and Laine divorced.

His dream had died a sudden, brutal death, but after only a few weeks of wallowing in misery, it dawned on him that he didn't need to have a wife or kids or even a "person" to hand down his land. He could still leave a legacy. It would simply be in the form of a foundation—a trust that would keep this ranch running exactly as it was right now for a hundred years after his death.

Just as he always did, he persevered. But only because he didn't deviate from the blueprint he created to achieve his goals.

So no. Sophie Penazzi and her baby were not staying. Might as well start the ball rolling now on finding her replacement.

Two seconds after Jeb strode into his house, Sophie had realized her offer to leave if he would pay her for expenses had been a terrible lapse in judgment. Her horror at making such a stupid mistake must have shown on her face because after Slim had taken her to her room, he'd told her to give him a few minutes and he'd straighten out this mess with Jeb.

Standing in the sitting room of the three-room maid's quarters, admiring the hardwood floors, traditional sofa and chair and big screen TV—quarters much nicer than any apartment she could afford—she took a long breath and said a prayer that Slim would be successful. Not only did this job pay enough to wipe out the debt she owed the hospital for Brady's birth, but also she had nowhere else to go. The thousand dollars she'd demanded as compensation for driving to the ranch wouldn't pay the first month's rent on a new apartment; forget about the additional security deposit required on most places. If she lost this job, she and her baby would be dead broke and homeless.

With her little boy asleep in the bedroom, she cursed Brady's dad for dumping them the way he had, putting her in the predicament of having no money and a child to raise. But rather than fall victim to self-pity, she reminded herself that Mick wasn't as much to blame for bailing on them as she was for trusting him. She'd been brought into the world by parents whose careers always came first. She shouldn't have been surprised that when she got pregnant, Mick no longer saw her as a partner, but a burden, maybe even an obstacle to the life he had planned. He'd never hidden his determination to arrange his world just the way he wanted it. She hadn't been blind to his self-centeredness. But she had stupidly believed love could cause him to make room for the new addition to their lives.

She shook her head in wonder. Thinking love would cause him to make room for Brady was just another way of saying that she believed that with enough love Mick would change. After twenty-two years of jumping through hoops for parents who never found a way to have any time for her, she should have known better than to take up with someone as career oriented as Mick. But she hadn't. He had to dump her before she finally got the message. People didn't change. And she wouldn't again make the mistake of believing they could.

A knock sounded on her door, then Slim opened it and poked his head inside. "You're set for a while."

"A while?"

"It sometimes takes Jeb a bit of time to realize everything's going to be okay, but he'll come around. You just do a good job."

Sophie smiled and nodded, but from the guarded expression on Slim's face she knew he hadn't really made any headway with her stubborn boss. Jeb Worthington wasn't happy with her and her baby and though he'd told her to stow her gear that didn't really mean she was staying. She appreciated the ranch foreman going to bat for her, but she wasn't the kind to let somebody else fight her battles. Once Slim disappeared down the hall, she checked to make sure Brady was sleeping soundly, scooped up the baby monitor and went in search of Jeb.

She walked down empty corridors and through half-furnished rooms confused that a man who seemed to have money didn't surround himself with creature comforts. Eventually she found him in his office. Pacing behind the huge cherrywood desk and tall-back black leather chair, he talked on the phone, his boots clicking on the hardwood floor.

"I'd like to speak with Mrs. Gunther, please." He was so absorbed in his pacing that Sophie knew he hadn't noticed her in his doorway. She let her gaze slide up his jean-clad legs, the lightweight plaid shirt, his broad shoulders. "It's Jeb Worthington."

If his jerky strides were anything to go by, patience wasn't his strong suit… Or maybe he wasn't a man accustomed to sitting or even being inside? The natural tan of his face and hands said he was more at home in the elements than his office. Plus, his body was trimmed, toned, muscled—probably from hard work, not a gym.

Her gaze moved up again, until it reached his face. Straight nose. Silky looking black hair. Her breath stuttered in her chest. Wow. How had she missed that he was gorgeous?

Thinking back on the day she interviewed with him, she winced, remembering that she *had* noticed. In fact, she remembered wanting to swoon when he walked into the room. She'd been so excited about the great pay and benefits he'd offered her that she'd forgotten that.

"Mrs. Gunther?"

He stopped his pacing, turned to the heavy drapes that covered a wall of windows, affording Sophie the opportunity to see his strong back that tapered into a taut waist and trim hips.

"When you sent me a woman with a baby, I think you forgot my housekeeper has to live in."

Jeb's conversation brought her back to the present and reminded her of another complication with her employment at this ranch. She was ready to fight to keep a job that meant she'd have to live with a man who was so attractive she'd wanted to swoon the first time she'd seen him.

Was that smart?

"The ranch is so far out in the country we only go into town for supplies once a month. She can't commute. And it's impractical for her to hire a baby-sitter. That is, if she can even find one. I had to go the whole way to California to find her."

His voice went from businesslike to impatient to downright angry so quickly that Sophie blinked. Maybe she was the one being too hasty? He was a grouch with little to no patience with mistakes. Not even honest ones. Yet instead of running for cover before he saw her eavesdropping, she stood gazing at him like a star-struck teenager, as if how he behaved didn't matter; he was so good-looking that she could forgive his being a little grouchy.

That wasn't like her at all. And it also wasn't right.

"Okay, let's just say we both agree that mistakes happen. I can appreciate that your staff got the instruction wrong. That doesn't change the fact that her having a baby is a deal breaker. I can't keep her."

Sophie's mouth fell open in dismay, but as he paused to listen to Mrs. Gunther, he turned in her direction and she jumped away from the open doorway into the hall, flattening herself against the wall so he wouldn't see her.

"I know that under the circumstances, especially with the flexible schedule, it doesn't seem that a baby would be a problem. But they're a hindrance, a distraction. I can't risk everything I've put into this company because she can't get her work done."

Though her heart had been pounding a hundred beats a second, his argument caused it to settle down and she frowned. *That* was all he was worried about? That she wouldn't get her work done? Was he nuts? Every mother in the world cooked and cleaned while caring for her children. Of course she could get her work done.

"Just start gathering résumés again. Get me somebody who can do everything I need done and this time without a baby."

He slammed the phone receiver into the cradle and Sophie hightailed it out of the corridor. But as she scrambled back to her quarters, she smiled, suddenly inspired. She might not have been able to get her parents or Mick to change, but the problem she had with Jeb Worthington wasn't about getting him to change. It was only about getting him to change his mind. To keep this job, all she had to do was *show* him that she could get her work done even *with* Brady in the room, underfoot, in the baby carrier slung over her back.

Actually that really was the way to go. Rather than tiptoe around Brady, the best thing to do would be to demonstrate that—just like every other mother on the planet—she could get her work done with her baby, not in spite of her baby.

And forget all about the fact that he was good-looking.

CHAPTER TWO

THOUGH Sophie didn't know what time ranchers woke for morning chores—there had been no reason to tell her because breakfast wasn't her responsibility, only supper was—she set her alarm for four-thirty and bounced out of bed when it rang.

Her plan was to make Jeb the breakfast of his dreams and serve it to him with Brady sitting in the high chair only a few feet away. The baby might goo and coo, but who could object to happy baby sounds? No one. Her boss would have good food and good company and he'd see there were more reasons to like having Brady around than reasons to kick them off the ranch.

Piece of cake.

After dressing herself in a T-shirt and blue jeans, she raced to the kitchen taking the baby monitor with her so that she'd hear Brady wake. Then she quickly brewed a pot of coffee, and ran to the refrigerator for fruit. A Tex-Mex omelet would be the main course, but she intended to do this up right and prepare the kind of hearty meal a rancher needed. Fruit cup first. A little oatmeal. Then the omelet, bacon and toast.

Running around the huge kitchen with solid oak cabinets and pale granite countertops surrounding the stainless steel appliances, she sliced fruit until five o'clock. Still scurrying, she fried bacon. At five-thirty, she put toast into the stainless steel toaster and by the time six o'clock rolled around she was becoming nervous.

The coffee was stale, the toast cold and the fruit soft. She thought ranchers got up at the crack of dawn? Where the heck was Jeb?

Expecting him to stroll through the door any second, she located everything needed to cook the omelet, which she couldn't actually prepare until he was ready to eat. When all the ingredients sat on the counter by the stainless steel stove, she stopped moving.

Where was he?

Six turned into six-thirty. The sound of Brady waking crackled through the monitor, and she went to the bedroom and quickly got him dressed. Then she came back to the kitchen and slid him into his high chair that she'd already placed at the table. At seven-fifteen, Jeb finally strolled into the kitchen and stopped dead in his tracks when he saw her.

Leaning against the stove, arms crossed on her chest, she narrowed her eyes at him. His dark hair and brooding gray-green eyes could stop the heart of any normal woman, and Sophie had to admit hers stuttered a bit just at the sight of him. But she reminded herself that her need to keep this job trumped any romantic notions. She needed employment, not to be a lovesick puppy over a self-absorbed man.

* * *

Jeb almost asked Sophie why she was standing in his kitchen. He liked being alone when he first got up. That's why breakfast wasn't on her list of duties.

Instead he reminded himself he had to be nice so she'd not only stay and clean the house for the clients arriving in three weeks, but also to mend his reputation. When she left, he'd give her the thousand dollars she'd requested so that her only complaint could be that her baby hadn't fit into ranch life. And if she just happened to stop in town on her way back to California, and mention that Jeb had given her a nice bonus, so much the better.

Walking to the counter with the coffeemaker, he said, "Good morning."

"I'm not sure I'd drink that. I made it at four-thirty."

He turned and gaped at her. "Why?"

"Because I thought all ranchers got up early and I was trying to please you."

This time his eyes narrowed. "Trying to please me?"

"Because I'm sorry."

"What the hell do you have to be sorry for? You said the agency told you it was okay to bring your son."

"I should have confirmed that with you."

At the repentant expression on her face, Jeb turned away from her. It wasn't her fault that the agency had got his instructions wrong. Yet, the woman he would fire as soon as his prospective clients had seen the house, had apologized *and* made him breakfast.

A wave of guilt rode through him like a wild stallion. He glanced over, ready to thank her for her trouble but also to tell her that her work was all for nothing because he wasn't a breakfast person. But when he looked at her, the words froze in his mouth. Her dark brown eyes snagged his gaze and he totally forgot the speech he had planned.

"I haven't yet made the omelet and I can make fresh toast," she said, her eyes brightening with hope and her lips teasing upward into a smile. "So, if you're hungry, I can have a hot breakfast for you in no time."

He swallowed. Good grief, she was pretty. But more than that, she was nice. Nice enough that he forgot all about counteracting Maria's claims that he was a grouchy boss. Staring into her dark brown orbs, it didn't matter what anyone else thought. He'd feel like a heel all day if he didn't eat the breakfast she'd planned.

"Sure. I'd love an omelet."

"Great! You sit. I'll put on a fresh pot of coffee."

She made the coffee first, and without another word to him, busied herself breaking eggs into a bowl and adding chopped vegetables from a plate beside the stove.

Taking a seat at the round oak table, Jeb finally noticed the high chair…and her baby. The little boy with hair pointing to all four corners of the world sat no more than three feet away from him.

The kid grinned toothlessly at him. Jeb sucked in another breath, debating how to remind Sophie that she was supposed to keep her baby out of his way, but within what seemed like seconds she appeared at the table, delicious smelling omelet on one of his everyday dishes.

"I'm really sorry about all this."

The room suddenly felt small and cramped. To his right was a baby. A perfect, healthy, happy child. To his left that little boy's mom. A perfect, healthy, sexy woman.

Lord, he should have kept Maria. She might have been attracted to him, but he hadn't been attracted to her and that situation he could have controlled.

Prepared to eat his omelet in record time and get the hell out of here, he picked up his fork. Much to his horror, Sophie took a seat, putting herself between him and her baby. She lifted a tiny spoon from a small plate of mushy food and directed it to her baby's mouth.

"I wish I had known you didn't want a woman with a child. I wouldn't even have interviewed."

The kid smacked his lips at the taste of the putrid looking yellowish mush. Jeb forced breath into his lung. "It's not your fault."

The baby clapped his hands together with glee as Sophie got another spoon of the mush and said, "I feel responsible."

Jeb's muscles began to quiver from the effort of not reacting to her or her child and he knew that was stupid, foolish. She was just another woman. His housekeeper. His *employee*. Being attracted to her was wrong in so many ways he couldn't even count them. He tried to convince himself that the spike in his heart rate was from having a baby so near, but he knew the real reason was Sophie herself. She was feeling guilty for things that weren't her fault and injustice always made him want to fight for the underdog. He couldn't fight for the woman he was firing. *He* was the enemy.

"Look, you have to stop taking the blame for everything."

"I can't help it." She laughed. "It's been woven into my DNA."

Her laugh skimmed along his nerve endings like a

spring breeze dances through new grass, but her words worked their way past his hormones and found his brain. He'd never wondered about this single woman's reasons for taking a job at a ranch so far out of town she had to live in, but her last comment was very telling. Though his parents would have happily let him become a beach bum, he'd had plenty of school friends who couldn't quite measure up to family expectations.

He glanced at the baby, and then caught Sophie's gaze again. He couldn't be so crass as to come right out and ask if her parents had frowned on her having a baby without being married. So, he took a shortcut and asked simply, "Crappy parents?"

"Depends on whose perspective you get. My dad's a doctor. Salt of the earth. Wins awards."

"And your mom?"

"University professor. Brilliant. Her students hang on her every word and she lets them hang out in her living room."

"But she doesn't have any room for her daughter?"

"It's more that her daughter never really fit." She fed the baby another spoon of yellow mush then smiled at Jeb. "With either of them. Not the surgeon filled with heart or the university professor everybody loved."

"And you think that's your fault?"

She shrugged. "Yes and no. I mean, logically, I know that my parents have to take responsibility for not making time for their daughter, but I also know we create our own destinies. I'd rather take responsibility than be a whiner."

Her comment was so unexpected that he nearly spit out his coffee on a laugh. And that scared him more than feeling sorry for her. He always was a sucker for a woman who could make him laugh. And this woman had not only gotten him to sit down to breakfast, and talk about her personal life, but now she'd made him laugh. If he didn't straighten things out between them and quickly, she'd have him spilling the story of his life. And that couldn't happen.

He rose from the table. "Okay. Here's how this is going to go down. I don't want you taking the blame for things you didn't do. I don't want you making breakfast. I never eat when I first get up. I just take coffee to the barn with me." He walked to the cupboard, pulled out his travel mug and set it on the counter with the coffeemaker. "I don't want anything special like this from you again. The job description doesn't include breakfast. So don't make it." He poured coffee into his mug. "I want the house clean, my laundry done and supper made. Nothing else."

He strode to the door, grabbed the knob and faced her. "You got that?"

She nodded.

"Good."

But as Jeb was walking to the barn, he wondered if Sophie really did understand what he'd said. It was easy to tell from her few comments about her parents that she'd probably spent her childhood trying to please them, which made her one of those people who was always working to fix everybody around them.

Lord, if she ever found out the truth of his life, she'd have a field day.

He stopped walking. Actually that wasn't funny. In less than a day, she'd already gotten him to sit down to a breakfast he didn't want, withhold a reprimand for not keeping her baby out of his sight *and* engage in a personal discussion about her parents. She'd grown up looking and listening for clues of how her parents felt. If he spent too much time in her company, she'd sense he was hiding something and she might even make it her life's mission to get him to talk about it so she could help him.

He was strong enough—stubborn enough—that he didn't believe he'd spill his guts and tell her things he didn't want anybody to know, but why risk it?

Her primary function was to prepare his house for his clients. He could easily take cooking off her list of duties and never even have to worry that their paths would cross.

That was a much better idea than sitting three feet away from her and her child, risking that she'd work whatever magic she wove and somehow get him talking about himself.

Sophie was in the middle of supper preparations when Jeb opened the back door and strode into the kitchen talking. "Sophie, can you come back to the office with me for a minute?"

She looked up from the pepper she was chopping then glanced at the baby monitor on the counter. Brady had just gone to sleep. She didn't believe he would wake up. She could leave him for five minutes without the monitor…right?

"This won't take long."

She smiled and said, "Sure," but waited until Jeb was in the hall leading to the front foyer, before she snatched the monitor from the counter as she passed it. He hadn't said a word about Brady that morning, but that was actually the problem. She'd never met a person who didn't oohh and ahh over her baby. The fact that her boss hadn't even addressed the adorable child sitting in the high chair next to him could mean he really was one of those people who didn't like babies. If that was the case, she might have to rethink her strategy. Stuffing the monitor into her apron pocket, she followed Jeb into the office.

"Have a seat."

She sat with a smile. A big smile. He wouldn't have called her into his office unless he had something important to discuss. She had to show him that no matter what he wanted she'd do her best to accommodate him. No matter what he said, she would agree.

He sat on the big leather chair behind the desk. "I've decided to modify your duties."

Great! More work! Finally a way to prove herself! If she had any luck, he'd changed his mind about breakfast. She was a much better cook than housekeeper, and breakfast was her specialty. She could easily impress him with omelets and waffles. If he'd simply add breakfast into her duties, he'd beg her to stay the entire year of their contract.

"I'm taking *all* cooking off your list of responsibilities."

All the breath whooshed out of Sophie's lungs. "What?"

"The cooking. I'm taking it off your list of job duties. You have plenty to do without it."

"No, I don't!"

He fiddled with some papers on his desk, then looked

up at her. "Yes, you do." He leaned back in the seat.
"You were surprised this morning when I didn't get up
with the sun because you thought that's what ranchers
do."

Heartsick because she'd lost her best way to impress
him, Sophie nodded.

"Usually that's true, but in our case I don't really run
the Silver Saddle. I run the ranch management company
that owns the Silver Saddle. As ranch foreman, Slim
gets up and gets the day going with the hands. That's
what every foreman at every ranch my company
manages does. I personally don't run the ranches. I
have great foremen who do that."

"And what do you do?"

"I market my business." He sat up again, leaning
forward on his desk, obviously comfortable talking
about his company, looking like a lethal combination
of sexy rancher and savvy businessman. "This house,"
he said, pointing around in a circle, "is a big part of my
marketing plan. Remember, during the interview I told
you I had frequent guests?"

"Yes."

"The guests are wealthy people who buy ranches so
that they have a private country retreat. Somewhere
they can go and be themselves. Be comfortable. But
after a year or so of owning a ranch, they realize how
much trouble it is to run it, so they go looking for
somebody like me. Or a company like mine. We do the
work for the ranch. They reap the benefits."

"I'm still not sure what this has to do with me."

"If it were just me living here, I wouldn't have a
housekeeper. I'd let the dust pile up. But because of my

guests I need the place to be clean. Which means you're part of the business. You're not really a maid. You're more of an extension of the ranch management company, making sure everything sparkles for clients." He relaxed and leaned back on his chair again. "So that's all I want you to do."

Knowing he was waiting for a reaction from her, Sophie stalled for time by running her tongue along her lips. A smart woman would simply say okay. Sophie told herself to say okay. To smile. To accept his order. Not to argue that cooking was her forte and if he'd just allow her cook for him, he'd never let her leave.

She took a breath. Told herself again to simply say, "Okay."

Just say okay!

She opened her mouth, but instead of her one-word agreement, she found herself saying, "This is because of Brady, isn't it?" But once the words were out of her mouth, she wasn't sorry. The guy was going to fire her for something that wasn't her fault and she'd be damned if she'd roll over and play dead.

"No."

"Yes. It is." She rose from her seat and leaned across the desk. "You didn't even look at him this morning."

He rose, pressed his hands on his desk and leaned toward her. "I asked you to keep him away from me. If we push everything else aside in this discussion, the bottom line is you disobeyed an order from your boss. Now you're paying the consequences."

"But Brady's a sweet kid!" She paused, drew in a breath. "You know what? Maybe if you'd spend some time with him *you* might get a little sweeter."

He gaped at her. "Are you kidding me? After disobeying a direct order, now you're sassing?"

Sophie reared back and pressed her palm to her mouth. In her zeal to prove that she could work with Brady, she'd *forgotten* that he didn't want the baby in the room. But he was right about the sassing. *That* didn't help her cause at all. And she knew better. But when it came to Brady, her motherly instincts always surprised her.

He sighed. "Look, I have potential clients arriving in three weeks. What I need... No, what the *business* needs is for this big house to be clean, looking like the perfect retreat from the hustle and bustle of a busy life. After that you can leave. I'll even give you the thousand dollars. I just want you and your baby gone."

Tears filled her eyes. *She was being fired because she had a baby.* She shook her head in disbelief. "He doesn't talk. If he makes a sound it's a gurgle of happiness. How could you possibly be opposed to that?"

"It doesn't matter. This is my ranch. My business and my home. I set the rules. I told you I didn't want to see your baby, but you either chose not to keep him out of my way or *couldn't* keep him out of my way as requested. The arrangement failed." He leaned back in his chair again. "Now, you can stay three weeks because I do need the house cleaned for the clients, and I'm even giving you the extra thousand you asked for. But after that you're gone. I won't have a baby here."

CHAPTER THREE

SOPHIE watched television until eleven that night, hoping to make herself tired. But even after hours of mindless TV her upset over losing her job made her too restless to go to bed.

After checking to make sure Brady was in a deep sleep, she slid into her one-piece bathing suit and the matching terry-cloth cover-up then grabbed the portable baby monitor from the bedside table. Slim had shown her a swimming pool when he gave her the tour of the house and said she was free to use it. Of course, that was before she had been fired, but she didn't care. She was restless and needed to make herself tired. She was having a swim.

She opened the door to her suite slowly, not wanting to run in to anyone since her cover-up was short and she felt uncomfortable walking around only half dressed.

Common sense told her she had no reason to fear. It was late. She was on the first floor. Her boss's suite of rooms was on the second floor. Slim had a cabin behind the homestead. Only a few hands actually slept in the bunkhouse, but even they were so far from the house that no one would see her. She was perfectly safe.

She took a breath, stole down the short hall that led to the kitchen and then slipped into the family room with French doors that led to the pool. In another two steps, she was standing on the stone patio.

Silence descended on her like a warm blanket. The city always had sound. Background noise. A person might grow accustomed to it and not "hear" it, but it was always there. On this ranch, so far away from civilization, she learned the meaning of the word silence.

Removing her cover-up, she glanced around in awe. Except for dim lights illuminating the blue water of the pool, this world was also inky-black. Remembering something about seeing stars in the country, she quickly glanced up and sighed.

"Oh, my gosh."

"Oh, my gosh what?"

On a gasp, Sophie spun around to find Jeb walking out of the shadows behind her. Water flattened his thick black hair and droplets cascaded from his shoulders and down his broad chest, making trails through whorls of dark hair leading to six-pack abs. Wet black swimming trucks clung precariously to lean hips and a butt made for a woman to sink her fingernails into in the throes of passion.

Even as her mouth went dry, she groaned inwardly. How could she be attracted to the man who had just fired her?

"Oh, my gosh what?" He repeated his question as he walked over to her, stopping within arm's reach.

Awareness shimmied through her. With her cover-up in her hand and wearing only her bathing suit, she wasn't quite as naked as he was, but they were both scantily dressed, alone, in the darkness.

She pulled in a breath. This was ridiculous. Not only were they were both sufficiently covered, but also she was furious with him and he clearly didn't like her. There was no reason to remind him of that, but she wouldn't cower from him, either.

She forced herself to meet his gaze. "The stars. There are so many."

"You have big city syndrome," he growled, back to being the grouchy boss. "The sky is always lit over a city, blocking one of nature's greatest gifts. A starry night."

He looked up into the star-spangled darkness and her gaze skimmed his broad chest and perfect tummy. He was, quite literally, the sexiest man she'd ever seen.

"Yeah. We certainly don't have stars like this in the city." She swallowed, desperately trying to will away her attraction. He was a self-centered grouch, who had fired her. He was the last person she wanted to feel anything for. But she couldn't deny that being this close to him, her whole body hummed. She told herself it was just plain foolish to be attracted to a man she didn't even like. Yet, here she stood, her breathing erratic, her nerve endings on red alert.

"I'll go back to my room."

He snatched a huge green towel from a nearby chaise. "No, I'll go. I'm done with my swim. In about ten seconds the patio will be all yours."

A nervous laugh bubbled up from her. There was no way she'd force him to leave his own swimming pool. No way she'd give him another thing to complain about. "No. That's okay. You stay. I only came out here to get a breath of fresh air."

She watched his gaze move from her face, down her one-piece suit, pausing on the length of leg exposed beneath the high-cut bottom.

"If you only came out for fresh air, then why are you in a swimsuit?"

Her breathing, which had been erratic, stalled in her chest. His voice might have been strong, detached, but the look he'd given her had been long and slow. He'd taken in every square inch of her and lingered on the part of her that usually drew a man—her legs.

She swallowed.

Knowing she had to get herself out of this and quickly, she tried to fall back on humor. "All right. You caught me. I'm guilty as charged. I wanted a quick swim, but I didn't realize you were using the pool or I wouldn't have come out."

He took a step closer. "I didn't picture you as the one-piece suit type. I figured you more for a bikini girl."

Another nervous laugh escaped her. Was it her imagination, or was he flirting with her? If he made a pass at her, she wasn't sure if she would melt or faint.

Of course, she could be jumping to conclusions. One little comment didn't necessarily mean he was flirting. He could actually be confused by her choice of swimwear.

"Why a bikini?"

"Don't you surf?"

"No."

"Hum. A California girl who doesn't surf. Another myth debunked."

Relief skittered through her. He wasn't flirting but

confused by her. She could breathe again. "You think all California girls surf?"

He caught her gaze, his pale eyes soft and serious in the moonlight. "Yes."

Realization of how close they were slid over her. He was a very different man when he wasn't yelling at her. In fact, from the way he was looking at her she'd never guess he had a problem with her at all.

She licked her suddenly dry lips, feeling reactions and emotions that were more instinctive than conscious. Her eyes desperately wanted to move down again, soak in the beauty and masculinity of his chest, and she struggled to keep them locked with his. Her nerve endings sparkled like the stars overhead.

He stepped back, his gaze still locked with hers. "You'd do well to remember that I'm a grouch and check to make sure the pool isn't occupied the next time you want to swim."

Embarrassment poured through her in a rush of heat. So much for him being a different man when he wasn't yelling.

But even if he couldn't rise above their differences, she could. "I'm sorry. Next time I want to swim I'll ask."

"There's no reason to ask. Just remember that I swim every night around ten-thirty and we'll be fine."

Though his words were appropriate, his voice went back to being soft, hypnotic, resurrecting the sprinkle of gooseflesh that covered her body. She peeked at him, confused again. What was going on here?

Before she could say anything, he turned to the French doors and within seconds was gone.

She shook her head. If she didn't desperately need the money she'd get working here for three weeks, she might be tempted to simply pack her bags and go now. But she did need the money. Not for herself, but for her child. Once again, her motherly instincts won out. But as soon as she had her three weeks pay and the extra thousand dollars, she was out of here.

The next morning, Jeb waited until he heard Sophie head upstairs before he walked into a blissfully empty kitchen. He poured himself a cup of the coffee she'd brewed, and with a huge sigh of relief made his way to his office.

Listening to the messages on his answering machine, he rooted through the stacks of paper looking for a pad to jot down a few numbers, but instead found a note of complaint Maria had left about a leaky faucet. At the time she'd lodged it, she'd been shamelessly coming on to him and he hadn't been sure if it was a genuine complaint or a way to get him to her bedroom.

He cursed. He'd never checked this out and now that he had someone using the suite again, he couldn't let it slide. With Sophie upstairs, he knew he could sneak into her rooms and try the faucet without her even knowing there'd been a problem. After the episode at the swimming pool the night before, that was probably for the best. He'd decided he wasn't even going to be in the same room with her again, if at all possible. So it was good he found the note now when he could check it out.

He left his office and stealthily made his way to her suite. The door opened to a sitting room that smelled soft and feminine. Brady's baby powders and soaps mixed with more mature scents of something smoky and sexy, undoubtedly belonging to Brady's mom and a picture of her in her innocent one-piece bathing suite popped into his head. He could almost feel the warmth of the night, hear her soft voice as she told him about the stars, and his groin tightened. He didn't know what it was about that woman that got to him, but she had something. He thanked his lucky stars she'd be leaving soon.

On his way to the bathroom, his gaze fell on a four-foot-by-four-foot square thing that sat in the corner of the sitting room and he stopped. Covered in net, with a bumper guard decorated with childish characters and images, the thing was obviously a convenient place for the baby to sit and play while his mother worked. But he didn't know that for sure. He didn't know anything about babies.

He glanced around. With no one in the room to see him, he could indulge his curiosity. He walked over to it and ran his fingers along the smooth plastic that formed a soft rim, probably to protect the kid in someway. He stooped down, peering inside at the toys Sophie had left behind. A stuffed bear. A doll made of soft-looking fabric with yarn for hair. Brightly colored balls and rattles. They were curious things, foreign, almost exotic to a man who hadn't spent two minutes with a baby until his housekeeper had brought one to his home.

"Oh, I'm sorry!"

At the sound of Sophie's voice, his heart all but pounded out of his chest. But with the ease that comes with years of practice, he glanced over indolently, as if she were the one in the wrong.

She stood in the doorway, wild-haired baby on her arm. Her eyes shone brightly with fear, and her breath stuttered into her chest. She should have been angry that he was in her quarters without her permission or even her knowledge. Instead she shook with fear over being in his presence—with her baby. The baby who belonged in this room more than he did.

The guilt he'd felt when she made him breakfast reared its ugly head again. He didn't have a qualm about firing someone for not doing her job; but he wasn't firing Sophie for not doing her job. He was firing her for having a baby.

The little boy cooed, drawing Jeb's gaze to the smiling imp and he swallowed. Did a man ever get over a life blow like the one he had received? Would he ever be able to look at a child without feeling the horrible emptiness?

It didn't matter. His only concern right now was getting himself out of this room before "the fixer" realized something was wrong and asked another one of her damned questions.

He pulled himself up from his crouched position. "My last housekeeper said the bathroom faucet leaks. Does it?"

"I…" She cleared her throat. "I never noticed it leaking."

He strode to the door. "That's what I figured."

He left without another word. Walking down the hall, he tried to focus on being furious with Maria for making his life miserable, but his mind wandered back to soft blankets, sweet smelling toys and blue eyes filled with life and wonder.

He might feel guilty over firing Sophie, but there was no way around it. If the house were clean, he'd give her the three weeks' pay and bonus today just to save his sanity.

CHAPTER FOUR

RIDING the fence line the next day on Jezebel, with Slim beside him on his black stallion, Thunder, Jeb knew he should be enjoying the easy camaraderie with his foreman. The sun was hot and a breeze shimmied through the wildflowers in the shiny green grass. Typically this was when Jeb's focus was its sharpest. Instead the easy pace of the ride lulled him, and his mind wandered back to the sweet smells in Sophie's suite, then to Sophie herself.

She'd been at the ranch three days and every one of those days he'd done something wrong. He knew that the curiosity he felt looking at Brady's toys was an aberration that would leave as soon as the baby did. He also wasn't worried about the conclusions Sophie might have drawn seeing him staring at her baby's things. She'd been so surprised to find him in her suite that he doubted she'd had time to really think about what she'd seen.

But the way his barriers had fallen at the swimming pool couldn't be dismissed so easily. He was her boss, yet he couldn't help asking why she didn't wear a bikini. He couldn't stop himself from looking at her legs. He couldn't keep his voice level, disciplined, authoritative. So he'd planned to simply avoid her, but that hadn't worked out, either. After their contact in her suite, he had to admit he was considering working in the barn and even staying out of the kitchen except to get coffee.

He shook his head in disgust. He hated being out of control. Shouldn't he be able to handle this better?

Of course he should! So what if she was attractive? He was an enormously successful businessman, whose big, bad ranch foremen all but shivered in their boots when they had meetings with him. How could one five-foot-six California girl cause him to forget everything he knew about keeping employees in line?

They were almost back at the barn when Jeb came out of his thoughts and asked Slim about the trouble they'd been having with hikers walking the ranch trails.

"Did you hear anything I said?"

"I heard everything you said."

"Then you'd know I already told you I met with the guy who seems to be organizing the hikes and told him it was no problem for him to bring people on the ranch as long as they stayed in the back of the property, away from the cattle and picked up after themselves."

As Slim said that, Sophie came around the corner of the barn. "Hey!"

"Hey!" Slim called, waving to her. "How's Brady?"

Jeb glanced over at him. He knew the kid's name?

"He's fine. We're both great." She turned and displayed a backpack-like baby carrier in which Brady sat, chewing on a thick plastic ring. "We're going for a walk."

Slim nodded and smiled and Jeb took advantage of everybody's preoccupation with chitchat to peek at the length of leg exposed beneath her jean shorts. Today her thick hair was caught up in a bouncy ponytail and she wore a fancy top with seashells or something dangling from the U-shaped neckline, but as always Jeb's attention was caught by her legs. They were perfect.

"Oh, don't mind him. I don't know where the hell his mind's been all morning." Slim poked him in the arm. "Are you in there, Jeb?"

Jeb's heart froze in his chest. He hoped to hell they simply thought he'd been woolgathering and no one had caught him staring at Sophie's legs, but one look at Slim's sly expression and he knew his foreman had caught every second of it.

Shading her eyes from the sun with her right hand, Sophie smiled up at him as Jezebel began to do a two-step, once again picking up on his nervousness around his housekeeper and her baby.

"I asked if you minded if Brady and I explore."

"No. I don't mind if you take a walk." He tugged on his horse's reins, directing Jezebel toward the barn. "But you're not familiar enough with the ranch to explore. Stay on the dirt roads."

Sophie nodded and walked off. Jeb watched Slim's gaze follow her, before he yanked on the stallion's reins and turned him in the direction to catch up with Jeb. "Well, I'll be damned."

"Probably for the sins you've committed," Jeb agreed.

"You like her."

Jeb stopped his horse. "No. I just think she's got great legs."

"And a pretty face and a sweet personality—"

"And a baby."

Slim laughed. "You can fool most people with that gruff voice and apparent hatred of kids, but you forget I know things about you that most people don't know."

Jeb headed for the barn again. "Whatever."

Slim laughed again. "Don't whatever me. Especially when I think it's a damned good sign that you like this girl."

"Right. And you think the fact that she has a baby makes her perfect for me."

Slim grinned. "And from the fact that you brought it up first, I'm guessing you've already thought of it, too."

He hadn't. Not until that very second. But as Slim pointed out it was a "sign" of sorts that the thought had even popped into his head. But where Slim saw it as a good sign, Jeb only felt stupid. Desperate. He hated both.

He looked Slim in the eye. "I keep you around because you're good at your job. But even you don't get to poke into my personal life. Let this alone or Sophie won't be the only one going in three weeks."

With the dusting and window washing done and nothing else to do, Sophie cleaned the kitchen after lunch the next day.

"What are we going to do once this kitchen is cleaned, Brady?" she asked the baby who sat in the high chair, chewing a teething ring, watching his mom with his big blue eyes. "The man doesn't even have furniture in most of the rooms. Once I dusted the woodwork and windowsills and ran a dry mop over the hardwood floors, I was done.

"Our top priority is keeping you out of his way, but even when we tried to go for a walk we ran into him."

Stacking her few lunch dishes in the dishwasher, she sighed. "I always thought being an efficient house-keeper was the one good thing that came from being left with maids, but in this case I'm sort of working myself out of a job. Julianna would love the irony of this."

She smiled remembering her parents' first maid, who'd not only taught her to clean, but she'd also taught her to cook. Miss Julie—as she liked to be called—had explained that moms taught daughters to cook, not just to feed their families, but as a way to bond.

Sophie had bonded with Julianna and Julianna had taught her everything she knew, not just about cooking but also about housekeeping.

When Julianna had retired, Florence had also been happy to teach Sophie even more about housekeeping. She'd depended upon Sophie so much that Sophie had felt like she was the maid and Florence was the lady of the house. Luckily she only lasted three months before Sophie's parents discovered what was going on and, horrified, had hired someone a tad more willing to do the work herself rather than "share" it with Sophie.

Laughing, Sophie remembered how mortified her parents had been that Sophie had been housecleaning with the help.

But they didn't realize how that had worked in her favor. In spite of the fact that she didn't have either of her parents' genius IQ, she now had a marketable skill.

She could cook and clean well enough to be anybody's housekeeper. It might not please her highbrow parents, but it did pay the bills.

Thinking of her parents made her incredibly sad. Not just for herself but also because they didn't understand what *they* were missing. She loved Brady so much that she would have given up anything for him. Yet her parents didn't have any more time for their grandchild than they'd had for their daughter.

But she and Brady had each other. For the first time in her life she had someone who loved her and she wasn't shortchanging him of the love a child deserved. She'd move heaven and earth to show him he was loved. Wanted. Which was exactly why she wouldn't stay with grouchy Jeb Worthington any longer than she had to to earn the money she needed to get back on her feet. She wouldn't neglect Brady the way her parents had neglected her. She might have to keep herself and Brady off Jeb's radar, but she wasn't hiding him for anybody.

She finished cleaning the kitchen, talking baby talk with Brady and when everything was tidy, she scooped him out of the high chair and carried him through the nearly empty formal dining room and into a hall, which passed two other empty rooms.

What was with this house? Why had Jeb left it so empty? Why would someone as rich as he was not buy furniture?

Looking around as she walked, she decided a busy guy like Jeb might not have had had time to choose sofas and chairs, end tables and lamps, and he most certainly wouldn't know how to "decorate." Not like Paul, the one and only male housekeeper her parents had hired. If Paul ever saw this house, Sophie didn't know if he'd die from the trauma of the neglect he'd perceive or if he'd be in hog heaven. Paul would probably convince Jeb to let him furnish and decorate every empty room—

She stopped. "Oh, my goodness, Brady! I think I just found the way to keep us out from under the boss's feet!"

The next morning when Jeb walked into the kitchen, Sophie was waiting for him. Wearing jean shorts and a tank top, with her dark hair piled on her head in a haphazard way that was somehow sexier than all get out, she stood in front of the kitchen sink, her eyes bright with enthusiasm.

His first instinct was to ignore her. But a fire of in-dignation ignited in his belly. This was his home, yet he couldn't eat or cook in his own kitchen. Couldn't go for his nightly swim without checking over his shoulder to see if she was sneaking out to join him. And now he couldn't get coffee?

No. Hell no! He was not losing his morning coffee!

He walked to the counter, reached into the cupboard for his travel mug and pulled it down. On his way to the coffeepot he'd noticed the high chair was empty. She was doing as he'd asked. Keeping the baby out of his sight.

"Where were you all day yesterday?"

She broke the silence with her question, but Jeb looked away, pretending great interest in putting cream in his coffee.

"I searched everywhere but I totally missed you. You're a hard man to find."

"Not really. I've got a company to run. This ranch is part of it."

"Unless I misinterpreted you, you also have a house that needs fixing before your guests arrive."

"It doesn't need fixing…it needs to be cleaned."

"Well, see, that's where you and I differ." She motioned to the table, indicating they should sit but he didn't budge from the counter. "Come on, this will only take a minute."

"Slim and I are flying to Wyoming today to look at the ranch of another potential client. We can't be late."

"I'll talk fast."

"Fine."

She pulled in a breath. He kept his eyes on her face, knowing damned well that her breasts had risen and fallen, but he wasn't allowed to look. Wouldn't look. *Refused* to look.

"I've noticed that your house is barely furnished."

He brought his coffee to his mouth and peered at her over the rim of the mug. "Because I don't want prospective clients to see my furniture. I want them to see the place empty enough to envision their furniture in the rooms."

"Good point. Except these ranches you manage are second homes for your clients. They won't be moving their furniture to a ranch they bought as a second home. And when they come here to check out your ranch, they may be looking for inspiration."

Confused, he scrunched up his face and said, "What the hell are you talking about?"

"I think you mixed up real estate concepts. If you're selling a house, it is true that you want everything to be neutral so buyers will see their own things when they walk through the rooms. But you're not selling this house. You're selling the idea that the second home of a ranch is cozy and comfy and private. You're selling privacy."

"I think the secluded nature of most ranches accomplishes that."

"Yes, but not the comfort part."

He was losing the battle to keep his eyes on her face, mostly because she was pretty enough that gazing at her face also resurrected a few thousand male fantasies. Knowing he had to get the hell out of here, he glanced at his watch. "What's your point?"

"That most women would come into this house and not be comfortable. If you're trying to create a mood, and I think you are, your house needs to be decorated."

"Oh, no. No decorator! No fancy sofas, sea of knick-knacks and glass tables that can be broken."

She laughed. "Agreed. When I pick some new things for this house, I'll be going on the same principles you've already established. Comfort. Peace. Privacy."

His eyes narrowed. "When *you* pick some new things?"

"Yes." She pulled in a breath. "Okay, look. You already know I need the money or I wouldn't be here. I'm going to be really honest with you and admit that I could probably get this house clean by the end of the week. But if I clean everything this week and leave, by the time your clients get here in three weeks, it'll be dusty again."

He frowned. "What you're really saying is you'd like something to do in between dustings?"

"Yes."

He didn't cotton to boredom himself, but her idea of

how to fill her time wasn't practical. "Even if I agreed with you about the house needing a little more furniture, how are you going to shop? Town is forty miles from here and once you get there you won't find a big selection of furniture or anything beyond household necessities."

"Ever heard of the Internet? I can buy anything you need and have it delivered to your front door."

He gaped at her. "I'm supposed to give you a credit card?"

"Nope. All you have to do is set up an online account that has limited uses and limited access. You can give me a budget. You can check my purchases every day." She paused and smiled. "Unfortunately it will mean I'll have to use your computer."

That stopped him. If she stayed in one place for several hours a day, avoiding her would be abundantly easier. "You'll be using my office?"

She grimaced. "Sorry. I don't have a laptop."

"But you'd be in the office all day?"

"Not all day, but a good bit of the day."

"How many hours?"

"I'm not sure."

"But several?"

She grimaced again and nodded.

For several hours a day, every day, she'd be out of his hair? He could use his kitchen. Make a sandwich with cold cuts instead of grilling a burger for lunch. Have a salad.

He picked up his mug. "Sounds like a good idea. You go cruising online today, looking for things you like and I'll set up an account tomorrow."

"Just like that?"

He nodded. "Just like that."

"You aren't going to tell me what you like?"

"You're supposed to be decorating for a woman. I'm not a woman. I just want the place to be comfortable. And not foo-foo. And no pink."

"What's my budget?"

Halfway to the door he paused, faced her. "Let me think about that a bit. Try to come up with a ballpark figure on big ticket items so I have an idea of the least amount of money you'll need, and then I'll give you a number."

Closing the kitchen door behind himself, Jeb smiled. They'd done it— Well, she'd done it. She'd come up with a way to stay out of his hair for the three weeks he was forced to keep her. He didn't care if it cost him half a million dollars. But there was no way he'd let her know that. All he wanted was for her to be busy and out of his way.

Problem solved.

After Brady awakened from his morning nap the next day, Sophie dressed him in clean clothes and headed out for her first day as a decorator. She was glad it had been easy to convince Jeb to let her furnish his home, but walking through the downstairs, seeing just how empty the house was, she worried that she'd bitten off more than she could chew.

A semiempty house might provide the opportunity to keep herself and Brady out of his hair, but it gave her no clue as to Jeb's taste in furniture, what he would like, or even what he disliked.

Brady on her arm, she roamed from room to room,

becoming more and more overwhelmed. The house wasn't merely empty, with virtually no clue of how to fill it, but also it was huge.

Her parents were well-off but this guy was *rich*. Handsome, sexy, grouchy and *rich*.

What the heck made her think she could please him? A man who could afford this house on a piece of property this big could have anything he wanted; and people who could have anything they wanted could be as hard to please as they wanted. What if he'd put off furnishing the place not because he didn't want furniture and not because he didn't have time to do it himself, but because he was so picky nothing appealed to him?

Volunteering to decorate was absolutely the stupidest idea she'd had in a long time.

Finding a stairway off a hidden corridor, she made her way to the lowest level only to discover another entire floor of rooms. Seeing hardwood floors, a huge white sectional sofa, mahogany bar and a fireplace as she descended the stairway, she assumed the space had been designed to be a family room. Further back she found two suites that she speculated should be guest areas if only because each had its own bath, but on the other side of the family room was a media room—at least partially furnished with a big screen TV and a row of comfortable lounge chairs. Beside that was a gym.

She stepped into the gym and smiled wryly at the weight benches, treadmills, stair climbers and every type of exercise equipment she could think of. Now that she knew Jeb didn't do much ranch work, she wasn't surprised to find a room like this. This was definitely how a man got a great body like the one her boss had.

She ran her fingers along the bars on the sides of two treadmills, wondering why he had two of everything. Did he exercise with a buddy? Did Slim join him?

Even as she thought the last, she opened a door off to the side, thinking it was a closet, and instead discovered a dressing room and beyond that a shower and tub with jets. He had absolutely everything a person would need, but none of the little touches that made a house or any one of the rooms personal—not even a splash of color in paint.

She returned to the dressing room and, looking around, found the closet, filled with fat white towels, soaps and other necessities. Everything was so white it gave her no clue as to her boss's taste. She was just about to close the door when a bit of color caught her eye on the bottom shelf. She stooped down and came face-to-face with a box. Sliding it forward so she could peek inside, she saw nothing but pink. Pink towels, a pink terry-cloth robe, pretty pink hairbrush, even pink weights.

She laughed, thinking it looked like a box of Pepto-Bismol, but her laughter gave way to an unexpected understanding. This gear was for a woman. The second treadmill and stair climber and weight bench were for a female friend.

Oh boy. He had a girlfriend. As if there wasn't enough pressure on her to do a good job, now there was a woman in the picture. Someone else who would judge her taste.

What she didn't expect was the rush of disappointment that followed this discovery. Telling herself it was ridiculous to be disappointed her boss—her *grouchy boss*—had a girlfriend, she shoved the box back into place and wound her way through the hollow-sounding empty room that led to the steps and the first floor.

In the office, she set Brady in the playpen she'd brought in the day before and walked to the desk. Pulling his tall-back leather chair away from the desk to sit, she suddenly felt like an interloper. The rest of the house was so empty it was possible to look around and not discover anything, but this was his domain.

A chunky chocolate-colored leather sofa and chair created a seating area atop a Native American print rug that protected the hardwood floor. From the papers strewn over the rough-hewn wood sofa table in the center of the grouping, she guessed that was where Jeb and Slim created the proposals for clients.

A bookcase took up the entire wall to the left of the desk. She glanced at a few titles, mostly mysteries and thrillers. Nothing that give her a clue of how to furnish his huge house.

She pulled open the top desk drawer, looking for a legal pad to make notes and sketch designs. She found nothing but file folders arranged in a long row. With a sigh she began to close the drawer but the name on a tab caught her eye. *Samuel's House.*

If this file contained pictures of the house of a friend—especially a rancher friend—she'd at least get an idea of how his friends lived and know if she was going in the right direction.

She eagerly lifted the file folder from the drawer and opened it on the desktop. To her dismay there were no pictures. Only correspondence.

Dear Mr. Worthington…
On behalf of the staff and children of Samuel's
House, we'd like to thank you and your parents
for your recent generous donations…

Donations? Samuel's House was a charity?
She told herself to close the file, but curiosity got the
better of her and she flipped the first letter over and
found a second.

Dear Mr. Worthington…
Thank you again for remembering Samuel's
House with your recent generous donation.

After the third letter, her mouth had dropped in awe.
Samuel's House was obviously a home for children.
She glanced down at the other file folders and quickly
scanned the identity tabs, but found no other charities.
She flipped the next page of correspondence in the
Samuel's House file.

Dear Mr. Worthington…
Words can't express our gratitude for your com-
mitment to build a new facility for the children at
Samuel's House.

Sophie's eyes popped. He was building an entire
facility?

The generosity exhibited by you and your parents
touches us deeply. The children who come to us
are as much in need of emotional help as they are

basic necessities of life. The new buildings to be erected by your family will provide us with opportunities to instill confidence in our children, even as they learn good sportsmanship and get much needed physical activity.

We hope you'll visit us again soon. The children always enjoy seeing you.

Closing the file, Sophie tried to catch her breath. If she'd thought he was rich before this, her eyes had been opened even wider. The man could afford to build an entire facility for what appeared to be an orphanage.

But his money took a back seat to an even bigger realization. Grouchy Jeb Worthington, the man who supposedly hated kids, supported an orphanage. She leaned back on the chair. That didn't make any sense at all.

CHAPTER FIVE

JEB ambled into the empty kitchen, smiling to himself. With Sophie busy elsewhere in the house, he no longer had to avoid her. Their paths legitimately didn't cross.

He laughed as he made a sandwich to take back to the barn office. He could be very clever when he needed to be. Now it didn't matter that his hormones went crazy when they were in the same room. They'd never be in the same room.

He finished his sandwich and headed out again, but at the kitchen door he realized he needed a file from his desk. He pivoted and marched to his office and found Sophie already in his desk chair.

All right. Fine. So his plan wasn't as good at keeping them apart as he'd thought. But this would be a simple encounter. A minute tops. Nothing to worry about.

"Don't get up," he said, talking as he walked in. But the scent of something heavenly sweet—like roses or peaches—instantly engulfed him. He didn't know what brand of soap or shampoo she used, but it filled the air with a scent so feminine it instantly transmitted a message straight to his groin.

Great.

Brady cooed and Jeb glanced in the corner. The baby sat in the playpen Jeb had seen in her suite, chewing on the ear of a stuffed bear. This time his chest contracted. It was as if all the things that made a woman ultra-feminine had gathered in this one space and decided to torment him.

At the desk, he bent and reached for the handle to open the drawer. On its own volition, his gaze drifted to the right, taking in the smooth length of thigh partially hidden beneath his desk, as her scent swirled around him.

This is ridiculous!

His logical side immediately took control, but his masculinity instantly disagreed. Why was it ridiculous to be attracted to a beautiful woman?

Because nothing can come of it.

He grimaced. Unfortunately his logical side was correct.

He turned his attention to sliding open the drawer and reached for the two files he needed—applications of potential clients. But Sophie shifted on the chair, her elbow bumped his shoulder and their gazes met.

Her eyes were dark, smoky, sexy. Her complexion smooth, perfect. Her lips plump, kissable.

His heart speeded up, scrambling his pulse. His gaze locked with hers. He told himself to pull away and get the hell out of this room, but he didn't move. Didn't speak. Barely breathed. Not because she was so pretty, or even because she was suddenly so close. But because she had the same look of confusion on her face that he was sure was on his.

She was attracted to him, too. Though he'd suspected

that from their encounter at the swimming pool, he hadn't realized the intensity of what she'd felt. Now he knew she was as powerfully attracted to him as he was to her.

Male confidence filled him. The kind that nudges a boy to ask his first crush to dance. The kind that inspires an adolescent to sweet-talk his first date into a real kiss. The kind that leads a man to seduce his first lover. With one smooth movement he would be close enough to kiss her and he didn't think she'd back away—

Her baby yelped and Jeb jumped as if someone had exploded a firecracker. He grabbed his files and headed for the door without a word. What could he say? I damned near made the biggest mistake of my life and kissed you? An employee? A woman with a baby? He couldn't himself believe he'd almost kissed her. How would he explain it to the woman who looked as confused by the attraction as he was?

When he was out of sight, Sophie sucked in a breath and fell back on the chair. He— she— he…

She squeezed her eyes shut then popped them open again. As crazy as it sounded, that man was attracted to her. She'd seen the spark of it in his eyes, felt the electricity of it arching between them. The man who had more money than Sophie could even imagine—enough money to support an orphanage—and was so handsome he made her heart stop… He *liked* her.

Her. Simple, sometimes silly, her.

Even as she realized it didn't make any sense, her heart soared. But Brady screeched again and she shook her head to clear the haze. He might be attracted to her and she might be attracted to him, but he didn't like kids. Support of an orphanage notwithstanding, she'd seen how angry he got around Brady. How standoffish. For Pete's sake, he was firing her because she had the audacity to bring her baby to his ranch.

They could be as hot as Cleopatra and Mark Anthony and absolutely nothing would come of it. She shouldn't even *want* to be attracted to him.

She *didn't* want to be attracted to him.

"I'm sorry, buddy." She rose from the chair and ran to the playpen. "Your mom is here. She isn't going anywhere."

Two days later, having not seen Jeb even once since the episode at his desk, Sophie headed for the barn office. She had waited until he'd been alone for an hour and Brady had been sound asleep for ten minutes, before she took a deep breath for courage and walked the thin sidewalk leading to the barn.

She understood why he was avoiding her, but she'd come to terms with being attracted to him and wasn't going to let it stand in the way of her doing the best job she could. The truth was he was firing her, and that wouldn't look good on a résumé. She could state that she left his employ because the job was live-in and she had a baby and the ranch had no accommodation for Brady. That would probably even work. But it would work better if Jeb would give her a letter of recommendation.

The only way to get a recommendation would be to do a good job. And the best way to assure that was by getting his approval before she actually made any purchases.

Clutching her yellow legal pad, she followed the sidewalk around the neat-as-a-pin white barn to the back, where Slim had told her she would find the office. She knocked on the frame of the open door before she stepped inside.

"Got a minute?"

He glanced up from his work, his eyes dark and serious. "Not really."

She took a timid step into the room. "This won't take long. I don't feel right spending this kind of money without going over the list of purchases with you first. I don't want to accidentally order thousands of dollars of things you hate."

"We'd just send them back."

"I know, but work with me on this. It would be so much simpler if you'd just take a quick look and tell me I'm going in the right direction."

He sighed and dropped his pencil. "Let me see what you have."

With the trepidation of a schoolgirl about to show her artistry to her favorite teacher, she handed the legal pad across the desk. With the menacing scowl of the lord of darkness, he flipped it open.

She'd cut out prints of furniture, lamps and accessories that she'd made from the pictures she'd found on the Internet and pasted them onto the sheets in the legal pad, creating the groupings she intended in each room.

He flipped from page to page, examining the things she'd chosen. His expression went from grouchy to curious to happy in four flips.

He looked up at her. "These are great."

She winced. "The cutouts leave a lot to be desired."

"No. They're fine. I can see exactly what you intend to do." He glanced down again. "How did you get pictures of the furniture I already have?"

"I found the Web sites for the brand names and there they were."

"This is all good."

"Really?"

He peered up again, the curious expression back on his face. "Why would you think they weren't?" Before she could answer he shook his head. "Your parents, right?"

She grimaced. "Yes and no. I'd love to blame them for absolutely everything wrong in my life, but the truth is I'm not a decorator."

He flipped back and reviewed the pages he'd already examined. "You may not be a trained decorator but these are really, really good." He caught her gaze again. "I think the fact that you aren't a pro works in your favor. I don't want too polished of a look. I don't want things to be too perfect. These rooms are just the simple rooms of a normal house."

She finally took a seat. "I hope they aren't too simple."

He laughed, turning to the next page. "Maybe what I should have said was that they looked comfortable."

"And not as much as a pink pillow among them."

He worked his way through the sheets in the legal pad again and with every flip of a page, confidence spread through Sophie. This grouchy guy, who to this point seemed unpleaseable, genuinely liked her plans for his home.

After studying the final page, he closed the tablet and handed it across his desk. "Do it."

The joy of accomplishment swelled her heart until it was so big she could barely breathe. "Really? Everything?"

"Everything. I didn't see anything that made me want to run for cover. Every room looks comfortable and homey. Just what I want."

The joy that had swelled her heart gave way to another, more elemental feeling. Connection. She'd finally done something that he more than liked. She'd finally pleased him.

But the brush of their hands as he handed the legal pad to her reminded her that his real problem with her had little to do with her work. They were powerfully attracted to each other. Sexily, steamily attracted to each other. And after the episode in his office, they both knew it.

She pulled in a breath, caught his gaze, forced him to look at her, deal with her, as an employee. Not a woman.

"I really appreciate your confidence in me. I won't disappoint you."

"No," he said slowly, holding her gaze, obviously getting the subliminal message she so desperately wanted to send. "I don't think you will."

"Thank you. I can start pulling this all together tomorrow morning."

"And don't skimp on shipping. I want as much of this done as possible for the client visit. If it means we pay extra to get things here, then that's what we do. Money is no object."

"Okay."

She turned and began to walk out of the room, but he called her back. "Hey, Sophie?"

She swallowed, worried that something negative

had occurred to him, so when she faced him again she made sure her expression displayed nothing but confidence. "Yes?"

"Are you going to need any help?"

"Help?"

"You know. Lifting furniture, painting, that kind of thing?"

She hadn't thought of that. Though she worried it might count as a strike against her, she chose to go with the truth. "Probably."

He glanced down at his work again. "When you need someone, talk to Slim. He'll know who he can spare for a few days or a few hours."

Success tumbled through her. He was treating her totally like an employee. "Thanks."

"You're welcome." He didn't look up. She didn't take offense, but scurrying up the sidewalk to the house, her flip-flops slapping her heels as she ran, a realization occurred to her. He'd treated her well because she'd behaved ultraprofessionally. Proud of her work, she'd let it speak for itself and when he asked a question, she was ready. Her flip-flops again slapped her heels as she made her way through the foyer, and she stopped dead in her tracks. As usual, she wore shorts, a tank top and flip-flops because they were easy to work in, but they really weren't very professional. Which was probably why he didn't see her as an employee first, but a woman. Maybe if she dressed a little more professionally she could add another layer of protection for him?

With Jeb's permission, Sophie began her shopping spree. For days, she searched the Internet making comparisons, looking for bargains. Though Jeb had told her money was no object, she knew a budget was coming and she didn't want to waste her resources. Slim asked her when she would need assistance from his hands and she said she'd need his guys the next day. That was when the furniture would begin arriving.

"That's cutting it mighty close," he'd said, eating a dish of apple cobbler while Jeb was on the phone schmoozing a potential client. "So, I'm scheduling myself in your team, too."

That surprised her. "Really?"

"Sure. I want to see you succeed." He smiled sheepishly. "You remind me of my oldest daughter."

"You have a family?"

Slim rolled his eyes. "No. They found me under a rock."

She laughed. "I didn't mean that! I'm talking about being married. I didn't even know you had been."

"Was. Like Jeb, I'm a victim of divorce." He took a bite, chewed and swallowed. "Ranch life isn't easy on a marriage."

Sophie held back an "Oh," of understanding that lifted her spirits. If Jeb had been married to the woman who had owned the pink weights, pink robe and pink everything she'd found in the workout room that meant they didn't belong to a girlfriend. Of course, jumping to the conclusion that those things belonged to an exwife might actually be wishful thinking, if only because that meant he was free.

Still, it wouldn't do her any good that he was free. She wouldn't pursue him and he wouldn't pursue her. He didn't like kids and she had one. Plus, she'd be gone in two weeks. No worry about them connecting in any way but professionally.

But she was curious.

And she couldn't ask Slim. If there was one thing she'd seen about ranch life, it was that the people who worked here were loyal. She'd never ask Slim a question he'd have to refuse to answer because she sure as heck knew he'd never betray Jeb.

"So what did you do in California?"

"Do?"

"I thought I'd start sneakily asking you questions about your life and what you like and don't like so I could figure out a gift to buy you as a way to thank you for the pie."

She laughed. It was cobbler, but she didn't correct him. His groans of appreciation while he ate kept her confidence high. "You don't have to buy me a gift."

"I know I don't have to. I want to."

She shook her head. "Just having you appreciate my cooking is thanks enough."

"Since you don't want a gift. How about a ride? Maybe you'd like to take one of the horses out for a few hours."

Her eyes widened. She'd never ridden a horse, but being at this breathtaking ranch had awakened that desire in her. "I'd love to see more of the ranch."

Jeb knew Slim was up to something the second he walked into the kitchen.

"I was just telling Sophie we have a new mare, perfect for someone like her to ride."

He faced her. As had now become the norm, her

thick dark hair was swept to the top of her head and pinned out of her way, but tendrils escaped to frame her face. Her bright eyes were shining. Her smile made him want to smile back at her. Which was a really great reason to stop looking at her, but he couldn't very well stare at the coffeepot while talking to her.

"You've never ridden?"

"No."

Her excited expression was almost too much for him to bear and he couldn't stop the chuckle that escaped. "And you want to go riding this afternoon?"

"I've got all the furniture and fixtures ordered. Now I have nothing to do but wait until everything arrives."

"Okay. Great. Whatever."

Slim smiled down at the dish of pastry in front of him. "That's exactly what I told her you'd say. I also told her she couldn't ride alone on her first time. She'd need a guide."

"Right again."

"Which is why I told her I'd watch her baby."

Jeb frowned. "How can you watch the baby when you're going with her?"

"Well, I could go with her but then you'd have to watch Brady."

Jeb's breath caught. He pictured himself…alone… with the little boy with the wild hair and the bright eyes and the smile that could lift the spirits of a man on death row. Terror filled him. He'd never even held a child. He most certainly didn't know how to care for one for several hours.

What if he cried and Jeb couldn't get him to stop?

What if he—required a diaper change?

What if he choked?

"I can't do either."

"You have to do one," Slim pointed out, his smile sly and victorious.

Slim was baiting him! He wanted Jeb to backhand-edly admit he had the hots for his new housekeeper by refusing to be alone with her. Or in the alternative, he wanted Jeb to actually go on the ride and spend some time alone with the woman who could make him want to ravish her just being in the same room, hoping some-thing would happen between them. Either way he was meddling, which Jeb had specifically warned him not to.

Jeb took a breath. Slim knew Jeb would never fire him. Their bond went beyond a little teasing about a woman. So he was being clever, but Jeb could be pretty crafty himself. He decided to do exactly what Slim wanted him to do. Go with Sophie. But not with the result Slim expected. His foreman might think he was matchmaking, but Jeb had willpower enough to resist her. He would return without stars in his eyes or lipstick on his mouth because he would make this ride as innocent as possible. He'd shown new employees around the ranch before. And Sophie appeared to like behaving like an employee. So if he treated her solely as an employee when they were alone, in a fairly romantic environment, this ride could actually purge their attraction once and for all.

"Fine. I'll ride with her."

CHAPTER SIX

WHILE Jeb got the horses, Sophie changed into jeans and sensible shoes. She eagerly raced to the barn, ready for the adventure of riding a horse and finally seeing more of the ranch than what was within walking distance.

But, she also had another reason for wanting to take a ride alone with Jeb. It was the perfect opportunity to reinforce that he had nothing to fear from their attraction. She'd already set a tone of professional behavior. This would show him that even in a relaxed setting they could interact like mature adults.

When she reached the barn Jeb stood by two saddled horses. One she recognized as the horse he'd been on the day she arrived at the ranch. The other was a brown mare, a lot less commanding than Jeb's sleek bay.

"Well, let's get going."

After leading the two horses outside, Jeb pointed at the stirrup. "Put your left foot in there, then hoist yourself up, toss your leg over the horse's back and settle yourself in the groove of the saddle."

That sounded simple enough. "Okay." She nodded

and slid her foot into the stirrup. But in spite of a decade of aerobics, she couldn't quite hoist herself up and over the broad back of the horse. Not even after three tries.

With a sigh, Jeb put his hands on her waist and said, "All right. I'll say one-two-three-go, then you sort of leap and I'll help you the rest of the way."

Sophie took a shuddering breath and nodded, unable to speak. How was she going to keep this trip innocent when his big hands made her waist seem tiny, and having his fingers curled around her middle so intimately also felt—right. Wonderful. Perfect.

"One-two-three-go!"

With one foot in the stirrup, she pushed off with the one still on the ground. When she got about halfway up, Jeb pressed his palms to her bottom to give her a boost and her mind went blank. She forgot the part about swinging her leg around and nearly went flying headfirst over the horse. She screamed, stopping her out-of-control forward momentum by slapping her palms on the saddle, which caused her to fall backward, almost on top of Jeb.

Knowing he was probably furious she quickly said, "I forgot the thing about swinging my leg around."

"Well, don't forget this time!"

His angry voice caused her to face him. "Hey! Don't yell! I'm new at this."

But when she caught his gaze, his eyes were bright and aware, taut with male need. Everything she felt from the touch of his hands on her was magnified a hundredfold in his eyes.

He very quietly said, "Let's try this again."

She almost told him to forget the ride. Not only was

she still on the ground and still in need of his hands on her waist to hoist her up again, but she didn't think her plan to stay neutral, like a boss and his housekeeper, was going to work. Their attraction was too strong and they were about to take a ride, alone.

Thinking of the two of them all by themselves in the wide-open spaces brought a million possibilities to mind—including the fact that he could absolutely ignore her for hours. But she didn't think so. If just having his hands on her behind caused her to forget everything but her name, out there in the wilderness, with no one to see, and the real world so far behind them, it was more likely that their attraction would get the better of them and one of them would act on it.

Then what would she do? If he was the one to lose control would she resist? *Could* she resist? If he kissed her, would she let him touch her? And if he touched her, would she be able to stop them from making love? All this time she'd been so sure she could keep herself in line, but what if she only kept her wits because he kept his? And what if he only kept his because of prying eyes? What if, totally and completely alone, they couldn't resist the force that made her shiver with need?

He turned her around to face the horse again, grabbed her foot and tucked it in the stirrup. Before she could argue or even get her bearings, he said, "One, two, three go!"

Rather than give her time to launch her leg over the horse, he put one hand on her butt to boost her at the same time that he grabbed her leg and helped it over the saddle. In what seemed like three seconds, she was straddling the mare.

Excitement raced through her and she forgot everything she'd been worrying about. "I did it!"

He shook his head with a snort. "Yeah. It's more like *I* did it."

"What does it matter?" Atop the mare—who might look small next to Jeb's horse, but who made Sophie feel as if she were sitting on top of the world—Sophie experienced a wave of sheer power. *This*—this feeling of power and control—was probably part of the draw of working on a ranch, but it was probably also the reason Jeb didn't appear concerned about their alone time. With this high view of the world, she genuinely believed she was strong enough to do anything. Including resist her boss.

Jeb led the way, his horse walking at a leisurely pace. Not yet accustomed to straddling the huge beast, Sophie swayed from side to side, thanking God Jeb was in front and couldn't see her.

"You better find your center. Get yourself settled."

"Do you have a rearview mirror or something?"

"I just know how greenhorns sit."

Irritated that he'd called her a greenhorn, even though she was, Sophie fidgeted until she stabilized. The mare glanced back at her as if voicing her approval. Sophie totally relaxed.

In only a few minutes they left behind the ranch buildings, and were riding a dirt trail. Leaving the hustle and bustle of Jeb's business, they rode into silence. Sunshine reflected off green grass with a dark mountain backdrop.

After a while, Sophie could no longer stay silent. "This is spectacular."

He half turned. "The view?"

"The whole thing. The view. The peace and quiet. The privacy." She peeked over at him. "When you're guaranteed that your mother's students will fill up the downstairs of your house every day, privacy becomes very important."

"Nowhere to run?"

"No. I could always find a place to run and even more places to hide. That was the problem. I would have spent my teen years in a closet."

He laughed. "*Would* have?"

"Julianna, our housekeeper, typically found me and put me to work."

For that he turned. "Really?"

"I think she knew what my parents refused to see."

He slowed his horse, allowing her to catch up with him. "What's that?"

"That we weren't really rich. I don't think she was trying to teach me a skill for a job, but she recognized that I'd need to know how to scrub my own kitchen and dust a bedroom."

"And you turned those few lessons into a career."

"You scoff, but because this job had room and board, the money I made here would have paid off the hospital and doctor bills from Brady's birth in no time."

He looked away, obviously uncomfortable, but Sophie wouldn't take the comment back or even amend it. She wasn't sorry he now knew how much this job had meant to her, and even mentioning Brady might have been for the best. He didn't like kids and she had one. That had cooled his attraction every time.

They rode for another ten minutes in silence. She hadn't intended to insult him because the silence was strained, oppressive. Even meaningless small talk would be better than this.

She took a breath and casually said, "What brought *you* here?"

"What makes you think I'm not from here?"

"Slim and the other guys talk with a barely discernible twang, but still with a distinct way of speaking. You don't have one." She waited a beat then said, "So where are you from?"

"Nowhere."

She laughed. "Right. Everybody hates their roots, but a person can't claim not to have any."

"I can. My parents were everything your parents pretended to be. Rich. Sophisticated. Jet-setters."

Her eyes widened. "No kidding."

"They had so much money they didn't need to put on airs or even stay in one place. They lived where they wanted, did what they wanted when they wanted."

"And ignored you?" she asked, almost hoping he'd say yes because then they'd be kindred spirits.

He shook his head. "No such luck. I was on every fishing boat, at every party, on every yacht."

She gaped at him, angry that he didn't appreciate his good fortune. "Pardon me for not being sympathetic."

He laughed. "Right. It was a joy to be exposed to things a kid shouldn't see."

She'd never thought of that. Adults partying on a yacht probably forgot to be discreet. She pictured pitchers of margaritas, bikini clad women and men ogling, maybe getting a little free with their hands.

Jeb pulled on his horse's reins. "Let's stop for a minute, give the horses a chance to get a drink."

He'd brought them to a small stream that wound through a grove of trees. Sophie gazed around in awe. "Okay."

He easily dismounted. Sophie watched him then mimicked what he had done.

"Hey, look at that." She grinned. "I got myself down."

"The trick will be whether or not you can get yourself back up."

She laughed, but her laughter suddenly faded. He was nice, funny even. Fun to be with. It was hard to believe he didn't like kids. Especially since he supported an orphanage. Why would a man who didn't like kids support an orphanage?

In the ensuing silence, she glanced around, rummaging in her brain for something to say and remembering he'd never really finished the explanation about his childhood. "So, with such wacky parents, how'd you grow up to be so normal?"

He grabbed the reins of both horses and walked them to the stream. As they drank, he said, "I didn't. I was the most confused person on the planet until I went to university. I lived on campus for the first two years, but eventually I got an apartment next door to some really stable guys. People who were in school because they needed to learn accounting and business practices and even history."

"Let me guess…ranchers?"

"Yes." He glanced over. "As soon as the horses are done drinking, we'll turn back."

"But we hardly went anywhere!"

"We've gone far enough."

Yeah. They'd gone far enough in the conversation! He'd told her a bit of his past but this was as far as he intended to go. And the only reason she could think of why he'd refuse to tell her facts so far from the past that they shouldn't matter anymore was that they did matter. Which meant school or his friends somehow connected to one of their two taboo topics. Their attraction or her baby.

Curiosity tingled through her. How could friends cause a man to dislike kids? It didn't make any sense. And because his dislike of kids had cost her her job, she couldn't let it go.

She walked over to him. "You know what? I don't think so. Everybody else might have to scrape and bow when you talk, but I'm already fired. So I'm not taking no for an answer. I want to hear about the guys who impressed you enough that you copied them."

He sighed. "No."

She groaned. "Why not? What's the big deal in telling me?"

"It's none of your business."

"Really? I'm guessing the reason you don't like kids is all wrapped up in this story, and since I lost this job because you don't like kids, I think I have the right to know."

He turned away, but she caught his arm and spun him around again. "What are you so afraid of?"

His gaze latched onto hers, his stormy eyes revealing his anger. "Seriously, you don't want to mess with this right now."

"Yes, I do! And I'm not going to stop—"

As quickly as she'd spun him around, he grabbed her by the waist and hauled her against him, his lips falling to hers. He didn't kiss her gently like a man expressing an emotion. He kissed her roughly like a man in the grip of a need. He swallowed her gasp of surprise and took advantage of the slight parting of her lips to slide his tongue into her mouth. Her head spun and liquid warmth fell from her chest to her toes.

But she didn't stop him. The same thing that had its hooks in him took a hold of her. Her mind went blissfully black and she kissed him back, every bit as greedy as he was.

He abruptly pulled away, his breathing raspy, his voice equally so when he said, "Now, can we go back?"

She stared into his stormy-gray eyes. Saw the heat, but also the confusion. He hadn't kissed her to demonstrate their attraction. He was warning her. Their chemistry was a little too hot and a little too strong. At some point it would get the better of them. If they didn't stop talking, getting close, that "point" would be today.

"Yes. We can go back."

But could they?

CHAPTER SEVEN

A LITTLE after eight the next morning, the kitchen door swung open. Sophie peeked up from feeding Brady to see Jeb stopped in the doorway. Their gazes caught. The same syrupy warmth that had flooded her when he kissed her poured through her, but he hardly registered a reaction. If anything, he looked confused.

Quickly glancing down again, she saw the baby spoon in her hand, remembered Brady was right beside her in the chair and her heart stopped. Jeb liked her well enough—maybe too well—when they were alone. When it was just them. A man and a woman who were incredibly sexually attracted. But put Brady into the picture and he had absolutely no interest in her.

He walked directly to the coffeepot. "I got a call about three o'clock this morning. Slim's mom had a heart attack. He's in Texas. He'll be out for a while."

Sophie's breath backed up in her lungs. Sympathy for Slim enveloped her, along with sudden understanding. Jeb's confusion had nothing to do with her or Brady. "Oh, my goodness, I'm so sorry."

"Yeah. He's a mess." Jeb filled his travel mug with

coffee and faced her. "He called me as soon as he got off the phone with his sister, borrowed the plane and flew down." His gaze found Brady and his eyes narrowed. She expected him to chastise her, but he kept the conversation on Slim. "I imagine he's pacing a hospital corridor about now."

His eyes flicked back to Sophie, and she tried not to feel anything when their gazes met, but a wave of sensation rolled through her. She couldn't turn off or tone down her reactions to him. She'd never felt any of the things with Mick that she'd experienced the day before when Jeb had kissed her. Her off-the-charts response to him was confusing, frustrating, seductive—and absolutely insane.

The man didn't even want to be in the same room with her son and she suspected he wasn't saying anything about Brady right now only because he had more pressing concerns. She couldn't possibly be attracted to someone who disliked her baby so much that he wouldn't keep her as his housekeeper. So why had her heart flip-flopped and her chest tightened, just because he looked at her? Hadn't she already made this mistake with Mick?

"Can you manage without him for a few days?"

She shook her head as if to clear a haze. "I'm sorry. I missed what you said."

"I asked if you could manage without Slim for a few days."

She hesitated. Furniture would begin arriving today. Slim had assigned two hands to help her, but she had no idea if two men would be enough. Still, Jeb's plate was full. She wouldn't add to his stress.

"Yes. I can manage."

Jeb shook his head. "That pause you took says you're not sure you can."

"I'm not. I don't know how much of the furniture will get here today. And we're also on a deadline. Every pair of hands helps."

"Okay, see how it goes and if you need more men, don't pussyfoot around, ask."

She nodded. He snapped the lid on his travel mug and left the kitchen. Sophie let out her breath. She had to get a hold of herself. Not only was her attraction to Jeb so strong it was frightening, but she had to work here for another two weeks. If nothing else, she had to keep her reactions to herself. With Slim gone Jeb didn't need the added burden of having to tiptoe around her. If anything, she should find a way to pitch in and help.

It didn't take much thinking to figure out what she could do. Though Jeb had told her dinner was no longer her responsibility, with the change in his workload all bets were off. Nine chances out of ten he wouldn't have time to get his own supper and if she fixed him something, he'd appreciate it.

The question was could they handle being in the same room for twenty or so minutes while he ate?

Furniture began arriving at noon. The two men Slim had assigned to her, Bob and Monty, assisted the delivery men with unloading trucks and carted the sofas and chairs, boxes and crates to rooms Sophie designated. They didn't unpack anything, merely got everything to its proper place, knowing they'd have their work cut out for them the following day.

In between deliveries, Sophie put a pan of three-cheese ziti in the oven. She wouldn't beg Jeb to eat. If he refused dinner, she would simply smile and let him go his own way. But her conscience wouldn't let her shirk her responsibility in a time when everybody should be pitching in.

At dark, Jeb entered the kitchen, his face drawn and tired. The steps he took were slow. He even closed the door softly, as if he barely had any energy.

Sophie turned to the stove, making her appearance in the kitchen as casual, normal, as possible. They were supposed to be housekeeper and boss, not potential lovers. She'd already proven that when she behaved professionally, he did, too, so maybe if she stuck to that principle, he'd follow suit.

Her back to him as she stirred, she said, "Have you had supper?"

"No."

"Good. I made three-cheese ziti." She faced him again and smiled cautiously. "It's one of my specialties. I could have it on the table in ten minutes, if you're interested."

For a few seconds he didn't reply. Sophie held her breath. She knew he was thinking about that kiss, about their attraction, about whether or not spending this much time alone was a good idea. She couldn't believe he was so afraid of being alone with her that he'd go hungry rather than let her cook for him but she also didn't really know him. And that was another thing she had to remember when their attraction began to get the best of her.

Finally he said, "I don't have to eat in the dining room, do I?"

"It's easier for me if you eat in the kitchen."

"Can I clean up first?"

"Sure. That'll give me time to toss a salad."

He left the kitchen and Sophie sucked in a breath. Her preparing supper for him was the right thing to do. If they behaved like a normal boss and housekeeper, it might also be a way for them to get beyond the attraction neither one of them wanted.

But just as she grabbed the pot holders to pull the ziti from the oven, Brady's soft cries issued from the baby monitor and she froze.

Oh, no!

She raced to her crying baby, hoping she could coax him back to sleep before Jeb returned from cleaning up, but from the way he bounced and yelped when she entered the bedroom she knew he was too awake to drift back to sleep with a back rub. And she didn't have time to rock him.

She glanced from the door to the crib and back again. She had no choice. She had to take Brady to the high chair.

Jeb walked into the kitchen to find Sophie busy at the stove. He pulled a chair away from the table and immediately noticed the baby in the high chair beside it. The kid grinned up at him.

He pulled in a silent breath. This had to have been the worst day of his life. Not only was his foreman gone and his ranch in total confusion, but he'd spent the day thinking about a kiss that had been a whopper of a mistake. Now, he had a baby six inches away from him.

But just like everything else that had happened in the

past fifteen hours, even this meal wasn't part of the agenda. Having the little boy at the table must have been unavoidable, or Sophie wouldn't have him here. The woman had done nothing but try to please him since she'd arrived at the Silver Saddle. Tonight she'd been ready with supper—even though he hadn't asked. Surely, he could muster twenty minutes of civility for her baby?

He glanced over.

The kid grinned again.

His lungs felt as if they had filled with cement, but he refused to give into the sorrow, the loss, the self-pity. None of his troubles were this baby's fault.

"Hey…" He paused. What had Slim called him? Brody? Bradley? *Brady.* "Hey, Brady."

The little boy pounded his rattle on the high chair tray.

Sophie brought a salad to the table and this time when Jeb's heart turned over in his chest it was for an entirely different reason. His blood hadn't ever boiled in his veins the way it had from a thirty-second kiss meant to dissuade himself and the woman setting a salad in front of him. He'd wanted to show her they shouldn't play with fire, and all he'd accomplished was to throw gas on the flames.

With the salad in front of him, Sophie headed back to the stove. He squeezed his eyes shut, told himself he was thirty-five years old, owner of a thriving business, too smart to let a little thing like emotion ruin his plans.

"I'm sorry that I had to bring Brady to the kitchen. He was sleeping and I thought he was down for the night, but—"

Jeb stopped her with a wave of his hand. "It's fine."

She sucked in a relieved breath. "Thanks. I'm sorry—"

Yet another apology from a woman who really hadn't done anything wrong. Her fear of him shamed him. Life had treated this woman abysmally. He knew it. Now he was adding to her misery. "Don't say you're sorry. This is fine. I'm fine. We're all fine."

"Okay."

A few seconds passed in silence as he grabbed a dinner roll and buttered it. The baby pounded his rattle on the tray. Made soft cooing noises. Laughed at nothing.

From the stove, Sophie called, "Are you having fun back there?"

He giggled.

Jeb put another pat of butter on his roll, desperately trying to ignore them.

But when she came to the table with a bowl of green beans, she looked at Jeb, not the baby.

"Can I ask you a question?"

The loner in him, the man who'd realized five years ago when Laine had left him that he'd always be alone, wanted to say no. But his fair side, the part of him that knew just how wrong it was to make a woman feel embarrassed for her child, wouldn't let him. He focused on his roll. "Sure. You can ask a question."

"What is it about babies that you don't like?"

His knife stopped. She'd gone straight for the jugular. The moment of truth. The point where he either spilled his guts or gave her just enough of an answer to satisfy her curiosity.

He cleared his throat. No matter how much he

wanted to be fair, the bottom line truth she was digging for wasn't any of her business. So, he simply said, "I don't dislike babies. I just haven't been around them much."

"Oh."

He dug into his salad.

"Because of your parents' lifestyle?"

He nodded.

"Not a lot of people with kids on yachts?"

"Not a lot of people who live to party actually have kids. And if they do, they're typically hidden away with a nanny."

"Do you ever wish you'd been left with a nanny?"

He had. A million times over he'd wished his parents had purchased a home. *Anywhere.* In the country. In the city. Anywhere. They could have even left him with a nanny. They could have left him with an army of nannies and he wouldn't have cared because he could have consistently attended school, made friends, known stability. Then he wouldn't have made his mistake with Laine. He wouldn't have hurt her or himself. He wouldn't have the feeling he was tumbling over a waterfall every time he looked at the woman serving him dinner.

But, again, that was his private misery. Not something he'd share with a woman he'd known about a week, a woman who'd be leaving his ranch in another two.

"My parents did what they did. I learned long ago not to wish for things that didn't or can't happen." Before she could ask another question, he quickly said,

"What about you? Have you ever wished you'd married Brady's dad?"

It was a low blow to turn the tables so harshly, but when she paused and licked her lips, Jeb forgot all about Brady's dad and her possible reply. His gaze fell to her mouth and he remembered every second of kissing her. The fire in his blood. The silkiness of her lips. The way they seemed to fit together so perfectly.

"Like every unmarried pregnant woman, I thought getting married would solve all our problems. So, yeah, at first I did wish I could have married Brady's dad." She rolled her eyes. "Boy, would *that* have been a mistake!"

"What was he like?" Jeb asked, hoping against hope she'd tell him that her ex was just like him so he could easily talk himself out of liking her, wanting her.

"He was very focused."

"Really?" Apparently he and her ex *were* alike. "Was he building a business or something?"

"He was building a life. He had a great job, made lots of money and could afford to have absolutely anything he wanted. So what he was doing was creating a lifestyle, a home."

Jeb frowned. From everything he'd seen, Sophie was exactly the kind of woman a man would want to create a home with. What she planned to do with his house was magazine worthy. So her boyfriend dumping her didn't make any sense.

"If he was building a life I'm not sure I understand how you didn't fit."

"Oh, I fit," she readily replied. "It was Brady who didn't."

Jeb's heart flopped over in his chest and he glanced at the perfect, happy boy in the high chair. Righteous indignation exploded in him for the child unwanted by his dad and he could have happily found the man and beat him to a pulp. But even as part of him condemned Brady's dad, the other part reminded him that he wasn't any better. And *that,* the truth he avoided more than confronted, was his real avenue to obliterate his longing for a relationship between him and his housekeeper. And maybe it was time he not only faced it, but also he gave her enough of a hint that she'd get the stars out of her eyes, too.

He cleared his throat. "The truth is, Sophie, some people aren't cut out to be fathers."

"That's what Mick said."

Jeb waited a beat, then another, until she returned to the table with a glass of iced tea. When her gaze found his, he quietly said, "I'm not, either."

He saw from the way her eyes sharpened, then darkened, that she got his message. Women with babies shouldn't get too attached to men who weren't cut out to be fathers. Though he'd been subtly telling her that by his behavior since the moment she pulled Brady from her car, saying the words aloud pounded home the point.

She stiffened and shifted ever so slightly, putting herself between him and her son, as if protecting him, and he got *her* message. Her baby would always take precedence. Especially over something as fleeting as a potential romance.

Good for her.

He ate the rest of his dinner in near silence, while

Sophie puttered behind him, storing leftovers, stacking dishes in the dishwasher. When they did talk it was about Slim's mother's upcoming surgery. Sophie volunteered to call her father and get background information about the procedure, but Jeb reminded her that he could look it up on the Internet, closing the door because he didn't want to get cozy with her. He didn't want to depend on her for personal things. Hell, he didn't even want to have personal discussions with her. He just wanted to be left alone.

After the main course, he refused cobbler and walked out of the kitchen as if nothing major had happened. But as he strode through the downstairs corridor to the stairway that led to the family room and ultimately the weight room, he knew that was a lie. Something major had happened. She hadn't merely cooked for him. They'd talked and he'd told her something he hadn't ever told anyone else.

But it had been unavoidable. They had to deal with their attraction once and for all. They'd hit the point where he had to come right out and say he wasn't cut out to be a dad, so there'd be no more guessing. No more confusion. No more wondering. She'd simply stay away.

It was exactly what he wanted.

So, why did he feel so awful?

As he passed the hall closet on his way to change into sweats to exercise, he noticed the door was ajar. With an absent movement, he raised his arm to close it, but as he did he saw a swatch of pink and he stopped.

Seeing the box of things Laine had left behind, his entire body hummed with emotion. Anger. Sadness. Anticipation. Wishing. Hoping.

Not wanting to go down that road again, he tried to close the door, but the corner of the box hung out, over the thin metal runner for the sliding panel. That's why the door wouldn't close. Somebody had been in here.

Sophie.

She knew there had been a woman in his life. One of the men might even have mentioned that Jeb had been married before.

He stifled a groan. No wonder she'd been so quiet when he'd told her he wasn't cut out to be a dad. She'd probably been jumping to all kinds of conclusions. She might have even envisioned a sad wife, longing for children, leaving because Jeb refused to have any.

Damn Laine for leaving these things.

Steeled for a rush of pain, Jeb stooped beside the box. He looked down at the pink weights, pink towels, pink everything. He pictured Laine working out, using the weights, laughing as they ran side by side on the treadmills, drying off with one of the hideous pink towels.

He picked up the weight, forced himself to feel it, to remember the sound of it crashing through the mirrored wall across from the weight bench.

Pain strong enough that she'd lost her temper, lost control and done something she never would have done in a million years. Just as she'd said things that she never would have even contemplated had their situation not been so heartrending.

That's why he wouldn't even consider exploring his feelings for Sophie. He wouldn't put Sophie through the kind of emotional pain that arose when a woman got involved with him.

* * *

After dressing herself and Brady the next morning, Sophie made her way to the kitchen, where she found Jeb leaning against the counter, waiting for the coffee to brew.

She paused in the doorway, not sure if she should pretend she forgot something and leave before he made an issue of Brady being in the same room, or push the envelope. The night before he hadn't minded Brady being at the table. After a bit of hemming and hawing around, he had admitted he wasn't cut out to be a father, but, oddly, that had actually made sense of many things. A man who supported an orphanage couldn't possibly be opposed to a baby, but he might worry that with a fatherless kid underfoot he'd be forced into the role of surrogate dad. A role he didn't want.

"I started the coffee."

She took a cautious step into the room. "So I see."

He turned to the counter, reached for something on the other side of the coffeepot and faced her again, displaying the pink weight she'd found in the box of junk in the gym.

"There's a box of this stuff in the closet in front of the weight room shower. It belonged to my ex-wife. Have one of the boys put it out in the trash barrel."

She said, "Okay," but her mind was going a million miles a second. Not because he'd admitted he'd been married before, but because he still wasn't reacting to Brady. Did this mean that with his objection to being cast in the role of father out in the open, he now didn't mind being around Brady—as long as she didn't try to get him to play daddy?

She took a few careful steps into the kitchen, walking to the cabinet where she stored Brady's cereal. Unfazed, Jeb turned to open the cupboard door above the coffeemaker. He pulled down his travel mug and poured in cream, as if it were any other morning. Nothing wrong. Nothing amiss.

He *didn't* mind having her baby in the room!

The coffeemaker groaned and he picked up the coffeepot to fill his travel mug.

With her baby on her hip, she walked to the refrigerator to grab the milk to make Brady's cereal, still watching Jeb out of her peripheral vision, checking for any sign that he wanted her baby gone. But as she opened the refrigerator door, she caught him staring at Brady with a look of longing so intense it nearly stole her breath.

She ducked into the refrigerator before he realized she'd seen it, but that expression totally confused her. That was the look of a man who loved kids. Yearned for kids. Not a guy who didn't want to be a dad. How could he believe he wasn't cut out to be a father?

Pulling out of the refrigerator, she glanced at the pink weight. Maybe it wasn't a coincidence that after spending time with Brady the night before Jeb had been thinking of his ex-wife, maybe even deliberately going through her old workout gear? Thanks to Mick, she knew that people sometimes said terrible things to each other when a relationship was breaking down. Maybe, disillusioned over their failed marriage, Jeb's wife had told him he wouldn't make a good dad?

Telling herself that was none of her business, Sophie set the milk on the counter and reached into the cupboard for a bowl. After placing it on the countertop, she shifted to the drawer to retrieve a spoon, and again caught Jeb gazing at her son.

That absolutely was *not* the look of a guy who wasn't daddy material. If the expression on his face was anything to go by, he longed to hold her son.

Taking the cereal ingredients to the table, she told herself to let it go, but it was no use. The man was curious about her baby. Wanted to hold him. Maybe even get to know him. But he wouldn't ask, and after his declaration that he wasn't cut out to be a dad, she couldn't make the offer.

She frowned. Maybe offering to let him hold her son wasn't the way to go about this. If she made it seem as if he was doing her a favor by holding Brady, he probably wouldn't think twice about it.

Before she lost her courage, she turned to Jeb and asked, "Would you hold him while I mix his cereal?"

Without giving him a chance to question if he could handle it, she shoved Brady at him. He grasped the baby around his tummy. "Wait. Stop. I can't—"

Sophie turned away, busying herself with the cereal and jar of strained fruit. "Sure you can. Just put his butt on your forearm and he'll settle in himself. Remember what you told me about finding my center on the horse. It's sort of the same principle."

She glanced over out of the corner of her eye, ready to spring into action if Jeb bobbled her baby. Looking simultaneously horrified and terrified, Jeb quickly did as she instructed. Within seconds Brady was comfortably nestled on his arm and against his chest. Jeb put his big hand across the baby's back, securing him.

Sophie relaxed, but she prepared Brady's cereal

quickly, not wanting to test Jeb's abilities or his patience. When everything was ready, she pulled the baby from Jeb's arms and carried him to the high chair.

Jeb picked up his coffee. Several seconds ticked off the clock in total silence. But he didn't leave the kitchen. He wasn't scowling. If he was really angry, he would have stormed out of the room. Wouldn't he?

"So he likes that mush?"

Sophie smiled. He wasn't angry. And he was curious. "Yes. He loves this mush."

"What is it?"

"Rice cereal and strained fruit." She lifted the jar and examined it. "Bananas today."

"I'm guessing it tastes better than it looks."

She laughed. "It does."

"I hope so." He turned to the counter again, found the lid for his travel mug and snapped it on before heading for the door, where he paused. "You wouldn't mind making supper again?"

"No. I love to cook."

"Okay, then I'll see you later."

When he was gone, Sophie let out the breath she had been holding. They might not ever get together romantically. Her leaving precluded that, but she had the sudden, intense feeling that that didn't matter. Jeb Worthington was a nice guy, who supported an orphanage, who believed, for some reason, that he'd make a lousy father. She understood accusations being hurled by an angry lover. She understood believing them, if only because of being vulnerable in the moment. But Jeb had been divorced a while. It was time for him to get beyond the accusations. And happy Brady was maybe just the baby to help him along.

After breakfast, Sophie found Monty and Bob waiting in the downstairs family room for her. Mug of coffee in one hand, Brady on her arm, she greeted them. "Good morning."

Monty took off his hat. Bob blushed endearingly. "Morning."

Maneuvering through stacks of boxes, she said, "Okay, nearly everything has arrived for this room and today we're going to pull it together."

Monty's eyes widened. "Please tell me we don't have to get that sofa up that thin stairwell."

Sophie glanced at the "S" shaped monstrosity that had been in the room when she arrived. "Nope, I decided to keep it." She walked to the play yard, which she'd taken from the office and set up in the corner of the big room the day before. Sliding Brady inside, she said, "But we do have to move it to the middle of the room."

Monty frowned. "The middle of the room?"

"We have to surround it with color. Otherwise, no matter where we try to hide it, it will stick out like a sore thumb."

She pointed across the room. "See that big long tube over there?"

Bob nodded.

"That's the rug that goes under it."

"Under it?" Bob and Monty said in unison. But Bob added, "We're going to need another pair of hands."

Sophie looked around. "Actually another pair of hands isn't a bad idea." Jeb had told her that if she needed help, she shouldn't pussyfoot around. So, she wouldn't. "Bob, why don't you go ask Mr. Worthington to join us?"

His eyes grew large and his mouth fell open. "Jeb?"

"Yes."

He pulled in a breath. "Okay, but he isn't going to like this."

"What he'll like is the beautiful home he'll have to show his potential clients," she reminded Bob with another smile. "Seriously. This is important."

"Okay."

Bob left and Sophie and Monty worked at unpacking lamps, artwork and other accessories for the room. Within ten minutes, Jeb was clomping down the stairway with Bob.

Before he could say anything, Sophie said, "Thank goodness you could help us. This room is huge, but the couch is a dinosaur. We definitely need you if we're going to have this space ready for your clients."

Knowing he wouldn't argue that, Sophie smiled. Jeb scowled. "With Slim out of town, I'm swamped."

She knew that but she also knew that the only private time she'd have to show Jeb he could be okay with kids would be when Slim was gone.

"Well, we could spend the next ten minutes arguing over why you should help us. Or we could just get everything moved so you can leave."

"Fine. Whatever. Let's get started already."

She directed Bob and Monty to the left side of the sectional sofa. "You guys move that over there," she said, pointing to the far corner. "Jeb and I will position this section in the center of the room."

Bob and Monty nodded. As she and Jeb shifted the center curve of the sofa to the right, the two cowboys walked the bottom of the "S" shape out of the way.

She brushed off her hands and stood back to examine the center placement. "That's it. That's exactly where the sofa belongs."

"Great," Jeb said, heading for the stairway.

"Oh, no," Sophie scolded. "Not yet! We have to get the rug in place, and then put the sofa on top of it, then you can go."

Jeb sighed.

Sophie assigned him to help Bob remove the bold print rug from its shipping container. Blocks of burgundy, brown, beige and gold brightened the hardwood floor when they rolled it out. Sophie and Monty placed the center curve of the white "S" on the left end of the rug. Then Jeb and Monty returned the bottom of the "S" to its place beside the center of the sectional sofa.

With the big "S" in place, Sophie instructed Jeb and Bob to maneuver other furniture around it but suddenly Brady began to fuss.

Sophie turned to Monty. "See if he'll take a rattle."

Monty scurried to the play yard. He picked up a rattle and shoved it at Brady who only fussed all the more.

Jeb sighed again. "Let me." He grabbed the rattle from Monty's hands, shook it to make the pleasant sound and smiled down at Brady. "Here, little guy."

Sophie held back a smile. He was a natural with kids! She couldn't believe his ex-wife had somehow convinced him he wasn't cut out to be a father. From here on out, she would expose him to Brady every chance she got, until he realized how wrong he was to believe that.

Brady sniffed and stopped crying, but he didn't take the rattle from Jeb. Seeing another opportunity, Sophie called, "Can you pick him up?" from the other side of the room, where she was holding a picture for Monty to hang. "As soon as I'm done here, I'll take him upstairs."

Jeb reached down and lifted Sophie's son. As inconspicuously as possible, she watched him settle Brady on his arm just as she'd shown him only a few hours before in the kitchen.

It was everything Sophie could do not to laugh out loud. Getting Jeb accustomed to her baby, and beyond the belief that he wasn't cut out to be a dad, would be a piece of cake.

When Jeb arrived in the kitchen for supper, Sophie and Brady were already there. That didn't surprise him. Neither did her request that he hold Brady while she tossed a salad. He glanced over at the empty high chair, knowing that's where Brady should have been and pulled in a resigned breath.

He could come right out and confront her about challenging his statement, except he didn't think she was forcing him to interact with Brady out of a challenge. At least not a romantic one. He didn't have the sense that she was trying to prove to him that he could get along with Brady to obliterate his excuse for not wanting to get involved with her. She'd hardly looked at him all day—except to boss him around. Now that he was okay with her baby, it almost seemed she wasn't interested.

Realizing just how "okay" he was with the little boy, Jeb felt a rush of happiness. He had to admit that now that he'd held the little guy without disastrous consequences, he didn't have to run anymore if the baby was around. Actually he could probably enjoy this baby.

The idea brought him up short. He'd never even considered "enjoying" Brady. But he knew he would. And when he recognized that, he realized something that stunned him.

Technically he no longer had an excuse for wanting Sophie off his ranch.

He frowned, wondering if she'd gotten him accustomed to her baby just to keep her job. But curiosity about her motives took a back seat to the sudden vision he had of what life would be like if Sophie stayed on with her little boy. Jeb would probably be the one to take the kid out to see the ranch. He'd be the one to teach Brady to ride. Actually, if Sophie stayed long enough he could take this little boy under his wing. Teach him the ropes of being a man.

The joy that rose in him at just the thought of "playing" dad caused him to swallow hard and squeeze his eyes shut with pain. How foolish, how needy, to so desperately long to use someone else's child as if he were his own.

He set Brady in his high chair. "I need to wash up."

He refused to be so pathetic that he'd settle for a few months or a few years being the pretend dad to his housekeeper's son.

At this point in his life he had little more than his pride. He wasn't giving up that, too.

CHAPTER EIGHT

AFTER dinner, Sophie cleaned the kitchen then returned to the basement room, Brady on her arm.

Lowering him into the play yard, she said, "I know you're getting tired, but you need to stay up another hour in order to sleep through the night. So I might as well try to get a little more work done."

He gooed up at her. She smiled. "You are adorable."

He giggled.

She ran her fingers through the downy hair on his head, ruffling it even more. "You better hope that mane of yours tames before you're a teenager."

He giggled again.

"I'm serious. That could be a definite handicap with the girls."

"What could be a handicap with the girls?"

Hearing Jeb's comment, she glanced up and saw him coming down the stairs. She straightened away from the play yard and their eyes met across the huge room.

Subdued yellow linen curtains now matched the yellow in the multicolored throw pillows piled on the sofa and chairs. A sun-shaped clock smiled from above the fireplace mantel. Books and wood sculptures filled the wall unit.

Fearing his reaction to the nearly finished room, Sophie swallowed before answering his question. "His hair. If it doesn't settle down a bit before he hits his teen years he could be in real trouble."

Jeb laughed and said, "No doubt about it." Then he glanced around.

Sophie didn't know if he'd come down to inspect the job she was doing or if he was on his way to his workout room, but whatever his reason, he was here. Seeing a nearly finished room. About to pronounce judgment.

"I like it."

"Really?" Her heart began beating again. "The yellow doesn't put you off?"

"It's not my favorite color, but I'm guessing the other colors—" He pointed to the burgundy, brown, yellow and burnt orange throw pillows "—like the ones in those pillows are so dark you felt you needed something to offset them."

She sagged with relief. "Exactly."

Silence descended on the room. Jeb didn't rush off as she expected him to. Instead he stood in the center of the room, looking uncharacteristically nervous.

He rubbed his hand along the back of his neck. "There's something else we need to discuss."

His ominous tone caused her to step back. "Okay."

"All along I've been saying you couldn't stay because of your baby, but with Slim gone and every-thing confused, I sort of got over that."

Her heart tripped over itself in her chest. That was not at all what she'd been expecting. "You did?"

"Yes. The kid's not really as much of a problem as I thought he was going to be."

"Are you saying I can stay?"

He met her gaze. "You've proven yourself. You fit here. And now I'm okay with the kid. So, yeah. I'd like you to stay. But there is a condition."

Stunned, Sophie could only nod.

"This is a business and I am your boss. And we've got to start acting more like that."

Though he didn't come right out and say it, she got his point. No more kisses on horse rides. Just the reminder of being in his arms that afternoon sent sensation careening through her, but she ignored it. The man did not want to be attracted to her and she needed this job. Agreeing to that was a no brainer.

"Okay."

"Another thing. Just because I'm in my house it doesn't mean my work is done for the day. I'm on the clock 24/7. Even when I'm not working, I'm thinking about work. That's how I get so much done in a day. You can't be handing your son to me. It's a distraction. He can be in the kitchen. When he gets older, he can roam around the house. But I don't want him underfoot. Understood?"

"Yes." For a home, a decent salary and benefits she'd be a fool to argue. "Understood."

"Good." He looked around. "Now, could you use some help?"

The change in his tone confused her as much as his question. "You just reminded me of how busy you are. Now, you're volunteering to help me?"

He laughed and Sophie gaped at him. But it suddenly

sunk in that she was staying. *Staying.* She and this man would live together until she left his employ. It could be years. Hell, it could be *decades.* Now that the ground rules for her permanent employment had been laid. He was setting the tone.

"I might be busy, but this is my company. I have the most to gain from everything being done right. With you staying, I'll be around a little more often, checking into things."

Okay. She got it. And she could handle it. She could behave like an employee. No problem. "You're welcome to watch, but I'm only going to be putting on some finishing touches."

His gaze circled the room. "I'm not sure what kinds of touches you think the place still needs. It looks finished to me."

"Well, technically it is, but a few magazines on the table will help a woman to see herself relaxing down here." She pointed at the bar. "Cocktail glasses and some open liquor bottles will help a man to see himself standing behind the bar, mixing drinks. Unless you have a few half-empty liquor bottles upstairs somewhere, I'm going to have to open those new bottles and toss a shot or two."

The look he gave her was half mortified, half shocked. "You're going to have a drink?"

She laughed. "No! I'm going to drain a bit off each bottle to make the liquor appear more inviting. Nobody wants to open the bottle, but if the bottle's already open, people will help themselves." She gazed around proudly. "I want this to be a help-yourself room. I want it to be ultracomfortable."

He looked around with her. "Okay. I buy it."

Brady began to fuss and Sophie sighed and walked over to him. She might be an employee, but she was also a mom. And it appeared this was the first test of that part of their arrangement.

"Well, that settles that. He's too tired to finish." She clapped her hands as a signal to Brady she would pick him up. "He has to go to bed."

She said the words casually, but out of the corner of her eye she watched Jeb to see how he would react to her leaving a project because of her baby.

His expression never changed. He didn't flinch. He didn't react at all. "Okay. See you in the morning."

Happiness exploded inside her. It was going to work! She could stop sassing. He could handle her baby. They could work together!

She lifted Brady out of the playpen, but as she turned toward the stairs, he dropped the little blue teddy bear he'd been chewing on.

Jeb was beside them in seconds, scooping it up. "Don't forget this."

Smiling, he handed the soft bear to her, but their fingers brushed and electricity danced up her arm. Their gazes caught and her heart skipped a beat.

But Jeb quickly turned away, adhering to their new condition that they behave more like a boss and house-keeper. And she agreed. She didn't know why he didn't want to be attracted to her, but she needed this job. She couldn't afford to be attracted to him any more than he wanted to be attracted to her.

She walked to the stairway. "I'll see you in the morning."

In her suite, she bathed Brady, slid him into pajamas and fed him a bottle while telling him a story. When he was done eating, he went out like a light.

Grabbing the baby monitor, she headed back to the basement. Though she'd given Jeb the impression that she was done for the day, that had only been a test. She needed to put the finishing touches on that room or she'd never get everything done before his clients arrived. It was only a little past eight. She had at least two hours she could work.

At the bottom of the stairs, she was surprised to see Jeb sitting at the bar.

He lifted his glass in salute then displayed a whiskey bottle that had been opened. "I found a way to help you."

She laughed. He was a funny guy. But she didn't think that's why he'd made the joke or stayed at the bar. They could make all the agreements they wanted about behaving like a boss and employee, but their electric moment earlier proved that their attraction wasn't going away just because they wanted it to. The only way to get over it or to learn to ignore it would be through practice.

And that, she guessed, was why he'd waited to see if she'd return.

"Very funny." She puffed a pillow. "Shouldn't you be on the treadmill by now?"

He swiveled on the bar stool. "I thought about it, but I also had a sneaking suspicion that after you put Brady to bed you'd come back down here." He nodded at the stepladder in the corner. "It's not good to be using one of those when you're alone. The shot of whiskey was just a perk."

She laughed again. "Seriously, I'm only going to be fluffing pillows and dusting."

He shrugged. "All right. I'll finish my drink and get out of your hair."

He took a small sip from the crystal glass and Sophie turned away, not surprised he intended to nurse his drink. He knew as well as she did that they had to get accustomed to each other.

Still, understanding what he was doing was one thing. Being successful at it was another. It wasn't exactly good practice to sit in the same room without talking. If they really wanted to get accustomed to each other, they had to talk. She just had to think of something normal to talk about. Brady was off-limits. They'd talked about him enough for now. Their attraction was taboo. She couldn't talk about the hands. Jeb wouldn't participate. She knew about his parents and childhood. He knew about hers.

She pulled in a breath. The topic range had slimmed to one not-exactly-spectacular subject. "My parents once had a male housekeeper."

He swiveled on his chair to face her, clearly glad she'd picked up the conversational ball. "Oh, yeah?"

"He taught me everything I know about decorating." Maintaining a casual tone, she stood in front of the sofa, studying the placement of a painting on the wall across from it. "He had a past a lot like mine. He learned to keep house and cook because both of his parents worked."

"Makes sense."

"The decorating thing just came naturally to him. He knew how to put furniture and accompanying pieces together in a room in such a way that they'd be stylish and still homey."

She turned just in time to see Jeb looking around again, obviously analyzing her placement of furniture and choice of accents. "If he taught you this," he said, motioning around the room, "he didn't need to go to school. He might have been just a guy who wanted to be comfortable."

She gazed around, too, trying to see the area from Jeb's perspective and realized that what he said was true. What she'd learned from Paul was how to make a space comfortable. Homey. Paul had wanted a stay-at-home mom and a dad who could have gone to his baseball games. Instead he had to cook, clean and do his own laundry *and* be his own cheerleader at Little League games. In a way, Paul had been as displaced as Jeb. And maybe that was why Jeb appreciated his style. They both wanted a home. And here she was creating one for Jeb.

Telling herself that turning Jeb's house into a home was her job and nothing else, she turned away and her eye caught the picture across from the sofa at another angle. Deciding she didn't like it, she grabbed the stepladder from the corner of the room where it had been stashed.

Settling it under the picture, she said, "It looks like you were right about the ladder."

"I knew the temptation to use it would be too strong."

She chuckled. "Right. I'm changing one little thing, not painting the entire room."

She climbed the two steps and lifted the picture from the wall, but it was heavier than she'd imagined. When

she fully took its weight, she swayed and so did the
ladder.

Jeb was beside her in seconds. He grabbed the
picture, leaned it against the wall then caught her as she
fell backward.

Sliding his one arm around her shoulders and the
other beneath her knees, he swung her off her feet and
away from the teetering ladder.

For several stunned seconds, she simply stared at
him wide-eyed, her heart pounding from the near fall.
Then she realized she was in his arms, cradled against
his chest, and the pounding of her heart changed
meaning. She'd never felt smaller or more feminine
than she did right then. She was the woman making his
home and he was her hero, her rescuer.

She stifled a groan. Why did she always think of him
like this? Why couldn't he touch her without her brain
hopping right over common sense and landing smack
dab on a fantasy?

He set her on her feet, but they were standing face-
to-face, so close their bodies almost touched.

This was not the way to get over an attraction.

Yet, she couldn't pull her eyes away from his. She
couldn't take the step back that would have separated
them.

And he couldn't, either. Several seconds passed in
stunned silence then, as if in a trance, he began lowering
his head to kiss her. Their gazes remained locked. They
both knew what was happening. They both had several
seconds to change their minds.

Neither did.

Their lips met softly. Warmly. Wetly. She closed her

eyes, realizing how well they fit. How perfectly. Then all thought vanished in the wake of the landslide of feeling that tumbled through her. His kiss didn't merely convey the depth of his desire. A thread of genuine emotion wove through it. Where his physical needs had caused him to take in their first kiss, this time he gave. He pulled responses from her she didn't even know she was capable of giving, and once led down that path, her appetite was suddenly as strong as his.

Placing her hands on the sides of his face she brought him closer, her breasts crushed against his chest, and she deepened the kiss. Intense emotion vibrated through her blood. Her pulse pounded. She pressed herself against him, wanting to be closer, feel more, take more, but he abruptly pulled away.

The breath heaved in both of their chests. Their gazes caught and clung. The silence in the room was thick, filled with unspoken questions.

He was the first to find his voice. "This isn't right."

Sophie touched her tingling lips. That kiss hadn't simply been a pulse-pounding exchange between two sexually attracted people. It had been an insight into how much he wanted her. He couldn't resist her any more than she could resist him. This attraction wasn't going away. In spite of their good intentions, it was somehow growing stronger.

Because she was getting to know him. His personality was now as much a part of the attraction as his sexuality. He was a nice guy. A smart man. A generous man who helped an orphanage. A logical man who had accepted her baby. How could she not want as much of him as he was willing to give her?

She cleared her throat. "It felt pretty right to me."

"No. It isn't. Not even a little bit."

She'd never been a bold person, but his kiss had filled her with courage. He more than wanted her. He *liked* her. And the only reason he'd given her that even hinted to why he didn't want to get involved was his fear that he wouldn't make a good dad. But in only two days she'd taken him from shying away from Brady to holding him while she finished dinner. Just as his reason for firing her was no longer valid, his reason for not wanting a relationship didn't wash, either.

She pulled in another breath, stilling her heart, calming her own hormones and spoke quietly, in truth. "Okay. I get that you don't want Brady underfoot. But you saw yourself with him today. He likes you and you're a natural."

He stepped away then turned away. "This isn't about Brady."

"I say it is."

"It isn't." He faced her again. "I don't want to hurt you."

She smiled. She'd never met a man so considerate of her feelings that he'd hurt her to prevent hurting her.

"How do you know you would?"

"I hurt my wife."

"From what you told me this morning, it sounded more like she hurt you."

"No. I hurt her." He pulled in a breath. "That's how I know I'll hurt you."

She honestly thought about that for a second, wondering if the angry statements of a wife losing her marriage could convince a good man he was bad. She couldn't see Jeb deliberately hurting anyone. Unless he had been preoccupied with the ranch? Slim had said ranch life was hard on marriages. So if Jeb had hurt his first wife it could have been through neglect.

"You didn't spend enough time with her?"

He laughed. "We were practically joined at the hip."

Which explained the side-by-side workout equipment, but also totally confused her. How could he hurt someone he had been so close to?

"Then I don't get it."

"Maybe you just need to believe me when I say I'm not cut out to be a husband?"

"Okay, that's enough. You can't be not cut out for everything. In fact, I don't believe you're not cut out to be a husband any more than I believe you're not cut out to be a father. This very day you proved you could be a good dad. You were great with Brady."

"I never said I wasn't good with kids. I said I wasn't made to be a father."

Angry now because he seemed to be talking in circles, she gaped at him. "There's a difference?"

"Sophie, my wife left me because I couldn't give her the one thing she wanted more than her next breath. A child. It isn't that I simply decided one day that I wasn't the kind of guy to be a dad. Mother Nature told me I'd never be a dad. I can't have children."

JULIA JAMES

CHAPTER NINE

SOPHIE froze, stunned into silence, and realized he'd been telling her this in one way, shape or form all along.

He stayed rooted to his spot, quietly waiting for her reaction, but words simply failed her. Of all things, she was sympathetic with his ex-wife. Now that she'd had a child, she knew she had been created just for that task. She *needed* children. She loved being a mom. As much as housekeeping gave her an income, being a mom gave her a reason to get up in the mornings.

Jeb took a step back, smiled ruefully. "Look, you're a wonderful mom. Brady's an adorable child. You should have more kids. Brady should have brothers and sisters. If you get involved with me those dreams end."

He caught her gaze, held it, the intensity in his eyes searing her with truth. "So let's not talk this to death. When I tell you getting involved with me would be the worst mistake of your life, just believe me."

The next morning, Jeb didn't immediately head for the kitchen and the coffeepot. Instead he slipped down a few hidden corridors finding the stairway to the basement. Though the family room Sophie had created was silent, he could still hear the echo of their voices as they talked the night before. Still feel the heat of his body's reactions as his mouth had mated with hers. Still feel the disappointment in her silence to his admission that he couldn't have kids.

That spoke louder than if she'd said a thousand words. A woman who had no real connection to her parents would want a family. Hell, he understood her need because *he'd* wanted a family. And Sophie was a wonderful mother. A good person. A generous, genuine woman. She deserved a family.

He should be glad she'd been stunned speechless. Every morning for the past five years he'd awakened wishing Laine had had the knowledge before she'd tumbled in love with him, created a life with him, and then had a doctor tell her he wasn't the man she'd assumed. At least Sophie had options. She might have come to the precipice with him, but there was no way he'd let her tumble over.

Unwittingly remembering the kiss again, he closed his eyes. He could feel her eager mouth beneath his, feel the impatient way she pressed herself against him.

He shook his head. He had to stop reliving that kiss. What he felt for her was wrong. And as soon as he punished his body with a good hour or two of exercise to get rid of the sexual tingle that still heated his blood, he would go into his kitchen, grab a mug of coffee and pretend he had absolutely no feelings for her.

He made it to the exercise room and performed a regimen of stretches to prepare for the real workout to come. After awakening his muscles, he sat on the weight bench. Every lift and movement required his full focus and attention, so he didn't have time to think about Sophie, about being attracted to her, about wanting more than what he knew he could legitimately have with her.

Yet, when he was done, when he'd punished himself for two grueling hours, she was the first thought to pop into his mind. The tingle of need returned, along with it the usual arguments. He told himself that maybe he was jumping to conclusions. That maybe if he gave her a day to think about what he told her, she'd come around. Maybe her silence was actually a statement that she wanted time before she commented. Maybe after she thought things through, she'd decide having one child was enough.

And while she was malleable he could seduce her, bathe her with so much affection and attention that she wouldn't have time to get tangled up in the reality that she'd only be a mom once.

Cursing, he walked to the shower. His entire body instantly got onboard with the idea of seducing her. But though he knew that with a few kisses he could have her in his bed, he also knew the price for that kind of success was too high. Seducing her was no guarantee of keeping her in his life. What if they did have a brief time of happiness but in the end she left just as Laine had?

Worse… What if she stayed and lived her life miserable, deprived of any more children? She'd never have a little girl with her big brown eyes. Or another wild-haired baby boy. Or even a son or daughter with her father's surgical skills and Sophie's kind heart.

Adoption was a solution but it was hollow. Yes, they'd have children to raise but they wouldn't be hers. They wouldn't be *theirs*. His circumstances demanded that any woman who wanted him in her life gave up the possibility of leaving her own legacy. Her own flesh and blood.

He knew the value of that. He'd found a way around it with his ranch. But a money legacy was one thing. The emotional connection of a mother and child was quite another. How could a woman in her twenties make such a dramatic choice?

She couldn't.

Not if she was smart.

When Jeb walked into the kitchen, Sophie didn't have to turn around to know it was him. All of her nerve endings went on red alert, as if they recognized his presence.

She knew he was upset and would probably revert to the cold, distant persona he'd used when she first arrived but she was determined not to let him. What he'd told her the night before flabbergasted her. In a sense, he'd forced her into the position of making *all* the decisions about their relationship after just two kisses. He'd basically said there was no point of a courtship, stolen kisses, moonlight walks, discussing possibilities. Unless she could tell him right now that she didn't want another child, he didn't want anything to do with her.

Well, she couldn't tell him that. What woman could? How could she say that loving him was worth giving up the possibility of ever being pregnant again, ever bearing another child, ever tickling the tummy of a being who had her genes?

She needed time, and not time spent tiptoeing around each other. They needed time interacting like normal people, getting to know each other, experimenting with what they felt in a normal way. And if it killed her she would take them back to the place they were yesterday. The teasing, fun, share-duties-with-Brady place where they could get to know each other enough that if decisions had to be made, they'd both have the knowledge to make them.

Ready to force him back to that place, she turned with a smile, but when she saw him, everything she wanted to say evaporated from her brain.

He stood in the doorway, a white towel wrapped around his neck, no shirt, no socks, only sweatpants clinging to his lean hips. His dark hair shone wetly from a recent shower. His gray-green eyes dark sparked with emotion.

Her breath stuttered in her chest. Wow.

What would it be like to wake up beside this handsome, sexy, passionate man every morning? Getting kisses every day that turned her blood to fire? Feeling his solid muscles curled around her as they drifted off to sleep?

He walked to the coffeemaker. "You and I need to talk about that kiss last night."

Not yet! She didn't want to discuss the night before. She didn't want him to tell her they should pretend nothing happened, pretend they didn't like or want each other. She wanted them to have time!

"That's not going to happen again."

"We're two people who are very attracted to each

other. Common sense tells me that's going to happen a lot."

He turned from the counter. "It can't. I will never again commit to another woman. Especially not a woman who so obviously loves her child. Do you think I would deprive you of everything you truly need? Do you think I'm that selfish?"

She laughed. "Actually, yes, I do."

He gaped at her and she laughed again, knowing that if she tried to have this discussion in a serious way she'd probably tremble into oblivion. She had to be light and friendly in a pushy, honest way.

"How else do you explain cutting off the possibility of any relationship by forcing me to make a decision before I even know whether or not there should be a decision?"

"That's my point, Sophie. There shouldn't be a decision. I'm saving you the heartbreak of falling in love only to be disappointed."

She pulled a paper towel from the roll and cleaned up a spill by the sink. "How vain you are. You're so absolutely positive I'll fall in love that you won't even give me the options."

"Trust me. You don't want the options."

"How do you know?"

"I know."

"Because you hurt your ex-wife or because she hurt you?"

Taking a sip of coffee, he studied her over the rim of his mug. Finally he said, "When you love somebody enough that's the same thing."

She stared at him in silence. Technically he'd just

told her that he believed he could love *her* enough. This man who knew his mind, knew himself, knew what he wanted, was afraid of a relationship with her, not because he didn't think it would result in real love, but because he knew it would.

She turned to the counter again, wiped at the spot of the spill that she'd already cleaned. Now, she understood why he'd forced her into the position of making her choice the night before. He'd already made his. He might not be in love with her, but if they went any further, shared any more kisses, touched enough, he'd put himself in a danger zone. Unless she could say she accepted the fact that she'd have no more children, he knew he'd be hurt.

And she wasn't ready to make that choice.

So he was right. They couldn't take this any further.

He laughed emotionlessly, took another sip of his coffee and said, "Why don't we just say the whiskey made me kiss you last night and leave it at that?"

What a wonderful way out for two people in a situation so intense she could barely breathe. "Okay."

"And let's not be upset about this."

She blushed as guilt rattled through her. How could she be so cold to a man who deserved her warmth? Why couldn't she simply say she accepted that she'd never have another child? She had one. She'd had the experience of being pregnant, bearing him and nestling a newborn against her breast. Why couldn't she say one child was enough?

Because she'd had that child alone. Because that pregnancy hadn't been happy. It had been scary. Lonely. She'd made every discovery, experienced every "first" by herself. Not with the man she loved.

And that was the real bottom line. She didn't merely want another child. She wanted the experience of a pregnancy with a man who loved her. She wanted the whole package. She wanted him to buy her pickles and ice cream. She wanted to know what it felt like to have a husband holding her hand in labor. Telling her she was beautiful. Thanking her when it was over and he was holding a wailing newborn in his arms. His son. His progeny.

Still turned away from Jeb, she squeezed her eyes shut. Now she understood. As proud as Jeb was, he'd never feel right about depriving her of those things. He knew the depth of the loss she envisioned because it was his loss, too. He longed to thank somebody for giving him a child. He longed to hold a hand during labor. He might even yearn to be the one to buy pickles and ice cream, to satisfy cravings, to be a part of all those firsts.

Dear God. No wonder there was no argument for him. He knew what he was asking her to forfeit because he'd done it. And not out of choice. She couldn't push him or argue with him any more than she already had. That would only make him feel worse.

She feigned a smile and faced him. "All right. No fussing. No sulking."

He studied her a few seconds, undoubtedly recognizing her smile was forced, but at least her thoughts were clear. She agreed. They couldn't do this.

"So we're good? We both know anything romantic between us would be a mistake."

"Yes." All the emotion that had been riding through her suddenly turned into a blank space, a feeling of emptiness so intense it stole her breath.

He picked up his travel mug and walked out of the kitchen, obviously on his way to his bedroom to dress for the day.

Sophie watched the door swing closed behind him.

She liked him.

He liked her.

And that emptiness she'd just felt wasn't her own. It was his. It had hurt him to deprive his ex-wife. He wouldn't be so cruel as to deprive her. But in protecting everybody else, he hurt himself.

Ironically that was part of why her attraction to him continually grew. He deserved love. Real love. Selfless, abiding, I'll-fight-for-you-forever love.

But she wasn't the woman to give it to him.

That afternoon Brady wouldn't take a nap. He fussed so much Sophie pulled him from the crib. "Is something wrong with you today, little buddy?"

He sniffed then rubbed his nose against her chest before starting to cry again.

Walking him to the kitchen, she hugged him tightly. "What's the matter?"

He only cried all the more.

"Are you sick?" She glanced down, as if she expected him to reply, and of course, he didn't. Remembering he'd gone through something similar when he'd gotten his first few teeth, she sat on a kitchen chair and rubbed her finger along his gums. On the bottom row she felt a bump. Remorse filled her. She hadn't immediately recognized his problem because she'd been preoccupied with Jeb's. Her guilt grew, as she realized yet another reason not to get involved in her boss's life. She had a baby who needed her.

"I'm sorry it took me so long to figure this out, but now that we're on the right page we'll be fine."

The door swung open and Jeb walked into the kitchen. "Everything okay?"

The air always left the room whenever Jeb entered and Sophie struggled for breath. Without even trying, he crackled with life and energy that translated into raw male sexuality. She couldn't imagine a woman loving him, knowing what it felt like to touch him and taste him, knowing what it felt like to be the object of his desire, and still leaving him. Though she understood his ex-wife's wish to have a child, she had a new set of doubts about the woman who had left Jeb. How could a woman love a man and desert him in *his* hour of need?

As she thought the last, Brady squirmed, as if Mother Nature was reminding her that her top priority wasn't her boss, but her son. She had to stop thinking about Jeb.

"He's getting a tooth."

"Poor little guy." He ran his fingers through Brady's downy hair sympathetically. "Do you have medicine or something to help him?"

She looked up, caught his gaze and swallowed hard at the emotion she saw in his eyes. In one day of inter-acting with her son, he already had strong feelings for her little boy. And she suddenly realized something that she should have seen before this. He didn't want her to keep Brady out from underfoot because he didn't want to be around her son. He'd wanted her to keep him away so he didn't grow attached to her child. He loved kids and didn't want to get attached to Brady only to have Sophie take him away when a better job came along, or she grew tired of ranch life…or she found love with someone else.

She looked away. There were so many ways she could hurt him. Was it any wonder he had been wary of her?

"I have gel for his gums. It numbs them enough that he can sleep. He's usually fine in a day or two."

"Then you go take care of him. I'll make my own supper."

"No. I'm—"

"No arguing. I realized today that you haven't taken a day off since you got here. Your boy needs tending. I can get my own supper."

"I know but—"

"No buts!" He put his hands on her shoulders and guided her to the door. "I'm fine."

The touch of his fingers on her shoulders made her close her eyes. Even a simple gesture shot sparks of fire through her.

She ignored them. Not because she didn't like Jeb, but because she did. Too much. And if she wasn't careful she'd sacrifice her dreams for a man she barely knew.

CHAPTER TEN

BRADY finally fell into a deep sleep around eight o'clock that night. Knowing he'd be good for several hours but not wanting to leave him, Sophie had settled on the sofa, pillow on her lap, ready to unwind by watching some television, when there was a knock at her door.

Confused, she sat up and set the pillow beside her. "Who is it?"

"It's me. Jeb."

She rolled her eyes, laughing at herself. Of course it was Jeb. Who else did she think it would be?

Shaking her head at her own stupidity, but forgiving herself since the past few hours with Brady had been difficult, she rose from the sofa and opened her door.

"Sorry." She smiled sheepishly. "It's been a hellish few hours."

He produced two brown bottles of beer from behind his back. "I sort of figured, so I brought you a beer."

Surprised, she smiled at him. "Thanks."

"I also need to talk with you about a few things."

"Oh?" The tone in his voice sent shivers of fear

through her. He was a very observant man, and busy as she had been with Brady, she hadn't been careful about her reactions to him that day. What if he'd figured out the conclusions she'd been drawing by the expressions on her face? What if it embarrassed him to realize she had been thinking about him, about his life, about what he'd gone through?

She opened the door a little wider. "Come in."

He stepped into the room, handed her one of the bottles and took a seat on the chair, which seemed to disappear around him.

Laughing, she sat on the sofa. "Chair's a little small."

He frowned down at it. "Not very comfortable, either."

Knowing they could chitchat all night when she'd rather get this over with, she said, "What did you need to talk about?"

"I got two phone calls this evening."

"One from Slim I'm hoping."

He took a swig of beer. "Yep. If his older sister can't handle caring for their mom, he's out for the summer."

He said it in such a somber way that Sophie's spirits lifted. Maybe his guarded mood wasn't the result of her making him feel bad about himself, but worry over running the ranch and his business without Slim.

"That's awful."

"We can manage. Especially since the other call was from the clients. They've canceled their visit."

"Oh, no! Do you have any *good* news?"

He chuckled, leaning back in the chair, looking casual and sexy and totally unconcerned, almost as if he functioned best when others needed him to be strong.

"It gives us more time to get ready for them."

"So, they're still coming?"

"Yep."

"How long do we have?"

Jeb shrugged. "Mrs. Baker said they just need a week or two. Mr. Baker's current picture ran over and he can't get away from the set."

Sophie's eyes widened. "He's a movie star?"

"Director."

"Oh."

"Don't be disappointed. Directors are important, too."

"I know. I was just kind of hoping to meet somebody cool."

"Oh, trust me. He's cool. He wears sunglasses in the house."

She laughed and took her first swig of beer. "I can't drink this whole thing."

"You're a lightweight?"

His horrified expression caused a giggle to bubble from her. "No. I can hold my own. I simply can't get tipsy tonight. I'll probably have to get up with Brady."

"He won't sleep through the night?"

"Not when he's teething."

"I'd take part of the watch for you, but that means I'd have to sleep on that." He pointed at the square sofa. "I don't think that's a good idea for my back."

She glanced down at her beer. Just as she'd suspected, he was such a natural with kids that he didn't think before he volunteered. If Brady was around, he'd be involved. If she didn't keep to the rules he'd set, he'd be the one to be hurt.

"I can handle it, but thanks for offering."

"Why are you always so surprised when somebody does something nice for you?"

"I'm not. I expected you to offer to help. What surprises me is that you don't realize how nice you are."

He burst out laughing. "You need to have a conversation with my last housekeeper. She'd totally disagree with you."

She took a drink of her beer. "Right. I'm guessing she's the reason you don't realize you're nice."

"Stop saying I'm nice. I'm not."

She winced. "That's right. I forgot men don't like to be thought of as nice."

He scowled. "Now you're making fun of me."

"Sort of. But you can't deny that you're worried about Brady, or that you pay well—or even that you treat your ranch foreman like a brother."

"I threatened to fire Slim for teasing me the day you asked if you could take a walk around the ranch."

"Yet he still orchestrated the two of us going out on a ride." She smiled. "And when his mom got sick you lent him your private plane. Without a second thought."

His scowl deepened. "I'm not nice."

"Again, you're not going to get *me* to believe that." She motioned around the room. She might not be the woman to love him, but that didn't mean she couldn't make her mark on his life. And her best way would be to get him over the hurdle of thinking he didn't deserve to be loved. He did.

"This place is a hundred times better than what I could afford on my own," she said, ticking off the things he'd already done for her. "You're keeping me on, when you could have stuck to our three-week deal, because you know how much this job means to me. If I stay long enough, you'd eventually treat Brady like a son."

She stopped, suddenly realizing what she'd said.

Silence cloaked the room in oppression.

He took a long drink that drained his beer bottle, and then very quietly said, "We both know that's not a good idea." He rose. "I'll see you in the morning."

Filled with remorse for not thinking through her stupid, offhand remark, she rose, too. "Okay."

He headed for the door, but suddenly faced her. "And I'm not nice." With slow, deliberate steps, he closed the distance between them. "Given half a chance, I'd ravish you. I'd kiss you until you couldn't breathe for wanting me and then I'd take my time making love to you. I wouldn't think about tomorrow, consequences be damned." He slid his palm to her cheek, his thumb caressing it softly, seductively. "You'd be in my bed, simply because I want you and some days I can't control that."

She looked away, and he lifted her chin until she caught his gaze. "Think about that the next time you're tempted to believe I'm nice."

With that he kissed her. Dumbfounded by the raw need in his voice and the truth in his words, she hadn't steeled herself for the touch of his mouth against hers. When their lips met, she simply melted, fell into the sinful sensations, opened to him, accepted the rub of his tongue as it swept into her mouth.

Heat poured through her, causing her stomach to clench and her breasts to expand with life and need. Of its own volition, her body pressed against his, finding the hard evidence of his desire. Her hands skimmed the strong arms holding her, until they reached his broad shoulders, his neck, and slid into his thick, silky hair.

He pulled away, brushing his lips from her mouth to her chin, down her neck to the sensitive crevice there. Running them along her collarbone, he quietly said, "I won't tie you to me when I can't give you what you need. But unless you can tell me that it's okay for us to make love—even if it's only once—you're going to have to be strong enough for both of us."

The strength he spoke of eluded her, but he stepped away. "Don't settle for less than what you want. Not even for me."

The next morning the air sizzled when Jeb walked into the kitchen. The kiss the night before told her exactly how much he wanted her, and reminded her of exactly how much she wanted him. He hadn't spoken of love. Hadn't made excuses or proposed alternatives for not being able to have children. He'd warned her away from him, even as he told her he didn't intend to resist her.

When their eyes met, the sizzle that had entered the room with him increased exponentially. Her pulse scrambled. Her chest tightened. Her blood burst into flame.

Just from a look.

What would happen if they ever did make love?

"Good morning."

She cleared her throat. "Good morning."

"How's Brady?"

"He was awake most of the night, so now he's sleeping like a lamb. He probably won't be up before noon."

A hush fell over the room, and she realized what she'd said. Her baby was tended. Jeb had given the hands a much-needed day off due to the client's cancellation. Slim was in Texas. They were alone in the big quiet house. And they burned for each other.

She quickly turned to the sink, shoved her hands in the dishwater and picked up a glass.

Without a word, he stepped behind her, pushed the hair from her neck and brushed a kiss across her nape. She squeezed her eyes shut, reveling in the sensation, knowing that one of these days she would succumb, not sure at this moment if he was warning her—or seducing her—and terrified that she didn't have the will to resist.

"Lucy, I'm home!"

Slim's voice rang through the downstairs and Sophie started, but Jeb slowly pulled away. His lips rose from her nape, leaving a cool sensation in their wake. His hands slid from her waist. He stepped back, away from her, just as Slim pushed open the swinging door.

Dressed in jeans and a lightweight plaid shirt, he walked toward the table and picked up the conversation as if he hadn't been away. "I hear you have news."

Jeb walked to the coffeemaker. "Clients canceled," he said simply, his voice gruff with sexual need that Sophie prayed Slim wouldn't notice.

"Monty wasn't clear," Slim said, appearing blissfully ignorant. "He wasn't sure if they weren't coming at all or if they'd just postponed."

"Postponed." Jeb turned from the coffeemaker, pot in hand. "Want some?"

"Sure. You got any pie?"

"Yes." Sophie heard the squeak in her own voice and winced. She cleared her throat. "How's your mom?"

"Good. Once she's out of the hospital, she's moving in with my older sister, but only for a month or so. She's adamant about going back home."

"So your sister could take her in?"

"She set up a bedroom in her den, near a downstairs bathroom." Slim took a swig of coffee. "So they're all set."

"That's good," Jeb and Sophie said in unison and though Jeb didn't seem to think anything of it, Sophie realized they were growing so close they were beginning to talk alike. Jeb might be able to compartmentalize his feelings for her and keep them purely sexual, but what she felt for him was personal, intimate, a real connection.

She suddenly understood what he'd been telling her all along. Too much time in each other's company and they would be in love. And then the choices would be snatched from her. Starry-eyed from intimacy and a life-changing connection, she'd downplay the fact that loving him meant giving up everything else. She wouldn't consider how she'd feel twenty years from now when she had only one child to walk down the aisle. Only one child to give her grandchildren. Only one child.

Jeb spent the rest of the day following Slim, telling himself he was getting his foreman reoriented, but he was really avoiding private time with Sophie and her son. He knew what he wanted. The woman *and* her little boy. The ready-made family. He also knew the kind of man he was. Strong. Determined. Not one to take no for an answer. If he pulled out all the stops, he'd win. He always did. And then what would happen? Ten years, five years…maybe even two years from now, she'd wake up one morning realizing she'd forfeited her dreams and she'd hate him.

In the end he really wouldn't win. And he'd hurt her. Maybe even Brady. If she left after Brady and Jeb had bonded, the little boy would see him as the dad he longed to be and they'd both scream in pain at the loss.

So he stayed away. Out of sight. Out of mind. Hoping to take things back to normal.

But as the day wore on, he suddenly remembered that Sophie now made his dinner. Knowing any private time with her would take them back to the place neither one of them wanted to be, he called Slim to the barn office.

"While you were gone, Sophie and I had some conversations."

Slim fell to the seat in front of the desk. "Oh, yeah?"

Jeb picked up a pencil and tapped it on his desk blotter. "Yeah. I was so busy she started making my dinner and before we knew it, I sort of got accustomed to Brady."

"Hey, that's great!"

"Yeah. Once we realized Brady wasn't a problem for me anymore, I couldn't see any reason she couldn't stay… So she's permanent now."

Slim's eyes widened. "What else happened while I was away?"

Not about to touch that with a ten-foot pole, Jeb pretended great interest in his phone messages, leafing through them, avoiding Slim's gaze. "Nothing, except now that I've got dinner on her agenda again, it might be a good idea for you to eat with me so we can debrief at the end of the day."

Slim laughed. "Are you asking me to supper?"

Jeb scowled. "It's not a date."

"If her dinners are as good as her cookies and pie I'm still in."

They walked to the house discussing the ranch. When they entered the kitchen, Sophie turned from the stove.

Her gaze moved from Jeb to Slim and she smiled with relief. "Hey, are you eating here tonight?"

"Yep." Slim rubbed his hands together in anticipation. He sniffed the air. "Pot roast." He sniffed again. "And mashed potatoes."

Sophie laughed. "You're good."

"Nope, just hungry." He ambled to the table. "Hey, Brady."

The baby cooed.

Jeb also took his regular seat. "Hey, Brady."

Sophie scrambled to the table with another plate and silverware. "I'll be ready in a second."

Seeing she'd only brought enough utensils for him, Slim frowned. "You're not eating with us—"

"I—"

"She—"

Sophie scurried back to the stove. Slim peered at Jeb. "What's this all about? She'll have to clean up twice if she waits to eat until after we're done." He glanced at Sophie, then back to Jeb. "You don't have a problem with her eating with us, do you, boss?"

Knowing he'd sound like an idiot if he admitted that

he did, Jeb said, "No. Especially if it means less work for her." He twisted in his chair to address Sophie. "Come eat with us."

She nodded, but she wouldn't look at him.

Jeb turned back to Slim. Sophie set her place then brought the food to the table. Slim grabbed a healthy helping of pot roast and between bites began asking questions about what had happened with the hands while he was gone.

Within seconds the awkwardness had passed, Jeb caught Sophie's gaze. She smiled hopefully. He took a breath then looked away. They could do this.

CHAPTER ELEVEN

TWO FRIDAYS LATER, Jeb awakened out of sorts. Grumpy. Groggy. Even after a steamy shower, he ambled to the kitchen feeling something like a bear with a thorn in its paw.

As always, Brady sat in his high chair. Sophie stood at the counter, fixing the baby's breakfast. Something stirred in Jeb's psyche, but before it rose enough that he could label it longing for what he couldn't have, he squelched it.

The little boy screeched at him.

"Hey, kid."

Sophie brought the cereal to the table. "He's in a rare mood today. Watch yourself."

Jeb laughed. "You think he's in a rare mood?" He grabbed one of the regular mugs from the cupboard, filled it with coffee and walked to the table. "He's got nothing on me today."

"Oh, yeah?" she asked, sliding a spoon of cereal into Brady's open mouth. "What's up?"

He could have told her that he wanted to sleep with her so much that some nights he actually plotted strategies to sneak into her room. He could have told her that he resented the easy way she fit into his life as a maid when he really wanted her for a lover. He could have said he resented the way she made him feel comfortable and edgy at the same time. Or that it made him mad that he could see she needed a job more than he needed to sleep with her.

Instead he said, "I have no idea," but something tripped in his brain. A memory that wouldn't quite form.

Something *was* nagging at him. And for once it was something more than wanting to sleep with her. He just couldn't put his finger on it.

"I have this weird feeling that I've forgotten something."

Silence descended as Sophie aimed a spoon of cereal at Brady's mouth and Jeb took a sip of coffee.

Slim entered the kitchen through the back door. Sophie said, "There are cookies. Oatmeal. Just out of the oven."

Jeb fought the urge to squeeze his eyes shut. Did she have to be so sweet? If she were a tad more selfish, or inconsiderate, or even a bit grouchy he could probably sleep with her simply for sex. Instead with someone nice like her, emotion had gotten involved and it shook an angry finger at him every time he even casually considered seducing her.

Slim headed for the cookie jar. "Great. I skipped breakfast."

Jeb turned in his chair and faced Slim. "So what's on the agenda today?"

"Nothing for you. I've got a handle on it. You can go about your business as usual."

"With the Baker postponement I'm sort of at loose ends."

Slim shoved a cookie into his mouth and headed for the door. "Not my problem."

As the door closed behind Slim, Jeb turned to Sophie. "What are you doing today?"

Sophie paused in feeding her son and he pounded on the tray, screeching angrily. She sighed. "Whatever I'm doing, I'll be doing it with Brady on my arm."

He glanced at the baby, then back at Sophie and knew the real reason he wouldn't seduce her into something she didn't want. She had a baby, responsibilities. His natural inclination would be to ask how he could help, but he knew that wouldn't be wise. He couldn't fall into the role of her baby's daddy, no matter how much he wanted it. And some days he resented that.

He pulled in a breath. He *was* in a mood.

"But it doesn't matter. With the extra time we've had," Sophie said, still feeding Brady. "Even I'm down to putzing around. To tell you the truth I'm kind of getting bored."

"Yeah, me, too." He rose from the table and grabbed his coffee. "I'm going to check my emails."

He left the kitchen and strolled back to the office, wishing he could get rid of this feeling. But he couldn't. He tried to remind himself that he and Sophie were wrong for each other. They were different, had different needs, wanted different things, so he shouldn't like her. But he did. And he paid for it. Every damned day she and her baby sat at the tips of his fingers, as if fate were taunting him with everything he wanted but couldn't have.

His life sucked.

At his desk, he grabbed the calendar, flopped into the tall-back chair, lowered his gaze to that day's entries and forgot all about being angry and moody.

Today was the day of the groundbreaking for Samuel's House. Not only did he have to be a hundred miles away in less than three hours, but he also had to write a speech.

Damn.

That's why he'd forgotten. He hated speeches, so he'd pushed the whole event to the back of his mind, hoping it would go away. But it wouldn't. It was here. And he had to say a few words on behalf of his parents as well as himself. There was no way out.

He bounced out of his chair as if his butt were on fire and ran into the kitchen. "Call Slim, have him call the pilot and tell him I've got to be in the air in an hour."

She turned from the sink. "In the air? I guess this must be the thing you forgot? Where are you going?"

Good grief. Had he ever met a woman so curious, or one who had such a clever way of getting him to talk about himself—

He stopped his ranting because he'd hit a relevant truth. She *could* get him to talk. She pulled things out of him no one else had ever been able to.

"You haven't done any writing by any chance, have you?"

"Writing?"

"I need a speech."

"A speech? Whatever for? Does this have something to do with Samuel's House?" She winced. "Working at your desk I found the files."

"Then you'll know I'm a sponsor. Today is the groundbreaking for a new facility and I'm supposed to say something."

"Just speak from the heart."

"Yeah, right. I'll get up in front of a hundred people and say 'uh' about fifty times." He gave her his best pleading look. After the sleepless nights he'd endured because of her, she owed him. "Come on. Fly along. Help me think of something to say."

He'd sounded so desperate and the invitation had sounded so innocent that Sophie had forgotten how powerful their attraction was and she'd agreed.

She felt the first wave of reminder when he walked down the stairs to the foyer. Wearing boots, black jeans and a white shirt with a bolero tie, he looked sexily Western. Everything female in her responded.

And she was going to spend an entire day with him? Without stuttering or falling into his arms?

Fastening his watch on his wrist, he said, "You ready?"

She peered down at her simple sundress and sandals, then took another look at him. He was the epitome of a rich rancher. She looked like a surfer girl.

Maybe she didn't have anything to worry about?

"Yeah, I'm ready."

Finally done with his watch, he glanced at her. "Wow."

Then he saw Brady sitting in the travel seat beside her. His expression changed from normal man gazing hungrily at a woman he found attractive, to normal man looking at a baby.

And everything fell into place again.

He'd never act on his attraction to her, not even in a teasing kind of way because of Brady. He didn't mind having her baby around, but he also didn't want to grow too fond of him, too attached to him, too close to him, because he didn't want to end up hurt. Or Brady to end up hurt. Or her to end up hurt.

He'd thought it all through and acted out his conclusion by not ever mentioning his feelings for her. If he even still had them. It had been so long since they'd been alone or talked, he might have grown immune to her.

She had nothing to fear.

"The kid's coming?"

"Is that okay?"

He shrugged. "Doesn't matter to me. Let's go."

They got into an SUV and drove to a landing strip on the ranch. Stepping into a plane that looked more like a living room, she just barely held back her gasp of awe. At the back was a bar. Silky drapes decorated the windows. Her feet sunk into thick carpeting. Two rows of buttery-brown leather seats sat across from each other.

She walked to one side. Jeb walked to the other. After settling Brady in the baby seat, she buckled herself in.

Jeb pushed a button that activated an intercom system. With a word to the cockpit, the plane began to move. It didn't take them long to get into the air. Once they were cruising, Jeb removed his seat belt. "Anything you want? A sandwich? A drink?"

"No, I'm fine."

"Then let's get started." He pushed a button that caused a little table to slide out from the wall beside him then pulled a few note cards from his jacket pocket. "I guess I'll start off with good afternoon."

She laughed. "Makes sense. Then thank everybody for their hard work. Somebody somewhere did something to get this thing going… Even if you don't know who or what, so thanking everybody will cover it."

He nodded. "Okay. That's good. Then what?"

"Well, if it were me, I'd just say what I feel about the building. What does this project mean to you?"

He took a breath. "A lot."

She leaned her elbow on the arm of her seat, and put her chin on her closed fist. "Really? How'd you get involved with an orphanage anyway?"

"It's not an orphanage. It's a transitional care facility."

She frowned. "What's a transitional care facility?"

"It's a place where kids who can't make it in foster care go."

"Oh, hard cases. So how'd you get involved with something like that?"

"I caught a kid—Billy Clark—stealing a few years back, and by the time I drove him into town to the sheriff, I'd bonded with him. Parents were drug addicts. He was stealing to feed his sister."

"That's awful!"

"Yeah, well, I thought so, too, and I didn't press charges. But we sent social services out to their house. Billy and his sister were to go into foster care and though his sister easily adapted, Billy couldn't. He ran away and ran away and ran away until—"

He stopped. Sophie reached across the aisle and touched his forearm. "Until what?"

"Until he fell in with the wrong crowd and was

involved in an armed robbery where a man was killed. He's now in a state facility, probably for life."

"I'm sorry."

"Not half as sorry as I was. I thought I'd failed him. He wasn't my responsibility but he had no one else and somehow I just kept missing the mark—probably because at the time I didn't have much real world training. My upbringing hadn't prepared me for anybody like him and I didn't know what to say to him. I didn't know the signs that he was in trouble. I was such an airhead." He shook his head in dismay. "Anyway, my parents visited me about a week after his sentencing, and their cavalier attitude about life infuriated me. I exploded and we got into a fight and before I knew it I was telling them they needed to do something about Billy…or at the very least kids like Billy." He smiled. "Imagine my surprise when they did."

"So your parents aren't as bad as you thought?"

"They're still beach bums." He paused to laugh and Sophie could see that he and his parents might have different goals and ideals, but they loved each other. "They could see I was serious about starting this facility and they put up some cash, too."

"And you keep up with it?"

"Hey, it's a good cause and something worthwhile for my parents to spend their money on. I'm happy to throw in a few bucks and make a few trips."

"You just don't like speeches."

He rolled his eyes. "Who does?"

"Good point. Okay, so once you thank everybody, just talk about the service you believe the facility provides for the community. Say you and your parents are proud to be involved with it." She smiled. "Then sit down."

He laughed. "That part I can handle."

"I don't know why you're so nervous."

"I don't like speaking to groups. I'm much better one-on-one. And when there's no emotion involved." He caught her gaze. "I hate this emotion junk."

"No kidding." But she smiled. He really had a heart of gold. Which was really why he hated speeches. No man wanted to look soft and vulnerable. Especially not with the media watching.

But that was also why he didn't want to get too close to Brady. He knew the little boy would pull him in and make him feel like a father, and when Sophie left he'd be lonelier than if he'd never experienced what it would be like to be a daddy.

They finished the speech and then Sophie closed her eyes, not forcing him into any more discussions. She respected his feelings and he respected hers. There was no point belaboring the issue.

Slim had called ahead and made arrangements for a car to be waiting for them at the airport. They drove a short distance to the building site and, within minutes, Sophie was being introduced to a long line of people.

Every person, from the lowliest social worker to the tycoons who made up the board of directors for the facility, grinned at her. From their comments it was easy to see this was the first time Jeb had ever brought a woman to one of their events, and most of them believed they were romantically involved.

She wanted to say, "Nice to meet you but I'm Jeb's housekeeper." Instead, not wanting to cause a stir, she only said, "Nice to meet you."

The ceremony began, Jeb said his few words after

Pete Malloy, executive director of Samuel's House, gave a long speech. Shovels angled into the dirt, Jeb, Pete Malloy and the executive board posed for pictures.

Sophie smiled, her heart turning over in her chest. She knew how much he hated this, yet he did it anyway. Not because he was good but because he was wonderful. Selfless. Generous.

She let her gaze ripple across the crowd and back to him. So many people depended on him. Including her. Yet, he didn't brag. He quietly did what he perceived needed to be done.

Pete Malloy hustled over to Sophie, beating Jeb by two seconds. "We're serving cookies and punch, if you're interested."

Jeb said, "Maybe another time," at the same time that Sophie said, "I'd love a cookie."

Pete said, "Great! Just follow my SUV."

When he walked away, Sophie winced. "Sorry."

"That's okay. Neither one of us had anything to do today anyway."

They made their way to the existing Samuel's House facility, which was only around the bend from the open field where the new building was to be built. Sophie got out of the SUV and unbuckled Brady who was waking up from the long sleep he'd drifted into listening to Pete Malloy's speech.

"Hey, buddy," she crooned as she lifted him out of his seat.

Jeb came around to her side of the car. "Want me to take the carrier in for you?"

His question surprised her. But then she wondered why. True, he might not carry the little boy around on his shoulder, but he'd folded her and Brady into his life so naturally that the three of them lived together comfortably.

Like a family.

She shook her head to dislodge that thought. That was crazy. "No. I think I'll hold him."

They walked into the building that was nothing like Sophie expected. The furniture appeared to be new and though magazines and books littered the end tables of the main room, the fresh scent of cleaning solutions greeted them.

"Wow. This house is great! Why did you think you needed a new one?"

Jeb put his hand on the small of her back and directed her back down the hall to a dining room. From the easy movement, Sophie suspected he didn't even realize what he was doing, but Sophie did. He was so casual with her that he really did treat her like family. Not a housekeeper. He wasn't trying to make them fit. He didn't have to. He was so accustomed to her and Brady, that he was now adding them into this part of his world.

"We're building a new place because this house is no longer big enough." He glanced around, pulled in a breath and faced her. "There are thousands of kids out there who need us. We'll never even know about most of them. But I want to have room for everybody we find."

His serious expression caused Sophie's heart to melt. He genuinely cared about these kids. He was such a good man that it was hard not to like him. But he'd proven himself to be a good person long before this.

She'd even grown to like him long before this. And that was the problem. Seeing this side of him, she was falling over the edge. Up to this point they'd both managed to stop short of that one little word that could cause so much trouble. But here she stood, face-to-face with his generosity, his commitment, and it was simply too much.

Unless she got a hold of herself, before this trip was over she'd be head over heels in love.

They entered a room filled with a combination of adults and teenagers, all of whom seemed to know Jeb.

"Hey, Mr. Worthington."

"Hey, Aaron." Jeb offered his hand for shaking. "How've you been?"

"Good. Gonna graduate next spring."

"I told you that if you stayed it would be worth it."

"Yeah, we'll see. When I can't get anything but a fast food job, I'm coming to you."

"No, you're going to college."

"Right."

"The funds are already in place."

"Yeah, for tuition. Where am I gonna live? On the street?"

"We'll work something out."

Sophie pulled in a breath. He was so good with these kids. It amazed her that he'd ever believed he wasn't cut out to be a dad. But more than that, it amazed her that she'd ever been able to resist him. She was no longer worried that she'd fall in love with him because it was too late. She was already in love.

And that was going to be trouble.

As more teenagers gathered around him, Sophie got pushed to the side. Pete Malloy strolled up to her.

Pointing to Jeb with his punch glass he said, "He's quite an interesting man, isn't he? There's never a dull moment when he visits."

The urge to tell Pete that he didn't know the half of it bubbled up inside her. Instead she turned to the Samuel's House director with a smile. "You should try living with him."

"So you're living together?"

Sophie winced. If nothing else, she had to nip that rumor in the bud right now. "I'm his maid."

"Oh." The embarrassed expression on Pete's face was priceless. "I'm so sorry."

"Don't be." Not only had he clued her in that she was probably looking at Jeb with stars in her eyes, but also Pete had given her the opportunity to dispel the rumor before it caught fire and couldn't be pulled back.

More than that, he'd reminded her of her real place in Jeb's life. His maid. He might be interesting enough, kind enough, generous enough that she'd fallen in love with him. But she was his employee. A single woman with a child who'd desperately needed a job. A woman who sassed him. And who'd been stunned speechless when he'd told her his biggest secret, that he couldn't have kids. She hadn't been supportive. She'd frozen.

How could he possibly like a woman who'd thought of herself first, not him. Even the memory of that night shamed her.

"We've obviously crossed the line from boss and employee into friendship. So it's not a big deal."

"I can see how that could happen."

She followed Pete's gaze to Jeb and her heart ached. How she must have hurt him by her silence. It was no wonder he'd stopped any possibility of a relationship between them. Here he was, a man who didn't care about biology, who cared for dozens of children. Why would he attach himself to a woman whose heart didn't expand any further than herself?

"He's a genuinely nice guy. Bit of a curiosity, though. If I spent any more time with him, I'd probably be poking into his life. Trying to get the inside scoop."

Sophie laughed. "Trust me. You wouldn't get it."

"Close mouthed?"

"Extremely."

"Too bad. I'd love to know what happened in the Zoe situation."

"The Zoe situation?"

"Yeah. Zoe's a little girl Jeb and his ex had considered adopting."

Her eyes widened. "Oh?"

Pete nodded. "She was the youngest kid we'd ever had come here and she clearly didn't fit. Jeb and Laine developed a soft spot for her and the next thing you know the word adoption had come up. Then out of nowhere her mom appeared—clean and sober—with a job and an apartment. She took Zoe and from all accounts everything worked out."

Sophie said nothing. She wasn't amazed that Jeb would consider adopting a child. She'd seen his commitment to this place, these kids. What surprised her was that she'd had no clue.

"Everything ended well for Zoe…but the next event we had, Jeb arrived as a divorced man."

Sophie's mouth fell open. She told herself not to

pry, but she couldn't stop herself. "You think losing the child had something to do with Jeb's divorce?"

"Yes."

Jeb ambled over. "Are you telling her all my secrets?"

Pete had the good graces to look embarrassed. "Just the ones I know."

"Then I'm glad I never really told you anything." He faced Sophie. "Pete and I need a minute with the board of directors. Do you mind?"

She shook her head, looking at Jeb with a whole new perspective. He'd been told he couldn't have kids, then the one child he'd wanted to adopt had been snatched from him. It was no wonder he believed he'd never be a father. "No. Go on. I'll be fine."

"Great." He motioned for Pete to walk with him. "There are apparently some papers we need to sign."

"Okay," Pete said as they disappeared into the milling crowd.

"You Jeb's woman?"

Sophie turned at the question to see a young man looking at her curiously.

"I'm his maid."

"No kidding! He's got a maid?"

She laughed. "Yep."

"Hey, Jordie!" the kid called, motioning to a tall, slender boy to join them. "This here's Worthington's maid."

The boy walked over. "You're a maid?"

Hoisting Brady a little higher on her arm, Sophie said, "Yes."

"I'll bet he lives in a big old mansion."

"It's more of a house…" She stopped as two more kids joined them. Both girls. Both around fifteen. Both wearing too much eye makeup. One with a ring in her nose.

"Does he have a dog?"

"Horses."

A general affirmative sound rose from the group, as three more kids walked over.

"He's got a ranch, right?"

The question came from somewhere in the growing crowd and Sophie hesitated. She'd always known Jeb was a private person, but the few things she'd heard from Pete today magnified just how much he held to his privacy. He wouldn't want her talking about him and she didn't want to endanger his confidence in her. The only thing she could think to do to get the conversation away from him was to turn the tables.

"Yes, he has a ranch." She smiled at the first kid. "So what's your name?"

"Orlando. This here's Jordie. That's Mark and Austin," He said pointing to the two boys to his right. "That's Birdie and Macayla's the one with the nose ring."

Sophie smiled at each one. "It's nice to meet you."

"Where are you from?"

Sophie should have realized she was no match for the questions of a group of curious kids, but at least the questions were no longer about Jeb. "California."

"California?" The girls gasped.

Orlando was much too cool for that. He nodded. "The big C."

"Yep."

They managed to fire off enough questions to fill the entire space of time that Jeb and Pete were gone. Though they laughed a lot, Sophie's gaze continually drifted to Macayla. The girl needed somebody. She didn't have to say the words. Her confused eyes told the story. They also told the story of why Jeb and his ex-wife had considered adopting one of the children who lived at Samuel's House. The boys and even Birdie had a maturity about them that didn't match their ages, but an innocent like Macayla stuck out like a sore thumb. If someone didn't catch her now, God only knew where she'd land when she fell.

Jeb strode over with a groan. "Are they grilling you about me?"

She laughed. "They tried, but I managed to change the subject."

"Great. Let's go."

The kids protested, but Jeb promised a return visit soon. Again, it was easy for Sophie to see that the kids admired him, loved his visits and trusted that he would take care of them.

They said goodbye and headed for the door. Though all of the boys and even Birdie disbursed casually, Macayla stayed where she was. She didn't speak. Didn't move. Simply watched Sophie and Jeb leave.

At the door, Sophie turned one final time. Her gaze caught Macayla's and she had the sudden, intense intuition that *she* was the person created to mother this child.

CHAPTER TWELVE

AFTER Jeb confirmed with the pilot that he and Sophie were settled in, ready to take off, he leaned back in his chair and feigned sleep. But after only a few seconds, he opened his eyes.

"I know what you're thinking."

"How could you possibly know what I'm thinking?"

"Because I thought the same things myself."

She laughed. "Right. So what am I thinking?"

"That that little girl needs a home."

She caught his gaze across the aisle of the plane. She blinked once, twice, but she didn't refute what he'd said.

"You need to remember that these kids are street kids. The kind of home you'd make for somebody like Macayla would stifle her."

"Or be exactly what she needs."

He shook his head. "What she needs is to learn how to live in a normal environment, to pull her weight in chores to earn her place. The last thing she wants to be is beholden to someone."

"And you know this because?"

"Because I read every file."

"You do?"

He nearly growled at his mistake. How was it that this woman could get him to tell her things he never told anyone? "Yes." He sucked in an annoyed breath. "Don't make me out to be a saint."

But he saw from the glimmer that came to her eyes that that was exactly what she'd done.

"I know you're not a saint, but I also see you don't give yourself credit for the good things you do."

"I give a few speeches, read a few files. If you want to direct those stars in your eyes at somebody, go look at my parents. They're the ones who put up the money."

But the spark stayed in her eyes and it killed him. He wanted to be everything she saw. But he wasn't good. He was flawed. And he'd best not forget that.

Sophie made a simple supper of macaroni and cheese and fried fish, still feeling the push of maternal instincts for Macayla that was as sharp and keen as what she felt when she first held Brady. Though Jeb didn't mention Samuel's House or their trip that afternoon and kept his focus on the discussion he was having with Slim, Sophie couldn't shake the thoughts of Macayla. She hadn't felt anything like this when she looked at Orlando or any of the other kids at Samuel's House. And for that reason alone, she didn't want to ignore it.

After Brady fell asleep, she went to Jeb's office and found the Samuel's House file. She retrieved Pete Malloy's email address, wrote an email asking if Macayla had an email address and sent it across cyberspace. To her surprise, Pete replied within a few seconds. Though he encouraged her to make friends with Macayla, he also set ground rules for Sophie, telling her to keep the emails light and friendly and not to play psychologist or stand-in parent. He reminded her that she wasn't a therapist and that there were trained staff members to handle Macayla's big problems.

Doing exactly as Pete suggested, she wrote an email simply telling Macayla it was nice to meet her and hit Send, knowing it was up to Macayla whether or not they'd become friends.

When Jeb didn't arrive in the kitchen for coffee on Sunday morning, Sophie suspected he was avoiding her. She confirmed that suspicion on Monday when she walked into the kitchen to find a pot of coffee had already been brewed and at least two cups taken, but Jeb was nowhere in sight. By Wednesday, having only seen him at meals with Slim, she knew the trip to Samuel's House, or maybe her reaction to it, had caused him to decide to keep his distance.

Which was fine, maybe even for the best. She hadn't meant to fall in love with him, but she had and now she had to figure out what to do about it. Her head told her to do nothing and given the way he was avoiding her, Sophie realized that was probably the right thing to do. The feelings she had for him were new. Fragile. She didn't think they would go away. But she also wasn't sure what she should do about them. Did she dare tell him and risk rejection? But if she didn't tell him, could she live with a man she loved, cook for him, clean for him…and never have his love in return?

After tidying the kitchen and putting Brady into bed

for a nap she went to the office to check her email.
Macayla had answered.

She let a day go by before answering Macayla, if
only because she didn't want to put any pressure on her,
and life fell into a casual routine with Sophie spending
most of her time alone with Brady, keeping up the
house and planning meals. She typically served Jeb
and Slim lunch, then sat down and ate supper with
them. The conversation didn't turn to her often.
Typically the meal was spent listening to Slim give a
report of what had happened at the ranch that day.

Both Jeb and Slim always thanked her for meals. But
her part of the conversation rarely extended beyond
that and she soon realized that things were actually
working out. She and Jeb could live in the same house,
and she didn't have to worry that her feelings for him
would cause her to do something that would ruin her
stay at the ranch.

So it surprised her when Jeb returned to the kitchen
on Thursday night just as she was finishing up the dishes.

For the first time in weeks, they were alone.
Everything she'd felt for him at the groundbreaking for
Samuel's House came tumbling back. He was good,
kind, generous. Sexy, sweet and funny. How could a
woman see that and not love him?

Their gazes met, but Jeb quickly looked away.

And Sophie forced herself back to reality. She might
love him. He might have feelings for her. But he also
had issues and she needed this job. She had to respect
that.

He walked to the table. "Can you give me a minute?"

She said, "Sure," but something about his ominous

tone caused her tummy to tingle. She swore she hadn't treated him any differently since she realized she loved him, but what if she had? What if he guessed or sensed that her feelings had changed? What if he couldn't work with her knowing how she felt?

He took a seat at the round table and Sophie sat across from him.

He slid an envelope from his pocket. "As you know, the ranch management company direct deposits your salary into your checking account."

Her heart stopped. "It's payday?"

He laughed. "Yes. Finally. We hold back two weeks pay and only pay once a month, so you probably thought you'd never see cash. But here's your paystub."

"Oh!" Joy coursed through her. She'd been dying to see money appear in her checking account like magic, and here it was!

"I want you to open that now because the money's a bit more than you expected."

She glanced up at him. His eyes were soft and serious. He worried about her reaction.

"The first month, you weren't just doing maid's work—you were also decorating. So I had my accountant check into average salaries for decorators and that's reflected in your deposit."

She looked down at the amount that had gone into her checking account. Her mouth fell open. "Holy cow."

He laughed. "The decorating you did was worth every penny."

She swallowed. The extra he'd paid her would significantly reduce her bills. In another month she'd be out of debt, two months from now she'd have a savings account.

How could a woman not fall in love with this guy? He never missed a trick. He saw everything that went on around him, rewarded people. Appreciated people.

She blinked back tears. "Thanks."

He rose from the table. "You're welcome."

She sat staring at the pay stub, a million things going through her mind. But no matter what direction her thoughts took they always came back to one simple fact. Jeb Worthington was a good man. And at Samuel's House she had realized that she loved him. He wouldn't have anything to do with her because he couldn't have children. But over the past weeks of emailing Macayla, her perspective of motherhood and mothering had changed dramatically.

But he didn't know that.

He walked to the door and for the first time Sophie realized how alone he looked, how deserted. Working for the kids at Samuel's House or on the ranch he was fine. At lunch and dinner with Slim, he was fine. But when he walked through the kitchen door, into rooms meant to be shared, the family room, media room—his bedroom—the emptiness of his life was obvious.

At the door, he turned and said, "I'll see you in the morning."

She nodded. But when the door swung closed behind him, her heart expanded in her chest. She couldn't stand to see him alone anymore. She loved him and she knew that if he'd give it half a chance he'd love her.

But she knew he wouldn't "give" it a chance. He wouldn't make a move. If anything was going to happen between them, it would be up to her.

Her mind made up, she rose from the kitchen table.

She was either about to change both of their lives or make the biggest mistake of her life.

An hour later, she stepped through the French doors out into the cool night air. Just as she expected, he was in the pool, cutting smoothly through the glistening water. His muscles rippled as he stroked, the faint sound of his movements cut through the silence.

He reached the edge of the pool, touched it and turned around again in one clean movement. Mesmerized, she watched, stripping her cover-up and dropping it to the chaise.

After a few seconds of watching him, her blood virtually sang through her veins. Physically he was perfect, but the arousal that shimmied through her took second place to the feelings swelling her heart. For two weeks she'd hidden the fact that she loved him. And it was time to quit pretending they could only be housekeeper and boss, when they could have so much more if he'd simply open his heart to the possibilities.

She knew there was only one way he'd accept her, a sacrifice. But tonight it seemed easy. They could have as many kids as they wanted. They simply wouldn't be biological children. But that was okay. There were plenty of kids like Macayla who needed her.

It was time to admit that they were meant to be more.

"Hey."

He stopped swimming, twisting to bring himself around to face her.

"Sophie?"

"Yeah."

He ran his hand down his face to scrape away the water. "What's up?"

"I just felt like a swim."

"Oh." He paused for a second as if needing to think that through then he said, "Okay." He hoisted himself out of the pool. "I'll leave."

"No!" Realizing how sharp her word had been, she took a light breath to soften it. "I mean… The pool's big enough for both of us. Why don't you stay?"

He yanked his towel from the chaise, dried his face and turned to her. "You know why."

She took a step closer. "Because we like each other?"

"Like isn't exactly the word I'd use."

She laughed. "All right. Maybe lust is a better word. But don't you think time's been working on changing that?"

She saw from the look on his face that he understood, but the way he drew in a long breath also told her that didn't make him happy. "Sophie, don't."

She caught his hand, yanked lightly in the direction of the pool. "Come on. Stay with me. Give us a chance."

He shook his head sadly. "It wouldn't work. And you know why."

"Yes, because you can't have children. And you don't want to deprive me." She sucked in a breath, steamrolling on before he could stop her. "But the past month with you and the trip to Samuel's House has changed things for me."

He caught her gaze. "What are you saying?"

"Well, you don't know this but I've been corresponding by email with Macayla."

"Sophie—" Her name came out as a growled warning.

But she laughed. "I know she's not anywhere near ready to go into a private home. I know she's still working things out. But someday she's going to be ready and when she is I'm going to be here for her."

"This isn't a good idea."

"Yes, it is," she insisted. "You might have read her file but her file doesn't tell the whole story. She had a normal life until her parents died. It's their deaths that made her so out of control. She only ran from two foster homes before they gave up on her and shipped her to Samuel's House. She's different from the other kids. More than anything else she needs to get over her parents' deaths. We could help her with that."

Jeb stepped back, away from her. "Don't."

"I know you're skeptical, but that's actually good. You'd keep me grounded. When I'd want to adopt every child who came through the Samuel's House doors, you'd remind me that adoption isn't right for some of them. That they need their space. And the best thing we could do for them would be simply to be their friends. But Macayla is different."

He took another step back, didn't say anything.

She stopped the argument that instantly sprang to her head, finally realizing he wasn't disagreeing. He wasn't saying anything at all. "Jeb?"

He pulled in a breath, let his gaze ripple down the length of her body then squeezed his eyes shut. "If anybody could make me consider adoption, it would be you."

She would have laughed. Would have given into the glorious sensation that just having him look at her aroused, but she knew he'd only given her half a statement. He'd said if. *If* anybody could make him consider adoption…

If…

"What are you saying?"

"I'm saying that you're reaching for a solution I rejected long ago. I'm saying I've been down this road before and I know where it ends because I've been there."

Zoe. The little girl Jeb and his wife "almost" adopted. Pete hadn't known the whole story. He only had part. Even he admitted that.

"It was *you* who didn't want to adopt, wasn't it? Your wife would have taken Zoe, but you said no."

"I said no."

Her heart stopped and so did her breathing. She couldn't believe what he was saying. "But why?" She shook her head. "I don't get it."

"Of course, you don't! You're young and healthy and could have a hundred kids if you want. You have choices. I don't."

"So what you're really saying is that you're mad that you don't have choices. If you could have children, it wouldn't bother you to adopt."

"No… Yes…" He turned away. "I don't know."

"Oh, you do know. You know very well. You're standing your ground because you're mad."

"Yes, damn it!" He spun around to face her. "I spent my entire life on the outside looking in. Never enough. Lots of times the kid everybody pitied. I don't want to be pitied anymore. I don't want to make excuses and take handouts of affection somebody tosses at me."

"I'm not tossing you a handout!"

"Aren't you?" He took a slow step toward her. His gaze rippled down her body, then strolled back to hers. "You came out here to seduce me. But instead of jumping into the pool, surprising me, catching me off guard, you called me out. Told me how you were going to compensate for my deficiency. Should I have been grateful? Were you expecting me to fall into your arms? Weep for joy? Tell you you could have me and everything I own because you were willing to sacrifice?"

"It wasn't like that." Shame burned through her. He made her sound so cheap. "You said you wouldn't have anything to do with me unless I knew what I was getting into. I thought that was what you needed to hear."

"Which just goes to show how little you know me." He laughed harshly. "You know what? It doesn't matter."

"Of course it does. We can work this out—"

"I don't want to work it out!" His angry shout reverberated through the quiet night. "Don't you get it? I want to be enough. I want a woman to come to me for me."

Sophie stared at him, working to understand what he was saying until she broke it down to the most simple terms. He wanted what she wanted. To be loved. Accepted. But where she would hug everybody in the world to her, hoping to find the person or people who could fill the void, he rejected everybody. Never believing he was really loved. He'd probably done this very thing to his ex-wife.

And now he was rejecting her.

No wonder he'd told her to stay away from him. She was a fixer. He didn't want to be fixed. They were the worst possible combination.

A lump formed in her throat. Tears filled her eyes.

Would she ever stop being the little girl trying to make a place for herself looking for love?

She turned and raced to the French doors. He didn't call her back.

Running back to her suite of rooms, she suddenly envisioned her and Jeb in the kitchen the following morning.

He wouldn't regret what he'd said, but he would regret hurting her. So he'd apologize, trying to make up for embarrassing her. Apologize for not loving her. Because he couldn't love and *she* was the one who was desperate for it, not him.

Humiliation tightened her chest. She ripped off her swimsuit, but rather than put on pajamas, she stepped into clean jeans and a T-shirt. She pulled things from the dresser drawers and closet, tossing them into her two suitcases. She now had thousands of dollars in her checking account. True, she'd wanted to pay off Brady's hospital bills with that money, but circumstances had changed.

She was done being the woman who tried to make everybody else happy. The fixer. The one who scurried to find a way. Only to be rejected every damned time.

This time she really would be on her own. For real. Not dependent on anybody for anything.

CHAPTER THIRTEEN

JEB walked into the kitchen at noon the following day expecting to smell lunch and finding the room cold and empty. The coffee he'd made at seven that morning sat on the still warm coffeemaker, smelling stale and strong.

"Sophie!" he called, striding through the downstairs, angrier than he'd been in a long time. He refused to take the blame for this. She'd started the episode the night before, offering something she really didn't want to give, and making him feel like a damned fool. Somebody so needy she had to give up what she wanted to make him feel okay.

Well, he wasn't having it. He was okay. Just the way he was. He didn't need anybody fixing him.

Assuming she was in her suite, maybe even holed up with Brady, he calmed himself before knocking on her door. It wouldn't do any good to yell. He'd yelled the night before but he'd been angry. Today he wanted to get them back to normal. A boss and housekeeper. A woman who needed him. Not the other way around.

When his knuckles hit the wood, the wood panel creaked and fell inward.

He frowned and peered inside. "Sophie?"

The room was dark and cool. The end tables were clear of the books and magazines she typically had lying around. "Sophie?"

Nothing.

He peered into the bedroom. The bed had been stripped. The crib was gone.

His heart stopped. "Sophie?"

He walked back to the sitting room, looking everywhere for any sign of an explanation but there wasn't even as much as a note.

She'd left him. No note. No goodbye.

He pulled in a breath. *She'd gone?*

He almost couldn't believe his eyes, but the argument they'd had the night before played over in his head and he realized something he hadn't thought of before this. He'd been so angry, so caught up in the drama of his own troubles, that he hadn't really considered her feelings. In the light of day, he'd figured she'd be mad, but he'd handled her anger before. Now, looking at the empty room, he suddenly realized he hadn't just rejected her the night before, he'd embarrassed her. And that was the one thing she couldn't handle.

Rubbing his hands down his face, he held back a sea of regret by deciding that maybe this was for the best. He couldn't be what she wanted. He didn't doubt that she believed she'd be okay with adoption, but he wasn't okay with it. She didn't realize that when he'd said he'd never be a father he meant it. He'd taken control by accepting who and what he was. It was the only way he could reconcile himself. So, no matter how much he liked and wanted Sophie and how much she liked and wanted him, he wouldn't deprive her.

This was for the best.

Turning, he strode to the door but a swatch of blue caught his gaze. He stopped. Brady's shiny blue bear lay on the floor. He stooped and picked it up. His eyes squeezed shut, but he willed away the pain, the regret, the sense of loss.

She'd gotten him to say and feel a hundred times more than what he knew was good for him. He was limited. Pretending he was okay—normal—when he wasn't, only made him feel worse.

Walking to the kitchen he opened the trash and tossed the bear inside. She wouldn't be back for it and hadn't left a forwarding address for him to mail it to her.

It was time to get on with the rest of his life.

Again.

Sophie awoke along a deserted stretch of highway with Brady crying in the car seat behind her.

She groaned at the stiffness of her body from sleeping sitting up. "Sorry, buddy." She'd left so late at night that around three o'clock, her eyelids had grown heavy and she'd known she had to stop to get some sleep. Brady slept soundly in the car seat, so she pushed her seat back and nodded off.

"I'll feed you and we can get back on the road."

Pulling a bottle from the cooler, she told herself not to think about Jeb. Not to wonder if he'd noticed her gone. Not to feel a spark of hope that he might come after her, look for her. Because she knew he wouldn't.

The embarrassment she'd felt—not from his rejection but from her stupidity in putting herself out to him—washed over her like a tsunami, but she decided the intense humiliation was a good thing. If she remembered the desperate expression on his face when he looked at Brady, her feelings softened. If she thought too long or too hard about what he said, she understood him. Because their battle was the same battle. Neither one of them really had anybody who loved them.

But if she remembered the humiliation, remembered that he refused her love, then she could get mad and probably even stay mad, and hopefully forget the crushing blow to her heart.

She fed Brady, forcing her mind to more pressing concerns. She had enough money for the first and last month's rent and even a security deposit, but if she didn't soon find a job she wouldn't have money for food. She drove the remainder of the way to California focusing her energy on the task at hand. She had to find work…and quickly.

Just over the border into California, she stopped at a diner and grabbed a copy of the local newspaper for something to read while she ate her late dinner. The paper automatically opened to the classified, she looked down and saw the ad for a two-bedroom apartment over a garage.

"I see you're looking at the ad for the Murphy place."

Smiling up at the waitress, Sophie closed the paper. "Not really. The paper just sort of opened."

The middle-aged woman handed her a menu. Dressed in a pink uniform with her hair pulled back in a severe bun, the waitress looked about fifty. "It's a great little apartment. Cheap, too."

"Yeah, well, it would have to be free next month because I don't have a job."

"What kind of work do you do?"

"I'm a maid."

The waitress sighed. "Too bad you're not a cook. I happen to need one."

"You own this place?"

She nodded. "Yes."

"I'm not a trained cook, but I *can* cook."

"We don't get too fancy here. It's not like you have to know anything more than eggs and beef stew."

Sophie laughed, but inside her heart stuttered. If she got this job she wouldn't have to go back to her parents and admit she'd lost her maid's job. She could rent the available apartment, live in an entirely different town, make new friends—make a new life.

"I get a little fancier than that."

"How fancy?"

"I make a wicked ziti."

The older woman laughed, extended her hand for shaking. "I'm Maggie. I lied when I said we didn't get too fancy because I was desperate. We need a cook so I was willing to take what I could get. But we're also just off the interstate and we get all kinds here. Truth is if you cook well, I'd happily make it worth your while to say."

"I cook well," Sophie said, deciding she might as well toot her own horn. If she was turning over a new leaf, no longer looking out for anybody but herself, she might as well start now.

Maggie slid onto the bench seat across the booth from her. "If we call this a job interview, dinner's on the house."

* * *

Jeb was standing by the sink trying to decide if he should grill hamburgers for himself and Slim for lunch, when he realized he would have to break the news to his foreman that his wonderful dinners were now a thing of the past. Slim was going to throttle him.

Just as he thought that, Slim burst into the kitchen. "Clients are here." He stopped, glanced around. "Where's Sophie?"

Jeb shrugged. "No idea."

"She's gone?"

"Yep. And we're back to grilling burgers and steaks for every meal." He caught Slim's gaze. "You got a problem with that?"

Slim shook his head as if resigned. "Nope. I'm fine."

"Right." Jeb caught the backhanded implication that Jeb was the one with the problem, but he already knew that. Slim wouldn't say any more than he already had. He didn't have to. And Jeb wouldn't defend himself. He already had. Sophie was the one who'd thrown the monkey wrench into everything. It was time for his life and Slim's life and the ranch life to get back to normal.

"Let's go. Clients are waiting."

Two weeks later, Jeb got an urgent message from Pete Malloy. There was a problem at Samuel's House that needed his attention. Immediately.

His first thought was that something had happened with Macayla, that Sophie opening a line of communication and then leaving had thrown her for a loop. But he squelched it. She hadn't been that important. He wouldn't let her be that important. Whatever was wrong with Macayla, one way or another, he would make it right. Without Sophie.

He napped in the plane and as always a car awaited him at the airport. He jumped inside and drove to Samuel's House.

Pete greeted him at the door. "Thanks for coming."

"You said it was important."

Pete laughed. "It is. Come on."

He followed Pete to the dining room. At the door, Pete more or less pushed Jeb in front of him, and nudged him inside.

All sixteen of the Samuel's House kids shouted, "Surprise! Happy Birthday."

Much to Jeb's own surprise, he laughed. No one had ever thrown him a birthday party.

"Who is the squealer who told my birthday? I didn't think anybody knew my birthday." He really didn't. He'd never told anyone. Not even Slim.

Pete grimaced. "It was me."

Jeb turned to face him. "You? How did you know?"

Macayla stepped forward. "I'm not going to let Pete take the heat for me. I Googled you."

Jeb tried not to think of Sophie when he looked at her, but it was no use. This teenager with the big brown eyes, scraggly brown hair and nose ring had stolen Sophie's heart, changed how she felt, taken her away from Jeb.

He shook the thought from his head. No one had stolen Sophie. He'd let her go. That's how he had to remember it.

"You found my birthday through Google?"

She shrugged. "I have my ways." Then she turned away as Pete carried a big cake into the room.

The group of kids broke into a noisy rendition of Happy Birthday and Jeb stood speechless. He couldn't remember the last time anyone had told him happy birthday. Let alone made him a birthday cake.

Eating a piece of cake, he made his way through the group thanking them. Each of the kids had his or her own reason for being thrilled to throw the impromptu party. But Macayla had glossed over her part in things and had immediately begun talking about Sophie.

"She worries about you."

He turned away, pretending uninterest, but just as quickly turned back again. Was it so wrong to want to know she was okay? To at least know she had a job?

"How is she?"

Macayla shrugged. "Good. She loves California."

"Oh, she moved home?"

"Not hardly. Her parents like a visit now and again, but they're not much on having a baby around."

It broke his heart to think of Brady. Broke it again when he realized Sophie's parents treated the baby the same way they'd always treated her. Okay for sometimes, but not somebody they liked having around. Their own child and they neglected her. At least his parents had wanted him around.

"So where is she then?"

"Diner just outside the Nevada border."

"A diner?"

Macayla laughed. "She loves to cook."

He knew that, of course. He also knew she wasn't a snob when it came to finding a job. All she ever wanted was a way to support her son.

And him.

She'd wanted him, too. She'd loved him. It was the first he'd let himself admit it, but he knew it as well as he knew his own name.

He tried to silence the little voice that nudged the memory of the night at the swimming pool to the front of his brain. She'd wanted to make love that night. She'd wanted to commit. To offer him a life and he'd thrown it all back in her face.

The pain of that washed over him. He hadn't meant any of what happened that night the way she'd taken it. He'd only been protecting himself. But he'd never before seen how protecting himself affected other people.

He'd embarrassed her. Humiliated her. Hurt her.

He told himself not to care. Not to worry. Not dwell on her. She'd be fine.

"Yeah, she lives in an apartment above a garage. Owned by some guy named Murphy. She says he's been coming on to her big time."

Macayla laughed but Jeb's blood boiled. Though he could tell himself he didn't care that she'd moved on, he did care. He cared a lot.

"Is she making okay money?"

Macayla shrugged. "By your definition probably not. By my definition, she's got a place to stay and free meals for herself and Brady. She's doing great."

Macayla walked away casually, without offering the reassurances Jeb needed. Instead she'd planted seeds that caused him to go crazy with worry. For the next twenty-four hours he suffered with images of Sophie struggling. He pictured her apartment as being one room, with a tiny bath. He saw her eating one meal on her shift at the diner and going hungry the rest of the time.

Finally, when he couldn't take it anymore he called Macayla, swore her to secrecy and got the name of the diner where Sophie worked.

His hat low and sunglasses covering his eyes, he walked into the diner the next day. He didn't want to talk to Sophie. Simply wanted to know that she was okay. And—maybe—to check out the guy named Murphy. He strode to a booth in the back and when the waitress came with a menu, he ordered coffee.

"Oh, I am *sooo* glad you're here."

Sophie laughed at Maggie as she raced into the kitchen with an order. "I'm glad I'm here, too."

"No, I'm *seriously* glad," Maggie said, slapping her order receipt on Sophie's work table. "There's a cutie in the back booth ordered a Tex-Mex omelet. I'm not even sure I know what that is, let alone how to make it."

Maggie said Tex-Mex omelet and Sophie instantly thought of her first full day of working for Jeb. She told herself she had to stop letting her mind wander back. Jeb didn't want her. They were two different people. She'd always want to bring friends into her life. He'd always want to live in seclusion.

"I make a wicked Tex-Mex omelet."

"I know!" Maggie said, clapping her hands together with glee. "I was so lucky that you strolled into my diner!"

Sophie laughed, broke eggs into a bowl and began to make the omelet. When it was ready, Maggie hustled it out to the dining room.

A few minutes later, she returned, omelet in hand. "He says it's dry."

Sophie gaped at her. "Dry!" She'd never made a dry omelet in her life and after a night of Brady crying she wasn't in the mood for random complaints. She headed for the door. "Who is this guy?"

At the doorway she glared back into the dining room to the corner booth. When she saw Jeb her heart stopped. She ducked back into the kitchen.

"That's my old boss."

Maggie peered out into the dining room again. "That's the guy you used to work for? The mean old man."

Sophie cleared her throat. "I never really said he was old."

"Yeah, but you did say he was mean."

"He sent back the omelet, didn't he?"

Maggie laughed. "Yeah, but he's sweet as pie. Flirted with me the whole time he ordered."

Sophie whipped off her hairnet. "Don't let that fool you."

She grabbed the omelet and marched out into the dining room, shoving the plate under his nose. "You sent this back?" she asked, talking to the top of his hat because he hadn't taken it off.

Jeb's head came up. She saw her reflection in his sunglasses. "It was dry."

"If it's so dry, how about if you take off that hat and I dump it on your head?"

He pulled his sunglasses down. "You've gotten ornery."

"You always were ornery. So we're even."

She turned to walk away but he caught her hand. "We're not even close to even. You left without giving notice."

"Oh, I pretty much figured you knew I wouldn't hang around."

"You see, that's just it. I didn't figure you'd be leaving. I thought I'd at least have time to apologize."

"That's too bad, huh?"

"Well, that's sort of why I'm here."

"To apologize?"

He nodded. "And to say you were right."

"I'm always right." Except this time she wasn't sure what she'd been right about. "What was I right about?"

"Macayla doesn't belong at Samuel's House. I reread her file. Went a little farther back than the two foster homes she ran away from. Saw the part about her parents."

Her heart lifted. "So, you'd let me adopt her?"

He gave her an odd look, as if he was pondering something, then he smiled. "Why don't *we* adopt her?"

She took a step back. "Very funny."

"Not funny at all." His smile grew. "Actually it's the best idea I've come up with in a long time."

She slapped the omelet on the table, so she could put her hands on her hips. "What are you doing? She's already been through enough trauma! You can't promise her something you can't deliver."

"Oh, I'm delivering. My mind is absolutely made up. From where I sit it's you who's balking."

"I'm not coming back to be your maid."

"I didn't ask you to." He took off his sunglasses and caught her gaze. "I'd like you to be my wife."

Her heart stopped. Her breathing stuttered. "I... You..."

He pointed at the seat across from him. "Sit. Let me

apologize. Let me tell you that I love you and I probably have loved you since the second day you were at my ranch."

She sat.

"I was afraid. And you were right. I was pushing people away. But you were also right when you said we handled the people in our lives differently. You gathered. I pushed." He reached across the table and caught her hand. "It doesn't seem to be working for either of us, so what do you say? Do you want to get married and work on meeting in the middle? Gather some people, push away others?"

The surprise of it shook her. Part of her wanted to shout yes and throw herself in his lap. The other part remembered the hurt, the humiliation of their last meeting. She swallowed. How could she trust him? "I don't know."

He tugged on her hand, forced her to look at him. "Do you love me?"

She nodded. "Yes. Unfortunately."

"Just what every man wants to hear."

"You're not an easy person to love." She didn't really mean that. He was probably the easiest person she'd ever met. She'd fallen in love with him in only a few weeks... Fear held her back. She'd held out her heart. He'd stomped on it. Now he expected her to believe he loved her...

He loved her.

Her head jerked up. "You love me?"

He nodded. "And want you to come home with me. We'll adopt Macayla. Give her the home she wants. I'll teach Brady how to rope and ride. And if you want more kids we'll look into adoption." He pulled in a breath. "Or, if you really want more of your own kids, we could look into that, too." He blew out his breath. "There's nothing wrong with you. You could have oodles of kids. And there are ways you could have them."

"But…"

"But nothing. They'd be yours but they'd also be mine because you'd be mine."

Tears filled her eyes, brimmed over, spilled down her cheeks. "That's a change."

He sat back, smiled wickedly. "I missed you."

She laughed through her tears.

"I've never been able to say that about anybody. My parents taught me not to depend on people, so I learned how to get by without everybody. You…" He shook his head. "It's not so easy to get along without you."

Without a word, Sophie got up from the booth and started to walk away. He caught her hand, tugging her back. "Where are you going?"

"To tell Maggie she needs to find a new cook."

He tugged again, brought her down to his lap. "Without answering me, first. I seem to remember putting a proposition on the table."

"I've decided to let you suffer for a few hours."

"While you pack?"

With a laugh, she nodded.

He shook his head. "You've gotta work on your punishment skills. The way I had it figured I'd have to camp out in this diner, work on you, maybe even seduce you into coming back with me for at least a week."

"You could still work on seducing me."

He lowered his head to kiss her. "Oh, yeah?"

"Yeah."

Then he kissed her and she knew everything was going to be okay. Not because he'd come back for her or because he agreed to adopt, but because he loved her. And she'd always heard people who genuinely loved each other could work anything out.

Now she knew they would. It was all a matter of finding the right person, the right love.

* * * * *

A sneaky peek at next month…

By Request

RELIVE THE ROMANCE WITH THE BEST OF THE BEST

My wish list for next month's titles…

In stores from 19th July 2013:

☐ Bedded for His Pleasure — Heidi Rice, Kate Hardy & Trish Wylie

☐ What Happens In Vegas… — Katherine Garbera

3 stories in each book - only £5.99!

In stores from 2nd August 2013:

☐ Claimed by the Rebel — Cara Colter, Michelle Douglas & Jackie Braun

☐ Princes of Castaldini — Olivia Gates

Available at WHSmith, Tesco, Asda, Eason, Amazon and Apple

Just can't wait?

Visit us Online

You can buy our books online a month before they hit the shops! **www.millsandboon.co.uk**

0713/0

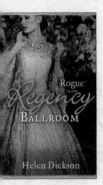